I0652989

Cherise At The Altar

Woman of Faith, Book One

Phylicia Joannis

Published by Brave Girls Press, 2025.

CHERISE AT THE ALTAR
First Edition. April 8 2025.
Copyright © 2024 Phylicia Joannis
Imprint Brave Girls Press
Paperback ISBN: 979-8-9881438-4-0
Written by Phylicia Joannis.
Cover Art: Image courtesy of MadebyNath via Canva
All quotations of scripture are from the New King James Version of the bible unless otherwise noted.

Cherise
At
The
Altar

By Phylicia Joannis
Woman of Faith Series Book One
Copyright 2024

Brave Girls Press
Raleigh, NC

For the ladies
You are thoroughly known and genuinely loved by the God
of the universe.

For You formed my inward parts;

You covered me in my mother's womb.

I will praise You, for I am fearfully and wonderfully made;

Marvelous are Your works,

And that my soul knows very well.

My frame was not hidden from You,

When I was made in secret,

And skillfully wrought in the lowest parts of the earth.

Your eyes saw my substance, being yet unformed.

And in Your book they all were written,

The days fashioned for me,

When as yet there were none of them.

PSALM 139:13-16

1

Lucky Me

I haven't had the greatest luck with men. I used to think it was bad timing. Pursuing a doctorate while working to pay for my tuition didn't leave much time for dating, let alone something real. And my mother raised me to be ambitious and independent above all else. When my college boyfriend, Garrett, told me he wanted to get serious, I wasn't ready. So, I turned him down, and, well, Garrett moved on.

In a plot twist worthy of daytime drama status, Garrett drowned his relationship sorrows in my best friend's very ample bosom. Briana and I had spent every summer together since kindergarten, so naturally I played the role of supportive bestie right up to their wedding day. Yes, it *was* as awful, and awkward, as it sounds. I had a front row seat to their happily ever after on a too-bright Saturday morning. A flock of cardinals chirped their agreement to the union as I wondered if maybe I'd wasted too much time, a thought that would have sent my strong black mother into apoplexy if she knew.

Degrees and careers are great. Ambition is fine. But in that moment, I wanted what Garrett and Briana had. I wanted church bells and flower girls and an *ahem* white dress. I wanted a man to look at me the way Garrett looked at Briana.

It turns out finding a man like that is hard. And keeping him? Even harder. Three years and one soul-crushing break up later, I still haven't figured it out. But I haven't given up, either.

That's why I'm standing at the entrance of Red Hot BBQ in uptown Raleigh, freezing in the unseasonably cold September air in a cropped dress that inches up my thighs whenever I move.

Brunswick should have been here by now. I met him last night at a club, and after a few drinks he asked me out to dinner. I took it as a good sign. Some guys ask you out to their place, or to a motel, or some other skeevy spot. But Brunswick was a gentleman. His waist stayed a respectable six inches from mine as we danced, he kept his hands to himself, and he had an amazing smile. So, I said yes.

"Sorry I'm late." Brunswick slips next to me and smiles. We're close enough for me to notice his teeth are crooked, the bottom row a shade yellower than I remember, with silver crowns on the back molars. But hey, nobody's perfect. I follow him inside, prepared to starve myself because I always order salads on first dates.

"Just two tonight?" the hostess asks.

Brunswick looks at me, licks his lips slowly, then nods. "Yeah. Can we get a corner booth, please?"

I start talking to myself, as is my habit whenever a flag pops up. *His lips are probably just dry. And it's loud in here. Corner booths are quiet, cozy, intimate. He wants to get to know me better.*

By the time we reach our seats, I've talked myself out of running away. Brunswick slides in first, and I intend to slide in right beside him, but this dress, coupled with the friction of my thighs against the vinyl seat, forces me to abandon that quest. I sit, awkwardly, at the edge of the rounded booth. Brunswick notices and grins with all his teeth showing.

"Don't worry, I don't bite." He chuckles and licks his lips again.

I clear my throat and lift my rear just enough to get over another inch. "Oh, it's not you. These booths aren't the best with this material." I gesture to my dress, and he nods absently. We order appetizers and drinks. Brunswick starts picking at his fingernails, and I try my best to ignore it. "So, I had a really great time last night."

"Me too." He looks at me. "You're very pretty, Cherise."

I dip my head and smile, pretending to be flattered. I know I'm pretty. Petite and chunky with an even, brown skin tone thanks to my mother's constant nagging about self-care. It's not that I mind being told that I look good. It's just that it's an easy thing to say, and I want a guy to put in some effort, you know?

There you go again, Cherise. Being too much.

"Thank you, Brunswick. You're very..." For a moment, my mind blanks. Handsome? Not exactly. And while his smile looked amazing in the tipsy haze of a dark club, tonight it's just average. "I like your smile." *Close enough?*

He offers me another. "Yeah. People say it's my best feature." He leans into the table. "What do you do for work?"

Oh. That's different. Points for Brunswick. "I'm a physical therapist."

"Oh yeah?"

"I work with athletes, mostly, and help them rehabilitate."

"That's very cool. Professional, or?"

"Some professional. Mostly college athletes, though."

"Ah. Was that your dream? To become a physical therapist?"

A loaded question. With an answer too complicated for a first date. I settle for simple. "I've always liked helping people. And I've always loved sports. This path gives me the best of both worlds."

He looks me up and down. "You love sports, huh?"

He doesn't mean anything by it, I'm sure. Lots of people take in my oversized hips and tummy and make assumptions. It's a common misconception. "I played volleyball in high school and college." To his air of disbelief I add, "You're looking at a state champion."

"Oh yeah?" He laughs and leans back, rubbing his hands together. "You'll have to show me your moves one day." He winks, and I'm beyond grateful when the waitress brings our appetizers.

I throw my initial plan out the window, stuffing my face with fried pickles and onion rings while I overshare with Brunswick. I've abandoned any lofty ideas of a future together, so I may as well eat and get a free therapy session while I'm at it.

"My mom played volleyball in college. She got a scholarship to UNC, so of course, she says to me, 'Cherise, the best way to pay for college is to use every resource at your disposal. Sports are a valuable resource for brown folks, have been for years.' I didn't love volleyball, but I was good at it, you know? So, I kept doing it. I didn't realize I'd be stuck playing volleyball the rest of my high school life, you know? I wanted to try dance, or theater, but mom was like, 'Cherise, you'd make a terrible actress, and nobody wants to see you dance.'"

"I loved watching you dance." Brunswick cuts in, licking his lips a third time. Or is this the fourth?

I ignore him and keep going. "So, I never got to try dance, and I only got one year of chorus before it was back to volleyball. Not that I didn't enjoy other sports. My brothers played basketball and baseball, and..." I pause. Not because I've run out of things to say, but because Brunswick's right hand has slipped under the table.

He can't be doing what I think he's doing. I pick up where I left off and stare at the last fried pickle. "So, my brothers. I, um, I went to all of their games as a kid."

"Mhm."

"And I loved watching them play."

"Uh huh."

I ramble on as if everything's alright, but my eyes are flying around the restaurant, searching for a distraction, or a waitress I can call over. Or the nearest exit. Somewhere in the middle of a story about my dead dog, Brunswick slips the other hand under the table.

"Cherise?"

I've been on bad dates before. I've been ditched, stood up, and even gone on dates where a guy brought his brother in case he got bored. But there's no way I'm going to sit at this table while Brunswick–

"You stopped in the middle of your sentence, Cherise."

I stare at his arms. They're still squirming under the table, and I can't take it. "Brunswick, what are you doing?"

He blinks. "Huh?"

"We're in public, for goodness' sake! Can't you do that at home, or, or in the bathroom or something?"

He has enough sense to look embarrassed, at least. "I thought you wouldn't notice."

"How could I not? I know what playing with yourself looks like."

His brows go up. "My therapist said so long as I only do it once a month, it's okay."

I'm not sure what to unpack first.

"Look, don't take offense. You should take it as a compliment, actually. It's a comfort thing. It means you make me feel safe."

Gross. "Brunswick, I don't think–"

"You wanna see them?"

Everything starts moving in slow motion. I start to push out a firm, irrefutable 'No,' but my brain lags. Meanwhile, Brunswick fiddles with his below-the-table space and pulls out something I was not expecting.

"This one is Loki, and this one is Jimmy."

Two pocket-sized plastic figures lay on the table in front of him. I'm not familiar enough with that world to be able to identify the characters, but does it really matter? I'm as relieved as I am horrified when the waitress pops up again.

"Y'all ready to put in your dinner orders?"

I make eye contact with her, then her eyes follow mine to the toys on the table. "We're gonna need another minute." She exchanges another look with me and disappears with a nod.

Brunswick clears his throat. "Cherise."

"You brought toys to our date?"

"Jimmy and Loki are limited edition collectors' items. And, as I stated before, they are prescribed by my doctor."

I clear my throat and shake my head, because dizziness helps me hear better, I guess? "Okay, so your doctor, or therapist, or whatever told you to bring toys to our date?"

"Limited edition collectors' items. Not toys."

I offer a placating smile. "I'm gonna need you to walk me through this, Brunswick. Surely you can understand why I would be alarmed that a grown man would bring his," I pause, "limited edition collectors' items to our date."

"If I were taking medication on our date, would you be this bothered by it?"

"Depends on the type of medication." I mutter this under my breath with my head turned away. But loud enough for him, I say, "No, of course not."

Brunswick clears his throat. "Well, just think of this as my anxiety medication. It's not an addiction or anything. Every month I take them out one time."

"And you chose our date as that one time?"

"You're a beautiful woman, Cherise. I knew I'd be nervous."

I can give him that. "I guess I can understand. Sometimes when I'm nervous, I–"

"It took me hours to decide who to bring. Loki has really smooth edges, which I find very soothing. And Jimmy gives me good advice."

"Jimmy does what now?"

"He's shy, so he won't talk to you now." Brunswick grins at me. "But he'll open up after a while. You're a good woman, Cherise. I can tell."

I guess I should amend my initial statement. I have the *worst* luck with men.

2

My Squad

"He did what?" Shantell, my favorite cousin, stops sipping her boba tea. I'm recounting my latest dating debacle in a café with her and Adrian, my bestie-by-default. As my closest and most trusted friends, the two make up my official squad.

"Tell me you walked out?" Shantell's look says she knows I didn't.

"Oh, Cherise." Adrian gives me a pitying look.

"Well, we'd already gotten our appetizers. I couldn't just leave." It's a lame excuse, I know.

"Did you think the night was going to get better?" Shantell asks.

It didn't get better. It got worse. Much worse.

Shantell glares at me, waiting for a response. "Cherise, you didn't?" She lets out a sigh that kind of hurts my feelings. I know what she's asking, and though I'm not above making poor decisions, I'm not *that* desperate. Not yet.

"I didn't!"

Adrian looks from Shantell to me. "Didn't what?" Adrian has trouble keeping up sometimes, but it's not her fault. Shantell has known me my entire life. Adrian's only known me for a year. My best friend position has been vacant ever since Briana left me for wedded bliss. Adrian happened to sit with me and Shantell at breakfast one day and has been filling the role ever since.

"So, what happened next?" Shantell picks up her tea again and takes a very judgmental sip.

"He misplaced his wallet."

Adrian scoffs. "Oh, for the love. Cherise, you paid for dinner, too?"

Shantell's glare is hotter than my coffee, but I trudge ahead, because there's more to tell. "And his car broke down, so we had to call a tow truck. Which I also paid for."

"Of course you got in a car with him," Shantell mutters. "Let me guess, he offered you a ride home, and you couldn't say no?"

I make a face, and Adrian rubs her temples. "Cherise, you are a cautionary tale wrapped in adorable brown skin."

"Apparently Brunswick thinks so too. He asked me for a second date."

Adrian laughs out loud. Shantell goes quiet, and the top of my lowered forehead burns hotter than our summer in Cancun.

"Cherise Michele Williams, you told that broke behind Brunswick that you'd go out with him again, didn't you?"

"Come on, Shantell." Adrian chuckles. "Even Cherise wouldn't..." She looks at me and the rest dies on her lips. "Cherise? Noo! Why?"

"I won't!" I defend myself with fire in my cheeks. "I just told him I would so he'd leave me alone."

"Right, because a grown man obsessed with his toys *totally* won't become obsessed with you."

"Don't need your sarcasm, Shantell. I already feel bad."

"There's nothing to feel bad about." Adrian pats my shoulder. "And who knows? Maybe he *will* lose interest."

Shantell sets down her tea. "Adrian, that's real cute, but Cherise wouldn't have called a squad meeting if Stew Boy lost interest." Her eyes travel back to me. "How many times has he called you since your date?"

I rub my forehead with my palms. "Sixty-two times." Weakly, I add, "And 42 texts, not counting emojis."

Adrian's mouth drops open. "Should we call the police?"

"Give me your phone, Cherise." Shantell holds out her hand, and I deposit my phone into it. I wait, fingers drumming on the table while the two of them peruse through the messages. After a few minutes of whispered discussion, Shantell hands me back my phone. She and Adrian place their hands in front of them, fingertips together. The universal symbol of agreement.

"So, what says the squad?" I ask.

"We have decided," Adrian pauses and looks at Shantell, who nods in agreement, "that you should take a break from dating for a while."

I open my mouth to protest, but Shantell holds up a finger. "We're not done, Cherise. Adrian, please continue."

"Thank you, Shantell. Cherise, you know we love you, right?"

"Right."

"And we're only here to help you, right?"

Uh oh. "Where is this going?"

"Cherise, you are hands-down my favorite cousin." Shantell's voice is soft, and I cringe. She's using her daycare voice on me. "Sweetheart. Lately, your life choices have been, um, Adrian help me out here?"

"Questionable."

Shantell snaps her fingers. "Yass."

Well, they've got me there.

Adrian gives me the gentlest, most patronizing of hand squeezes. "Thing is, Cherise, we, as people who love you very much and know you very well, have come to the conclusion that you're a little burnt out from dating."

"And you know me." Shantell chuckles. "I'm the first to say 'do you, boo' but um, you've been dating some real duds, lately." She starts counting them off on her fingers. "Shawn, Trevor, Bailey, all one G, two tops."

Adrian nods. "There was Kyle and Chadwick and Jeffrey, too. And let's not forget that disaster with–"

"Don't say his name!" Shantell cuts her off. "Not unless you want a bucket of Cherise to carry home with you." Shantell sighs and pats my hand. "Our point, Cherise, is that Brunswick ain't for you. Not by a long shot."

"But I already told you I'm not gonna go out with him again."

Shantell taps her lips with her finger. "Then why haven't you blocked him yet?"

I open my mouth, but no words come out. Oh.

"I'll tell you why." Shantell folds her fingers again. "Because you don't know how to set boundaries."

"That is completely untrue." It's a lie, but I stick my chin out in defiance, anyway.

"Oh yeah?" Shantell raises an eyebrow. "All Brunswick Stew's gotta do is wear you down and wait you out. Sooner or later, you're gonna talk yourself out of all the reasons you should say no and tell that fool yes."

"No, I won't." Even as I protest, I know she's got me. It wouldn't be the first time.

"What happened to the determined, confident Cherise from three years ago?" Shantell asks. "The one who said she'd find a guy like Garrett with all five G's, no compromises? Face it, Cherise. You're slumming it."

"How many G's would you give Brunswick?" Adrian asks.

I can't help but feel betrayed. My squad is using my own standards against me. The Five G's, inspired by Garrett himself, are my must haves for my future husband. Great Looks, Great Personality, Great Credit, Great Manners, and Great Stamina. But finishing my doctorate wasn't half as hard as finding another guy like Garrett.

"You said he's got a nice smile, so that's great looks, I guess," Adrian continues. "Judging by the way the night went, he probably doesn't have great credit."

"And we know he's got no manners," Shantell cuts in. "So that leaves, what? Great stamina?" Shantell wiggles her eyebrows. "Did you take a peek under the table, Cherise?"

Adrian gives her a look. "Not helping."

Shantell giggles an apology, then mouths, "Tell me later."

I bite my lip and consider their advice. Maybe I am a little burnt out. A break might help me refocus and get my head in the game. I want my happily ever after, and I shouldn't settle for anything less than Garrett-level greatness.

But in three years' time, only one guy has even come close. And he broke my heart into a million pieces. Maybe Garrett was my one chance, and I missed it.

3

The Story of My Life

I hate the warbling sound of a call not answered. Every long, stretched-out tone is an obnoxious reminder that I'm the needy one, and not the other way around. Then there's that stretch of silence in between that leaves me hanging in suspense, wondering if the person on the other end sees my call and is ignoring it. It's my third dial before nine, and still nothing.

"Cherise, your 9:00 a.m. is here."

"Thanks Tammie." I slip my phone into my scrub pocket and head to the work room. The familiar scents of metal, sweat, and antiseptic hit me with a triple dose of adrenaline, and my earlier agitation floats away. I spot my first appointment of the day and smile.

"Good morning, Natalie! How are you feeling today?"

The five-year-old shrugs, but offers me access to her right foot.

"Has it been giving you trouble?"

She nods her head, and I press two fingers gently along her ankle. "No swelling. Has she complained of any pain, Mom?"

"Now and again, she complains that it's tender." Natalie's mother gives me an exasperated look. "The real struggle is getting her to rest it. She's definitely her father's child."

"Wanna see me tumble?" Natalie finally speaks.

"In a minute, but let me massage your ankle and foot first, okay?"

Natalie lets out a sigh and leans back on the bed. I pester her with questions I hope are relevant to a girl of five, then release her to her exercises. Natalie's mom looks on as we practice tumbles and do trampoline jumps. Thirty minutes passes quickly, and I end her session with another massage.

"Remember to rest this leg and keep it elevated at night to improve blood flow and circulation."

"Huh?" Natalie reminds me that she's five, and I reword my instructions. "Put your leg on a pillow before you go to bed. Put it on the couch when you're not at school. If it gets puffy and hot, put a bag of ice or peas on it for as long as one Blippy episode. Make sure you do the stretches I showed you today before you do any tumbles. Your bones are still growing, and we want to make sure they stay super strong." Natalie gives me a thumbs up and a fist bump.

"Thanks for doing this, Cherise." Natalie's mom gives me an appreciative pat. "Her dad trusts you, and after she got the cast off, he refused to take her anywhere else."

"It's my pleasure. How is he, anyway?"

"Busy." She shrugs. "His club has meets all month, and the girls are training extra hard, which means Natalie and I don't see much of him. He couldn't make it today, but he should be at Natalie's next appointment."

"Oh, it's no problem. Tell him hi for me, and to mind that rotator cuff."

"I will, though I don't need to. The girls at the club fuss over him worse than I do after his surgery. Won't even let him carry a gym mat."

I see them out, then check in with Tammie. "When's my next appointment?"

"Not until ten." We both jump as a loud sound shakes the walls. "Oh, for Pete's sake!" Tammie shakes her head.

"What was that?"

"Remember I told you we were going to have new neighbors? They're remodeling the space. You were off the last two days, so thankfully you're coming in on the back end of it." The whirring of a drill sends her lashes into her brows, and she blows out a breath. "I'll be glad when they're done. It was so disruptive yesterday. Monica had to shout over all the noise for her patients to hear her."

"The woes of sharing a wall for the sake of cheap rent. Who's moving in, anyway?"

"I can't remember the name, but it's a fitness center. Though, last time I took a peek, it looked more like a garage. So many tires and chains."

I make a face. "Ugh. Not a bunch of meatheads?"

Tammie laughs. "I know. But it'll probably be good for business. Lots of people injure themselves after taking things too far in these extreme workout places."

"Tammie, we shouldn't wish misfortune on others for our own gain. But, if a bunch of jugheads with no real training are leading the simple-minded astray, I suppose it's inevitable." I wiggle my eyebrows, and Tammie takes a sip of her coffee.

My phone rings, and I snatch it out of my pocket. Tammie must notice the look of disappointment on my face, because she puts her coffee down. "Your mom hasn't called you back yet?"

I scoff. "What? Of course she did. We arranged lunch months ago. I was just hoping to get a call back from someone, but it's a spam call." I yell at the still buzzing phone. "I already have enough insurance! Give it a rest, guys!" My awkward laugh gains me a raised eyebrow from Tammie as she takes another sip of her coffee. I extract myself from the lobby and head to my office.

I dial Mom again, but it still goes to voicemail. It finally dawns on me that my mother has two phones, and I dial her work number. She picks up on the first ring.

"Linda Realty, this is Linda. How may I help you?"

"Mom, it's Cherise."

"Why are you calling me at work? I need to keep this line clear for important calls."

That stings. "Sorry, yeah, I know. I just wanted to make sure we were still on for lunch today." Silence on the other end. "You still there?"

"Yeah, hang on a sec, Cherise." I wait for several seconds, resisting the urge to chew my fingernails. "Cherise, I don't have anything on the calendar for you today."

"No, Mom, we arranged this months ago. You, me, and the Cheesecake Factory at one o'clock. You said you'd block out your schedule."

She sighs into the phone. "Well, I've got a showing at one, and I don't think I can make it today, Sweetheart. Why don't we reschedule? I'm booked up most of the week, but I'm sure I can find something."

"No, Mom. You said you would have lunch with me today. It has to be today."

"Cherise, must you be so dramatic whenever you don't get your way? Honestly, I don't see what difference it makes if it's today or another day."

"You know what? Forget it." I wait three seconds. I don't know why, but in that three seconds I'm hoping for a protest, or a concession. Dare I say an apology? But the silence in that three seconds is more uncomfortable than I can bear, so I end the call.

At least I didn't make a reservation. I made that mistake a few times before, once at an expensive restaurant that charged a fee for cancellations. Mom offered to reimburse me, but I learned my lesson.

I take a few minutes to reset, then get ready for my next appointment. When lunchtime rolls around, Tammie finds me in my office.

"Hey, you."

I wave from my desk, my head slumped in my arms.

"Guess you're not going to lunch with your mom this year?"

I shake my head. "Nope."

Tammie places a small, white box in front of me. From the clear plastic on top, I spy lemon frosting. I open the box and swipe my finger across the top of a giant cupcake.

"Happy birthday, Cherise."

I stick my finger in my mouth, and my lips pucker. "You remembered."

"Of course I did! Double dark chocolate chip cupcake with lemon frosting. Strange combination, which is what the girl at the shop said when I ordered it."

"It is a complex flavor pairing that represents the bittersweet nature of my life." Tammie raises an eyebrow. "Don't judge me, okay?"

She raises both hands. "No judgment here. Enjoy!"

Tammie leaves me to inhale the cupcake in private. I abandon all decorum as I wolf it down, then scrape the last bits of crumb and icing from the box. My stomach rumbles in dissatisfaction, and the irony isn't lost on me. As delicious and thoughtful as the cupcake was, it still leaves me hungry. Because what I really want is to have lunch with my mom, on my birthday, *for once*. Having Linda Williams give me the time of day would mean the world to me.

But to her, I'm just an unwanted call.

4

I'm Fine, Everything's Fine

Two weeks later, I'm still fuming over my missed lunch with Mom. She forgot my birthday, but didn't realize it until days later. Which somehow became my fault? We argued about it for about three minutes on the phone, which was three too many for her, I guess. After declaring me too emotional and high strung, she retracted her offer to reschedule lunch and ended the call.

"How was your weekend?" I ask Jacob, my afternoon patient. I gesture for him to keep walking, my mind still distracted by my latest phone call with Mom. She said she'd call another time, once I'd gotten myself under control. I won't hold my breath.

"Oh, you know, this and that. Nothing out of the ordinary." Jacob's response snaps me out of my brooding. I scrutinize his walk as he follows the red-taped line on the floor. Something's off with his left leg. He's listing, but trying to hide it.

"Take that line one more time for me, Jacob." He walks back, and I gesture to a chair for him to sit. "Talk to me about this left leg?"

He winces. "You noticed that, huh?"

"Don't underestimate these brown eyes, Jacob. They don't miss much. What's going on?"

He fidgets in the chair and I wait. "Well, I'm not getting the speed I used to."

"Perfectly natural after a stress fracture. I told you to be patient."

"Yeah, well, Coach sent me to a personal trainer for some extra conditioning."

My hackles rise, but I shove them down. "Okay. Can you tell me what this extra conditioning entails?"

"Sprints, intervals, some weights. I'm still having trouble with the starting block, so we've been practicing techniques."

"Well, you're experiencing muscle weakness in this left leg, so I need you to ease up on the extra conditioning."

"Kendi says that studies show athletes recover faster with muscle break down."

"Kendi?"

"He's my new trainer. He suggested I up my weights to build back stronger muscles."

"Did he?" I measure my next words, reminding myself that it's not Jacob, but his meathead trainer that's to blame. "Well, Jacob, I need to remind you that you've already fractured this leg twice. An additional stress fracture on top of the two you've suffered could yield long-term consequences."

"Kendi seemed confident he could help me improve my speed." Jacob's eyes go wide at my glare. "But if you'd like to talk to him, I could have him call you?"

"Mhm." With some effort, I dial down my irritation and smile. "That would be great." I finish up our appointment with some additional instructions, then walk Jacob to the lobby to check out.

Shantell texts me about my lunch plans, and I send her the address for a spot I want to check out. Her daycare is just a few blocks from the clinic, so I offer to pick her up on the way. As an afterthought, I text Adrian to see if she's free. It's been a while since our last squad meeting.

ADRIAN AND SHANTELL sit in the seats across from me as we sample the six different sauces we ordered with our chicken tenders and wings. We're not above talking while we eat, and Shantell only has a half hour before she's got to be back at work.

"Can you believe this guy?" I ask in between bites. "Who does he think he is? Good for Kendi, he knows how to perform a Google search. But that doesn't replace a doctor's professional opinion."

"You right, girl." Shantell nods and dunks a wing into the honey mustard sauce. "Kendi's got a lot of nerve, and he crossed the wrong one, ain't that right, Adrian?"

"More information is needed." Adrian dips a fry into the barbecue sauce and shrugs. "It's possible that your client wanted to push himself, and Kendi simply gave him information. This could all be a misunderstanding."

Shantell and I both stare at Adrian.

"Whose side are you even on?" Shantell clucks. "Unless you want to pay for your own lunch today, I suggest you get with the program. I know not to bite the hand that feeds me." Shantell gives me a high five, and I nod.

Adrian sighs. "I can pay for my own lunch, and besides, our job isn't to tell Cherise what she wants to hear. Our job is to help her." I make a face and Adrian laughs. "On that note, how's the not-dating going?"

I let out the longest sigh and throw up my hands. "It's going great. I am the happiest I've ever been, and completely fulfilled by work. I don't need fancy dinners with hot guys, or even medium heat guys."

Shantell whispers to Adrian in a not-so-discreet way. "I think she's struggling."

"No, seriously! Ladies, I'm fine." I place my hand on my chest, close my eyes, lift my brows, and perform an award-worthy piece I like to call 'Cherise Is Just Fine.' "You two ladies are all I need. I don't need a man. Someone to love me unconditionally, who holds me at night and wakes up every morning telling me that he chose me and would choose me again and again."

"Uh oh." Adrian frowns. "Cherise?"

"The holidays are coming up, and all I have to keep me warm is a ratty old blanket, but that's okay. I'm a strong, independent black woman. I can just buy another blanket. And my own birthday presents. Who cares if no one remembers the day I was born, or the stupid lunch we planned months in advance? So what if no one gets excited when they see me calling?"

Shantell raises her hand. "I get excited when I see you calling."

"You get excited because I pay for your meals," I huff.

Shantell pouts. "That's not the *only* reason."

"I think what Cherise is trying to say is that she's..." Adrian catches the heat from my glare and throws up her hands. "Perfectly fine."

Shantell gives her a thumbs up. "Yup. Super fine. Like all the members of the Justice League."

"She could be a member of the Justice League."

"Shoot, my cousin could start her *own* Justice League."

I laugh, despite the pain in my chest. They see it. And knowing I don't want to cry in a basket of chicken fingers, they keep the jokes coming.

5

Meatheads

"Good morning, Dr. Williams!"

I return Tammie's greeting with a smile and a brave face as I grab a cup of water from the lobby. "Good morning, Tammie. My ten thirty cancelled today?"

"Yep, she's got strep."

"Oh, poor thing!" After an evening spent crying myself to sleep, my throat doesn't feel too great, either. My phone chirps, and I pull it from my pocket. I don't recognize the number, though, so I ignore the call. "When's my next appointment, Tammie?"

She taps her computer keys and shrugs. "Nothing until after lunch. Light day today."

"Hah. I could have gotten some shopping done this morning."

"You still can! And probably should. Tomorrow is busy. Back-to-back appointments."

I do a mental scan of my refrigerator. If memory serves, it's as empty as my love life right now. This stupid no dating thing is harder than I thought it would be. I've got way too much time on my hands. Ironic that I haven't made time to restock the fridge.

Still, I'm not looking forward to another solo night on the couch watching reruns of *Living Single* and feeling sorry for myself. "I'll just organize my office and go to the store tonight." I need the distraction.

"Suit yourself."

I hole away in my office, straightening files that don't need straightening and searching for dust I know isn't there. I keep my work spaces neat and in order. Why can't every part of my life be like this?

I tap out a text to Shantell, hoping she can get Big Mama's recipe for macaroni and cheese to me before I get to the store tonight. I'll need the comfort, no doubt.

My phone rings again, and I check the number. It's Shantell.

"You know I don't like calling Big Mama."

"You lived with her for half your life, Shantell."

"Exactly. She's got too much dirt on me, and we both know it. Every time I call, she tries to guilt me into coming over. *You* call."

"Big Mama will laugh me off the phone if I ask her for a recipe. She still thinks I can't cook after what happened at Thanksgiving that one year."

"She's still holding on to that? It was an honest mistake, and you were seven. See? That's why I don't want to call. She never lets anything go."

"But you're her favorite granddaughter. Even if she fusses at you, she'll do whatever you want. Me? She'll tell me I'm my mother's child and should just give up."

"Oh yeah. I forgot she doesn't like Auntie Linda too much."

I don't know when the grudge between my mother and her mother-in-law (now ex mother-in-law) began, but it's been a wedge between me and my father's side of the family for years. Shantell's really the only one that keeps in touch with me.

I sigh, and it's long and sad, and Shantell takes the bait. "Okay, Cuz. I'll call her. But if I end up spending the weekend cleaning collards or chitlins or something, I'm blaming you."

"You're the best!"

I hang up with Shantell and stare at my office. There's really nothing for me to do for the next several hours, so I meander to the fitness center next door. Construction's over, and business seems to be flowing nicely. People tend to flock to whatever's new in town. I suppose, since I'm snooping and lurking by the door, I'm not an exception.

"Can I help you?"

I swing around in full fight mode, but relax when I see it's just an attendant. I even manage to uncurl my fists as I offer a nonviolent greeting.

"Hey there! I'm Cherise. I work next door at the PT clinic."

My eyes work over the sleeveless orange and grey tee and the muscles it's doing a poor job hiding. No doubt the intended effect. I blink and force my eyes up at the brown brother in front of me.

"Do you have a membership here?" he asks.

I don't care for his tone, or the quirk of his eyebrow. I've been profiled as suspicious in grocery stores and gas stations. But a fitness center?

"No," I say. "I work next door."

"Would you like information on a membership here?"

What is this guy's deal? "No, I just stopped by to check the place out."

He nods and keeps staring, as if he's waiting for further explanation. I don't owe him any. I'm allowed to be here. But having eyes that intense glaring a hole into me is unsettling.

"I should have brought cupcakes or something. You know, to welcome you to the plaza. Since we share a wall and all."

The brow lifts even higher. "This is a serious gym. We train elite athletes here, some of the best in the state. They come here to work out, *privately*, and none of them, or the staff working here, want cupcakes sitting around."

"Wow. Did I offend you, big guy?" This is why I can't stand meatheads. So full of themselves.

"No, but if there's nothing else you need?" He waits a beat, then gestures toward the door.

I throw my mouth open. "Are you serious right now?"

"Unless you'd like to ask after our membership plans?"

"Nope. I'm good." I try to storm out with dignity, but I'm short and the universe hates me. So of course I trip over the threshold. I don't fall, but knowing Mr. Grumpy Pants gets a full view of my stumble-walk on my way back to the clinic doesn't make me feel any better about it.

Tammie sees the look on my face when I walk in and stands up with a worried one on hers. "You okay?"

I clear my throat, holding back the string of expletives begging to be released. "Let's just say our new neighbors rubbed me the wrong way."

Tammie lifts one side of her mouth. "Have you *seen* our new neighbors?"

Realizing my mistake, I hold up a hand. "Don't."

It's too late. Tammie chuckles and sips her tea, but whispers under her breath. "I don't think there is a wrong way."

My phone chirps, and it's that same unknown number. I'm too worked up to be bothered with an extended warranty call, so I send it to voicemail and head back to my office.

Not a half hour later, Tammie pings me on the intercom.

"Dr. Williams? You've got a visitor in the lobby."

I'm not expecting anyone. "Who is it?"

I hear Tammie whisper to my mystery guest. "What'd you say your name was again?" Then, to me, "His name is Kendi. He says Jacob Whittler asked him to contact you."

Perfect. "I'll be out in a sec."

I'm still miffed about my encounter at the gym, but I check myself before I walk out of the office. In the end, we're all professionals, right? No need to rip his head off for giving my client bad advice. We'll settle a few things about Jacob's care, I'll give my professional opinion about Jacob's workout regimen, and that'll be that. Kendi's probably lovely, and this is all likely a misunderstanding between Jacob and his meathead trainer.

By the time I reach the lobby, I've just about convinced myself not to use the term 'meathead' in our conversation. But then, I come face to face with Mr. Grumpy Pants. "You?"

His eyebrows arch up, and his smile rescinds. He still offers me an extended hand. "Miss Williams? I'm Kendi Ready. Jacob Whittler told me you wanted to speak with me, and—"

"That's *Dr.* Williams." I ignore his hand and level cool eyes at him. Or maybe they're boiling with rage. I can't tell, since I can't see them. I just know they're angry eyes.

"Excuse me. *Doctor* Williams." Kendi clears his throat. "I was hoping to talk over the phone, but I haven't been able to get through."

Huh. That explains the mystery number. "I'm a very busy woman." I ignore the mocking tone of his glare and its underlying message.

"That makes two of us. Listen, Dr. Williams, I can assure you that the workout plans made between myself and Jacob are in full agreement with his coach and his goals. I'm happy to discuss any issues you may have with my methods, but I'd appreciate it if you didn't interfere."

I scoff. "*You* don't want *me* interfering with your training methods?"

Tammie's eyes float from Kendi to me. She shifts back to her computer and pretends to work.

Kendi sighs. "Please, don't take offense when I say this, but Jacob is an elite athlete. That comes with a certain amount of risk that, yes, the average person shouldn't take, but he isn't average. He knows it, I know it, and respectfully, as his physical therapist, you should know it, too."

Tammie chokes on her tea, then returns to her typing. I step into Kendi's space, so close I can feel the heat emanating from the muscles at his core and chest. He's got at least six inches on me, almost everyone does, but it doesn't matter. I lift the name tag hanging from my lanyard and shove it in his face. "Kendi, read this."

He exhales. "Dr. Williams–"

"Yes, that's right. It says Cherise M. Williams, DPT on this name tag. Do you know what that means?" I don't wait for him to answer. "It means Doctor of Physical Therapy. That means I am a medical professional, educated and certified to assist my clients with their rehabilitation. I attended a highly competitive doctorate program for six years, post grad. And yes, I do understand that Jacob is under an enormous amount of pressure. But you want to know what else is under a lot of pressure? His femur, which has been weakened from prior injuries. Tell me, Kendi? What does it take to become a meathead trainer like you? Let me guess? A six-month certificate program you found off the internet?"

"Dr. Williams, I don't think that's called for."

"Personal trainers are *not* doctors. They are not trained in the medical profession, and they are not qualified to make medical decisions for *anybody*. Do you even know what a stress fracture is? More importantly, do you know what happens if Jacob trains too hard, too fast? If you want to push him over his limits, you should at least know the consequences. Reinjury, nerve damage, a permanent limp, the list goes on.

"So before you try to lecture me on what elite athletes need, you need to understand two things. First, I am Jacob's physical therapist. I'm not the one overstepping here. You are. Second, Jacob doesn't get back on the field without medical clearance from his PCP and from me. So, if you want to modify his workout, or increase his weights, or try *anything* beyond what I have currently recommended for his rehabilitation, you clear it with me."

Kendi frowns and dips his head. "My mistake, Dr. Williams."

"Yes. It was. Now, if there's nothing else?" I gesture toward the door. I can't help the smirk that follows.

Kendi looks like he wants to say something else, but he doesn't. He turns on his heel and walks out. I'm a little disappointed that his exit is way smoother than mine was, but I guess I can't have everything.

"Wow, Dr. W. I didn't know you had that in you." Tammie's look of awe sends heat to my cheeks. "You've always drawn a firm line when it comes to your clients, but that was just..." Tammie does a chef's kiss, and I chuckle.

I've gotta admit, it felt good.

6

The Ex Factor

I forgot how much I hate grocery shopping. I'm not very good with ingredients. I can remember that I want macaroni, chicken, salad, but the things that make those things taste good? Elusive. I prefer to shop from a recipe. It takes out all the guesswork.

At least Shantell came through with Big Mama's mac and cheese recipe. She listed all the ingredients for me, as well as the steps to glorious, cheesy heaven. By the time I find all the ingredients and seasonings for that, I've decided to grab a premade salad and rotisserie chicken from the deli.

I peruse through a dozen types of bagged salads with my finger on my lips, wondering which one will pair the best with dinner.

"When did they get so many salad options?"

I *know* that voice. It sends a jolt through my toes that zips up my legs, through my stomach and straight into my heart. I grab the closest bag in a panic and bolt in the opposite direction. Halfway to the register, I realize that I left my purse and shopping cart right there in the deli section.

Real smooth, Cherise.

I walk back on shaky legs. Peek out from behind the bread aisle. Try to wring the tremors from my hands. The coast is clear, so I make a run for it. I snatch my buggy and creep back up the way I came, heart pounding in my throat.

I can't get my fingers to stop shaking. I haven't seen him in, what? Eight months? Three? A year? I stopped counting, and now, apparently, I've stopped breathing too. I need to think of something else. Anything else. Sunsets, Big Mama's macaroni and cheese, Kendi's stupid face.

That's right. I told off that meathead Kendi Ready today. And even if I haven't been the most successful, relationship-wise, I'm still Cherise Michele Williams, DPT. I have nothing to be ashamed of.

Why am I hiding, anyway? I didn't do anything wrong. He's the one that cheated, and betrayed me, and shattered my heart, to say nothing of my confidence.

I lift my head and walk to the register like a normal human being. There are only two lanes open, and a small line at each. I feel exposed, standing in line, and anxiety tries to claw its way up. I press it down, one affirmation at a time.

You don't have to run.

You did nothing wrong.

You are beautiful.

You are successful.

"You forgot the ranch dressing."

You forgot the ranch–

I freeze, willing myself not to turn around. I want to run. I want to scream. I want to wake up and realize this is a dream. Or a nightmare. Or a mistake. Maybe it's not him. Maybe it's just someone with a similar voice, skin tone, and build. Maybe...

"Cherise? You not gonna talk to me?"

I turn around, as if I were a puppet and his husky voice my string. "Hey Calvin."

His eyes roam, stopping at my mouth before they reach my eyes. The ranch dressing in his hand floats up. "I thought it was you. Noticed you didn't have any ranch in your cart. It's still your favorite, right?"

He remembered.

Don't be moved. At least half the people on the planet like ranch dressing.

"Thanks." It comes out croaky, and as I take the bottle from his hands, our fingers touch. The familiar spark of heat is still there, and it sears my skin long after the bottle lands in the cart.

"You look good, Cherise."

I study his face. It's exactly the same, from the bushy brows and wide bridge of his nose right down to the light stubble kissing his cheeks. It's been two, maybe three days since he's shaved, by my estimation. He usually doesn't let it get past the fourth day. A part of me wants to run my fingers along his jaw.

No, Cherise. He broke your heart, remember?

I blink. He's talking to me, still. So, I talk back. The conversation is light and easy, and I feel warm all over. Checkout is a blur, and when I walk to my car, he follows me out.

"Cherise?" His voice is soft. Impossibly so.

"Hmm?" My voice comes out high-pitched and sweet, and I know I'm in trouble. I'm losing my resolve and slipping into Pick Me Cherise. But Pick Me Cherise is too nice for her own good. If I don't get it together, there's no telling where I'll end up tonight. I need to set boundaries and stick to them.

"I'm not with Candace anymore."

It shouldn't matter. I should pack all my groceries in my car and drive home. I don't belong with Calvin. He made that abundantly clear.

"What's that got to do with me?" A brave part of me shouts inside my brain, begging me to walk away. I know the longer I linger here with Calvin, the quieter that part will get.

"Cherise."

I'm not the same Cherise I was a year ago. And he's no Garrett, despite having passed my Five G test. Despite the fact that even mentioning his name has broken me more times than I can count. *Don't let him back in, Cherise. He hurt you.*

"I'm sorry, Cherise."

I shake my head. The tears fall. I know I should go home and forget about Calvin, but what am I going home to? An empty apartment where I'll spend the evening cooking more macaroni and cheese than one person should eat and watching tv until I doze on the couch?

"Can we talk? Grab a drink somewhere?"

"I have to put my groceries away."

"Okay. Can we grab a drink at your place?"

No! "Okay."

He turns me around to face him. "I've missed you."

I nod my head, wanting to believe that this time he really means it. "I've missed you too."

7

Blue Skies and Dirty Pigeons

I don't remember the sky being so vividly blue. The clouds are bright and happy, and the birds that congregate on the far end of the parking lot, the ones that bomb every car beneath them with wicked precision, seem twice as pretty. My smile is wide as I walk through the lobby doors, and Tammie greets me with a grin of her own.

"Good morning, Dr. Williams."

"Good morning, Tammie! Beautiful day today."

She wiggles her brows. "It's so-so. The sun's got nothing on that smile. Do you have good news?"

I shake my head. "What makes you ask?"

"Well, you walked in here like a cat with a canary in its mouth, honey. Ray Charles could see that something good happened. You gonna spill?"

"Stop it!" I wave a dismissive hand her way, but the smile stays as I sashay to my office and slide into my chair. I tap out a text to Shantell.

ME: Got back together with Calvin last night. *Screams*

I pull out the files for my first few clients and start reviewing. My phone buzzes twice. A reply from Shantell.

SHANTY: WHAT?
SHANTY: CALL ME! RIGHT NOW!!!

I giggle to myself and keep working. My phone buzzes several more times, but I finish my reviews before checking it.

SHANTY: YOU'D BETTER CALL!
SHANTY: CHERISE MICHELE WILLIAMS, DON'T MAKE ME CALL YOU FIRST!

I send a text to Calvin.

ME: Last night was amazing. Want to have lunch today?

My phone buzzes again, and I snatch it up. More texts from Shantell in all caps. None from Calvin. Shantell calls while I'm reading her texts. I've got another half hour before my next client, so I've got a little time.

"Girl." I hear the restraint in her voice, but I've already rehearsed what I'm going to say.

"It's different this time, Shantell. He apologized for everything."

"As he should have. But that doesn't mean you get back together. Every time he comes back, you get hurt."

"But this time is different. We were still technically together before, and things were fuzzy between us. This time, we made a clean break. And it's been months since I've even talked to him."

"Is he still seeing that chick? Did you even ask him?"

"He's not seeing her anymore. I didn't have to ask him. He told me right away."

"Cherise!"

"Just listen for a second." Shantell growls, but she stops talking. "Last night was incredible. We went to my place and we talked for hours. He told me how much he missed me, and he apologized for all the things he said. For the lying, the cheating, all of it. I was worried, too, at first. But after we talked, I realized that he really missed me. And I missed him, too."

"You gonna sit here and tell me that all you did with Calvin was talk?"

I wait a beat. "Well, that's not *all* we did."

"Cherise!"

"It was afterwards!"

"Cherise, you know I love you, and I really want to be happy for you."

"Then end that sentence there, and be happy for me. Because we're officially together again." My phone buzzes and I check my messages. Another smile weaves its way to my face. "And we're having lunch this afternoon."

"Cherise." I can hear the frustration in her voice, but I'm not interested in any naysaying. I'm having too bright a morning for that.

"Shantell, I gotta go. I've got clients. I'll talk to you tonight. Bye!" I disconnect before she can protest, then send Calvin a list of possible places for lunch.

Between a busy morning with back-to-back clients, and constant texts to Calvin in between, I don't circle back to Shantell's messages until I'm walking out the door.

> **SHANTY: I'm calling an emergency squad meeting. Tonight.**
> **SHANTY: Adding Adrian to the chat to weigh in.**
> **SHANTY: Adrian, Cherise has recoupled with Calvin. Care to weigh in?**
> **ADRIAN: Calvin the Cockroach? Cherise, NO!**

I stop reading after that. I've got about 90 minutes to drive across town to the sushi place Calvin and I used to frequent when we dated, grab something to eat, then head back to the clinic and prep for my next appointment.

I find Calvin inside, already seated at the bar and sipping a seltzer water. Our eyes meet, and my heart does a skip, jump, crash, bang, boom, slide. He doesn't smile when he sees me. Something is wrong.

"Hey." I lean in for a kiss, but my timing is off. He's turning his head for another sip, and I end up kissing his ear instead. I wipe at his ear with my finger. "Sorry about that. I'm so glad you could make it to lunch with me. It's been ages since we've been here, but it still feels exactly the same to me. Does it feel the same to you?"

Calvin nods and stirs his seltzer with his straw. "Yup."

I situate myself into the stool, not liking the way my legs dangle a foot from the ground. "Hey, you mind if we sit at a booth or something instead?" I gesture to my legs and shrug. "Short girl problems over here." I laugh alone. Calvin sighs and stands up.

"Alright if we sit here?" Calvin pulls out a chair at a small table and sits.

"Sure." The chair is better, but Calvin's mood isn't. "Hey, is everything alright?"

Calvin runs his hands through his hair and sighs. "Why do you ask?"

"Because you've been a bit snappy since I got here. Is something wrong?"

Calvin pulls out his phone. "I don't know, Cherise. You tell me."

"I thought we were good. Last night, things between us were good, weren't they?"

He nods. "Yeah. Last night was good. And after our talk, I thought, maybe she's changed, you know? But you haven't. After all this time." He stops and shakes his head. "Listen, maybe we were wrong. Maybe this was a mistake."

My hands tremble beneath the table. This cannot be happening again. "No. Last night you said all those things. About how you missed me and you were wrong to leave."

"That was last night. I mean, Cherise, we hooked up for one night, and this morning I woke up to 20 texts. You were blowing up my phone all morning talking about lunch."

"I wanted to meet someplace nice." I shift my purse to the floor. "I didn't realize it would bother you."

He shakes his head. "I can't do this with you."

"Do what with me?" I hate the desperation in my voice.

He waves his hand in the air. "All of this. Where you micromanage every aspect of our relationship."

"Putting in effort isn't micromanagement. It's called work. Relationships take work."

"Well, maybe I don't want to be in a relationship that takes work."

I lean back. "What is that supposed to mean?"

"I mean you're exhausting, Cherise. Our entire relationship we always had to do what *you* wanted to do. You want to go see friends, you want to celebrate every random, asinine couples holiday. You wanna dress up in matching outfits and go to festivals. Then you get mad at me if I don't."

"Excuse me for wanting to spend time with my boyfriend."

"Some days, I just wanted to chill out on the couch, or hang with my boys, but you tried to micromanage that, too. If we were watching Netflix, we had to have a theme. Our snacks had to match. Our clothes had to match. Whenever I'd go out without you, you texted me nonstop. I couldn't breathe!"

Every word feels like a bullet. And Calvin's a good shot. As he echoes the same complaints he'd listed when we broke up, every dream I had for us slowly shrivels and dies.

"And so yeah, I cheated. It was wrong, and I apologized for that. But Cherise." He sighs and takes another sip of his seltzer.

Please don't say it.

"You're just too much."

I anchor myself by grabbing the sides of the chair. He's right. I did all those things, and maybe I am too much. But I want this to work. "I can be less."

He scoffs.

"No, really." I lick my lips, swallow my pride. "I can tone it down, Calvin. I won't text you as much, I promise. And we can do whatever you want to do."

Calvin stares at me. "No, Cherise. You can't. It's not in you. And besides," he stares at his phone as it starts to ring. The name 'Candace' pops up on the screen.

Oh no. "You're still talking to Candace?"

His shoulders deflate a little. "Cherise, it's not like that."

"You never broke up with her, did you?"

His eyes answer for him. His phone stops ringing, then buzzes three or four times with messages. He taps out a response. His phone buzzes again, and again he replies. All the while I sit, watching Calvin text his *real* girlfriend. Who, from where I'm sitting, seems just as needy as me. I can't help but wonder, what does Candace have that I don't?

Is it just... me?

At some point, I scrape up what little dignity I have and walk out. Calvin's in his own world and doesn't seem to notice. I'm just background noise.

The drive back to the clinic is slow, and I spend every minute fighting the flood. I want to scream, and cry, and find someplace to hide. But I can't do any of those things. I've got clients waiting for me back at the clinic, and my ugly cry isn't something a quick touch up can fix.

One tear falls, then two. I need a distraction. I turn on the radio, but every song is a song Calvin and I listened to together, so I shut it off. Another tear falls as I pull into the parking lot. I'm not sure how much longer I can hold it together. Calvin's accusation keeps playing over and over in my head, the same way it did when we first broke up.

You're too much, Cherise.

Another tear. I'm not gonna make it. I pull toward my parking spot, ready for the downpour, but then I come to an abrupt halt. A beat-up Ford with a cross hanging from the rearview mirror is parked in my space. I put my car in reverse and circle the parking lot. It's full. Lunch time is usually sparse around the clinic, but now that the fitness center is in full operation, the parking lot is packed. Today, it seems, there's not a single space available out front. I hate parking on the far side of the lot, but at least it takes my mind off of... other things.

It takes two full rotations before I find a spot. Someone pulls out, and I pull in, right beneath the stupid birds at the far end of the parking lot. I glare at them as I lock my door. "Y'all better not trash my car. I just had it washed." They chirp and coo a response that I can only interpret as birdie profanity. And to think, just this morning I called the dirty pigeons pretty.

I inhale. Exhale. Repeat.

I can do this.

I put on a brave face and walk into the clinic.

8

One is the Loneliest Number

"So, are we pulling up, or what?" Shantell stares at her nails, then looks at me. We're sitting in my living room with an open box of pizza on the coffee table surrounded by even more boxes of Kleenex. Adrian is on the opposite end of the coffee table with her laptop on her thighs.

"I'm pulling up his address now." Adrian turns the computer toward us. "He's less than 15 minutes from here, and I've got a pile of bricks in my trunk."

Shantell gives her a high five. "We'll unpack why you've got bricks in your trunk later, but that's what I'm talking about, Adrian. We need to show up and show out!"

I shake my head and bury my tears in a tissue. "He's not worth it, guys."

"No, but we're not slinging bricks and breaking nails for him. We're doing it for you." Shantell tugs a slice free from the box. "You know we'll only scare him a little."

Adrian nods. "Sure. But anytime you need a brick on someone's hood, just say the word."

Shantell and I exchange glances. "Again, we'll unpack that later. But yes, we're here for you, Cherise."

I dip my head as an ugly cry pushes its way out. "I really thought things would be different this time." That's what I say, but it comes out garbled and warped. Adrian and Shantell flock to my side with reassuring back rubs and promises to kidnap me if I ever try to get back with Calvin again. While they're with me, I'm okay.

But eventually they leave, and I'm left alone in a quiet room with my noisy thoughts. At first, they linger on Calvin, but eventually they travel to all the people in my life who've told me I'm too much. Their faces blur and fade the longer I sit. But that phrase stays behind, sticking to my brain like gum stuck to the bottom of a bench, or twisted pieces of paper on wet grass.

The hurt pulls at me hard, carving a message on my heart that I can't erase. And I wish I believed the problem was them, but I can't help but wonder if maybe, just maybe, the problem is me.

9

Side Swiped

I hate walking on gravel. It gets stuck in the grooves on the bottom of my sneakers, and the grinding sound as the rocks slide against each other grates on my nerves. This morning, mine are shot. By the time I reach the clinic, I'm ready to commit an act of vandalism.

"Good morning, Dr. Williams!" She makes a face when I don't reply. "Bad parking spot today?"

"The worst! Not only was that raggedy Ford in my parking space again, I couldn't find a single spot on our lot. I had to choose between parking on the public lot a quarter of a mile away, or parking on the street."

"You chose the lot, right? You could make a drinking game out of the number of side mirrors on the street."

"Oh, don't I know it. I'd have to be desperate to park on the street. Why is it so crowded, anyway?"

"Our new neighbors are popular."

"At ten in the morning?"

Tammie shrugs. "They're shooting a commercial in the back lot. Got a couple trailers back there taking up at least a dozen spots. I wouldn't go out for lunch today if I were you. It's gonna be even worse during peak hours."

I groan and rub my head. "This stupid fitness center has been nothing but headache after headache."

"I don't know about that. Business has picked up here, too. You've got ten new clients."

"And zero free time." I let out a flat laugh. *As if I have better things to do.*

"I wonder who that Ford belongs to," Tammie muses.

"Your guess is as good as mine, but when I find out who it is, I'm gonna—"

"Oh, look! Someone's headed to the car now." I turn toward the entrance and peer out the glass doors. "Looks like he's shuffling around for something," Tammie muses. "If he were leaving, I'd suggest you run back to the lot and park your car in the spot. Oh well."

My eyes narrow as he exits the car and walks back toward the center. I should have known.

Kendi.

I'M HAVING IT OUT WITH Kendi Ready. Today. Nothing outside of work is going right in my life, and I know it's a petty hill to die on, but I've had it. Thanks to him, I've had to park on the far side of the lot multiple times, and apparently the avian gang gets a kick out of painting my black BMW white. Parking in the public lot is a nightmare, especially when I have to walk back at night, and today? I had to park on the street. In downtown Raleigh. Where the streets are paved with broken side mirrors, because the streets are as narrow as the mindless drivers going 40 in a 25.

I thought my car could make it until lunch when I parked on the street this morning. I was wrong. And as I stand by Kendi's crappy car, my left side mirror in my hands, one thing is clear. This is a fight I am going to win. This is a shared lot, and he's got no right to swoop in and take my spot. I'm not going to let him.

That's right, Cherise. Stand up for yourself.

As the minutes tick by, it occurs to me that I have no idea when Kendi's coming out, if at all. The gym is open 24 hours, and I don't know his work schedule. It's a bit deflating, once I think about it. And broken as it is, my side mirror is getting heavy. Plus, it's cold.

Maybe I'll have it out with Kendi tomorrow.

Tomorrow. For sure.

There's no sense looking for a new parking spot, since my mirror has already gone to mirror heaven, so I set it in the backseat of my car and go back to the clinic. Tammie watches me with careful eyes when I walk in.

"Did you move your car?"

I shake my head. "They got me, Tammie."

"Oh no!" She shakes her head. "Did anyone leave a note?"

"Nope. Just pieces of glass all over the ground."

Tammie groans. "Is it in one piece, at least?"

"More or less. It made a clean break."

"That's something, I guess."

I let out a long sigh and get ready for my next session. By the time I greet my last client, I've all but abandoned my plans to confront Kendi. Technically, it isn't *my* parking space. And I'll admit the idea of telling him off has lost some of its initial luster. Putting him in his place for my client's sake is one thing. Arguing over a parking space feels like something a girl who's 'too much' would do.

At the end of the day, I linger in the lobby. Adrian and Shantell are busy tonight, and I don't really feel like going home yet. "Tammie, you need any help?" I grab one of the disinfecting wipes on her desk and start wiping the chairs before she can answer.

Tammie clucks at me. "You don't have to do that. Go on home, Dr. Williams. I've got it."

"It's no trouble. I'm waiting for someone, and I've got a little time to kill."

"Who are you waiting for?"

My mind goes blank.

Tammie gasps. "Oh, are you waiting for Kendi?"

No. "Yep."

"Sick of him taking your parking space?"

"Yep."

"You'd better go, then, because he's walking toward his car now."

"Say what, now?"

Tammie plucks the wipe from my hand and pushes me toward the door. "Go easy on him. Or don't. Just promise to tell me all the details tomorrow!"

She shoves me out into the evening air with a double thumbs up and a grin. Kendi is halfway to the car, now. I turn back toward Tammie, but she shoos me forward, mouthing, "Go on!"

I turn back toward Kendi and square my shoulders. I don't actually have to have it out with him. We could just have a normal conversation. I can explain my situation to him, and we can work something out. No need to be petty.

"Kendi, hold up!"

He turns, finds me with his eyes, and heaves a heavily exaggerated sigh. "Yes, Dr. Williams?"

Oh, that tone. I don't like it. A few hours ago, I would have slung it right back at him. But I'm not going to be petty. I'm going to be calm. "I'd like to talk to you about my parking space."

"*Your* parking space?"

"You see where you're parked right now? That's been my space for about four years now."

"It's my understanding that parking spaces aren't reserved unless they're handicapped."

I take a breath, wait for a beat. "Yes, I am aware. And I know you're new here, but there's this unspoken rule we have about parking spaces."

"Which is?"

"That this is my space."

Kendi folds his arms across his chest, and his annoying eyebrows inch up. "Okay. So, what do you want me to do about it?"

I think it's obvious, but I guess I've got to spell it out for him. "I want you to park somewhere else."

"That seems a bit unreasonable."

"Not to me. I've been parking here for years."

"So, park somewhere else."

I roll my eyes and do an internal *woosah*. "I *have* been parking somewhere else. I've been parking somewhere else for weeks."

"Then what's the problem? When I get here, the lot is empty, so I park in the place that makes the most sense. Why should I park somewhere different?"

"Because I can't find a space when I come in, I've got clients to attend to, and the public lot is a quarter of a mile walk each way."

"Come a little earlier. You can't expect me to cater to you over a mild inconvenience?"

That last remark makes my petty slip, just a little. "See? This is what happens when I try to be civil with you meatheads."

"Meatheads?"

"I thought we could have a normal, pleasant conversation about why I need this space, but no. Never mind that since you got here, my car's been pooed on, covered in gravel, and today, sideswiped on the street. This isn't a mild inconvenience, and if you weren't so full of yourself, you'd realize that!"

"Me? You're the one claiming I can't park in a spot that *everyone* can park in. Even if I park somewhere else, someone else is gonna take this spot."

"No, they won't, because everyone knows it's my spot!"

"That's ridiculous." Kendi pauses as his phone rings, and I get my next insult ready. He answers just as I open my mouth, and my southern upbringing forces me to put the brakes on. "What? Where? Is she okay?" Kendi's eyes go wide, and he presses his free hand to his head. "I'm on my way."

He disconnects, then spares me a glance, working his jaw. I see the struggle there, and I'm not sure what's going on, but I can tell it's something more important than a parking space. "Everything okay?" I ask.

He shakes his head and slides into his car. Inputs an address into his GPS. Squeezes the steering wheel. Looks at me again. "My mom was in a wreck."

"Oh. I'm so sorry." Our spat feels really petty now. "Is she okay?"

"I don't know. They took her to the hospital. I need to go, but I was on my way somewhere before you stopped me."

I nod and take a few steps back so he can drive off without running over my toes.

He squeezes the steering wheel again. "I need a favor."

I shake my head no, but he gets out of the car, dislodges a key from his key ring, and offers it to me.

"I was headed to the address on this key label here. It's a church, and they need to set up for tonight's soup kitchen."

I throw up my hands. "Got nothing to do with me."

"I need you to deliver this key to Maggie Oh."

"I'm not going anywhere. I don't even have a side mirror, thanks to you."

"They're already short-staffed, and if they don't open up the kitchen, they'll have to turn people away. I don't have time to track down anyone else right now. I need to get to my mother. Cherise, please?"

"No."

"You want the parking space? You got it."

I'm still shaking my head no as he presses the key into my fingers. "I'm not doing it."

"I'll owe you one, and I won't park in your spot again, I promise." He angles himself back into the car. "I've really, I've got to go."

Kendi drives away, though I never told him I'd do it. I stare at the key and sigh, knowing I probably will.

10

Soup's On

I can't remember the last time I stepped foot in a church. Maybe when I was six or seven? Big Mama didn't watch me often as a child, but if she happened to have me on a Sunday, she'd take me to a big, brown church with white wallpaper, sticky air, and squeaky pews.

The steepled brick building towering above me looks old. Not in a run-down sort of way. More an, "I've been around and seen some things" kind of way. A wheelchair ramp wraps around the front of the building, connecting with the thick, gray steps leading up to the double doors. The sign above the doors reads 'Raleigh Christian Fellowship Church.'

No one is here, as far as I can tell, so I wander the grounds for a bit. It's not fully dark yet, but the street lights are on. Light poles guard the church on each side, illuminating the walkways paved between thick patches of lush, green grass. Judging by the smell, freshly cut.

I make my way around back, following a concrete path and the distinct sound of voices.

"I've tried calling twice now, but I keep getting his voicemail."

"We've got to get this stuff inside, Maggie. Can you call the pastor, or one of the deacons?"

"They're all out of town, and the one who isn't gave the key to Kendi."

"Hi!" I interrupt two people, an older man, and a woman in a pink jacket. "Um, you mentioned Kendi. Are you Maggie?"

She nods. I pull out the key from my pocket and hand it to her. "He asked me to bring this over."

Maggie's eyes light up and she throws up her hands. "Oh, bless you!" She takes the key and hands it to the older man. "Cliff, can you open up the doors while I start unloading everything?"

He takes the key, then Maggie turns back toward me. "Thank you so much! We were starting to worry. Pastor Lee is out of town along with half the deacons at a conference, and our college helpers all came down with a stomach bug, so we're short on volunteers. Did Kendi say when he'll be able to make it?"

"Um, I don't think he's coming. His mom was in an accident."

Maggie's hand flies to her mouth. "Oh no! Is she okay?"

A few wet drops hit my nose and I wrinkle my face. "I'm not sure." More drops trickle down, and Maggie notices.

She looks up at the sky and frowns, then hops into action. "What was your name, dear?"

I follow her as she speed-walks to her car. "Cherise."

"Lovely name. Could you possibly help me bring these up to the back doors? I'd ask Cliff, but he's recovering from back surgery, and I don't want him lifting anything."

"Oh, actually, I–" Maggie shoves a box filled with vegetables into my arms and sends me toward the doors with a gentle push. Resigned, I bring the box inside, where Cliff stands ready to direct me toward the kitchen.

"You take a right down that hallway there, and through another set of doors at the end. Kitchen's on the left. Can't miss it."

I redistribute the weight in my hands and lug the box down the hall. Maggie passes by me on the way. "Thanks, Cherise! The kitchen is this way." I follow her into a gym-sized room and drop the box along the wall of the kitchen. Maggie drops her box and begins to unload.

"You need any more help with the boxes?" I ask. She'd had a trunk full of them, and we'd only carted up two.

She waves a hand at me. "No. Our other helpers arrived and should be bringing them in shortly." Noise echoes down the hall, and she grins. "There they are now!"

A handful of teenagers walk in with boxes in their hands. They're loud and a little sloppy, but obedient, taking boxes and food items wherever Maggie directs them.

I slip out in the midst of the chaos, but I take the scenic route, admiring the pictures in the hallway as I go. There are group photos for blood drives and other activities, as well as portraits and paintings. Many I recognize as social revolutionaries, like Dr. Martin Luther King, Deitrich Bonhoeffer, and Maya Angelou. When I reach the back door, the drizzle has elevated into all out rain. It's not a wash day for me, so I decide to wait it out.

"Cherise! There you are." Maggie's voice echoes behind me and I turn around, noticing the tension on her face. "Thank you again for your help tonight."

"Oh, you're welcome." I shrug and turn back toward the rain. I know a pleading look when I see one.

"If you've got nothing else going on, could I get you to help one more time?" Maggie steps into the space in front of me and smiles. "As I mentioned before, our regular team is out sick, and with Kendi gone, I've got to run point in the kitchen. Our numbers are always higher this time of year, and we need a couple extra hands, if you're willing?"

I'm not. "Oh, I was just waiting for the rain to let up. Sorry."

"Oh, that's too bad." She looks disappointed, but the spark in her eye tells me she's not giving up without a fight. "Normally, I wouldn't push, but we really need the help. Even if it's just for an hour at dinner, it would be such a blessing."

Though she claims she isn't, Maggie strikes me as the pushy type. I put on a fake smile. "I really wish I could stay, but–"

"Sorry I'm late, Maggie."

Maggie turns and steps aside, letting in a bronze statue disguised as a man. He pops his umbrella out toward the rain, gives it a shake, then blesses us both with a smile no mortal being should possess. "Evening ladies."

"Preston! I didn't know you were coming tonight?"

"Heard you were shorthanded."

"Yes! Come on out of the rain. You know where to go, right?" Maggie points toward the kitchen, and Preston nods, moving in that direction. She turns back toward me with a shrug. "Sorry you couldn't stay, Cherise, but thank you for bringing the key. We'd be stuck in the rain if it wasn't for you, and I'm sure the dining hall's gonna be full tonight."

I nod. "So, Maggie, what time is dinner again?"

"Dinner service starts at six."

I stare at my fitness tracker, pretending to calculate my very empty evening schedule. "You know what? I think I could spare an hour or two."

Maggie's eyes light up. "Really?"

I shrug, nonchalant. "I mean, I've got some stuff to get back to at home, but I can squeeze in an hour of community service."

Her smile falters. "Oh. If you're really busy, Cherise, I don't want to keep you. I'm sorry if I made you feel pressured. You've already done enough, and now that Preston's here, I think we can manage."

"No, it's really no trouble! I mean, everybody's gotta eat, right?" I shrug off my coat and hang it on the coat rack by the door.

"Really? You're not just saying that?"

I shake my head no. Mostly to catch the back end of Preston as he disappears into the hall. "Nope. Not at all. I would love to help."

Maggie loops her arm in mine. "Fantastic! Come on, Cherise! I know just where to put you."

If it's anywhere near that tall chunk of handsome, I'm all the way in.

STIRRING SOUP SHOULD have been easy. And maybe if I hadn't spent the whole time staring at Preston through the kitchen window, it would have been. Maggie doesn't scold the way Big Mama does, but they share the same raised-brow look. The one that communicates exactly what they think about my cooking skills.

"Sorry again about the soup, Maggie."

I watch as she scrapes away the thick, charred bits at the bottom. She's got hot water running into the metal pot from the industrial-sized sink. "Not to worry. We managed to salvage most of it, and I can get another pot going in a flash."

I clear my throat and pull at the apron across my torso. "Need me to help with anything else? I could serve the soup if you want?"

Maggie nods and checks the clock. "Dinner service is starting soon, so that'd be great. Could you hand me the ladle over there by the stove?"

"Over where?" I turn with a little too much excitement, and my hips bump into the large metal table behind us. Which would have been fine if it hadn't been holding the remaining soup. It sloshes over the top, and I jump back to protect my hands from getting scalded. But instead of pulling my hands to my middle, I send my hands outward and straight into the tower of cupcakes Maggie set down to help me with the soup. The cupcakes fly all over the table and onto the floor. For a few heartbeats, no one talks. Then Preston walks into the kitchen.

"Maggie, we're ready for you."

"I am so sorry," I whisper.

Maggie turns off the water, turns to me with a bright smile I know she's pulling from reserves, and lets out a short breath. "Preston, great timing! Cherise is going to help you pass out bread."

Preston looks from Maggie to me, then to the cupcakes spread out on the floor. "Sure."

"I thought I was going to serve soup?"

Maggie shakes her head and all but shoves me into his arms. "Oh, this job suits you perfectly, Cherise. Besides, Preston could really use the supervision, isn't that right?"

Preston opens his mouth but doesn't get much out as we're both booted out of the kitchen. He chuckles, looks at me, then gestures toward the service line. A large pile of assorted breads rests on a tray at the end of the line. "After you."

We stand behind the bread, and Preston shows me where to find the gloves. They're tight on his large hands and baggy on mine, and we share a laugh as we compare them. "What happened in there?" he asks, still chuckling.

"I burnt the soup." He raises his eyebrows. "And knocked over dessert. All in the span of a few minutes."

"Ah."

"I don't think Maggie trusts me with the soup."

Preston nods his head. "Me neither."

"No?"

"My first time here, I spilled dinner on the way out the kitchen doors. Second time, I left all the ice cream on the counter instead of putting it in the freezer. I've also knocked down more trays than I can count trying to get mashed potatoes out of a ladle."

"Oof. Clumsy much?"

Preston tilts his head from side to side. "You could say that. I'm only good for two things now."

"Two things?"

"Brawn and bread. I can carry boxes, chairs, tables, equipment, and grab anything from the top shelves, but the only food I'm allowed to be in charge of is bread."

I laugh and toss up a roll. "You've got my dream job, Preston."

He smiles again, and it's soft and shy and curious. "It's Cherise, right?" I nod, loving the way my name sounds when he says it. "I've never seen you here before."

"I–"

"Can I get a roll, please?" I don't know how I missed the announcement for dinner service, but when I look away from Preston, the dining hall is full of people. One of them, an elderly woman in a soft, brown dress, waits expectantly with her tray held up.

"Oh! Sorry." I place a roll on her tray, then another for the next person, and so on. The line is long, and the space between Preston and I even longer as I wait for the crowd to thin. Whenever we get low on bread, Preston runs to the kitchen for more.

I try to make a bread run, too, but Maggie points me back to the line with a shrug. "Send Preston. The bread is on the top shelf, and he can reach it."

I'm not sure if Maggie's concerned that I'm too short or if she's worried I'll destroy the kitchen in the process, but I call Preston over anyway.

One hour stretches into two before the line whittles down to a few stragglers. I'm glad for it. It gives Preston and I a little more time to talk.

"So, Preston what do you do for a living?"

"I'm a loan officer by day, bread hustler by night."

"Ooh. A man of many talents, I see?"

"I try. What about you, Cherise?"

"Physical Therapist. That's with a D," I add with a wink.

Preston takes a step back. "Uh oh. We've got a doctor in the house tonight?"

"Yes indeed." I'd be lying if I said I wasn't mildly impressed that he knew what the D stood for. He's got a great personality and great looks. That's two out of five G's. Let's see if we can make it three.

"So, Preston, do you work in the downtown area?"

"No, I live and work in North Hills."

"Oof, that's a bit of a drive to get here, isn't it?"

"Yeah, but I promised a friend I'd help out today."

"Still, that's a lot of gas to burn. Unless you drive a Tesla, of course."

He chuckles. "I don't. Figured a house would be a better investment. Besides, my Toyota doesn't do too bad on fuel, and I walk to most places, anyway."

"Makes sense."

"I am a loan officer. Fiscal responsibility is kind of my thing."

Indeed. Great stamina if he's walking everywhere. I can't check his score, obviously. But you can't buy a house in North Hills without great credit. "So, Preston, are you the, um, breadwinner for your household?" I hold up a roll and wave it in front of his face. His eyes rove over to my left hand, which is not holding bread. He's definitely checking out my ring finger.

"Technically, yes. But I'm the only bread eater in my house."

"Your wife doesn't like bread?"

"No wife."

"Your girlfriend, then?"

"Don't have one of those, either." His eyes lock with mine, but only briefly. The line picks up again, and we get back to putting rolls on trays.

As I watch him greet the people passing by, my interest in Preston grows. He's kind and attentive as he makes conversation with each person in front of him. Some of them only offer a grunt in reply, but more than a few appreciate his banter. Some already know him by name and ask after his family. The interactions are brief, but watching him fills me with warmth. And excitement. Great manners. That's five out of five.

I wonder if he'd think I'm too much.

The thought chases away the heat in my chest like a bucket of cold water, and a thousand what-if's barrel through my head like a train flying off its track, derailing a future that hasn't even taken off yet. I need to get out of here before I embarrass myself.

As soon as I spot Maggie, outside of the kitchen of course, I flag her down. I don't wait until she reaches the serving line, but meet her halfway, my apron already untied and ready to fly into her hands.

"Sorry, Maggie, but I've got to run. I forgot I need to be somewhere."

"Oh." Maggie grabs my apron and follows me out of the dining hall. "Cherise, thank you so much for all your help tonight."

I nod, feeling more than a little shame for leaving so abruptly. But if I stay, I'm just going to make a fool of myself.

I did what Kendi asked. I don't have anything to feel guilty about, really. Except not saying goodbye, I guess. Preston probably thinks I'm rude, or crazy. But Raleigh is a big place, and we're not likely to see each other again. It's probably for the best.

I step out of the church and into the rain.

11

Coffee, Cool

All clouds have silver linings. Today, cruising into work and sliding into my unofficial-slash-official parking space is mine. Kendi's Ford is nowhere in sight. Which means he kept his word. Or he didn't come in to work today.

My mood dips as I consider why Kendi may not be in. I hope his mom is okay. Mine drives me nuts, and our relationship isn't the greatest, but I don't know what I'd do if something happened to her. Or Dad, for that matter.

"Good morning, Dr. Williams!" Tammie greets me with her usual smile. "I see you're back in your spot today. I take it the talk with Kendi went well?"

I shrug, not sure where to even begin that conversation. "It went."

Tammie chuckles and her grin shifts into something more sneaky.

"Don't start, Tammie. I know that look."

"I didn't say a word." She returns to her computer, then pulls a sticky note from the screen. "Oh, someone called earlier this morning and left a message for you."

"For me? Who was it?"

Tammie squints at the note, then hands it to me. "A Preston Jones. He says he found your jacket?"

Preston? I take the note and thank Tammie, then head to my office. If I'm reading her chicken scratch correctly, it does indeed look like Preston has found my missing jacket. And he left his number for me to call back.

A slow grin creeps up my face. He could have just left the jacket in the church lost and found, or dropped it off at the clinic on his way to wherever. But he'd left a message for me to call him back. Which means maybe I didn't completely blow it last night.

I dial the number.

I'M A BUNDLE OF NERVES as I step into the coffee shop. Preston is already seated and waves me over to his seat by the window. He stands as I approach.

"Cherise!" He grabs my coat from behind the chair and offers it to me.

I give a shy wave and take it from him. "Thanks for getting this back to me."

"Good thing I found one of your cards in the pocket." I dip my head, prepared to bolt out the door, but Preston tugs at my shirt sleeve. "Oh, hang on a sec, Cherise."

"What's up?" I clear my throat and burn a hole through the floor.

"Uh, can I buy you a coffee while you're here? Or a tea or lemonade if you don't want coffee?"

"Coffee is good!" The words come out chirpy and way too high. Preston doesn't seem to mind. He pulls out a stool for me to sit, and I do. My legs dangle a few inches shy of the bottom rung, but I keep it to myself.

He slides in next to me and pulls up an app on his phone. "We can order from here. Just put in whatever you'd like. My treat?"

"Thanks." I tap in my order and hand him his phone back. A few awkward seconds pass between us as he finalizes his order and we wait. "Listen, about the other night?"

He makes eye contact with me, waiting patiently as I collect my thoughts.

"I'm sorry for running out like that. I had to get somewhere, and I was late, and I didn't mean to be rude."

"Oh." He clears his throat. "That's good to know. I thought maybe it was me."

"Oh, no, of course not!" The café feels a few degrees warmer. Maybe I should have ordered a frozen lemonade instead.

"I'm glad to hear that, Cherise. Can I ask you something?"

"Sure."

"Would it be weird if I asked you to go out with me sometime?"

"Out with you?" I have trouble pushing the words out.

"Like, on a date?" Preston waits, and I start to calculate how long a human person can hold their breath. I'm pretty sure I'm breaking records here. Preston crinkles his brow. "Cherise?"

Did he just say what I think he said? "What, uh, what do you mean by that?" Not the cleverest of follow ups, but at least I've got words coming out now.

Preston tilts his head to one side. "I mean, I'd like to get to know you better. I thought we connected at the church, and I'd like to pursue that. If you're interested?"

I let out an expletive in response.

Preston lets out a nervous chuckle and shakes his head. "Wow. I mean, I thought we had a... I'm sorry if I read this wrong. Am I making you uncomfortable?"

I shake my head and grab his hand. "No! You're reading right. Sorry, I just wasn't expecting you to ask me out."

Preston takes my hand in his, sending goosebumps up the length of my arm. "Okay, then. Let's start off small and introduce ourselves. I'm Preston K. Jones, UNC Chapel Hill Cum Laude graduate. I'm 32, never been married, love track and field, have no siblings and two doting, smothering parents."

"What's the K stand for?"

Preston hums and shakes his head. "If we make it to a third date, I'll tell you."

"Ugh. That bad, huh?"

"You have no idea. Your turn, Cherise."

I like him. So much so that the idea of telling him about myself, and maybe saying something wrong, makes me hesitate. What I'm most confident about, he already knows. And everything else feels like a risk. Maybe I can tag along with his details and leave mine out. "You went to UNC-Chapel Hill, huh? That's my mom's alma mater."

"Oh yeah?"

"Yup. She graduated last century, but who's counting?"

Preston laughs. "I hope you don't phrase it like that in front of your mother."

"She hates it when I do. But it's technically true, so she can't say much. She started a family late."

I wince, kicking myself for oversharing. A server drops off our drinks, and the conversation lulls. I take the silence as an opportunity to really soak Preston in. He's all angles with his squared jaw and broad shoulders. He's wearing a tie and looking very tidy in his button-down shirt, crisp slacks and sandy brown shoes. No jewelry on his hands or face, and no sign of a chain around his neck. The only adornment is the stainless-steel timepiece wrapped around his wrist.

"It's dumb."

I watch Preston take a sip of his coffee and lift my brows. "What's that?"

"My watch." He lifts it into our line of view. "It belonged to my grandfather on my mother's side. It doesn't count my steps or track the weather. I noticed you looking at it."

"Oh. You notice a lot." I take another sip. "You're not a stalker, are you?"

He shakes his head vehemently. "Not at all. Though if I were, I'd probably be good at it."

"You probably shouldn't admit that out loud."

"Yeah. Speaking of time, I'm afraid I've got to go. It's a bit of a trek back to North Hills from here, and I've got to get back to work."

He slips out of the stool and taps the table. "I'll give you a call tonight?"

I smile and raise my coffee in reply. It takes all the will power I possess not to stare at him as he leaves the café. But he's so well put together, I steal a glance as he passes the window. As soon as he's out of sight, I squeal and pull out my phone, ready to text Shantell the news. But I can't bring myself to hit the 'send' button.

Whatever this is between Preston and me isn't real. Not yet, at least. And after what happened with Calvin, I'm not sure it ever will be. I slide my phone back into my pocket and slink back to work. Technically, we haven't even had a real date yet. And what if he changes his mind? If I tell Shantell about Preston and things fall through, she'll be more disappointed than me. Well, maybe not *more* disappointed. Equally disappointed. Because nobody wants this more than I do.

12

Orbiting the Sun

My first date with Preston is happening in the daytime. Which is new for me. The only clue I got from his call last night was to wear comfortable shoes. I really hope he doesn't plan to take me running for our first date. He doesn't seem like the type, but I don't know him that well. He did say he loves track and field. So maybe I'm a little worried he is the type.

I can do cardio, but I don't run for the fun of it. I'm tempted to call Shantell so she can guide me on how to dress for a date where I may or may not have to run. I don't want my thighs sticking together, so my cropped dresses are out. Something with legs, then? November days are cool, but they usually warm up by the afternoon.

I really should have done laundry. I've got a surplus of sweatpants, yoga pants, and jeans, but I want to make a good impression. My hand lands on a red and blue striped jumper with flared legs. Comfy, stylish, pairs well with stilettos and tennis shoes. Doesn't hug my curves too tight.

I try on the jumper, and the level of irrational disappointment I feel when it fits perfectly defies logic. It's super comfortable, but I don't feel special wearing it. Nothing about me stands out, which means my personality will have to do all the work today. With my confidence below sea level, I just don't think I can swing it.

I try on a few other outfits, but eventually circle back to the jumper. It's my best option, unless I want to dumpster dive into my dirty clothes and throw something into a quick wash cycle. Which I don't have time for.

My phone buzzes. It's Shantell, and I almost answer, but I know I can't lie to her, so I don't. "Sorry, Cuz. I'll fill you in if this turns into something. I promise."

PRESTON TEXTS ME AN address, and I meet him downtown near the capital buildings. Parking is a nightmare, thanks to a festival going on, and I have to park a block away. When I reach my destination, Preston is waiting for me. He's cool and casual in a pair of slacks and a polo shirt tucked in only at the front of his pants.

"Hey!"

"Cherise." He smiles and opens the restaurant door for me. I've never been here before, but it smells like heaven.

"What is this place?" I ask.

"Only the best soul food spot in downtown Raleigh." I doubt that. There isn't a soul food restaurant within a ten-mile radius of me that I don't know about. Preston picks up on my skepticism and raises both hands. "Okay, soon-to-be best soul food spot in downtown Raleigh. It's fairly new, but I know the owner, and trust me, you're gonna love it."

"I don't know, Preston. I have very high standards." *Crap.* Why did I say that?

Preston waves at someone at the bar, then guides me to a private room at the back of the restaurant. When he opens the door, my breath catches.

If the restaurant smells like heaven, then this place? It smells like heaven's country club. Trays of food line the walls, each labeled with fancy cards describing their contents. "Where have you taken me?"

Preston presses a plate into my open palms and pushes me forward. "Restaurant Week is coming up in a couple months, and my friend needs customer reviews. He offered us a tasting room in exchange for our input."

"We have this all to ourselves?" I'm sure my eyes are starting to glaze.

Preston chuckles and begins loading my plate with food. Rib tips, macaroni and cheese, mashed potatoes, sautéed cabbage, greens, fried chicken, fried chops. The servings are small, but it doesn't take long to load up my plate. "The tastings are done in timed slots. The place is ours for the next 30 minutes."

I skim through the row of dishes, taking samples of meatloaf, collard greens, green bean casserole, and more. I pass on the Brunswick stew. The moment my bottom hits a chair, I go to work on my starches. I'm halfway through a roll before I realize I've broken my first rule of dating. And Preston's watching me.

He probably thinks I'm a pig. I set down the roll and dab at the sides of my mouth with a napkin. "Sorry. I'm not usually like this, but I skipped breakfast this morning."

"Oh, that's okay. I thought we could say Grace before we eat?"

My brows fly up as he grabs my hands and bows his head.

"Lord, thank you for this amazing food and the company we share it with. I ask you to bless it, and us, in Jesus' name. Amen."

I mumble an amen and stare at my fingers. Preston's hands are no longer there, but the warmth is. A tingle starts in my belly and works its way up. Eating is going to be tricky, now.

"Is there anything you can't eat?"

"Huh? Oh, no. No allergies, and I'll try anything at least once."

Preston nods his approval. "According to my mother, I was a very picky eater growing up. But now? I'll eat anything at least twice."

He winks at me and I laugh. The tingle is still there, but Preston's relaxed demeanor eases the tension from my shoulders, and I pick up where I left off.

"Do you have any siblings, Cherise?"

I finish swallowing my roll before answering. "I have two brothers about eight years older than me."

"Really? Man, I've always wanted siblings. I'd settle for cousins, too, but I'm the only child of only children. Don't get me wrong, my parents never let a day go by without telling me they loved me. But having a brother would have been nice, I think. Or a sister."

"Well, there's a significant age gap between us, but the two of them always seemed to be in sync. They were twins, though."

"Twins! That's awesome. Probably a lot of work for your parents, though."

"If you ask my mother, having a lone daughter is more work than having two boys at the same time."

"Oh, I'm sure that's not true."

My birthday debacle comes to mind, but I want to enjoy my date, so I shove the thought aside. "What's it like, being the apple of your parents' eyes?"

Preston wipes his mouth and chuckles. "You caught that, huh?"

"I did."

"Well, it's a lot of pressure. But it's also a lot of power."

"Explain."

"Well, it means I can never do anything wrong. But it also means I can *never* do anything wrong."

"Oh, it makes perfect sense now."

He raises both hands. "I know, bad explanation. How about this? Imagine being the center of the universe."

"Like the sun?"

He snaps his finger. "Yes, exactly. You're the sun, shining bright, bringing the heat, doing your thing. And all along the outer perimeter of the sun are these planets, right? These planets love you to the moon and back. You're the center of their world. They will rearrange their orbit for you they love you so much."

"Wow, you're really leaning into this metaphor." I giggle.

"I am a man of many talents. Now, back to you being the sun. In your planets' eyes, you can do no wrong. You're the biggest, brightest part of their day. Thing is, these planets? They depend on you for light and warmth. You are their future, the one they put their hopes and dreams into. They've invested everything in you, and deep down, you know that if you ever mess up, or stop shining, or I don't know, fall out of the sky because you're reeling from depression, your planets would be devastated. And you love your planets. You want them to know they can depend on you, no matter what. But sometimes you also resent your planets, because their love makes you feel stuck." Preston frowns, and there's something familiar in the way he looks at me. "Sorry to unburden myself like that. Am I even making sense?"

I recognize that look now. It's the same look I get when I've shared something embarrassing about myself. Something vulnerable. Listening to Preston, I feel the weight of the burdens he carries. I carry plenty of them myself. But in my case, I'm not a star, let alone the center of anyone's universe. I'd settle for being the moon, orbiting around the earth. At least then I'd know I have an impact.

But no. In my universe, my parents are the solar system, and I'm Pluto. A tiny maybe-planet-maybe-moon, barely acknowledged. I can't say that I've ever felt what Preston's feeling.

My parents have never told me they're proud of me. And though they've been plenty disappointed, it's always been more of a resigned disappointment. Like, what else can you expect from Pluto? She's not even a real planet. And if she accomplishes anything, we're not gonna give her a trophy for it. Can't have her thinking she's a real planet, like her brothers Mars and Jupiter. Never mind that Mars dropped out of college to sell junk on Craigslist and Jupiter hasn't even landed on a profession yet. But I can't tell Preston any of that.

"It makes perfect sense," I say.

Preston's shoulders visibly relax, and a new face enters the room. "Presto!"

"Change-o!" They exchange hugs, and Preston introduces me. "Cherise, this is my friend, Charles. Owner of this lovely establishment."

"Which I hope you'll visit again." He winks. Charles is all charisma as he points to a stack of small square papers by the door. "You've got another five minutes in the room. Please take the review sheets on your way out, and try as many of the dishes as you can."

"Everything's been delicious so far." I mean it. My stomach is so happy right now, it could sing.

"Thank you, Cherise." Charles bows. "Promise me you'll come again?"

"Oh, I'm definitely coming. And I'll bring my squad, too!"

That gets another grin out of him, and he leaves us to our own devices.

Preston gets a mischievous look on his face. "How many ribs do you think we can finish in five minutes?"

"Oh, no, my belly is full enough as it is."

Preston gives me a once-over. "I think you can get at least ten more in."

"Ten?" My cheeks burn with heat as his eyes continue their inspection.

"They're small." He rubs his hands together. "And it's free."

"I do like free."

Preston's already filling up a plate of the inch long rib tips when I give him the green light. He doubles the amount on his plate, then sets it between us at the table.

"Can I tell you a secret?" Preston leans in close enough for me to smell his aftershave.

"Mm," is all I can say.

"I'm really competitive."

"Are you now?"

He nods. "So, if you make it to ten before I do, I'll grant you a wish. But if I finish first, you have to grant me one."

"What kind of wish?"

He shrugs. "We can decide now, or we can decide later. But if we decide later, there have to be rules."

"Okay. Let's decide later. What are the rules?"

"Um, since this is just for fun, we can say no if it's something that makes us uncomfortable."

"Pfft. That goes without saying." Good to know Preston's not a creep. "Anything else?"

"I think that covers it, unless you have a rule?"

I give it some thought. "Okay. If I win, and I want to save my wish for later, I can. Deal?"

He takes my hand and gives it a firm shake. "Deal."

I really hope he doesn't think less of me after this. Because I have a secret, too. Maybe it's because I've spent my whole life trying to get my parents to notice me, or maybe it's my natural drive. Either way, Cherise Michele Williams hates to lose, and Preston has no idea what he's gotten himself into. "First one to ten is the winner, right?"

He nods. "Clean cartilage, no residue. On the count of three?"

I give him a thumbs up, and we count together.

"One. Two. Three."

The race isn't even close.

I STEP OUTSIDE OF THE restaurant and stretch, feeling full on all fronts. Preston slips out beside me and takes my hand in his. I stare at our interlocked fingers, and he lets go.

"Sorry. Is this okay?"

I slip my hand back into his and squeeze. "It is."

Preston suddenly jerks me forward, turning my body back toward the restaurant as his arms wrap around my head and shoulders.

A wayward cycler tosses back an apology as he continues speeding down the sidewalk. My face is flush with Preston's torso, my nose pressing into his ribcage. He realizes it, too, and all too soon, he releases me.

"Sorry. You okay?"

I nod, though his eyes circle my body anyway. "You've um, got great reflexes." Among other things.

He clears his throat, then takes my hand in his again. "Ready to go?"

"Where exactly are we going?"

"To walk off all this food, of course." He points toward the street festival and tugs me along.

We wander through a forest of food trucks and roped off tents and tables, stopping wherever we please to touch and smell, or listen to the tenors of performers and storytellers. There's a lot to see, and even more to sample, despite our very sumptuous lunch. Preston isn't above stuffing his face with treats and samples. To my surprise, I let myself enjoy it, too. There's no judgment in his eyes when I eat, and the warmth I feel between us grows.

"So, what's your wish, Cherise?" Preston asks the question as he lifts a wooden necklace from its spot on a table and places it in front of my neck. It's not my style, which Preston realizes within a few seconds.

I'm not sure what I'll wish for, but I don't want to waste it. I may need a get out of jail free card in the future. "If you won the challenge, what would you have wished for?" I ask, dodging the question.

"Easy." He places his hand in mine. "A second date."

I snort, then slap my hand over my face, mortified. "You didn't hear that."

"Oh, but I did." Preston laughs, then pulls my hand away from my face. "No need to be embarrassed, Cherise."

"I'm not embarrassed," I mumble, then speed-walk away. It's a lie, of course. But Preston lets it slide.

"Now you know my wish. Tell me yours."

"Um, I'm gonna save mine."

"And leave me in suspense?"

"Yup!"

He rubs his chin. "That's a boss move. I'd better be extra careful with you."

"Is the sun afraid to get burned?"

"Not exactly."

I turn around, expecting him to be further away, but he's right behind me. My nose stops an inch from his chest. Preston towers over me, his chin clearing my head by at least an inch. He smells amazing, too.

"Um, Cherise?"

"Yeah?"

"You're standing on my foot."

"Oh. Sorry." I take a few steps back and shake my head. He's got to think something's wrong with me. I put some distance between us to collect myself. But the silence feels threatening, so I fill it. "Such a beautiful day today, isn't it? So many people out here, enjoying the fresh post-pandemic air." An older woman waves at me as she passes, offering a bit of southern hospitality, and I wave back. The toddler walking beside her points at the building beside us.

"You want to go in there?" she asks. He nods his head, and I look at the building. It's white on the outside, with gold spirals at the tops and a cross and bell tower.

"Oup, that's a Catholic church, little man." I make a face and lower myself to his level. "You might not wanna go in there. But there's a kid's museum just a few blocks that way. Maybe you can get your grandma to take you there, huh?"

"I'm his mother." The words are clipped on the way out, and as her mouth forms a scowl, mine forms an O.

Way to stick your foot in your mouth, Cherise.

I stutter over an apology, but the woman huffs and walks off, taking her son with her. I turn toward Preston and shrug. He gives me an odd look before examining his shoes. Second hand embarrassment. I get it. Hopefully I can make it through this date without shoving my foot in my mouth any further.

13

One of These Things
Is Not Like the Other

Shantell and Adrian are both quiet as I finish telling them about Preston. Shantell stirs her hot chocolate. Adrian sips her tea. They look at me, at each other, at their nails. But they don't say a word.

"Guys, come on. You're scaring me."

Adrian takes another long draw at her tea, pupils lifted to the ceiling. Shantell blows at her cocoa as she raises it to her lips.

"You're seriously not gonna say anything? Nothing at all?" The silent treatment draws out another three minutes before I cave. "Okay, okay. I'm sorry I didn't tell you about Preston."

"Apology *not* accepted." Shantell snaps.

I groan and wrap my hands around her arm. "Don't be that way, Shanty. You're my favorite cousin!" I turn to Adrian, who still hasn't spoken. "Come on, Adrian. I am languishing here."

"What's the point of even having a squad?" Shantell continues. "You're just gonna do whatever you want, anyway."

"It's not like that." I pout and pull on their sleeves. "Come on, girl besties. After what happened with, with..." I can't say his name out loud. Not without falling apart. Which pisses me off. He shouldn't have this much power over me. "Anyway, I just wanted to get through one date, let myself figure out if there really was anything there. And then I told you both right away."

"And how did the date end?" Shantell asks the question without looking at me.

"He asked me on another date. We're all set for this Friday."

"Whatever," Shantell huffs. "I don't care. What are you wearing?"

I shrug. "I'm sure I can just throw something together."

Shantell slams her hand on the table. "Cherise Michele Williams! Get your head in the game, girl! You claim this guy is five G's but what? You're gonna just *throw something together*? Adrian, hold my bag, cause I'm about to beat this girl."

Adrian grabs Shantell's bag and we both look at her. "What? She asked me to grab it."

"Adrian, I'm not actually gonna," Shantell shakes her head. "Never mind. Cherise. What time is your date on Friday?"

"Seven."

"And where are you going?"

"To an outdoor show, I think?"

"I'll be at your place at 5:30 p.m. Adrian, can you make it?"

"I'll have to move some things around, but sure."

"We'll be there at 5:30 p.m., Cherise. Make sure you've got the thermostat set at 69 degrees. Don't shake your head, just wear a hoodie or something. You know I can't stand being hot, and you'd better feed us."

"Good snacks, and lots of wine." Adrian cosigns with a snap.

"Nothing younger than our cousin, Terrance, or I'm walking."

"Okay." I nod and offer a sheepish grin. "Thank you, ladies!"

Shantell scoffs. "Don't think you're off the hook, ma'am. She doesn't deserve us, does she Adrian?"

Adrian tilts her head. "Normally I'd say no, but when you add up all the free food and drinks we've gotten–" Shantell glares at her, and Adrian changes course. "Doesn't matter. Cherise, you don't deserve us."

They clown around and make jokes, but I could care less. With my girl squad behind me, I know I can't lose.

"I THINK WE'RE LOST."

Preston scans the map in his hands then looks at the trees around us. "You might be right about that." He takes a few steps past the trail, checking the bright, diamond-shaped marker hammered into the trunk. "This doesn't make any sense. The diamond trails are all over on that side of the lake. But we entered on this side of the lake and should be seeing circles."

"Ahh!" I squat, more than a little frustrated, and blow hot air into my hands. It's breezy today, and I wish I'd worn a warmer jacket. "Preston, we've been at this for an hour. I know you like to frolic outdoors, but it's November."

He squats beside me. "I'm sorry, Cherise. I thought hiking would be fun. A friend of mine told me about a beautiful spot, hidden on the north side of the lake."

"Is this the same friend who told you about the outdoor light show?" I put emphasis on the word friend.

"No. Hey, I thought you liked the light show?"

I backpedal. "I did. I just thought we were going to sit down to watch it. I didn't realize we had to walk five miles of park grounds to see it." Shantell had forced me into a pair of strappy heels, insisting they were the only shoes that paired well with my babydoll dress. It made for a painful night.

Preston looks at me a full ten seconds without speaking.

There you go again, Cherise. I break eye contact, searching for a way to salvage things in the trees. But they don't offer anything helpful. I'm left to my own devices. Which means, I start to ramble.

"Do you spend a lot of time camping?" I ask. "These trees look pretty tall. Tall enough to slap a hammock between them. Do you have a hammock in your back pack?"

"No. We're not camping." He chuckles. "And yes, I've spent a lot of time outdoors. My parents took me every summer to Asheville."

"No kidding? Me too."

"Really?"

Not at all. "Yeah. We spent every Christmas at the Biltmore."

Preston whistles. "Wow, that's pretty... expensive."

I don't know why I lied. Or why I can't seem to stop. "Yup. It's kind of a family tradition. Fourth of July at home. Juneteenth at Big Mama's. Thanksgiving at my maternal grandparents, and Christmas at the Biltmore."

He nods. "I think I can get us back on track."

The map transforms into the most interesting document I've ever seen, and I study it, pointing at landmarks as if I have a clue what I'm looking at. "I see the lake, and this letter "A" probably marks where we can park, right?"

"That's a covered picnic shelter. But you see this mark here?" Preston points to a blue line on the map. "This trail intersects with that one. I think I know where we are, but we'll need to figure out what side of the trail the lake is on to be sure."

"Oh, I see what you're saying." I do not, actually.

'So, let's just go a little further this way and see what we find? I promise this will be the last outdoor adventure for a while."

I kick myself internally, wondering if I offended him with my complaint about our outdoor excursions. But Preston doesn't seem irritated, and he helps me through another ten minutes of walking until we get a bead on the lake. From there we reset.

"Okay, Cherise. Can you give me five more minutes? I promise you we won't get lost again." He extends his hand with an easy smile, and I take it. I don't even care if we get lost again. I just want him to keep looking at me like that. Like I'm the most interesting, most important person in the whole of Umstead Park. I bet Preston would never forget my birthday.

We arrive at our destination, and Preston is thrilled. He lays his hand on the trunk of a carved tree, which fell ages ago and was later turned into a work of art hidden in the woods.

"Isn't this amazing?" Preston beckons me forward, one hand on his head as he squats down to get a closer look. "All of these animals were sculpted by a chainsaw. Who knew a chainsaw could be so precise?"

I shrug, not having the heart to tell him that I've seen this trunk before. Several times. And while it is impressive, I don't have enough love for the arts to give it more than a perfunctory nod.

"Look at the detail on these leaves! If a regular person could carve something so amazing out of something that was dead, how much more could God do with us, right?" He looks at me, and I lift my brows. "Come put your hand here, Cherise."

"Oh, I don't think so." He turns back to the tree and gives it a gentle pat. I clear my throat. What can it hurt? "Alright, I guess I'll touch it just a little." He guides my hand over the wings of an owl. It feels a little damp underneath my fingers.

"Can you believe the level of skill that went into this?"

"It's amazing." I hope I sound more enthusiastic than I feel. Preston nods in agreement, so I guess so.

"Cherise?" He releases my hand and leans against the log. "I wanted to ask you something?"

I stand, rubbing dirt from my hands, though there isn't much. "Sure."

"When we met at the church that night, I felt drawn to you in a way I couldn't explain."

Butterflies take over the space beneath my ribcage. "Yeah?"

He nods, leans closer. "I'm usually more careful about who I date, but after meeting you, and considering where we met, I guess I just made some assumptions. Assumptions that maybe I shouldn't have made."

His face goes serious, and I lick my lips. This feels like the prologue to a breakup scene. That thought sends a tingle up my spine. Preston's only flaw, that I can see, is that he loves being active way more than I have the stamina for. And if that's his only flaw, it's definitely something I can live with. I don't want to stop seeing him. "Preston?"

He sighs. "Cherise, I need you to know something about me. I'm a Christian. And when I say that, I don't mean that in a religious way. More than going to church, I believe in God with all my heart, and I want to follow Him with all my life."

Oh. Images of religious fanatics pop into my head, but none of them quite matches Preston. We've only been on a few dates, though. "Okay."

"If that's not what you're about, then that's fine. I wouldn't expect you to change because of me."

That's good to hear.

"But it's kind of a deal breaker for me."

I take it back. "I'm sorry? I don't really understand what you're trying to say."

He runs a hand through his hair. "I'll put it like this. My life is centered around my faith in God. Getting to know God and what He wants, and following that with all my heart. And I need to be with someone with the same center. Otherwise, we're not a good fit."

"Well, I think that's..." Ridiculous, for starters. What does it have to do with anything? We just have to like each other. And I do. I really like Preston. And unlike him, I could care less if he believes in God, or flying pigs, or Santa Claus. He's everything I want in a man.

I know that pretending to be something that I'm not is a bad idea. But the tension in Preston's face tells me everything I need to know. He doesn't want to break up with me. He likes me, too. The connection he felt that first day we met? I felt it, too. And I'm not willing to give it up. Not yet.

"Preston, I think that's perfect."

His eyes go wide. "Yeah?"

I nod, scrambling for the right words. "Yes. All those things you said about God are things I also feel."

"Really?" Preston looks relieved. He wants this as much as I do. "That's good to hear, Cherise. To be honest, I wasn't entirely sure after the last few dates. You said some things that..." he shakes his head. "Never mind." He studies my face, then takes my hand. "Cherise, I hope you don't take this the wrong way, but are you a new believer?"

Brand spanking new. "Uh."

"I'm sorry if that sounds offensive. It's just that you seem like you're new to the faith."

I nod my head emphatically. "Yes. I am." I clear my throat. "All this is very new to me."

Preston nods. "But you have a church home, right? The one we met at?"

An alarm goes off in my head. If I answer yes, and it's the same church Preston goes to, he'll ask me why he's never seen me there before. Better to say no. But if I say no, which church should I say? I don't know the names of any other churches. Panic slips up my neck, and I cough. "Church home?"

Preston raises his brows. "Or maybe a small group?"

A group seems like a safe answer. "Yeah, I go to a small group."

"Oh yeah? Who leads it? Anybody I know?"

Why does he have so many freaking questions? I can barely breathe, but Preston's eyes are full of light and excitement, ready to soak up every minute detail I give him about my fake spiritual life.

Okay, Cherise. Think! If you tell a bunch of lies, you're gonna be in a mess later. The best lies are wrapped in truth, right? Pick something you can remember.

Kendi's cross hanging from his rearview mirror comes to mind. "I go to a colleague's small group. You probably wouldn't know him. He works in the building beside mine."

"Ah. Does he go to the church?"

"Uh."

"That would explain why you were there that night. He invited you?"

"No, he asked me to drop off the key for the church."

Preston nods and seems content with that. Until he snaps his finger and turns around. "Wait. You go to Kendi Ready's small group?"

I almost don't catch the expletive in my throat. When I trust my voice enough to behave, I squeak out, "Huh?"

"Kendi and I go way back. We went to school together, and he asked me to help out that night, too. I go to a church on the north side of Raleigh, but RCF is like a second home." Preston seems unusually happy about this. "You're in good hands with Kendi. He's got a great handle on the scriptures, and he does a great job with foundations, too."

"Yeah." I dip my head, imagining a hundred different ways for this to blow up in my face. All it takes is one phone call to Kendi, and Preston will know I'm the worst kind of liar.

I can figure this out. I just need a little time. I'll come clean to Preston later, then present him my case for why we should keep dating despite our differences.

Unless he talks to Kendi. I can't let that happen. Or maybe I can. So long as Kendi doesn't contradict me, everything should be fine. Would he lie to Preston for me? Probably not. Which means it needs to *not* be a lie.

The idea of joining a group with Kendi in it isn't very appealing to me. But I like Preston way too much to let that meathead get in between us. Looks like I'll have to put my feelings aside and form a temporary alliance.

"It's Karrington, by the way."

"What's that?"

Preston clears his throat. "My middle name. I promised to tell you if we made it to a third date. This one makes three."

A smile spreads on my face. "Say it again for me?"

He dips his head in embarrassment. "Karrington. Go on, get it over with."

"Oh my. Preston Karrington Jones, your parents had high hopes for you, didn't they?"

"They did indeed."

"I feel like there should be some numbers after your name, though. Or a title. Doctor Preston Karrington Jones the Third, a surgeon in a long line of surgeons."

"My dad would have loved that. But I'm just a humble loan officer." Preston gives a self-deprecating bow.

"Aw. Well, I'm a doctor. Maybe that will be enough to cover the stain you've left on your family's reputation."

Preston smiles and squeezes my hand. "Maybe. And Cherise? One more thing, while we're on the subject?"

I load up another snarky comment, fully committed to our game. Preston's light peck to my cheek throws me completely off it.

"I'm not interested in a fling, or something casual. I'm looking for something real. Someone I could potentially spend the rest of my life with."

Warmth swarms to my cheeks, and I follow him out of the woods with a giddiness I can hardly contain.

Me too, Preston. Me too.

14

Saved, Saved

Three days after my date with Preston, I'm in full panic mode. I haven't seen Kendi since that night he dropped off his key, and every day feels like the day Preston's going to find out I'm a complete fake. Times like these, I need my squad. Which is exactly why I've bribed them with pizza, wings, and unlimited drinks at my place.

"So, Cherise, to what do we owe the pleasure of this meeting?" Shantell takes a delicate bite from her drum, careful to avoid mussing her nail with sauce.

"Things going poorly with Preston?" Adrian asks.

I shake my head. "No. At least, not yet. I found out the other day that Preston is a Christian."

Shantell snorts. "Girl, so what? Half the guys I date are Christians."

"Okay, think less pulpit pimp and more Big Mama fanatic. Preston says he won't date me if I'm not a Christian, too."

Shantell's mouth widens in an 'O' of understanding. "So, he's *saved* saved, like Big Mama?"

"What does any of that mean?" Adrian asks.

"It means Cherise over here is unequally yoked." Shantell drops that bomb on the table and grabs another wing.

Adrian shrugs. "Still don't understand what that means."

"Yeah, I don't get it either, Shantell."

Shantell rolls her eyes, sets down her wing, and wipes her mouth. "How long you been alive and you don't know what that means? Big Mama talks about it all the time."

"But I didn't grow up with Big Mama like you did. You know she and Mom don't get along."

"And I've never even met Big Mama," Adrian adds.

"Ugh." Shantell lets out a frustrated groan. "Alright, let me educate y'all little heathens since you're ignorant. Cherise, you remember when Uncle Charles brought home his little sidepiece from Georgia that one Thanksgiving? I think we were in sixth grade?"

"No?"

"Well, do you remember when Big Mama stayed in her room the whole day after cooking Thanksgiving dinner?" I give her a blank stare. "We had all the fixings, but not a single dessert that year."

I snap my finger. "That was the year there wasn't any banana pudding!"

"That's right! Big Mama always makes a big batch of banana pudding on Thanksgiving, but that year, after she took the turkey out the oven, she closed the kitchen. Not a pie or pudding in sight. Dinner was still bussin' but we had to dig out a tub of Neapolitan ice cream from the Reconstruction Era and some ice pops for dessert."

"Okay, I remember now. So, are you saying that she did that because Uncle Charles brought home his girlfriend?"

"Look, Girl. All I know is Big Mama spent that whole morning talking about how she didn't raise Uncle Charles in the church to watch him be unequally yoked with some hussie from Georgia."

I nod, but Adrian leans in on her hands. "So, what does it mean, Shantell?"

Shantell resumes her eating with a shrug. "Far as I'm concerned it means there won't be any banana pudding at Thanksgiving."

"Shantell!" I scowl at her. "You're just as ignorant as I am."

"Religion makes no sense to me," Adrian shakes her head. "This is why I don't believe in any of that God stuff."

Shantell freezes. "What do you mean by 'that God stuff,' Adrian?"

I clap my hands together. "Who wants more pizza?"

Adrian sniffs. "I don't mean any offense, but it's all a bunch of nonsense. There's no proof that God exists, and the bible is just a bunch of made-up stories."

"Hold up!" Shantell lifts her finger, sans chicken wing. "Adrian, are you telling me you're an atheist?"

I look from my best cousin to my best friend, sensing the tension. "Ladies, let's not get into this right now."

"It's not a secret, Shantell." Adrian scoffs. "There's no reason for me to believe in God."

"No reason? I believe the spirits of our ancestors would beg to differ, Miss Adrian. You hail from a long line of spiritual people, dating to the very beginning of civilization. Denying God is like denying the color of your skin."

"That's a stretch. And narrow-minded, I might add."

Shantell shakes her head. "Adrian, I don't know who raised you, but in our black and brown circles, and especially in this squad, you can do a lot of things. You can be introverted, extroverted, rich or poor, educated or ignorant, gay, straight, or whatever letter of the alphabet you want. You can worship Jesus, Allah, mazel tov, or Amun-Ra, if you like. Matter fact, you can put raisins in the potato salad."

"Ooh," I shake my head.

"Too far? Sorry, I was feeling liberal." Shantell lets out a *woosah* and continues. "There are two things our people don't do. We don't put fruit in our potato salad, and we don't go around calling ourselves atheists. If you can't abide by these rules, then kindly leave your black card on the table on your way out tonight."

"Shantell, stop it." I give her a play punch on the shoulder, but her eyes are on Adrian.

Adrian narrows her eyes, then throws up her hands. "Fine. What if I just call myself agnostic?"

"Skepticism is okay, but we don't do the label thing." Shantell sips from her wine glass. "If anybody asks, just say you're undecided."

Adrian rolls her eyes and tosses back her drink. "The things I do for friendship."

"Wow, Shantell." I regard her in a new light. "I didn't know you cared so much about this stuff."

Shantell snorts. "Oh, I don't. But after the last few years, we've had to tighten things up in our communities. Too many ideas slip through, and next thing you know, Thanksgiving is taken over by vegan mac and cheese and raisins are in *everything*." She snorts wine up her nose, which is a little satisfying. But I'm still a bit disappointed. If she doesn't know what to do about someone like Preston, and Adrian knows even less, then where does that leave me?

"Girls, I still don't know what to do about Preston."

"I know what I'd do." Adrian turns her hand into a pair of scissors and cuts an imaginary string.

"Oh, but Preston is so cute, and he makes our little Cherise happy," Shantell coos. "Don't worry, girl. We'll help you fake it til you make it."

"What's the issue, exactly?" Adrian asks. "He won't date anyone who isn't a Christian. So, what did he say when you told him you weren't one? Did he give you an ultimatum, or what?"

I stare at imaginary dirt underneath my fingernails and mumble. "I told him I *was* a Christian."

"What's that?" Adrian leans in closer.

I repeat the words, even softer the second time.

"Girl, you know we can't hear you, stop playing." Shantell snaps her finger in front of my face. "Out with it. In a normal volume, please."

Ugh. "I kind of, sort of, lied to him."

"So, he thinks you're *saved* saved, too, huh?" Shantell presses her lips together. I know it's to keep from laughing.

"Oh, this ought to be rich." Adrian grabs another slice of pizza. "Cherise, you are the highlight of my life."

"Then I know you'll love this next part." I let out a short laugh. "I told him I was a brand new Christian, and that I attend a small group with none other than, get this, Kendi Ready."

Shantell spits out her wine, thankfully into her cup and not onto my carpet. "Kendi Ready? The guy from work?"

"Yup." I begin to laugh, but it quickly devolves into whimpers.

"Uh oh, don't cry, Cherise." Adrian places a soothing hand on my shoulder. "Everything's gonna be fine, right Shantell?"

"Last I checked, those two hated each other." Shantell's shrug doesn't make me feel any better.

"Not helping, Shantell." Adrian scowls at her before cooing at me. "Don't worry, Cherise. Kendi hates you, but you did him a favor, right? That means he owes you."

"Oh yeah, that's right." Shantell joins me on my side of the floor. "You could get him to lie for you, right?"

I shake my head. "Kendi's not gonna lie for me. He and Preston are buddies, apparently."

Adrian makes a face. "Oof. Well, maybe if you word it right, he'll tell a little white lie?"

"I can't risk it! If I tell him what I'm doing, he'll tell Preston, and it'll be over. I'll have to lie to them both until I figure things out."

"Why you gotta lie to both of them?" Shantell asks.

I put my face in my hands. "Because I'm going to join Kendi's small group."

Shantell chuckles. "So you *do* plan to fake it til you make it."

"It's a terrible idea, I know."

Adrian tilts her head. "Well, it's not the *worst* idea." I glance up at her. "I mean, if you think about it, it's very common to take an interest in the hobbies of your significant other. Even to go so far as to pretend to like what they like, whether it's food, sports, music, or movies. It's not that big a deal."

"Preston seems to think it's a big deal."

"Well, maybe it's a big deal like the way white people are really into Hogwarts." Shantell offers. "People get into fights over this stuff, but if they really like someone, they're not gonna care if you're team Potter or team Smog."

"It's pronounced Smaug, and that's from Lord of the Rings, not Harry Potter. Also, the fandom is divided by the four houses of Hogwarts. Gryffindor, Hufflepuff, Ravenclaw, and Slytherin." Adrian's correction is met with blank stares from the both of us. Adrian shakes her head. "How are we even friends?"

"Guys, it doesn't matter. I don't think Preston's faith is like Harry Potter."

"Well, why don't you test it and see?" Shantell grins. "According to Big Mama, I know how to test the most faithful of saints. First thing you need to do, Cuz? Check the size of his bible. And I don't mean that as a euphemism." Shantell tilts her head to the side. "Or maybe I do."

"Check the size of his... bible?"

"Mhm. You also need to find out which Sunday service he attends. If he goes to night service, you're in the clear. If he goes to the morning service, eh, it's not looking good. If he goes to both? You don't have a snowball's chance in–"

"Let's not scare her, Shantell." Adrian makes a face. "I wish I could be more helpful, but honestly this is way outside my orbit."

And mine. The longer I listen to Shantell's outlandish advice on bible sizes, the more I realize I'm in way over my head. I'm gonna need an insider's advantage.

Unfortunately, that means Kendi.

15

Trying New Things

"Kendi, I need a favor."

Kendi barely affords me a glance as he travels from one end of the gym to the other. They're closed for maintenance, and he's wiping down and inspecting equipment. I'm in between clients, so I figure now's a good time to find a way into his small group. Shantell and Adrian weren't much help, especially once Shantell turned her advice into a game of religious innuendos.

"What sort of favor?" He finally pulls away from his work, I'm guessing once he realizes I'm not going away.

"The kind that you can't say no to, because you owe me."

Kendi scowls, but it's a soft one. "About that."

"No trying to get out of it, Kendi. You said you'd owe me."

He nods. "I did. And Cherise, I really appreciate what you did for me that day."

Not the answer I was expecting. "That's right. I really went out of my way for you." A silence passes between us, on my end because I realize I never asked him about his mom. But, in my defense, he hasn't been around to be asked. I'm not sure why he's suddenly gone quiet, but I figure, better late than never. "How's your mom, by the way?"

"Better. She's got some rehab ahead of her, but she's tough. Thanks for asking."

"Of course." Asking him feels awkward now. Like, 'Sorry about your injured mom, but I got problems, too.'

Kendi clears his throat and gives me his full attention. "Spill it, Cherise. What do you need?"

"I need you to let me into your small group."

His brows escalate to the height I've grown accustomed to. "You know about my small group? How?"

"Not important. What is important is that I need to go, and you need to let me."

"Why?"

"Are you not gonna let me in?"

Kendi tips his head to one side. "It's not that. I just didn't think you were, um, interested in that sort of thing."

I scoff. "Well, I mean, that's awful presumptuous of you. Pfft. Cause I'm totally, uh, into all that stuff. I'm just new to it."

"New to what?"

Ugh, just say yes, Kendi! "New to all of this stuff." I wave my hand in the air, gesturing toward The Man Upstairs, or angels, or whatever. "You know. Faith stuff."

Kendi studies me with that intense stare of his. I can sense his wheels turning, there's practically smoke coming out of his ears. I'm not confident that even my "favor" card is enough to grant me an invitation into his personal space. I hold my breath, waiting.

"Why do you want to come to my group? Specifically?"

Oh, what a tangled web we weave... Telling him I learned about his group from Preston is too dangerous. If the two ever get together and talk about me, they're gonna figure out I'm lying. I need a lie wrapped in truth. "I've seen the cross in your car, and after I went to the church, a lot of people had good things to say about you." What was her name? I snap my finger. "Mattie would be lost without you."

"You mean Maggie?"

"That's what I said. Maggie and um, the old guy with the heart surgery?"

"Carl. Who just had back surgery."

"Tomatoes potatoes. But yea. They love you, and the kind of guy that spends every week serving the less fortunate is the kind of guy I want to learn from."

"Really?" He crosses his arms, which forces the muscles to contract. I bet a t-shirt hates to see him coming.

I nod. "I'd love to be more involved in church, and in the community. It's always been a kind of passion of mine."

He doesn't believe me. I can see it on his face. He's going to tell me no, favor or no favor, and I'll be stuck trying to figure out how to explain to Preston why I'm never at Kendi's small group. Why I've, in fact, never *been* to Kendi's small group. I need to figure out a plan B, but I really don't think–

"Okay." Kendi shrugs. "We've got a meeting this Friday, but." He scowls and shakes his head. "Maybe you can come to the next one."

I don't know when Preston will check in on me. I need to get into this group as soon as possible. "No, I'm free this Friday. I can come!"

Kendi rubs his forehead. "We alternate locations, depending on who's hosting."

"Okay. Just tell me where to go, and I'll be there."

He makes a face. "This week it's at my place." My facial expression must be really loud, because Kendi immediately throws up his hands. "Next week is probably best. I'm not really comfortable with strangers knowing where I live."

Rude. "I promise I won't show up unannounced at your place. If I have a question, I'll just send you a text."

Kendi gives a skeptical nod, then holds out his hand. "If you promise to behave, I promise to be patient. But this group isn't a social club. We're a tight knit bunch, and we've all got the same goal."

"Keeping Chick-fil-A closed on Sundays?" I snort.

"Growing in our faith."

"Right! That. Of course!" I take his hand, before he can change his mind. This is all fine, perfectly fine. And who knows? Maybe it won't be so bad.

16

The Most Awkward Introduction

This is really bad. Kendi is in an obvious huff as I follow him down the hallway toward his apartment. In my defense, I had no idea the day would end the way it did. He stops at what I assume is his door and starts shuffling through a ring full of keys.

"You really should downsize that keyring." I say it to break the tension, but he only grunts in reply. I roll my eyes. "You know, technically this is your fault, not mine."

Kendi stops and turns around. "This I gotta hear." He folds his arms. "How? How in the world is you backing into my car *my fault*?"

"If you hadn't taken my parking space all those weeks back, my side mirror wouldn't have gotten smashed. And if my side mirror hadn't gotten smashed, I would have clearly seen your junkmobile behind me."

"You've got two other mirrors! Besides, you should have gotten that fixed by now."

I scoff. "Do you have any idea how hard it is to get an appointment at a body shop during the holiday season? The earliest they can do is January. Plus, I checked my other two mirrors, thank you very much, and you weren't in either of them." Kendi turns back around, sifting through his keys. I cross my arms and mutter to myself. "Maybe if you hadn't been driving like a bat out of hell, I would have seen you."

Kendi looks back at me, eyes sharp. *Oops. Gotta watch my mouth.* "Sorry," I mumble. "I just mean you came behind me out of nowhere."

He sighs and clenches his jaw. "I'll admit, I was probably driving faster than I should have in the parking lot." I half expect blood to come out of his mouth, those words seem so painful for him to say. He sighs again and runs his hand through his hair. "Look. Cherise, I'm a little on edge today, alright? I was already running late, and I didn't expect to have to deal with all this on top of everything."

"Deal with what? My car's the one with all the damage. Do you have any idea what it'll cost to replace a fender AND a side mirror? You just got an extra ding on your door to match the other dings that were already there!"

"It's not my fault my car is sturdy and yours is made of aluminum and plastic."

"Hey! That car costs a quarter of my salary, and probably most of yours!"

Kendi laughs. "Nice, Cherise. You got anything else?"

"Huh?"

"Come on. You've obviously got plenty to say to me. Let's get it all out now before everyone gets here."

"Why? Are you afraid I'll embarrass you in front of your friends?"

"No. You only get one shot to make a first impression. And if you plan on coming to this group, you need to understand something."

"What's that?"

"I told you already, we're close. And while we don't mind letting others join, we've learned to be vulnerable with each other. The group is a safe space, and I'd like it to stay that way."

"So what you're saying is, once I go through those doors, no calling you meathead?" I chuckle despite myself.

"More or less. And disagreements are okay, but we work really hard not to be intentionally combative with each other."

"Got it. Don't rock the boat." I roll my eyes. "Shouldn't be too hard. All I gotta do is say no to gay marriage and yes to legislating a woman's uterus, right?"

Kendi blinks. "Cherise, that's..."

"Incredibly offensive. But in some circles, probably true." I whirl around, and a young brother maybe an inch or two shorter than Kendi (but still several inches taller than me) winks and stretches out his hand. "Hi. I'm Larry."

"Oh. Hi." I take his hand, and he gives it a quick shake before turning toward Kendi.

"Who's the new girl?" he asks.

"This is Cherise. She's a new believer looking for a group to join."

"Ohh." Larry gives me a side eye. "Fresh off the brimstone path, huh?"

"Larry..." Kendi's tone carries a warning with it.

Wait. Is Kendi... protecting me?

"I'll go easy on her, I promise." Larry laughs. "Cherise, welcome to the group. I think you'll find our political views as wide and varied as they are passionate, but nothing outshines the word of God here."

While I wonder if there's a Christian version of an urban dictionary, Kendi finally opens up the apartment. Larry waltzes right in, Kendi behind him and me bringing up the rear.

"Make yourself comfortable." Kendi points to his couch, then hesitates. "But not too comfortable. I'm going to need some help getting the food ready."

Larry flops onto the couch and pulls a bible from his bag. I sit on the far side, smoothing the wrinkles out of my pants.

"So, Cherise? How do you know Kendi?" Larry opens his bible and begins slowly turning the pages. He's speaking to me, but looking at the book. As if he's searching for my rap sheet somewhere in the thin pages. I find it very distracting.

"We share a building." I clear my throat, and a half second later, Kendi's handing me a bottle of water. "Thanks." I force the word out between clenched teeth. Maybe if he hadn't acted like I was a massive inconvenience the whole way over, I would have left out the sass. But apparently Kendi's a real grump when he's late. It must have taken all of his Christian charity to offer me a ride. The drive over was painfully awkward.

Larry scans me head to toe, then returns to his bible. "Ah."

I take a sip of water and raise my eyebrows. "Why do you sound so disappointed?"

Larry shrugs. "No reason. Guess I was just hoping you were Kendi's girlfriend."

Something crashes in the kitchen, and I drop the water bottle. Of course it spills all over Kendi's couch. Which, of course, is the exact opposite of Kendi's crappy car. It's a soft, gray suede, and it looks extremely expensive. There's a bit of neutral chaos as Kendi rushes over with paper towels and his trademark scowl. Larry's lips curl into a half-smile as I stand and try to take the paper towel roll from Kendi. I fail, because the stubborn meathead keeps saying, "No, I got it."

"But I made the mess, so I should clean it up."

"I got it, Cherise."

"Just let me—"

"Stop! You'll just make it worse!"

I tug the paper towel roll, but he won't let go. "I know how to clean water off a couch, Kendi. It's not rocket science."

He tugs back. "I insist."

I scowl and pull harder, which causes the loose sheets to tear and me to lose balance. On my way down, I manage to knock a vase from the coffee table and get violated from behind by its very sturdy wooden corner before landing face first onto Kendi's floor.

I groan as Kendi and Larry stand at either side of me to help me up. But that fall wasn't pretty and it wasn't kind, and a string of expletives leaves my mouth as the pain in my rump, and my undignified wobble, take center stage. I'm not sure how many F-bombs I drop, but it's enough to send the rest of Kendi's guests, who choose this precise moment to walk through the doors, into a mild shock.

I freeze as six strangers stare at me from the door.

"Hey guys, come on in!" Larry waves them forward. "This is Cherise. She's Kendi's new girlfriend."

The glare Kendi sends his way could melt the polar caps.

17

Spaghetti and A Stupid Meathead

I twist pasta onto my fork as slowly as I can, rotating the utensil with concentration levels worthy of a surgeon. Eh, maybe that's taking it too far. But it keeps me from acknowledging the half-scowl Kendi's wearing from his spot in the living room. The rest of the group surrounds him on chairs, the couch, or the floor. Dinner was a simple meal of spaghetti and salad, and it was blessedly uneventful. But Larry's declaration threw Kendi even deeper into his mood, and I'm still a bit embarrassed from the fallout. Meatheads are the worst.

Kendi clears his throat, but I ignore him. Twist, twist, twist.

"Cherise, are you almost done? We're running behind and need to get started."

I press my lips together and remind myself that I asked to be here. Kendi's a steep price to pay, but Preston's the payout. And my gut says he's worth it. "Please, don't let me hold you up. You can start without me."

"I think that would be rude."

Hasn't stopped him before. "I'm almost done."

Kendi flexes his jaw, then glances at the door. He clears his throat again, then taps his thigh with his index finger. "Alright. Let's get started. We're going over the gospel of Luke, so Larry, Pam, and Charlie, can you pick up the reading from chapter 16?"

I listen in as they take turns reading. I find it oddly comforting. Larry's voice is deep and low. If I had him on audio, I'd fall asleep every night without fail. It isn't boring. Just soothing. The group itself is a nice mix. Swatches of brown faces and not-brown faces fill up the living room, replicating the diversity Raleigh is well known for.

Thousands of international students fly into the city every year. I graduated with students from China, Korea, South Africa, Iran, India, Nigeria and a dozen other places. The south is steeped in racial division, remnants of Jim Crow, and segregation, but seeing Kendi's group fills me with a little light in spite of it.

"Cherise?"

I lift my head from my bowl. All eyes are on me, and I have no idea why. "Hmm?"

Kendi's eyes flick from my face to the bible in his lap. "Did you have anything you wanted to add to the discussion? Now that you're finished with dinner?"

I glance at my empty bowl, then back at Kendi. "Someone else can go ahead of me."

"We've already gone around the room with our thoughts." Kendi stands from his seat and heads toward me. Larry's smirk isn't lost on me, but he's got the wrong idea. Or maybe not. I have no idea why Kendi's standing in front of me all of a sudden, his hand extended like a knight in shining armor. He's even... smiling at me. And not in a sarcastic way. In an inviting, don't-worry-you're-safe kind of way. "Come on and join us, Cherise." I don't take his hand, I can stand on my own, but I rise from my chair and follow him into the living room.

"Yeah, we don't bite, hon." One of the girls winks at me. Alice? I pass by her, and she pats an empty spot beside her on the couch. I take her up on it and she smiles. "I'm Asia."

"Cherise." It's not necessary. They all know who I am – and who I most certainly am not, thanks to Kendi. It's not like I *want* to be Kendi's girlfriend. I'd rather eat a dead possum half-baked in the sun on I-40 than be coupled with him. But did I say that in front of a group of near-strangers? I did not. Because I have manners.

Asia taps my shoulder. "Do you need help finding the verses?"

I shake my head. "Oh. Uh, I don't have my bible with me."

"That's okay. You can use mine. Here." Asia places her thick, leather-bound book in my hands.

"You're so sweet." My smile slips, but if Asia catches it, she doesn't say.

"We're on chapter 16." She points to a place on the page, and my eyes cross.

"Ooh, there are a lot of columns." The words are out before I can catch them. Larry chuckles, but the girl sitting beside him smacks him on the shoulder.

Asia's smile does its own slipping, and she tilts her head to one side. "What kind of bible do you use at home, Cherise?"

My mouth opens and closes several times as I scramble for words. "Oh, you know. One of the, um, new ones. With the, uh, regular Chicago style format."

"Chicago style?" I spy Larry out of the corner of my eye, mimicking what I've said, but it earns him another jab in the ribs.

Kendi comes over and sits on the arm of the couch. "Cherise, the scriptures are broken down into books that are organized by chapter and verse. Each chapter will have these larger numbers here, you see? And the verses are the smaller numbers. The columns read from left to right, top to bottom, and there are typically two columns on each page of a standard bible. There are other versions that may read slightly differently, and if you use a bible app, most of them use a single column, which might be easier for you."

There's an app for this stuff?

"If you look at the previous page, you can spot the chapter here. Sixteen starts on this page, but it continues on the next. Follow along until you reach verse ten, and that's where we are."

Kendi's gentle teaching throws me off balance. I should still be mad at him, but I find myself less so.

"So, guys, Cherise is a new believer." Kendi addresses the group. "She may not be as familiar with scriptures as we are, but that means we should help and encourage her." Kendi gives Larry a pointed look.

Larry places his hand on his heart and dips his head. "Cherise, I am so sorry. Kendi said you were fresh, and I forgot. Please forgive me." He makes a face. "And for earlier, too."

Ugh. Right. Earlier.

"You don't have to read out loud if you don't want to, Cherise, but we would like to know your thoughts?" Kendi directs me back to the bible in my hands.

"Oh. Okay." I chuckle, but it comes out shaky. I read the verse to myself, nodding as though I'm really soaking it in. The verse itself isn't hard to understand, but I want to make a good impression, and the night didn't start off well. "Um, Kendi? When you ask me what do I think, what exactly do you mean?"

"Anything you want to share, really." Kendi shrugs. "Does the verse resonate with you? Can you think of examples in your life that echo the message found in the verse? Does it give you something to think about? Those kinds of things."

I nod. "Ah. Yes, it definitely is something I've never thought about before. And I will definitely think about it now. What, uh, what do you guys think about the verse? Specifically?"

Kendi chuckles, and I realize my mistake. Everyone else has already shared. But I wasn't listening and missed the whole thing. No one calls me out on it, though.

"Personally, I think it's a great reminder that the little things matter." That from Kendi. "It's hard to manage big things if you can't be diligent with small things."

"Yep, especially when you consider how big an impact those little things have," Larry adds. "I had a friend who constantly lied. You ask him where he's going, he'll make up a story. You ask him if he ate the last cookie in the jar, he'll say no. You ask him if he could loan you a dollar or two, he'll say he's broke, then go to the arcade. After a while, nobody trusted anything he said."

"Weren't you that friend, Larry?"

The girl beside him pokes him in his side, and Larry laughs. "Yep. But by the grace of God, I'm not that guy anymore. Now that guy's just 'my friend.'"

"Funny, you told everyone here that Cherise is Kendi's girlfriend." The girl locks eyes with Larry, and I shrink deeper into the couch cushions. I'd rather not relive that moment again.

"That wasn't a lie, per se." Larry hems. "It was more like, uh, wishful thinking."

"Let's move on." Kendi leaves his spot on the arm of the couch. "Does anyone else want to add anything about the verse before we close out?"

Thankfully, the only additional comments are those relevant to the verse, and not Larry's 'wishful thinking.' Kendi ends the evening with prayer, and his guests shuffle out.

Kendi starts collecting cups from the coffee table, and I jump in to help.

"It was great meeting you, Cherise!" Larry winks at me on his way out, then sends Kendi a thumbs up.

"Go home, Larry." Kendi grabs the cup in my hand. "Cherise, don't worry about cleanup. I'll take care of it."

I let him take the cup, but I'm left with nothing to do. It's awkward and uncomfortable. So, I pull out my phone and search for a Lyft.

Kendi looks over my shoulder. "What are you doing? I'll take you home."

"You're busy cleaning up, and I don't want to wait."

"Fine." Kendi sets down the cups. "I'll take you home now."

I shake my head. "Don't bother. I think we've spent enough time together for one day, don't you?" I don't like the way my voice sounds. It's Kendi, for crying out loud. What did I expect? "Look. I know you don't like me, and the feeling is mutual. So, I'll get out of your hair, and we can just—"

"Who says I don't like you, Cherise?"

Is he serious right now?

Kendi scratches his head, then slips his hands in his pockets. "I'm sorry about tonight. About being so edgy."

"And about what you said to everyone in your small group about me, in very descriptive, poetic words?"

"That was..." Kendi dips his head. "I shouldn't have said that in front of everyone. It's not you, I just had other stuff in my head tonight." He holds out his hand. "I'm sorry for what I said. And if you decide to come back, I promise I won't embarrass you again. Can we call a truce?"

"A simple, 'No, Cherise is *not* my girlfriend,' would have been fine. But because you had *stuff in your head* you said, 'You don't go searching for bones in a lion's den.' What does that even mean, Kendi? Cause it sounded like you called me the last person you'd ever date."

He doesn't answer for a while. "My mom's Nigerian. It's a proverb she used a lot when I was a kid, and it just came out. I'm sorry, Cherise."

"And I'm over it. Have a nice life, Kendi." I turn to walk out, but I don't have anywhere to go, since I haven't actually found a Lyft yet.

"Let me take you home. It's hard to get a driver before nine."

I glare at him a minute longer. Mainly because I've never seen him look so pitiful before, and I kind of like the look on him. He seems almost bearable with his brows furrowed and worried. But a part of me is still mad. He embarrassed me, and much as I want to impress Preston, I do have my limits. "You swear you won't act like a jerk again?"

He opens his mouth, then closes it. "I can promise to do better. I set a poor example tonight, and the last thing I want to do is discourage you. Next week will be very different. And not just because I'm not hosting." He chuckles, and it douses the rest of the fire in me. Ugh. Fine.

"You can drop me off at the clinic." He raises an eyebrow and I shrug. "I don't like the idea of a stranger knowing where I live."

"I guess I deserve that."

I snort, then put on a more serious face. "Actually, Kendi, there's one other thing?"

"Sure. What's up?"

I'm not sure how long this cease-fire between Kendi and me will last, so I'd better glean as much information as I can while I can. "I've been thinking a lot about this bible stuff, and I'm wondering, is there something I can do to show that I'm, you know, one of you?"

"Something like what?"

"You know, like, stores give out discount cards or loyalty cards or something?"

"You wanna know if Jesus gives out loyalty cards?"

I chuckle. "I didn't mean Jesus, specifically. I meant for this group? Like if I come ten times, do I get a stamp or something?"

"Um." Kendi scratches his head and opens his front door. I step out, and he follows behind me with a smirk inching up his face. "This group doesn't really have a card or anything. We don't keep attendance, either. If you were interested in joining the church, that'd be about the only place where we have an official record."

"Oh. How do I join the church? And what would that involve, exactly?"

We walk down the hall at a comfortable pace, and Kendi rubs his chin. He's so fidgety tonight. It's unnerving, and I want to grab his arms and force them to his sides. Why does it take him a hundred minutes to answer a simple question?

"Are you busy this Sunday?"

"Huh?" Red flags pop up immediately. Does Kendi like me? Did I lead him on in some way? Oh no!

"You should come check out a service or two, get a feel for the church first. See if it's a good fit. Service starts at ten."

"In the morning?"

"Yup."

"Will you also be there?"

Kendi shakes his head. "Not this week. But most Sundays I'm there. If you decide to come, just give me a call and I'll wait for you in the lobby. If you want to."

I do not. But I nod my head anyway. At least he's not trying to ask me out. I think? Maybe in his world, that's how it's done? But I've had enough embarrassment for one night, so the rest of my questions will have to wait a little longer for answers.

"Should I really drop you off at the clinic?"

I check my watch. No one will be there, and I'd only been joking anyway. But not knowing if Kendi likes me presents a bit of a conundrum. What if he decides to just show up at my apartment one day and confess his feelings? And what if Preston happens to see him there? He's never been to my apartment, but won't it bother him if Kendi knows where I live? Or worse, has been to my apartment first?

I send a quick text to Shantell as Kendi waits for my answer. If she's home, I'll have him drop me off at her place. She texts back a smiley face and a wine glass emoji.

Problem solved.

18

First Kiss

Going to Kendi's bible study has worked wonders for my name-dropping game. In just two weeks, I've managed to slip Paul, Peter, Simon, and a dude named Barnabas very casually into conversations with Preston. He seems to really like it when I do. Today is no exception.

"Sounds like you've been paying attention at small group." He sips from a glass of lemonade, and I watch the Adam's apple in his neck move up and down.

Yes, Lord, I've been paying attention. "Yeah, I've been learning a lot. Like, how Jesus really called Peter Satan. That was wild."

Preston chuckles. It's deep and rumbly, like thunder trapped in an ocean storm. The sound sends a shiver up my spine. It escalates to a full tremor when he takes my hand, presses his index finger into my palm and begins drawing slow circles.

I take a deep draw of my sweet tea as heat rushes to my cheeks. He's kept his word, and our last few dates have been in restaurants, with one exception. We caught a late movie one night, but thankfully, that was indoors. Preston's so good to me. It makes me feel a little guilty.

"Cherise? Would it be alright if we take a walk outside?"

"Of course." His fingers are still making swirls, and it's hard to concentrate.

He dips his head under the table and makes a face. "On second thought, maybe a walk isn't a good idea."

I wave in dismissal. "I'd love a walk, actually. It's a nice night." It's a cold night in early December, but Preston seems impervious to the weather.

His eyes travel to my Jimmy Chu's, and I see the doubt on his face. "You sure? Those don't look like walking shoes."

"These? Pfft! They're extremely comfortable, and I will be just fine." It's a lie. One I hope he sees through. Walking in these shoes would be the death of me.

He laughs. "I've got a better idea. Do you want dessert?"

"Oh, no, I couldn't eat another bite." Lies, lies, lies.

Preston pays for dinner and we leave, my hand wrapped securely in his. Once we're outside, he squats down in front of me. "Hop on."

I'm so glad I opted for jeans tonight. Because there's no way I'd ever pass up an opportunity to ride on Preston's back and, frigid weather aside, the choppy dresses in my closet would have been a disaster. I giggle and squeal as I wrap my arms around his neck and cross my legs over his middle. His hands secure my thighs, sending me into another fit of giggles, and after a few adjustments, he whisks me away.

"Where are we going?" My lips brush over the top of his ear. It's not an accident. It's a signal. One I hope he picks up on.

"Just to the parking garage. But we're taking the long way. I want to talk to you about something."

"Oh yeah?" Butterflies dance with sugarplum fairies in the space formerly known as my stomach.

"Mhm. I have a trip coming up next week."

"Oh." *Is he going to ask me to go with him?*

"I'll only be gone a couple days, but then I started thinking about how much I'd miss you."

He's going to take me with him!

"That got me to thinking about what that means. And about what you mean to me."

I hold my breath, waiting.

"I like you, Cherise. I think you know that already. But I think about you all the time, and I miss you when I don't see you."

Far too soon we're in the parking garage, and the low ceilings force Preston to put me down. We walk to his car, but before he opens my door, he turns me toward him. Every cell in my body reacts to his touch, just a simple tug at my wrist. His eyes hold mine as he leans forward.

"Can I kiss you?"

I nod my head yes, and he lowers his face to mine. Our lips touch, and it's brief. He pulls back, but I move forward, wrapping my arms around his neck and standing on my toes as I draw him into me. We kiss again, but this time we linger. His hands wrap around my waist, pulling me closer.

I don't want to let go. I don't want to stop. I want him to keep holding me, kissing me. I feel safe in his arms. And precious. He asked for permission to kiss me. Who does that?

Preston does. And I know without a shadow of a doubt that I want this man. More than I've ever wanted anyone.

"Preston?" The word comes out in a whisper, in between kisses.

"Yeah?"

"Let's go back to my place." I kiss him again and again, pulling him closer and closer. "You can stay over if you want."

I shiver as our noses touch and his fingers graze my neck. He lifts his head, and the empty space between us feels cold. "Oh. I can't."

He shakes his head, but I pull him back to me, kissing him again. "It's okay. I have protection, and I'm on the pill."

Preston breaks contact again and pulls away. "No, it's not that. Cherise, I *can't*."

Panic forces the air from my lungs as I realize what's happening. He's rejecting me. A grocery list of reasons rushes in, sending my head spinning.

Is he married? No ring on his finger. Oh no, he's gay. But where were the signs? Wait. What if he's not?

I don't want to ask, but my heart is pounding so fast, it might burst. I have to know. "Is it me?"

"What? Cherise, no."

"I thought that you... that we were..."

Preston cups my hands in his and kisses my knuckles. "Cherise. I like you. I really, really like you. But you and I aren't married, and there are lines I can't cross."

I blink. "Lines?"

Preston bites his lower lip as he makes a humming sound. "I'd hoped Kendi would have already covered this with you, but maybe not. Part of walking with God means trading in our old way of doing things with His way of doing things. That's true for every aspect of our lives, including relationships. Cherise, if we're not married, we can't be physically intimate. It wouldn't be right."

All the fire in my limbs seeps out, replaced with a cold dread. "When you say we can't be intimate, do you mean, like, ever? Like, you're celibate or something?"

"Yeah. Something like that."

My enthusiasm thoroughly doused, I let my hands drop to my sides. I knew Preston's faith would be challenging, but this is a whole nother level.

What have I gotten myself into?

"CUT HIM LOOSE!"

Shantell shakes her head emphatically as the spa technician applies another coat of soft pink to her acrylic nails. I'm in a chair a few feet from Shantell. Adrian sits beside me, an Ebony magazine hiding her face from me.

"I thought you liked Preston?" Shantell's abrupt decision is not what I want to hear. Truthfully, last night I felt the same way. But then I went to bed. Alone. And then woke up alone, too.

"I did like Preston. But that was only because he made you smile. And you don't look like you're smiling now. Adrian, back me up."

"I've gotta agree with Shantell on this one." Adrian's face is still hidden from me. "Preston has too many rules."

"It's just the two," I say, but the words lack conviction. I'd hoped to have made more progress with Preston by now. A key to his apartment and half my stuff at his place by Christmas, or at least the new year. This is unfamiliar territory for me, and I'm worried.

"Celibacy is a pretty big rule, Cherise!" Shantell shivers, but goes still when the technician glares at her. "Last night was your first kiss. Might be your last, if he's worried you'll try to steal his virtue. Is that what you want?"

"No, of course not. But I think I can get through to him."

Adrian lowers the magazine. "This I gotta hear."

"Well, Preston says we can't be intimate because we aren't married. I've been doing some research on marriage customs from different cultures, and there are a lot of cultures that require sex first."

"Ooh, sign me up for one of those!" Shantell giggles.

"I think the whole 'no intimacy before marriage' thing is just a custom that's been passed down from colonial white culture. Once I prove my point, I think Preston will see that us having sex is really no big deal and is actually a better way to solidify our relationship."

"Your logic is sound, Cherise." Adrian lifts a skeptical eyebrow. "Unfortunately, logic doesn't always win. Especially in the realm of religion."

"Aht, aht!" Shantell points an already finished finger at my bestie. "Adrian, what I tell you about that?" Adrian shrugs and Shantell sighs. "At any rate, I still say cut him loose. Y'all are moving too slow for me. First kiss after over a month of dating? By the time y'all have babies, you'll be Big Mama's age."

I laugh, but it isn't funny. Shantell's right. Things are moving too slowly. Preston's not interested in casual dating, but how long before he decides I'm wifey material? We need to fast track this relationship if I want my happily ever after. He needs to see me as someone he can be intimate with. Which means I need to turn up the heat.

19

Hot Mess

I have three tried and true rules of seduction.

Rule number one: start early. Preston is going out of town, which presents a perfect opportunity for me. If I play my cards right, he may even take me with him. The plan is for me to cook dinner at his place Wednesday night, but I'm not going to wait until Wednesday to start working.

No, my plans begin Sunday night with cute texts and selfies. I compliment him whenever I can and make sure I wear and do all the things he likes. I name drop one of the disciples in every conversation, wear his favorite colors in my clothes and accessories, and make sure he knows how much I miss him.

Rule number two: smells are everything. There's a saying that the way to a man's heart is through his stomach. I think that's only partially true. In my opinion, the way food *smells* is what makes a man's heart go bubbadabup.

And the way his woman smells is no different. So, Wednesday night, I'm preparing lasagna with fresh herbs. Before I head over to Preston's place, I make sure I'm clean, fresh, and smelling my best. I add a little extra something to the spaces I want him to snuggle, like my wrists and the crook of my neck.

When I arrive on his front steps with two bags of groceries and a body mist that would make angels weep, Preston does just what I hope. He draws me into his arms, breathing me in as he rests his chin on my shoulder.

"You smell amazing."

I know. Just like I know rule number three will knock his socks off. I shuffle out of my winter coat, revealing the silky, black dress Shantell helped me pick out. It dips just a little in the front, has no sleeves, and flares out at the waist. It's short enough to showcase my legs, which are smooth to the touch and ready for just that. Preston drinks me in a full minute before taking the groceries to the kitchen.

Rule number three: give him plenty to look at.

As I make my way around his kitchen, I'm sure to give him plenty of jobs.

"Preston, can you help me with my apron?"

"Preston, can you chop this lettuce?"

"Preston, can you help me reach that bowl on the top shelf?"

Each request pulls him into my proximity, reminding him of how I smell, how I look, and how much he needs me.

It didn't work on Calvin.

I slam a jar of sauce on the counter a little too hard.

"You okay, Cherise?" Preston's at my side in seconds, his fingers on mine, his shoulders brushing my sides.

It won't last. He'll get tired of you and leave you just like Calvin did.

I plaster on a smile and shove the thoughts away. "I'm fine!"

"You sure?"

"Absolutely." I shoo him out of the kitchen. "You go relax, or finish packing for your trip, and I'll call you back into the kitchen when dinner is ready."

He wraps his arms around my waist and kisses my neck. "I'd much rather stay here and help you." I scream internally, feeling lighter already. Preston turns me around and plants a kiss on my lips. "What else can I do?"

The oven beeps, and the words I really want to say never make it out. "Dinner's ready! Preston, can you set the table with plates and those bowls for the salad?" He goes to work, and I fan my face. Never mind that the oven door is still closed.

I manage to get everything plated without a single klutzy mistake. It's a good sign. This is going to be a good night.

"Everything looks amazing, Cherise." He stares at the spread and grins. "You didn't have to go to all this trouble for me, you know."

"It's no trouble." I take his hand and squeeze it. "Ready to pray?" I've learned by now that Preston prays before every meal. His mouth quirks up, and he says a few words of thanks before grabbing his fork.

"Where should I begin? This bread looks pretty enticing. But the salad looks gorgeous. And the lasagna." He samples a bite and groans. "Mm. Cherise, where did you learn to cook like this? Did your mom teach you? Or your dad, maybe?"

The answer is neither. But that doesn't fit the impression I've been feeding Preston over the last month. "My mom. She used to cook for us almost every night when we were little."

"Tell me about your brothers? What was that like for you?"

Lonely. "They were the stereotypical big brothers growing up, you know? Always looking out for me and protecting me from bullies and boys. It was nice." There is an eight-year age gap between me and my brothers, and they weren't crazy about the idea of having another sibling. They basically ignored me until they graduated high school. Now, the only time we talk is when mom or dad do something to get on their nerves and they need an ally.

"I always wanted a sibling growing up," Preston says. "I thought it would be nice to share my secrets with someone. When things got hard, I could lean on my brother or sister for help, you know?"

"Yeah. It was so great having them around. I'm sure they'd love you, too."

"Yeah? You think so?"

"They've got big personalities, and great senses of humor." So long as Preston doesn't mind being the butt of every joke, he'll do just fine.

"I'm looking forward to meeting them one day. If that's alright with you?"

My stomach does a flip. "Of course. Why wouldn't it be okay with me?"

Preston puts his fork down. "I know the other night might have come as a bit of a shock to you, Cherise. But I want you to know I take our relationship very seriously. That I take you seriously."

Everything in me wants to kiss him, but not with marinara sauce pooling around my gums. I wait until we're done eating, then clear the table and excuse myself to the bathroom.

I stare at my reflection in the mirror. "Cherise, you've got this. You're beautiful, strong, determined. And he wants you. Preston wants you." I help myself to the mouthwash on Preston's countertop, touch up my makeup, and freshen my curls.

A few minutes later, I join him on the couch while he fiddles with the top of an ice cream tub. His face lights up when he sees me. "Hey Cherise. I wasn't sure which ice cream you'd prefer, so I took a shot in the dark. This shortbread vanilla is my favorite, but I have mint chocolate chip in the freezer, too. You took care of dinner, so I figured I'd handle dessert."

He scoops a spoonful from the top and offers it to me. "Have a taste?"

I sit next to him, push the spoon aside and kiss him. I feel him smile as he returns the gesture. The spoon disappears somewhere in the ice cream, and he wraps his arms around me.

I want to stay like this forever. Me and Preston fit so well together. But just as quickly as it starts, it's over. Preston drops his arms and puts space between us. I lean forward, not wanting any distance between us. I try to kiss him, but he moves further back. "It's okay, Preston. I trust you."

He caresses my cheek and sighs. "We should slow down."

"What if we don't?" I place my hand on his chest. "What if we just keep going?"

"Cherise, I already told you–"

"That it wouldn't be right. But that's not true. Lots of people get together before marriage, and in some cultures, couples are expected to have sex first before a marriage is agreed to. Like in some Hindu cultures–"

"Let me stop you there." Preston slides off the couch and grabs the ice cream tub. "Regardless of what other people do in other cultures, this isn't something that's up for debate."

I watch Preston as he makes his way to the kitchen. "Why not? It affects both of us. Shouldn't it be something we both discuss and agree to?"

Preston sighs as he places the ice cream in the freezer. "You wanna talk about it, sure. We can talk about it. And if it were anything else, I'd probably agree with you that we should discuss it. But Cherise, this isn't something that I'm willing to compromise on. And it worries me that it's not the same for you."

I take a deep breath and try again. "I don't understand why you won't even consider it."

Preston returns to the living room, but he doesn't join me on the couch. "Alright, Cherise. Let's consider it. You did your research on other cultures and their marriage customs, right?"

I nod. "Yes."

"But you and I aren't getting married. We just started dating, and we're nowhere near that stage. We aren't engaged, and we haven't made any promises to each other. So even if I were to use other cultures as a basis for having sex with you, the example doesn't apply."

"I thought you said you were serious about us."

"And I am. But that doesn't mean I'm ready to spend the rest of my life with you. And until I am, I can't cross that line with you."

It feels like all the air's been sucked out of the room. Suddenly, it's hard to breathe.

See? He doesn't want to be with you. No one does. "I see." A moment later I'm on my feet.

"Maybe we should call it a night." Preston reaches for me, but I pull away and grab my coat. "Cherise?"

I feel foolish. And angry. And hurt. But mostly foolish. Being rejected the first time hurt. Why would I throw myself at him twice?

"Cherise?"

I keep walking until I'm out the door and in my car. I can't wrap my head around it. Is something wrong with him?

Or is something wrong with me?

20

Rules of Engagement

I spend all of Friday angry, skipping small group. There's no point in going if Preston and I aren't gonna be together. I try to focus on my clients and their care, and for the most part it works. I ignore all of Preston's calls and leave his messages unread.

Halfway through Saturday I'm less angry, but still not taking his calls. What era is Preston even living in?

By Sunday, I'm feeling conflicted, but I'm not ready to talk to Preston yet. After two rejections, I'm still hurt, and reaching out feels like setting myself up for a third. But I need to talk to someone about this, and Shantell and Adrian will just give me more of the same advice. That leaves one person. Kendi.

Monday morning I take my usual clients, with plans to catch up with Kendi after work. But by lunch time, I'm a bundle of nerves. How do I even begin? Should I tell Kendi about Preston and me, or keep it vague? Does it even matter if there is no Preston and me? Are we really over?

That singular thought sends me spiraling into sadness. I really, really like Preston, even if he is being stupid. Either he's taking this faith stuff way too seriously, or he's confused. This can't possibly be an actual rule, right?

I can't wait. Instead of going out for lunch, I head over to the fitness center. I find Kendi near the weights spotting a wiry, young college kid on the bars.

"Why is sex off the table for Christians?" I ask.

Kendi chuckles. "Good afternoon to you too, Cherise."

"I'm serious. There's no actual rule in the bible, right? I mean, even if there is, nobody follows it, right?"

"Um, Cherise?"

I shake my head. "No, don't tell me. I don't wanna know." I walk away, then turn right back around. "Please tell me it's not a rule? Like, it's one of those things like eating food offered to idols, right? Some people think it's wrong, some people don't, and we shouldn't judge. Right?"

"Cherise, now's not a good time."

"I mean, how can you expect people to be celibate this day and age? Catholic priests can't even do it!"

"Cherise, that's not an appropriate thing to say."

"Well, it's true! And if the people most devoted to God can't do it, why should I? It's stupid!"

Kendi shrugs. "Well, for what it's worth, I'm celibate. And I don't think it's stupid."

I scoff. "Haha Kendi. Real funny."

"What's funny?"

"You being celibate." I laugh and give him a thumbs up. "Nice one."

"It's true."

"Pfft. Please! You're a personal trainer. Isn't that, like, the most debauchery-ridden profession in existence?"

"Not offensive at all." Kendi's flat tone and raised eyebrow send mine flying.

"You're serious? You're really not sleeping with anyone?"

Kendi shakes his head. "Cherise, again, not a great time to have this discussion." He gestures to the kid in front of him and I scowl. But he's right.

"Sorry. But Kendi, this is kind of an emergency."

"I don't see how." I give him a pleading look, and he sighs. "Fine. Wait over by the massage chairs, and give me about ten minutes."

"Can you make it five?"

"I can make it never, if ten doesn't work."

"Okay, sheesh! Ten it is." I meander over to the front desk and press my palms into my temples. The massage chairs are occupied, otherwise I'd park it in one. I really don't want things to be over between Preston and me. But no intimacy means I've got to win him over in other ways. And I'm already playing this game with a handicap.

"Alright, Cherise, what's the emergency?" Kendi meets me by the chairs with a sigh.

Can I trust him with the truth? Or even a tiny part of it? Honestly, this whole thing is exhausting. Maybe it's time I come clean. I really should come clean. Get everything out in the open.

"Earth to Cherise?" Kendi waves his hand in front of me. "You still with me?"

I shake my head. "Sorry. I'm just..." *Never enough. Never have been, never will be.* "...a little thrown by this whole no sex thing. Is it *really* a thing?"

Kendi's face softens as he steps a little closer. "I'm not sure I can explain it well enough here, but let's start with this. What do you understand about it, and what would you say is your biggest issue with it?"

I take a minute to think about Kendi's question. Honestly? I'm not sure. I like being close to the person I'm with. It makes me feel connected and, in some ways, secure. Not being able to have that closeness with Preston is scary. Whenever Calvin and I fought, we'd find our way back to each other through intimacy.

But Calvin still left. So I guess, I'm not sure I'm brave enough to explore a relationship without it. There's no way I'm telling Kendi that, though. It's too personal. "I guess I just don't understand why it has to be a rule."

Kendi taps his finger against his chin. "Let's take a walk."

I eye him warily, but he shrugs and steps outside the fitness center, holding the door as he waits for me to follow. I walk through it, and we meander down the sidewalk.

"When I came to God, I wasn't the greatest person."

I'm not sure where this is going, but I don't interrupt him.

"I was willing to do almost anything God wanted me to, but there was one area where I really struggled. I had a girlfriend at the time, and we were... active."

"I thought you said you were celibate?"

"I am. Now. But I wasn't always."

"What made you change your mind?"

Kendi blows out a breath. "A lot of really messed up things happened. Some things you know are wrong without anyone specifically telling you. Some things are easy to give up. I could fast for days. Saying no to a drink was easy. I could lay down a lot of old ways, but when I was presented with the idea that sleeping with my girlfriend was wrong, I just struggled.

"Being with her felt good. Sometimes it even felt right. But whenever you're presented with a different truth, it leaves you unsettled. I had no excuses. I didn't love her, though I loved being with her. I wasn't interested in getting married, but I didn't want to give up our relationship, either. Knowing I was being selfish, in spite of everything God had done for me, left me in this constant tug of war. Some days I'd try to justify it. Other days I'd just feel so worthless. Like God was wasting his time with me."

Kendi stops walking and looks at me. "When we choose to give our lives to God, that includes giving him our desires. But the truth is, none of us gets things right 100 percent of the time. I know some great couples who've made mistakes along the way. But I also know that those mistakes can breed a lot of resentment between two people. I hurt someone I cared about, because I chose to do things my way instead of God's way. And while there's forgiveness and grace for every mistake we make, there are also consequences."

"I'm not sure I'm following you?"

"In scripture, we're taught that everything is not good for us. We haven't really gone over sexual immorality since you've joined the group, but if you want, we can talk about it this week. We missed you last Friday."

"Yeah, something came up." I clear my throat. "But Kendi? What if you're in a serious relationship? Wouldn't it be okay in that context?"

Kendi chuckles. "Come to the group this week and we'll talk about it." He looks back at the fitness center, then looks at me. "I've gotta head back, but I promise to answer all your questions on Friday, okay?"

I don't really want to wait until Friday, but I've got clients coming in, and I don't know how to ask the questions I really want answered. "Alright. Group on Friday."

"It's at my place again this week. Let me know if you want to ride together?"

I go back to the clinic, and though I'm not on board with Preston's way of thinking, I do feel a little better after talking to Kendi. At least I don't have to wonder if Preston's just trying to spare my feelings. That thought did cross my mind a few times, but now I can put it to rest. Mostly.

I've gotta admit, Kendi's not that bad now that we've called a truce. A surprising discovery, especially for a meathead. At this rate, we might even become friends. Eh, maybe not.

First thing I need to do is decide if I can either convince Preston to change his mind about sex or find a way to live without it. Because I still want my happily ever after, and I still think Preston's my best shot at getting it. Shantell might disagree, and Adrian might shake her head, but I have to try. And if I think about it, I've been practicing celibacy ever since I broke up with Calvin. Okay, technically he broke up with me. But loneliness aside, it hasn't been *that* bad.

I'm hopeful that Preston and I can come to some sort of compromise. But if I have to trade cold showers now for hot nights later, I think I can do it.

21

Let's Talk About Sex

Asking a room full of adults about sex is as awkward as it sounds. To their credit, the group is mostly straight-faced when Kendi announces the topic of discussion.

"We're going to pause our study on Luke and do something a little different tonight." Kendi says. He promised not to embarrass me again, but that doesn't keep my cheeks from flushing with heat. "We'll be talking about relationships and Christian living, so I've asked Larry and Pam to take charge of tonight's discussion, since they've got a lot of experience and wisdom on the subject."

To his credit, Kendi doesn't mention my name or even glance my way. If I keep my eyes forward, maybe no one will know I'm the one causing tonight's topical shift.

Larry and Pam stay in their seats but wave at everyone in the group before starting. "Hey everyone," Pam begins. "Some of you may already know that Larry and I have been doing relationship studies for a long time."

"Those studies came in handy when we got engaged this summer," Larry adds. I perk up at that little tidbit. I had no idea the two were a couple, though now that I think about it, they always sit together. "After talking to Kendi, we thought it would be helpful to share our experiences and answer any questions that pop up about relationships. But first, let's go to the scriptures and see what the bible says about Godly relationships."

I still don't have a bible, but Asia helped me download an app a few weeks ago, so I follow along on my phone while Larry reads a passage in Hebrews. Afterwards, Pam reads a passage in one of the Corinthians. Pam reads:

"'You say, Food was made for the stomach, and the stomach for food. This is true, though someday God will do away with both of them. But you can't say that our bodies were made for sexual immorality. They were made for the Lord, and the Lord cares about our bodies.'"

She skips down a bit before continuing. *"Run from sexual sin! No other sin so clearly affects the body as this one does. For sexual immorality is a sin against your own body. Don't you realize that your body is the temple of the Holy Spirit, who lives in you and was given to you by God? You do not belong to yourself, for God bought you with a high price. So you must honor God with your body.'"*

"What do you guys think about these verses?" Larry asks.

Asia raises her hand. "I think what struck me most in those verses is the last part that says we must honor God with our bodies. Like, even beyond sexual purity, we need to honor God in all things. And I think sometimes we get caught up in semantics and ideologies that we hear around us, but at the heart of everything we do, honoring God comes first."

"That's a good point." Pam nods her head. "With Larry and I, it's the line we draw for every interaction. We may have disagreements about how to engage with one another, but when we stop and ask the question, 'Am I honoring God in the way I'm treating the person I want to spend my life with?' the answers become much more clear. Neither one of us wants to do something that would make the other feel ashamed or guilty in the eyes of God, because we love each other."

"That's right." Larry leans forward. "I'll give you an example. In my family, we're very affectionate. Lots of hugging and touching and slaps on the back and all that."

"But in my family, we don't do any of that." Pam continues. "When Larry and I got together, I had a really hard time with him touching me. If he tried to kiss me or hold my hand, it felt really intimate, and I was worried we'd fall into sin if we did those kinds of things."

"It frustrated me a little bit at first," Larry admits. "I wasn't trying to push. I was just trying to show affection. We got into an argument about it, and Pam said to me, 'Would it make you feel better if I let you kiss me? Even if I feel guilty about it afterwards?' And it really struck me when she asked me that. I wanted to show her how much I loved her, but at what cost? If my affection cost Pam her peace, was our relationship really honoring God?"

"We're not saying that kissing and holding hands is wrong." Pam waves her hands at the group. "Every relationship is unique, and some of the boundaries will be different for each person. But when one person tries to make the other feel bad about their boundaries, one of two things will happen. Either you cave and feel guilty and resentful, or you stick to your principles and part ways."

"And in some cases, separating is better." Larry glances at Kendi, then looks at Pam. "But thankfully, that wasn't our case. We realized that, more than anything else, we wanted to encourage each other to follow God. That meant making concessions for each other and being gracious and understanding in how we dealt with one another."

"But what if the other person really wants to kiss you?" I ask, a touch too eagerly in hindsight. "Like, wouldn't it be wrong to hold that other person hostage because you've got misconstrued ideas about right and wrong?" Hmm. That did not come out right. Judging by Pam's face, it didn't translate any better. "Uh, I mean, not that your ideas were misconstrued! I just, um."

"I think Cherise has a valid point," Kendi says. I gape at him. Did Meathead just agree with me? "From Larry's side, we see that he needed to adjust himself to make sure he didn't pressure you into doing something you thought was wrong. But what about you, Pam? Did you reexamine your stance on what is or isn't considered too intimate? Did you also have to make an adjustment?"

Pam shakes her head. "Larry never asked me to after that."

"Couldn't the fact that Larry was the one making adjustments, and not both of you, also breed resentment in your relationship?"

Pam nods her head. "Absolutely."

Not the answer I was expecting.

"Could you speak more on that?" Kendi asks.

"Yeah." Larry clears his throat. "Our wedding date is just a few months away, and the closer it gets, the more Pam and I have visited and revisited the same old arguments. When, if ever, is it okay to get a little bit closer? What if we technically don't cross the line, but try other stuff? At this point, we're definitely getting married, so why do we have to keep waiting?"

"And before you guys assume that it's all Larry," Pam interjects, "I want to tell you two things. First, these are questions we intentionally ask each other, it's not just Larry asking me. Second, the reason we ask ourselves these questions is because we've messed up, and we have to remind ourselves of why we set the boundaries we set."

"In the interest of being completely vulnerable with you guys, Pam and I wanted to share not just our successes, but our failures. Some of you already know about this, but a few months ago, Pam and I almost called off our engagement."

"What happened?" The question comes from Zev, who spends most nights in group pretty quiet.

Pam tilts her head from side to side. "Well, truthfully, Larry and I spent a night together. It wasn't planned, and normally we just say goodnight at the end of a date, but I'd been feeling really guilty about withholding so much of myself from him. I was worried that he might feel that resentment that Kendi mentioned. So, I decided to test my theory. I told him I wanted to stay, and we held hands and watched a movie. Then holding hands turned into kissing, and kissing turned into other things. And we just didn't stop."

"I felt really bad afterwards," Larry says. "Pam couldn't even look at me the next day, and I knew I'd messed up. We both felt guilty, but she took it really hard. We didn't talk to each other for weeks, and when we did, she'd just start crying and apologizing."

"I told Larry I wanted to call off the wedding. I'd never felt more ashamed. I was angry at myself, because I completely ignored all my boundaries. And I was angry at him for letting me. I didn't think we could get past it."

Larry takes her hand in his and squeezes it. "But we did. I told her we didn't have to talk about the wedding, but we needed to talk to each other about what happened. About what went wrong and why. And every few weeks, we ask ourselves those same questions. And we forgive each other, and remind ourselves that there's grace for every mistake. Because the last thing we want to bring into our marriage is baggage we don't have to carry."

A few more people ask questions, but I find myself at a loss for words. I'd expected a lecture about rules, followed by their perfect example. But Larry and Pam didn't do that. And even though I still don't get what the big deal is, I feel a little closer to the group after being a part of such an intimate discussion. This amazing group of people share literally everything with each other. And I've been lying to them this whole time.

The feeling fades as guilt creeps in.

"Hey, Cherise? You okay?" Kendi taps me on the shoulder, and I realize that we're the only two people left in his apartment.

"Yeah." I nod. "I'm fine."

"You get the answers you were looking for?"

And some I wasn't. "Yeah. Thanks."

"Come on. I'll walk you out."

My steps are slow on the way out, and I'm not sure if it's because I'm tired, or because I know each step is leading me to the inevitable. I've got to tell Preston the truth. I really care about him, and I can't keep lying to him like this. I've known for a while now that his religion isn't just a hobby, but tonight was so raw and real. It'd be a slap in the face to him, and Kendi, and everyone in the group to continue.

"Kendi?"

"Yeah?"

"What do you do when you have to tell someone something that's really, really hard?"

He turns around and looks at me. "I don't know."

"Helpful."

He shakes his head. "No, really. Sometimes I do the hard thing, but sometimes I don't. I mess up a lot, Cherise. I keep quiet when I shouldn't, and I say too much when I should hold my peace. The only thing I can say for sure is that trusting God never fails, even if we do."

Ah, herein lies my trouble. I've always believed in God, I guess. But like, He's up there in heaven doing his thing, and us people are down here on earth doing ours. God was never a topic of discussion at our dinner table, though Big Mama raised my dad in church. The invocation of Jesus' name only came in our house when Dad stubbed his toe on the couch, or when Mom paired it with an F-bomb during a heated argument.

While I believe in the Big G, I never imagined He'd want anything to do with me. Or that I'd need to trust Him for anything. As I follow Kendi out, all I can do is smile, nod, and wonder how in the world I'm going to explain myself to Preston.

22

Reset

Christmas comes and goes before I get up the nerve to talk to Preston. I've gone back and forth on what to say. Bringing in the new year alone is depressing, but there's more than that at stake. I've fallen hard for him, and I want to try again. I haven't returned his calls, yet, because I know I need to have this discussion in person. I've also been too terrified to dial his number.

A few days before the new year, I walk up to the front door of his house, completely unannounced, and hope for the best when I ring the bell. I shiver in the cold as I wait, despite the heft of my coat.

The door swings open, and Preston appears, his eyes drinking me in with what I hope is longing. "Cherise?"

"Hey Preston. Can we talk?"

He takes a step forward, framing the door with his shoulders. "If we're breaking up, I'd rather we not go inside."

A jolt runs through me, and I lick my lips. "Breaking up?"

He frowns and the muscles in his neck twitch. "You haven't been taking my calls. I spent the last two weeks wondering if you and I were done." He shakes his head. "I wasn't sure you'd have the decency to tell me if we were. I appreciate you coming here in person, but I'd rather we do this outside."

He's caught me off guard, and now I'm staring at him with my mouth hanging wider than a trout in the Neuse River.

He clears his throat. "I didn't want to leave things the way they were between us. I kept wondering if maybe I pushed you too far or didn't explain myself well. Maybe I gave you the wrong impression, or hurt you in some way. I wasn't rejecting you, Cherise. And if I made you feel that way, I'm sorry. But you walked out and you didn't come back. You didn't pick up Thursday night, or Friday morning, or the next day or the next. I left you dozens of messages."

I lower my head. "I know."

"I don't think you do."

He takes another step forward. He's close enough for me to catch the scent of his mouthwash, and a shiver runs down my spine. I gather my thoughts while I study his face. His frown hasn't gone anywhere, and his eyes are red. I can tell he's fighting back tears.

"Do you have any idea how many times I've stopped myself from showing up at your job like some nutcase?" he asks. "How could you not return any of my calls?" I start to explain, but the pain in his voice snatches the words right out of me. "I've never wanted anyone as much as I want you. And that scares me a little, but I thought I meant something to you." His eyes connect with mine, freezing time and space as the breath in my lungs goes still. "You hurt me, Cherise."

I'm locked in his gaze, feeling sick and more than a little dizzy. I have to remind myself to breathe.

"Maybe it's for the best. Maybe you and I aren't a good fit, after all. Maybe I expected too much, or maybe you're just too new in your faith. I mean are you even..." He sighs and shakes his head. "Never mind. It doesn't matter."

Now's your chance to come clean, Cherise. "Preston, about that?"

He doesn't seem to hear me. "I kept wondering if maybe I was the one in the wrong. Maybe I was too rigid, and I should've tried to compromise, or just give in. But Cherise, I can't do that."

The tears he's held at bay start sliding down his face. I reach out to wipe them away, but he pulls back and wipes them away on his own.

"Doing what's right isn't always easy. And I need to be with someone who shares my faith and encourages me in it. Not someone who asks me to compromise it."

A lump forms in my throat. Before I came here, I thought that if I explained myself well enough, Preston and I would find a way forward. But now I don't believe that. Not one bit. If I tell him the truth now, it's over. He might forgive me, but I doubt he'll ever give me a second chance.

Preston opened his door believing we were breaking up. In spite of that, he still opened his door. And instead of shielding himself from the hurt and pretending to be okay, he shared his heart with me. I don't want to take that lightly.

"I'm sorry, Preston." The words come out stilted, and it's hard to push out any more than that. My throat's gone and locked up, as though I've swallowed a box of Red Hots and it's lost its ability to function.

Preston nods, his expression resigned. He's misunderstood my apology. I study the man in front of me; his shoulders and jaw are tense, and his fists clench and unclench every few seconds. He's a tightly wound coil, and what I say next will either bring him closer to me or send him jetting off in the opposite direction.

He's being vulnerable with me. And honest. Only a coward would trade that for a lie.

"Preston," I begin again. "You're right. You deserve to be with someone who encourages you and shares your faith. And I—" I hesitate. Lick my lips. Stare at Preston's sad face. See the spark of hope in his eyes.

He wants me. He wants *us*. And that's all I've ever dreamed of. To be wanted by someone. Loved by someone. How can I pass that up?

"I want to be that person for you."

Preston blinks. "What?"

I guess I'm a coward, after all. "I don't want us to break up. I'm sorry I left the way I did, but I was angry and hurt, and I didn't understand."

"You completely shut me out, Cherise."

"I know. And I'm sorry." I take a step forward, but he takes a step back. Doubt clouds his face, and I scramble for words. "A lot of this stuff is still new to me. But I talked to Kendi about it, and he helped me understand things a little better."

"You talked to Kendi about us?"

I backpedal, recognizing the worry on Preston's face. "Not about us specifically. Just about celibacy and why it's a thing. We had a whole discussion about it at small group, and while I don't completely understand it, I have a better understanding now than I did before." Preston still looks skeptical, so I quickly add, "And I'm okay with it."

"Cherise, you don't have to force yourself to agree with me."

I take another step forward, feeling hopeful when Preston doesn't back away again. I pull his hand into mine and lace our fingers together. "I'm not. Preston, the truth is..."

I'm a coward for not coming clean. I know that. But I also know that I want the man in front of me, and I'll do whatever it takes to keep him. I'm not a Christian now, but I can change. It wouldn't be the first time I reinvented myself, and if I try hard enough, sooner or later it won't be a lie.

While I can't tell him the *whole* truth, there is one thing I can tell him. It's an equally terrifying confession, but I owe him this much.

"The truth is?" Preston tilts his head to one side, waiting, and I close the remaining distance between us.

I take a breath, close my eyes, and leap. "I love you, Preston."

"You do?" His voice goes soft, and I feel my insides melting.

"I do." I exhale and let out a little laugh. "That's a really scary thing to say, but–" The rest gets lost as Preston kisses me. It's shorter than I'd like, but after what I put him through, it's more than I deserve.

"That feels really good to hear." He leans his forehead against mine and sighs. "I'm not sure where we go from here, though."

I can think of a few places, but after promising him that I'm 100 percent on board with being chaste and proper, suggesting them would be inappropriate.

Preston caresses my shoulders and plants another kiss on my cheek. "I think I need a little time to sort things out."

A slow terror creeps into my stomach and I shake my head. "I don't want to break up."

"We're not breaking up. But we've obviously got some issues to resolve before we move forward. So, let's think of it as a reset."

A reset. Sure. With the new year just days away, a reset seems fitting. Except the only reset that comes to mind is the time I forgot the passcode to my iPhone and lost all my data. Pictures, emails, passwords, texts from Shantell I was saving to blackmail her with later. Everything.

Suddenly, a reset sounds like a terrible idea.

23

Sucker

It's my first time deciding where Preston and I go out, and I want it to be perfect. After all the turmoil of the past few weeks, I'm ready for a fresh start. To show Preston I mean business, I'm pulling out all the stops.

We meet up on New Year's Eve at a fancy steakhouse off Glenwood Avenue. We order appetizers, and I dive into my curated list of dating questions for Christian couples. And no, that's not a joke. I had to shave down the list to make it work.

"Preston K. Jones, where do you see yourself in five years?"

Preston hums and taps the table. "In five years? Maybe a regional branch manager, if I'm lucky. Starting a family, if I'm luckier."

My cheeks warm and I take a sip of my water. "Fantastic. Which would you rather attend: a concert, or a play?"

"Concert, definitely."

Rats. I love the theater. But this isn't about me, and I've got plenty of follow-up questions to keep us going the rest of the night. "Would you like to go to a Christian concert with me?"

"Sure! Anyone in particular you thinking about?"

Oh. I did mark some potential date ideas down, but honestly, I was more focused on the upcoming productions of *The Book of Mormon* and *Hamilton* than I was on Christian bands. I glance at the notes pinned on my phone, trying my best to be discreet. "Um, Jonah's Brothers?"

Preston chokes on some of his water and coughs. "What?"

My eyebrows go up. "What?"

"Was that a joke?"

"No, I–" I check my phone, much less discreetly, and browse the notes I made for this evening's topics of discussion. Unfortunately, I pinned the wrong list to the top of my phone. Adrian's birthday is coming up, and Shantell sent me a list of possible outings based on her favorite things. The words 'Jonah's Brothers' are typed out at the top of the list with dates and times. Apparently, they're Adrian's favorite group. So probably *not* a Christian band.

I smile and laugh, though it sounds pretty forced to my ears. "Yes. That was a joke."

Preston chuckles. "I was starting to worry. I like the Jonas Brothers well enough, but they're not what comes to mind when I think Christian concert."

I shrug. "I guess."

Preston squints at me. "Have you heard any of their songs?"

Maybe? I scoff. "Of course I have."

Preston, to my surprise, begins belting out the words to a song that's only vaguely familiar to me. If it's not R&B, Motown, or East Coast rap, it's not on my radar. This doesn't sound like any of those. Not by a long shot.

Someone else joins in from a table across from us, and I cover one side of my face. "Preston? What are you doing?" But Preston's found his stride. Even though the song's not my flavor, I'll admit he's got bars. I still don't enjoy our table becoming the focal point of the entire restaurant.

When he finally finishes, he earns a few whistles and tons of applause, to which he graciously bows. I couldn't cool the heat in my face if I tried. I've never seen this side of him before, and I'm not sure how I feel about it.

He leans in toward me with a smile. "Did you like the song?"

I return the gesture, despite my embarrassment. "Yeah, it was nice. But did you have to sing it right now in front of all these people?"

"I needed to test something."

"Well, if you wanted to see how well I do with attention, now you know. I'm not a fan."

Preston dips his head in apology. "Acknowledged. I will refrain from doing it again."

"Thank you." I keep my head down, face still burning. But Preston is quiet, and I start to wonder if maybe I've upset him. What if his song was meant as some grand gesture, and I just ruined everything? I lift my head, slowly, and try to offer him reassurances. "It was really nice, though. I didn't know you could sing like that."

He shrugs. "I picked up a few things here and there. But Cherise, have you heard that song before?"

I clear my throat and take another sip of water. "Yeah."

"Do you know the name?"

"What's with all the trivia?" I laugh, but underneath the table my right leg starts bouncing with nervous energy. I press my fingers into my knee to keep it still.

"Do you know the song, Cherise?" Preston glues me to my seat with his stare.

"Yeah, it's um..." I wave my hand in the air, but no title magically makes its way into my brain. "I can't put my finger on it. You know, it's one of those things where you've got the answer right on the tip of your tongue, but you just can't get it out. Aargh, so annoying, right?"

He leans back and sighs. "Never mind."

Our entrées arrive, and we eat quietly. Preston seems disappointed, but I know it's not the steak. Mine practically melts in my mouth it's so tender.

"Cherise, what's your favorite song?"

I lift my eyes from my plate. "Hm? My favorite song?"

He nods. "Yeah. What's your favorite song?"

I suppress the urge to blurt out "Yeah" by Usher, which is one of my top five. What would he expect my answer to be? Preston would expect a Christian song, right? Unfortunately, I don't know any. I wrack my brain, scanning for some obscure memory from my time with Big Mama at church, but nothing pops up.

I'm taking too long to answer. Preston stares at me, his fingers steepled at his chin. *Think, Cherise.* "*Joyful, Joyful!*" I force the words out quickly, hoping my awkwardness will be overlooked by my choice in song.

"Joyful... Joyful?" Preston repeats the words slowly.

I'm not really sure if that's the name of the song. It's not a memory from church, just a scene from *Sister Act.*

"Seriously?" He's staring right through me now. I can cave or double down, but my mother didn't raise a quitter.

"Yup. The first time I heard it, I felt goosebumps. I've loved it ever since."

He doesn't look like he believes me, but he doesn't say as much. "Okay."

"What's your favorite song?" I ask.

"*Everything I Do*, by Bryan Adams."

I groan a little on the inside. Looks like I'm 0 and 2 tonight. I jot it down in my phone, wondering if it's a Christian band. "That's an interesting choice."

"Yeah. My mom's a big Bryan Adams fan, and while I'm not, I do love that song. Have you heard it?"

I nod yes. A stupid move on my part. Preston's been quizzing me all night, and if I keep lying, he's going to catch me. It looks like he already has.

"Cherise?"

I nibble one of my asparagus spears and pretend not to hear him.

"Cherise."

"Is it just me, or is it a little warm in here?" I chug down the rest of my water, swishing it around the inside of my mouth to keep myself from talking. Or from sticking my heel any further down my throat.

Preston sighs, and when I look at him again, he's frowning. "Why are you lying to me?"

"I'm not lying. It's very warm."

"You know what I mean."

I'm caught, but I can't admit it. The last thing I can admit to is being a liar. There's too much at stake. "Why do you think I'm lying to you?"

"Because no one's favorite song is *Joyful, Joyful*, and when I told you I liked Bryan Adams, you gave me your fake face."

"My what?"

Preston rubs his head. "Your eyes go wide, your brows go up, and you only show the top half of your teeth."

Is he for real? "I don't have a fake face. I've been wearing a normal face all night."

"Every time I ask you a question, your face changes."

"That's just how I look."

"No. That's how you look when you're pretending, Cherise."

"Uh, what are you even talking about?"

"I'm talking about your walls."

"My walls?" There goes my leg again.

"You pretend you like things when you don't, you pretend you know things that you have no clue about, and you make things up for no reason."

I'm screwed. "That's not true."

"It's completely true. And it makes no sense."

For a moment, I'm at a loss. I'm caught, but I *cannot* let Preston know it. "I can't believe you're making a big deal out of a song." It's weak, but it's the best I can do.

"That's exactly my point. Cherise, it's not a big deal. It's just a song. If you don't know it or don't like it, why not just say so?"

"I told you I *do* know the song."

"Then what's it called?"

Me and my big mouth. "Which one? The one you sang, or...?"

Preston shakes his head. "Forget it."

I'm not sure how this evening got away from me, but I need to get things back on track. My eyes wander the room. *Come on, Cherise!* Blessedly, an answer comes. "*Sucker*, by the Jonas Brothers." Preston stares at me. "That's it, right? The song you sang earlier?" He nods, and I let out a slow breath. Our waitress passes by and gives me a thumbs up on the sly. I make a mental note to leave her a huge tip.

"You knew it this whole time?" he asks.

"I told you, I had it on the tip of my tongue."

"And *Joyful, Joyful* is really your favorite song?"

"It was life-changing for me." *Let's not overdo it, Cherise.*

He takes my hand in his and squeezes. "I'm sorry. I guess I'm still a bit on edge after everything that's happened."

"That's understandable." I clear my throat. "I guess you don't trust me."

He lets go of my hand, and I wonder if maybe I said the wrong thing. "You're right. I don't. I know that's not fair to you, but I'm not sure I can get past this. Maybe we should..."

"Keep trying?" I offer. *Please say yes.*

He waits a beat, then nods his head. "Yeah. Okay."

I pay for dinner, and we part ways for the night. Preston kisses me on the cheek before he slips into his car, but I can feel him pulling away long before he leaves.

24

Saint Cherise

"Why are the Jonas Brothers so popular?" I say this in between volleys, though I really shouldn't talk. Adrian returns the ball with a Wimbledon-worthy whack, and I have to rush to the opposite end of the court to knock it back. A swift tap sends it just over the net, but Adrian's ready with another swing that sends me sprinting back to the other side.

"They're devilishly handsome, for one." Adrian doesn't sound winded at all, but tennis is her favorite sport.

Shantell stands on the sidelines, angling her tush for the benefit of the male players one court over. Mid-January is too cold for outdoor courts, so we're playing indoors for my benefit. The cold weather would never keep Adrian from playing. Or Shantell from flirting.

"Y'all done yet?" Shantell asks, winking as one of the men catches her eye.

Adrian smashes the ball into a deep corner, and I don't even try to go after it. "I am. Adrian, you're killing me, here!"

We both watch the ball bounce off the back wall. "Sorry. I've got a lot on my mind."

"Like what? How to help me shave an extra ten pounds?" I dab the sweat from my brow with a towel and twist open the cap for my water bottle.

Adrian swings her tennis racket back and forth. Her brows crease and she sniffs. "They found a mass. At the doctor's last week."

Shantell stops taking fake swings for her fans and rushes over as I drop my bottle. "What?"

More sniffs, followed by the saddest sound I've ever heard come out of a human mouth, send both of us locking Adrian into a group hug.

"What do you need?" Shantell asks.

"You know we're here for you," I add.

Adrian shakes her head. "It's fine. I'm fine."

Shantell and I exchange looks. "What did they say?" I ask.

"They scheduled me for a biopsy in March to rule out cancer." She looks up and puts on a brave face. "It's probably nothing. Don't worry."

"Don't worry?" Shantell scoffs. "What time is the appointment? We'll go with you."

"You don't have to do that."

"We're not gonna let you go by yourself." I squeeze her, infusing all the comfort I can into the embrace. "Squads don't abandon each other, especially in times like this."

She nods and breaks down, which sends all three of us into a frenzy of wails and tears. By the time Adrian pulls away we're a mess of sweat, snot, and unattractive tear streaks. I dab at Adrian's face with her towel while Shantell rubs her back.

"I need a distraction from all this." Adrian waves her hands in the air, and we all settle down on a bench. "What's going on with you two?"

Shantell shrugs. "Not much. The daycare is growing, so I've gotten busier with work. But that doesn't stop me from being busy after work." Shantell waves at the male players as they gather their things. One of them pulls off his shirt, and Shantell stands up and starts catcalling. Adrian and I both pull her back to the bench, but it doesn't do much for the secondhand embarrassment.

"Girl, stop." I shake my head. "That reminds me, Preston decided to sing a Jonas Brothers song during our date."

"Ooh, which one?" Adrian perks up. "Cherise, you didn't tell us he sings?"

"I didn't know. And when other people started joining in, I thought I was going to die."

"Wait." Shantell tilts her head to the side. "He sang in the middle of the restaurant? Out loud?"

I nod. "Loud enough to get a standing ovation three tables over."

Shantell makes a face. "Are we sure Preston's not white?"

Adrian scoffs. "What's that got to do with anything?"

"Uh uhn, that's not how we do. That's a white people thing. Black folks sing in church and in bed."

"Why in bed?" Adrian asks, then quickly follows with a, "Never mind! I got it."

Shantell wiggles her eyebrows. "You sure, Adrian? Cause you're mighty ignorant to be one of us. Were you adopted by white parents? Blink if it's true and you're too embarrassed to say it out loud."

"Shantell, stop being ignorant." I give my cousin a look, but she shrugs.

Adrian chuckles and turns back to me. "So, which song was it?"

For the life of me, I can't remember the name. "It was popular enough for a random waitress to know it. But that's not the biggest problem." I recount my date with Preston, mildly annoyed at the way Shantell's lips puff out with each new detail. She has zero control over her facial expressions.

"What are you gonna do now?" Adrian asks. "Pretend that you know all the Jonas Brothers' songs?"

"No, I–"

"Because I have them. If you want to borrow them."

"Of course you do." Shantell rolls her eyes. "Cherise, enough is enough. You've been dating this guy for how long now? And you're still playing these games? Look, if he were putting out, that'd be one thing, but he's giving you *nothing*. I say cut him loose."

I shake my head. "I can't."

"Girl, why not?"

"Because I'm in love with him."

Shantell blinks at me, but Adrian's face breaks out into a wide grin. "Aw, Cherise! When did this happen?"

I shrug. "I don't know. But I do, and I want to make this work."

"But whyyy?" Shantell whines. "You've already resorted to gaslighting him to keep him. How far are you willing to go, girl?"

I laugh. "Shantell, I'm not gaslighting him."

"Uh, yes you are."

I shake my head. "No, I'm not."

"Huh. Okay." Shantell taps her finger against her chin. "So at dinner, Preston got mad at you, right?"

"Right."

"Because he thought you were lying to him. Right?"

"Yeah."

"But then, thanks to a waitress waiting in the wings, you proved to him that you weren't lying to him, and Preston apologized to you. Right?"

I don't like where this is headed. "Yeah, but–"

"So, you made Preston feel bad about accusing you of lying to him, even though you were, in fact, lying to him. I got all the facts straight?"

I open my mouth to protest, but only manage to squeak out a "Well."

"Classic gaslighting, Cherise."

I look to Adrian for backup, but she's shaking her head. "Shantell's right about this one, sweetie. But now that it's behind you, I say you–"

"Cut. Him. Loose." Shantell emphasizes every syllable with a clap.

Adrian shakes her head. "No. Double down. He thinks you're a saint? You become a saint."

I raise my hands in frustration. "Where do I even start?"

"Start by cutting him loose!" Shantell again.

"I dunno." Adrian shrugs. "But if you want to get a jump on memorizing the Jonas Brothers' latest album, I've got you."

"Not gonna happen," I say this to Shantell, who's turned both her hands into scissors. Then I turn to Adrian, who somehow has magically whipped up a Jonas Brothers cd from her bag and is trying to force it into my hands. "And Adrian, not relevant. I didn't say I liked the Jonas Brothers. I said I was familiar with them. I don't need to memorize," I skim the list and snap my fingers, "Oh! *Sucker*. That's the song. But I don't need to memorize the lyrics. I need to figure out how to keep Preston from breaking up with me, and it can't be something small. Girls, if I don't figure this out, we might not last the rest of the month."

"You could try bible verses?" Shantell offers.

"I've been trying that. He liked it at first, but now it just seems to annoy him. I need something bigger. Something next level."

"You guys met at a soup kitchen, right?" Adrian shrugs. "Maybe you could find another one and volunteer." I nod my head. Now we're getting somewhere.

"Or," Shantell grins. "You can cheat and ask Kendi. If there's some magical way to take your fake Christianity to the next level, I'm sure he'd know."

Hmm. "I'll try the soup kitchen first. And if that doesn't work, I'll go to Kendi." I really hope Adrian's suggestion works. Asking Kendi for help tricking my boyfriend doesn't sit well with me anymore.

25

The Next Best Thing

S unday morning I walk up the steps and into the foyer of Kendi's
church. My canary-yellow dress has sleeves, a choice Shantell was
weirdly adamant about. Apparently bare shoulders are sinful? I look
around at all the smiling faces, searching for the scowl I came here
for. I don't find it, but I do run into Maggie.

"Cherise, it's so good to see you!" She draws me into a hug and I
return the sentiment. "I'm sorry about the mix-up last week."

"Oh, don't worry about it." I plaster on a smile and try not to
think about that little disaster. Imagine forcing your boyfriend to
drive a half hour from his house to serve the homeless with you,
which you claim to do every week, only to discover that the soup
kitchen is closed and has been since Christmas due to kitchen
renovations. Doesn't exactly scream "I come here often." Preston was
not impressed.

In fact, Preston was the opposite of impressed. And though I
attributed my mistake to a brain fart, I'd be delusional if I thought he
bought it. Kendi's my only lifeline, now. Which is why I'm dressed
up like a pineapple (with sleeves) and waiting for him in the lobby of
this big, beautiful church. I just hope I don't go up in flames when
I walk into the sanctuary. Heaven knows I've told enough lies to
warrant a little smoke.

"Cherise!"

I turn around, and Kendi almost makes me spit my gum out. I've never seen him in a suit, and it, um, suits him. I'm so glad I decided against bringing Shantell. I'm no saint, but she'd leave puddles of drool all over the floor. It's not just Kendi. There are all sorts of good-looking brothers coming and going, dressed in pressed suits and snazzy ties. They've got nothing on Preston, but my goodness.

"Do you have a preference on where you sit?"

I shake my head and follow Kendi into the sanctuary. He's a little stiff when he walks, though I'm not sure if it's the suit or the knowledge that I'm walking behind him. He makes his way to the front, and I stop. He must have excellent hearing, because he turns around to look at me despite the chatter in the room.

"You okay, Cherise?"

"You like to sit in the front?"

"I'm nearsighted. Easier to see the screen."

I stare at the giant projector hanging from the ceiling and nod. "Oh."

"We can sit in the middle instead."

"No, it's fine." I swallow down the panic in my throat. It's irrational, really. It's not like whoever is preaching is gonna come down from the pulpit and point his finger in my face. Call me a big, fat, liar who's gonna burn in hell for all eternity–

"Cherise?"

"Huh?" I blink and turn around. Kendi's already settling into a chair at the midway point of the sanctuary. I park it beside him and let out a slow breath. My palms begin to itch, and I stuff them into the pockets of my dress, grateful that it has pockets.

"Service will probably be short today."

"Really? Why?"

"They're holding baptisms afterwards."

"Ah." I nod my head, though I have no context for what that means. Service ends after an hour of singing and sermonizing, then we shuffle out into the lobby. As the space around us crowds with people, Kendi shifts away from me, and his eyes dance to the door. But if he bolts, I won't be able to pebble him with questions.

He clears his throat and edges toward the door. "See you around?"

I grab him by the arm and tug him back. "Actually." Someone nearby sputters at the sight of us, and I immediately let him go. More than a few women are checking us out, now, and I hope this doesn't come back to bite me. The last thing I need is for some random rumor about me and Kendi to get back to Preston.

"What is it? You wanna go see the baptisms?" Kendi glances down a hallway, and my eyes follow. But I don't see anything, and I need to focus.

"Maybe next time. You wanna grab some lunch?" Kendi's suspicious glare sends heat into my chest. I didn't even do anything wrong, so why is he glaring at me?

"Why?" he asks.

I roll my eyes. If things were good between Preston and I, I would probably take this opportunity to walk away. But things aren't good. And whether I like it or not, I need the surly meathead standing next to me. "I just wanted to ask you some questions, that's all."

"You can ask me here."

It's a struggle to bite back my response. Ugh. And to think I thought we could be friends. "I can, but since I'm hungry, I thought you'd be hungry too. Sorry I offered."

Kendi relaxes his face and shrugs. "Oh. Um. Okay. There's a place down the block." He leaves before I can technically agree, but I shrug and follow him out. What else can I do?

I'm not sure why Kendi's acting weird all of a sudden, but it's on brand for him. His pace doesn't leave much room for chit chat, though, and I don't get a chance to talk to him until he stops in front of a food truck. Why there's a food truck out here in the middle of winter, I couldn't tell you. But there's a sizeable crowd, so I guess it's a thing. I also guess this means we're eating outside. Fantastic.

"Two gyros, please." Kendi orders first, then I put in my order and join him at a small table near the truck. He seems wholly absorbed by the metalwork of the table's legs, but we've all got our quirks.

"Can I ask you something, Kendi?"

He lifts up his eyes and clears his throat. "What's up?"

"Is there a way to show someone you're really a Christian?" He blinks, and I shrink down further into my seat. "What I mean by that, is, um. Is there a way to show someone that, uh, that you're serious? Like you're not just pretending? Like, it really matters to you?"

"You mean a public way to express your faith?"

Public way? "Uh, maybe?"

Kendi chuckles and his entire frame relaxes. "Oh! I mean, sure. We have our small group, but you could also join the church or be baptized." He checks his watch. "They're probably gonna be done by the time we get our food. It would have been nice for you to see, though."

"What is baptism exactly?"

"It's a public ceremony where you declare your faith, more or less. The early church practiced the custom, and Jesus commands us to preach the gospel, baptize people and make disciples. Anyone who believes in Jesus can be baptized, though every church may have a different process."

"Is it a big deal?"

He nods. "Yeah. It's one thing to decide by yourself that you want to follow Jesus. But to declare it in front of other people is kind of like deciding to follow Jesus with a community. And that community will hold you accountable to your profession of faith. It's a wonderful thing, and it's full of symbolism. I take it you've never been baptized before?"

I shake my head.

"Do you want to be baptized?"

I swallow. "Other than, like, saying I'm a Christian in front of people, what else would I have to do?"

"Well, we have a class once a month for anyone interested in being baptized. Whoever teaches the class does the baptism, and I'm on the rotation for that. Once you've taken the class, we put you on the schedule. You can invite your friends and family, if you want. You get baptized, and then we celebrate."

"Huh. So, is it a big party? Like a wedding?"

Kendi tilts his head back and forth. "Eh, more like a funeral, though I wouldn't say it's quite that formal."

"A funeral?"

"Metaphorically speaking, you're passing from death to life. But if you'd like to be put on the schedule for the next baptism, just let me know. I'm teaching the class in a few weeks, and baptisms are done every third Sunday."

Huh. "And baptism is considered a really big deal?"

He nods. "It's a pretty special event in the life of a believer. When I got baptized, I was so nervous, because I kept thinking of all the ways I'd messed up. I was still struggling with a lot of guilt, but someone said something to me that day that really helped me.

"One of the deacons of the church put his hand on my shoulder and said 'Kendi, the water is a symbol, and symbols are powerful. But you know what? It's just water. The real power comes from what Jesus did on the cross. And that work has already begun in you. So, if you're afraid because you think God won't accept you, I've got some good news. He already has. And if you're afraid because you think that people might reject you, I got some good news for that, too. They don't get the final say.'"

I nod as reverently as I can before asking, "So, when you say it's like a funeral, do people get dressed up, or...?"

Kendi lets out a short laugh. "Some do. I've seen plenty of people dress up to celebrate. It's a special occasion, after all. But it's not required."

Note to self, find a banging black dress. With sleeves. "Okay." Maybe a baptism will be enough to convince Preston that I'm serious. But what if it isn't? "Kendi, is baptism a one-time thing, or do you do it over and over?"

"Just the once."

Hmm. I'm not sure how long I can ride a single wave. "So, there's not a refresher, in case the first one starts to wear off?"

One side of his mouth ticks up. "Salvation doesn't wear off, but I think I know what you mean. While we don't rebaptize people, I do strongly encourage you to continue coming to small group and get plugged in to a church. Christian community is a huge part of our spiritual growth and development. And remember, baptism is just a symbol of the work God is already doing in you. When you mess up, or you find yourself falling back into old ways, the answer is repentance. You turn toward God, and away from whatever is pulling you in the wrong direction."

"Are you sure there's no rebaptism ceremony?"

"Cherise, have you ever been to a second funeral?"

I roll my eyes but catch his drift. "No."

"What's got you worried?"

We make eye contact, and for a few seconds, the air between us feels different. In this moment, I feel as if I could share everything with Kendi. About Preston, about the lies, about all the struggles and heartbreak that led me to them. This path I've chosen feels scary, and in the span of a few seconds, I'm tempted, more than ever before, to abandon it.

But then the moment passes.

"I'm not worried. But I think I want to do what you said. About joining the church. You said they take attendance?"

He nods. "They do, for Sunday school, and they do regular check-ins with all the members. Did you enjoy the service today?"

I nod. "Yeah. I felt pretty comfortable." No one pointed an accusing finger at me, for starters. "The music was good, too."

"I can get you started on the process, if you want?"

"What do I have to do?"

"Just fill out a questionnaire and have a counseling session. Most likely that would be with me, too."

Oh boy. "You sure do a lot in this church."

"Since you're already coming to the group, it might put you at ease to have a familiar face."

Does it have to be your *face?*

Kendi shifts in his chair. "Someone else can do it, if you'd prefer."

Apparently, I'm as bad as Shantell when it comes to facial expressions. I guess Preston was right about my fake face. "It's fine. But how long will that take?"

"Not long. You just fill it out, and I take it to the pastoral team."

I nod. "Okay!"

Kendi looks at his watch just as our order is called out. He looks at me and shrugs. "I hate to eat and run, but I've got to get going." He grabs our food, hands me mine, and takes off. I sit, peeling bits of bread off my sandwich as I chew on everything we talked about. This could work, but the same guilty feeling that kept me from coming to Kendi in the first place finds its way back into the pit of my stomach. Kendi's so serious about his faith. As serious as Preston. Faking interest is one thing, but their devotion is next level.

CHERISE AT THE ALTAR

The only thing I've ever spoken about with this much passion is Olivia Pope's entanglement with Fitz in the tv show *Scandal*, and I don't think that translates over. Lying to the person I love isn't what I want, either.

Preston deserves the truth. Deep down, I know that. But I also know that I'm a coward, and becoming a passable Christian is the next best thing. I just hope it will it be enough.

My phone buzzes, and I check the incoming text.

PRESTON: We need to talk.

26

Liar, Liar

By the time I walk into the Starbucks on the north side of Raleigh, the sleeves of my yellow dress are soaked at the pits. Which makes no sense in January and is not a good look on anyone. Preston greets me with a wan smile when I walk in.

"Thanks for coming." His eyes dance around my face, never quite meeting my eyes. A fresh pang of guilt hits me, but I shove it down. I've been on the receiving end of a "We need to talk" text enough to know what this is. Preston is breaking up with me.

I clear my throat and slide into a chair. "Did you already put your drink order in?"

He shakes his head. "No, I figured I'd wait for you. Traffic's insane on this side of town."

"Right." I'm glad he's not looking hard enough to see the tremble in my smile. I twist the silky fabric of my dress and remind myself not to lift my arms under any circumstances.

"How was the drive?"

Small talk? Okay. "Not too bad."

"Good. Good." He stares hard at his phone. "You want something hot or cold?"

"Cold. Thanks."

"Cold." He repeats the word to himself, scrolling through the options on his phone. He knows what I like, but he shows me the screen anyway. "Did I get it right?"

I nod, though inside I'm crying. He's so considerate it makes my chest ache. I don't want to lose him, but Preston's not an idiot. He's perfect. He's honest, and thoughtful, and vulnerable, and I'm none of those things. Not even close. Even if I wasn't lying to him about my faith, things would have wound up this way. Because they always do.

No matter how hard I try, I'm never enough.

Our drinks arrive. The silence between us stretches so tight, I almost feel the tension snap when it ends.

"How's the drink?" Preston asks.

I nod and smile. "Good. Thanks." An earthquake breaks out on my face, and I cover my head with my hands.

"Cherise?"

Preston's voice is tender. He's so, so good, and the wrongness of us claws at my throat. I have to tell him the truth. Lying hasn't gotten me what I wanted, anyway.

"Cherise, there's something I need to say."

I shake my head, not willing to hear more. The words are already tattooed on my heart. Hearing them from Preston would destroy me.

He pulls my hands away from my face. "Cherise?"

I snap my arms back and cover my face again, soaking my palms in tears.

"Cherise, are you okay?" I shake my head. "This is all my fault. Cherise, I'm sorry."

I let out a shuddering breath, but keep hiding behind my hands.

"That first night I met you, things were different. You were so confident and funny, and I thought you and I got along great. But somewhere along the way, things got messed up. I should have known how fragile you were."

Fragile? I peek through one of my hands. "What?"

"The walls, the lies, the random verses, I should have seen them for what they were. I guess I got so excited to be with you, I didn't pay close enough attention."

He knows the truth about me? But how? "Preston, I can explain."

He shakes his head. "It's not your fault, Cherise. It's mine. I should have known better. I've been where you are before, and I know what it's like."

He's lied to the person he loves about his faith? "You do?"

"Cherise, the last thing I ever want to do is discourage you. And if I've ever done anything to make you think that you're not good enough, please forgive me. It wasn't intentional."

Both hands slide from my face as I try to follow the threads.

"I told you I needed to be with someone who would encourage me in my faith. But you deserve that person, too. Someone you don't have to pretend with. I thought I could be that person, and I'm sorry if I let you down."

I'm not sure what's happening. Preston is apologizing, but this still feels very much like a break up.

"I know what it's like to feel like you have to pretend to be perfect, and I hate that I've made you feel that way."

The pieces finally start clicking together. "What you're saying is that I've been pretending to be something I'm not, because I'm afraid you'll think I'm not good enough for you?"

He nods. "Yeah. And that's not right. Cherise, living a double life is exhausting. Believe me, I know. And you can't develop in your relationship with God if you're pretending. As much as I want this, I'd never forgive myself if I came between you and your spiritual development. So I think–"

"You're not."

"What?"

160

This has to be a sign, right? Preston doesn't know my secret, not really. And this isn't a break up. Not unless I want it to be. And I don't. "Preston, you're not coming between me and my relationship with God. If anything, you've made it better."

He swallows and leans in a little. It's a small movement, but I notice the shift. The muscles in his face begin to relax as he dips his head. "I don't know about that."

"It's true. Do you have any idea how many times I've harassed Kendi in the last month about bible stuff?"

He rubs the back of his neck. "No."

"Well, it's a lot. Preston, you make my life so much better. In fact." I grab his hand, relishing the way the warmth of his fingers soothes the coldness in mine. I love this man, more than words can even express. And I know there's no going back for me. "I'm getting baptized."

His eyes light up at that. "You are? When?"

"Soon. I talked it over with Kendi today. And I'll be joining the church, too."

"Cherise, that's fantastic. I'm so happy for you." He smiles and presses a kiss to my knuckles. "I'll be there. Just let me know the date?"

"Of course."

He squeezes my hand. "I'm so excited for you. I can't wait."

"Me either." The lies catch in my throat, but I swallow and smile. I'll make it up to him. I'll be everything he needs and more.

27

On the Straight and Narrow

I need to find Kendi, so I sneak into the fitness center during what I hope is a slow part of the day. There aren't too many meatheads loitering about, so I guess I picked the right time. I tap the front counter and scope out the gym. Kendi's nowhere in sight. The counter is empty, save a small bowl of fruit chews. They really need to get better snacks in this place.

"Can I help you?" One of the front workers steps out from the employee area behind the counter.

"I'm looking for Kendi. Is he here?"

"He's on break. Did you schedule a consultation with him, or...?"

"No. I'll give him a call." Since he's on break, I'm sure he won't mind. Especially when he finds out what it's for. I dial his number, but the phone rings four times before going to voicemail. Hmm.

I try again, but this time the phone goes straight to voicemail and I get a text from Kendi.

MEATHEAD: Please text me.

Ugh. I tap out a text.

ME: Please schedule my baptism at your earliest convenience.

My phone immediately begins to ring.

"Cherise? It's Kendi."

Duh. "Hey Kendi! I just sent you a text."

"Yeah, I'm in the middle of lunch, but I didn't want to text you about this. You want to get baptized?"

"Yeah, I've given it some thought, and I believe this is a natural next step. What do I need to do?"

"The timing is perfect, actually. I'll be doing the next baptismal class, which is the third Saturday of February. You come to the class, find out all the details, ask all your questions, and you can get baptized that Sunday. What do you think?"

"Sounds perfect. What time Saturday?"

"Six o'clock."

Oof. I have a standing reservation with Adrian and Shantell that evening, but I'm sure I can work around it. "I'll be there!"

I SHOULD HAVE REMEMBERED my luck. Turns out that Saturday is not only my standing reservation with my squad and the night of the baptismal class. It's also the only date my hair dresser can fit me in for a silk press. I generally keep my hair in its natural curly state or in protective styles, but Kendi says you only get baptized once, and I want to make sure this is one to remember. I've already ordered a dress and shoes, and I want my hair to be as straight as the narrow path I'm pledging. Well, straighter.

My appointment's at four. In a perfect world, I'll be done and in class on time by six, but again, this is me. Also, my hair is deceptively thick.

Six thirty comes and goes, but the way my hair cascades down the side of my face makes me shiver in delight. At 6:45 p.m., I swipe my credit card, making sure to leave a hefty tip for the service, and give my head a little shake. My hair flows like water from one side to the other. Perfection.

I break a few laws on my way to the church, but it saves me a few minutes, and I clock in at around 7:05 p.m. when I slide into the study room. Kendi's reading from a bible at the front of the class. I try to concentrate, but my phone buzzes with a message from Shantell.

SHANTY: You're late.
SHANTY: Where you at???
SHANTY: ???
SHANTY: You coming or nah?

I switch my phone to silent mode as the people closest to me grumble. "Sorry," I whisper.

"Does anyone have any questions?" Kendi's eyes find mine, and I freeze, hoping he won't call on me. Is this that kind of class? Were we supposed to be taking notes?

Someone else raises their hand. "If we're not members of the church, can we still be baptized?"

Oh. Good question. I'm not a member yet, so I wait for Kendi's answer.

"No, you don't have to be a member of the church. We'd actually prefer you were baptized first, though it's not a requirement for membership. The most important thing for us isn't membership numbers. It's making sure people are secure in their faith and growing. Which is why we want everyone to take this class prior to baptism. Any other questions?"

A young woman raises her hand. "Can I invite more than one person?"

"Yes, of course! This is a big moment, and you can celebrate it with as many people as you feel comfortable with. I will say that the breakfast served in the morning is limited to one additional guest, but all are welcome at the actual baptismal ceremony."

"What time is the ceremony tomorrow?" I ask.

"It will be at one, directly after morning service."

Okay. If I skip the service, that's plenty of time to get dressed and ready.

"Just so everyone's on the same page, I want to talk to you about what to expect tomorrow. Breakfast will be at nine, and then immediately after service, you'll make your way to the baptismal lobby. We'll gather there for a word of prayer before we begin."

My phone lights up in my purse. Shantell's calling me now, which means she's probably irritated. I look up at Kendi, then back at my phone. It's almost 7:30, and I don't want to flake on Adrian and Shantell. I've got the gist of everything, so there's really no reason to stay. I know where to meet and what time. I'm sure the rest is just following along single file while they sprinkle water or oil or wine on your forehead.

I slip out while Kendi's distracted by another question. I'm sure he'll notice I've left, but the class was likely wrapping up anyway. I tap out a text to Shantell.

ME: On my way.

28

In Over My Head

I'm late. Which wouldn't bother me if I hadn't already told Preston what time to be there for the baptism. I'm hoping he'll get stuck in Sunday traffic coming in from the north side of Raleigh, because it wouldn't make sense for him to make it to my baptism before I do.

When I walk into the church, there are only a handful of people still loitering in the foyer. There's a bit of noise coming down the hall, and I walk over to the baptismal lobby where Kendi told us all to meet. When I enter the room, it's packed. I recognize some of the people from the class, but none of them are dressed up for a funeral. They're all in gray t-shirts with the church logo and shorts. I scan the room. There are only a handful of people in suits and dresses.

"Cherise!" Kendi calls me from across the room, dressed like he's going to the beach. He looks me up and down, then tosses a sack at me. "You're late."

I look down at the sack. "I had something to do this morning, and it ran over. What is this?"

"Come on, we're about to get started, and we don't have time to chat." Kendi reaches for my wrist, but another hand beats him to it.

"Cherise?"

I turn around, feeling giddy as Preston's warm tones wash over me. "Preston. You made it."

"Of course. Hey Kendi."

Kendi's face brightens at the sight of Preston, and they go in for a bro hug. "Hey. You two know each other?" He looks from Preston to me, but the scowl that was on his face just a moment ago is conspicuously missing.

"Yeah."

An awkward beat passes between us, but Kendi breaks the tension with a laugh. "Well, Cherise needs to go get changed, so we can get started. Cherise?"

I offer Preston a pout, and he squeezes my hand before letting go. "I'll see you after, Cherise. You look beautiful, by the way."

I giggle, and it's a slow walk to the women's room, because I keep looking back. Kendi's cheery disposition dissolves once we reach the doors.

"Cherise, we're going to have to rearrange the order a bit. You'll be last, so that should give you enough time to get changed and get to the pool."

My hand freezes on the door, and I swing my head in his direction. "The what?"

"Follow the stairs up, and it's right there in the middle." Kendi points. "You can't miss it."

I shake my head. "Why are we going into a pool? I mean, is that really necessary?"

Kendi stares at me like I'm stupid. He works his jaw a full minute, then speaks to me slowly. "Cherise, what do you think baptism is?"

"You told me the water is a symbol. Of a funeral and the old man dying and the new person being alive and all that. You didn't say anything about actual water."

"What did you think we were doing?"

I throw my hands up. "I don't know! The thing where you eat a piece of bread and someone makes the sign of the cross over your forehead with wine. I think I saw them do it at my grandma's church once."

Kendi rubs his temples. "You may be confusing it with communion, but we don't put anything on your head here, so I'm not sure where...?" He shakes his head. "Never mind. I'm pretty sure I covered all of this in the baptism class."

Right. The baptism class. Which I attended late. And left early. "Well, I don't remember any of that."

Kendi takes a deep breath and releases it slowly into the heavens. "Okay. Cherise, here's what's gonna happen. You're gonna change. You're gonna walk up the steps and into the baptismal pool. I'll be standing right in the middle. You walk straight to me. I'll ask you if you've accepted Christ as your savior. When you say yes, I'll make a declaration that I'm baptizing you in the name of the Father, the Son, and the Holy Spirit. You'll pinch your nose, and I'll guide your head down into the water and back up again. You'll walk to the other side of the pool and take the door that loops back into this hallway and the changing rooms."

With each word, the panic in my chest grows. My hair. I spent hours at the salon getting it straightened. And this dress? Does Kendi have any idea how hard it was to find an outfit long enough to kneel in but short and curvy enough to be fun and flirty? With sleeves, no less? And now Preston's barely gonna see it, because I'm changing into some frumpy gym uniform?

"Cherise?" Kendi waves his hand in front of me. "We've got to get started."

I shake my head again. "No. I'm not ready. I didn't know there was water. And there are all these people." I swallow and gesture toward the small crowd gathered in front of the baptismal pool. They came to see their loved ones, but they're gonna see me, too. Preston's going to see me. With baggy, water-logged clothes. This is not how I saw myself this morning.

"Don't worry about them. Remember what I said? About how God's already started the work?"

"Yeah, but–"

"It'll be fine, Cherise. Don't worry." Kendi shoves me into the bathroom, and as the door clicks shut behind me, another realization hits.

"Wait, you're *dunking me* in the water?" I shout the words as I rush back out, but Kendi is already gone, and Preston's in my line of vision. I shut myself back inside before he spots me, then slide to the floor.

Everything's under control, Cherise. No need to panic. Except I've got one too many reasons not to get in that water. On top of everything else, I can't swim. Water has always terrified me. I'm not sure if I should blame the trauma of having two big brothers who loved shoving me underwater, or the trauma of falling into a neighbor's pool when nobody was watching. Either way, the idea of being submerged fills me with dread. I don't even like wetting my face in the shower.

I clench the bag of clothes between my fists. Maybe I can slip out a back door? There's lots of ways in and out of the church, right? Preston will understand, and Kendi can go fly a kite. I'm not doing this.

Then I remember the way Preston's face lit up when I told him I was going to get baptized. The way he showed up today with the same bright smile. Maybe he'll understand. But what if he doesn't? The next baptism is a month away. Would he believe me if I told him I needed to postpone?

"I'll just tell him it's that time of the month." A solid excuse. I'm just about to leave, when a knock sounds at the door.

"Cherise? Everything okay in there?"

Preston? I lick my lips. "Yeah. Um. Everything's fine."

"I saw you dip your head out earlier. Did you need something?"

He's always so considerate. And I promised to be good to him. To be everything he needs and more. But if I can't handle a little water, then can I really believe that? I clear my throat. "Yeah. Uh. My shoes. I need something else to wear."

"I think they have flip flops you can wear. I'll go track some down."

I lean my head against the door and sigh. *You can do this, Cherise.* I slip out of my dress and into the clothes Kendi gave me. They aren't as baggy as I thought, thanks to my hips, but they're still not the most flattering threads.

I set all my things on a bench near the wall – it seems to be the official spot for everyone's clothes – then walk out of the bathroom. Preston joins me, a pair of flip flops in his hand.

"Hey," he whispers in my ear, sending a tingle up my spine. "You'll need to walk into the pool barefoot, but I'll leave the shoes in the hall on the other side, okay?"

I nod my head, and I must look pretty pitiful, because Preston leans in as if he'll kiss me. He thinks better of it at the last moment, and squeezes my shoulder instead. There's a line ahead of me, but it's small. Just two people. More are coming around the hall from the opposite end. They have towels draped along their necks, but they're still sopping wet. I shiver and turn back to the steps.

There are only three steps up into the baptismal pool. When it's my turn, Kendi gestures me forward, and I step onto the platform. Looking out, I spot Preston in the crowd. He's smiling with his phone up, no doubt recording.

Kendi gives me another wave, and I step into the water.

29

Lights. Camera. Action!

The water surrounding my waist is cold. Colder than I thought it would be after having so many other people in it. It laps at my midsection in tiny waves, despite the fact that I haven't moved.

"Cherise, have you accepted Jesus Christ as your Lord and Savior?"

Kendi's words sound far away. The most prevalent sound is the pounding in my chest. *I shouldn't be here. This is a mistake.*

I feel Kendi's hand at my back, and my eyes snap up. He gives me a leading look, and it takes me a while to get my brain to work. *He's waiting for me to say something. I'm supposed to say something.*

"Cherise?" His eyes look worried now. He glances out at the crowd, briefly, and I follow his gaze. Preston's camera is still up, but he's watching me with a furrowed brow. My brain starts working again. It sends a signal to my tongue, and I force out the lies lodged in my dry throat.

"Yes, I have."

Kendi's eyes linger on my face, and for a moment, I wonder if he's going to call everything off. He leans in closer to my ear, and every muscle in my body stiffens. *Please don't call me out. Not in front of Preston. Please!* "I'm going to keep my hand at your back. Make sure you pinch your nose as I guide you down, okay? I've got you, Cherise."

Oh. I nod, and he leans back and stares out at the crowd.

"In front of witnesses and before our Lord, Cherise Michele Williams, I baptize you in the name of the Father, and the Son, and the Holy Spirit." He nods, and I press my fingers over my nose.

As Kendi guides me down into the water, the cold shocks me into a yelp. But yelping underwater isn't great for breathing. Water rushes into my mouth, and I panic. Not in a small way. It's a full-fledged fight for my life as I thrash in the water. Kendi's hand slips from my back, and the next thing I know, I'm sinking. I dig my hands into anything I can grab, clawing and clenching with arms and legs.

I bang my wrist against the top side of the pool, then wrap myself around what can only be Kendi's body. His hand finds its way to my back again, and I find myself floating up. When my face breaks the surface of the water, I gurgle and splash, gripping him for dear life.

"Cherise, put your legs down." Kendi tries to pry my leg off of him, but I squeal in protest.

"I can't swim!"

"It's three feet of water, Cherise." Kendi growls. "Put your legs down!"

I pry open my eyes, noticing for the first time just how close I am to Kendi. Heat ignites my cheeks, and I let him shove my legs back under the water. His shirt is torn in two places, his hair dripping. I let him go and turn away, but it's a mistake. A crowd of people stare back at me from the lobby, mouths rounded. Cameras up.

Oh God.

I know I shouldn't look, but I do. My eyes find Preston. His eyes are wide with horror as he looks from me to Kendi.

I make a run for it.

30

Such A Brave Coward

There has to be a limit to the number of missteps one person can take. That's my thought as I sprint down the hall and toward the women's changing room. But I forgot my flip flops, I'm sopping wet, and the floors are slick. I hear someone call my name, maybe Kendi, I don't know. But I don't want to see him. I don't want to see anyone.

I round the corner just as my luck runs out. I slip on the floor, landing hard on my side. But the sound of footsteps behind me gets me back up on my feet. I didn't see the water fountain on my way down, but my face finds the corner of its metal frame on my way back up. Blood immediately starts dripping from my lip.

I whisper an expletive and cover my mouth in my hands, scurrying into the women's room and slamming the door behind me. I grab a paper towel from the dispenser and slide to the base of the door, pressing it against my lip. Blood stains the front of my shirt, and a small puddle forms beneath my rump. I whimper into the paper towel. This day could not get any worse.

"Cherise, you in there?"

I know it's unreasonable, but hearing Kendi's voice behind the door makes me angry. "Go away!"

"Cherise, are you okay?"

"No, I'm not okay! I almost died, thanks to you." If not from the water, then certainly from my humiliation.

"Cherise."

"You said you had me, but you didn't. Just leave me alone!" The whimper grows to a sob as the floodgates open. I came here today to show Preston the best side of me. Not act out my trauma in front of him. We're supposed to have lunch together after this, but I'm sure he's halfway to North Hills by now.

I'm afraid to look, but I don't need a mirror to know that my makeup is trashed, my lip is swollen, and my hair is a kinky, tangled mess. The sound of retreating footsteps makes me feel ten times worse.

I know I told Kendi to go away, but him actually leaving sends me into another fit of sobs. I hope no one else needs the bathroom, because I'm never leaving. If I could find a way to melt into the puddle beneath me, I would.

I jump as another knock sounds at the door. A wave of relief hits, followed by another irrational wave of anger. "I told you to go away, Kendi."

"Cherise? It's me."

I freeze. *Preston?*

"I've got a couple towels for you. Crack open the door, and I'll slide them through."

I swallow the lump forming in my throat and pop open the door. A brown hand clutching a white towel slides through. I take the towel, and another hand appears with a second. I take that one, too, then close the door back.

"I'm right outside if you need anything else, okay?"

More tears slip down my cheeks, and warmth fills my chest. Preston didn't leave. I made a pure fool of myself out there, but he stayed, anyway.

I stare at my dress, still folded neatly on the bench on the wall. I'm not sure how I'll get back into it, damp as I am. I'm not so sure I want to. I didn't bring a lick of lotion, and ashy legs aren't exactly attractive. Neither is body odor. I don't have any deodorant.

But Preston is outside the door, waiting on me. I scan the bathroom as my spirit lifts. There's a small shelf in the back of the room, and from here I can see it's got a few supplies. I pull myself up from the floor, gasping at my reflection as I pass by the mirror.

I find a bottle of scented hand lotion, a small basket of sanitary napkins, and a second, larger basket with a hair dryer and clips.

"It'll have to do."

I grab the lotion and dryer, set them on the counter and get to work. I wash away my makeup, it's ruined anyway, then dip into one of the stalls to peel off my wet clothes and dry off. Though I doubt anyone else will come in, I'm not taking any chances, and there's only so much embarrassment a girl can take.

The end result isn't ideal. My hair is frizzy without heat protectant and products, and the makeup I keep in my purse can only do so much. But I'm presentable, and if Preston didn't run away after that disastrous display, then I think I can trust him to see me in light makeup. At least, I hope so.

I take a deep breath, swallow, and open the door. Preston is leaning against the wall on the opposite side, a large bag in his hand. He drinks me in with a smile, then walks over. He raises the bag in his hand. "For your wet clothes."

"Oh." I turn back to the bathroom and grab the still-soggy items, plunking them into the bag. Preston tugs at my hand with his pinky, then wraps it firmly in his before raising it to his lips. He brushes a kiss over my knuckles, then squeezes my hand. A stray tear falls from my face, and I look down.

He wipes the tear away and presses his forehead to mine. "You ready to get out of here?"

I nod and let him lead me away. I keep my head down, but the baptismal lobby is empty. By the time we reach Preston's car, the tension in my chest has eased. But my throat feels heavy and thick, and I don't trust my voice, so the car is quiet as we leave the parking lot. I fiddle with the sleeves of my dress and wipe invisible lint from the edges. Preston looks at me from the corner of his eye, then takes my hand again.

"We don't have to talk, Cherise. But if you want to, I'm here."

His words are a soothing balm, and the tightness in my throat gives way. "Thanks," I whisper.

"I hope you don't mind me saying so, but," He pauses.

And in his pause my imagination runs wild. Maybe he's disgusted and doesn't want to hurt my feelings. Or maybe he's disappointed in me, or concerned that I'm not altogether well. Maybe he's ashamed of me. Or seeing me like that was hard for him to witness. I slide down into my seat and turn my head, bracing myself.

He chuckles. "That was probably the most memorable baptism I've ever been to."

I wait for him to tell me what I already know. That it was painful to watch. That he almost died from secondhand embarrassment. That—

"I don't think I've ever had this much fun at a baptism before." Preston gives my hand another kiss. "I'll never forget the look on Kendi's face." He lets out a snort, and I think it's the most beautiful sound I've ever heard.

"You're not... disappointed in me?" The words come out quiet and shy.

Preston's face turns sober. "No. Cherise, I'm sorry. I shouldn't have laughed."

I shake my head. "This isn't how I pictured my day going."

"I'm sorry." Preston sighs as he slows down for a red light. "You wanna skip lunch today?"

I nod my head, feeling dejected. He doesn't want to be seen with me like this in public. I don't really feel like being seen like this, either. "Yeah, sure. Probably for the best. You can just take me home."

Preston frowns. "Oh. I was thinking we could go to my place. Order takeout, snuggle on the couch. Watch a movie?"

"Oh." I love this man.

"If you're not up to it, I understand."

I shake my head. "No, that sounds perfect."

"Alright. My place it is."

The drive to North Hills feels more pleasant after that. Preston takes the local route and we listen to songs on the radio. *Sucker* comes on, and he gives me a look. A knot forms in my stomach, twisting as the silence between us grows palpable. Awkward silences are my kryptonite, and I begin to ramble.

"I bet you're wondering why I panicked like that in the water today?" I swallow as he nods. I should stop, but once I get going, it's hard to put the brakes on. "I had a pool accident when I was a kid. We'd been invited over to a neighbor's house, and I went to the bathroom. I saw the pool, I was four, and I was curious. When I fell in, I couldn't get myself out. I don't remember what happened after that. I just remember being terrified, you know? I stayed away from water for years. I never learned how to swim, and my brothers–"

At this I pause. Life with my brothers always felt like a competition. Not for them, but for me. For space, for a voice, for my parents' attention. Like Preston, they could do no wrong as far as my mom and dad were concerned. Even after my pool accident, my brothers would often ignore my protests and dunk me underwater, insisting that my fear was all in my head. That I just needed to get used to the water again. I hated it. But I'm not ready to share the dysfunction of my family with Preston.

"My brothers tried to encourage me to swim, but I just could never get over the fear, you know?"

Preston clears his throat. "So, you had all that going on in your head, and you went into the water, anyway?"

I squeeze my eyes shut, as if that will help stave off my apprehension. "Yeah. I guess it was pretty foolish."

He chuckles again. "I'd wondered why you weren't baptized already. I had no idea you were struggling with this. And making the decision to get in the water anyway isn't foolish, Cherise. It's really brave. I'm proud of you."

I open my eyes and look at him. Try to commit the awe on his face to memory. I am not brave, not by any stretch, but hearing him say so makes me want to be brave. "I honestly thought you'd leave me at the church."

"What? Why?"

I shake my head. "I haven't had the greatest experiences with relationships. I've been hurt a lot. And every day I wake up and wonder if today's the day I'll be hurt again."

Preston goes quiet. And as my brain catches up to the fact that I just spilled a piece of my heart, the panic starts. I feel vulnerable and exposed. And incredibly stupid. The tightness returns, and I begin rifling through my purse for something to soothe the ache in my throat. It also keeps me from looking directly at Preston. I wonder what he's thinking, but I'm terrified to find out. I've already told Preston I love him, but he's never said it back. A fact that rattles around in my brain the rest of the ride over.

We pull up to his house, and I follow him in. He offers me the couch, a blanket, and, after a few minutes, a warm mug of tea. He sits next to me, then fans out a stack of menus on the coffee table. "Got a taste for anything in particular?"

I shake my head. "No. You can decide."

He nods, then takes my hands, rubbing warmth into them. I inhale sharply as he pulls me into him and wraps his arms around me. "Thank you for sharing your story with me, Cherise. For sharing your pain. I know that was hard for you."

My heart slams against my chest. His mouth is close to my ear, air tickling the outside with each word. He's close enough that I can feel the steady thump of his own heart. He rubs my back in slow, steady strokes. It's the most soothing touch I've ever felt, and despite a very weak attempt to stop myself, I begin to cry on his shoulder. He tightens the embrace, seeming unbothered by the waterfall soaking his shirt.

I made a lot of mistakes today. But it turns out, being vulnerable with Preston wasn't one of them. He's proven again and again that I made the right choice. It's a comforting thought. And a sobering one.

While I'm certain I can trust Preston with my heart, I'm equally as certain I can never trust him with the truth.

31

Timing and Tapas

"Mom, it's me. Cherise. Again. I'm calling to see if you want to have lunch next week. Again. Give me a call back when you get this."

I hang up and stare at the phone, wondering if I should try her work number. But I'm not an eleven-year-old girl desperate for attention. I'm a grown woman, and if Mom doesn't want to carve out a little time from her busy schedule to have lunch with me, then the least I can do is keep myself from begging.

"She didn't pick up again?" Tammie's too keen for her own good, and I make a face before slipping my phone into my pocket. She clucks and shakes her head. "You wanna talk about it?"

"Nope!" I look at my watch and then out the door, catching the back end of Kendi as he makes his way to his car. It's been three weeks since my baptism fiasco, and I still haven't found the courage to face him. I also haven't told a soul.

Tammie sees Kendi, too. "Oh! Looks like Kendi's done for the day. You two still getting along okay?"

I huff. "Pfft. Me? And that meathead? We've managed a tolerable truce, but I wouldn't go so far as to say we get along."

Tammie shrugs. "Oh. I thought for sure I saw you two leave together a few times from the parking lot."

"That was, like, one time. And it was completely his fault, because he ran into my car!" I don't know why I'm getting so defensive, or why my voice has gone up two full octaves. Also, technically, I ran into him.

"I've seen you three times, but who's counting?" Tammie wiggles her eyebrows and returns to her computer monitor. "Your last client cancelled about a half hour ago, so if you want to coincidentally *not meet* with Kendi in the parking lot, you're free to go."

"Pfft. As if." I shuffle the magazines on the counter and clear my throat. "And why are you just now telling me about a cancellation?"

Tammie grins. "I'm a snoop, that's why." She laughs when I roll my eyes. "Don't pretend like there's nothing going on with you. I've known you for years, and I've never seen you as chirpy as you've been the last few weeks."

I can't help the smile that creeps up my face. "Well, that's because I'm seeing someone."

Tammie glances out the door, then back at me. "Oh really? I knew this spring air felt a little different. Who is it?"

"You don't know him."

"If he drives a Ford and is built like a Chevy, I think I can guess."

"Ew, Tammie, no. Get Kendi out of your mind."

"So you *have* noticed his muscles." Tammie does another silly eye wiggle.

"Anyway." I wait for Kendi to leave, not wanting to fuel Tammie's matchmaking any further. In the meantime, I grab my phone and send out a text to Preston to see if he's free. I really hope I'm not overdoing it. Memories of Calvin at the sushi bar send me into a brief panic, and I consider unsending the text. But it's already marked as read.

Shoot. I stare at the screen, each second I'm left on "read" sliding a needle deeper into my heart. Why isn't he responding? Am I being too needy? Ugh. Why is this so hard?

I slide my phone back into my pocket and grab my purse. "I'll see you tomorrow, Tammie."

"See you tomorrow, Dr. Williams."

The cool night air feels refreshing against my skin. The faintest whiff of seared meat traveling from the bar and grill a block away reminds me that I have no dinner plans. Yet.

I get into my car and check my phone. I've missed a call and have two new texts. All from Preston. "How did I miss these?" It doesn't take any major sleuthing to figure out my phone is still on silent mode, but I check the texts first before returning Preston's call.

ME: Got dinner plans tonight?

PRESTON: I do now. There's a nice spot in Midtown I've been meaning to take you to. I'll call you in a bit.

PRESTON: Cherise? You didn't pick up?

I call Preston back, feeling a little triumphant. Not because I left him waiting. Well, maybe a little bit because I left him waiting. But mostly because he's just as eager to spend time with me as I am with him. The last few weeks have been really good. Conversations between us have been easier, lighter. No more talks about getting in each other's way. No more texts stating "we need to talk." We've really hit a turning point, and I'm hoping to ride that momentum all the way to the altar.

After I apologize for keeping him waiting, and Preston gives me directions to the restaurant, I head right over. It's a swanky little spot, alive and brimming with hipsters and college kids. Preston spots me and waves me over to the outdoor seating. I check the trays passing by as we embrace. Looks like we'll be eating tiny foods tonight. But they smell delicious.

"I've heard good things about this place. They've got amazing tapas."

"Mm." I slide into my chair and check out the menu. From oysters and foie gras to chorizo and suckling pig, they've got a little bit of everything. "I'm having trouble deciding. Can you pick for me?"

Preston puts two fingers to his lips. "Hmm. Well, I do love a challenge. How about this? You tell me what you don't want, and I'll take care of the rest."

"Everything is fair game."

"Alright."

To my absolute delight, Preston orders eight small plates.

"Cherise?" He grabs my hands, caressing the palms. There's a tremble to them that's not usually there. "I actually wanted to talk to you about something tonight."

A stone drops into the pit of my stomach. "Oh?"

"We've been dating for a few months now, and I'd like to think things between us are good."

His statement sounds like a question, so I nod. "Yeah. Things are good." My heart rate goes up as Preston pauses. *It's too early for a proposal. Isn't it? Oh. My. God. Is he? He's not. But what if he is?*

He clears his throat and chuckles. "I don't know why I'm so nervous."

I squeeze his hand and reply with a chuckle of my own. "It's okay. Just spit it out, already." I shrug, nonchalant, despite the fact that a full orchestra has taken up residence in my chest.

"Well, um. Cherise. I told my parents about us."

I lean forward in my chair, expectant. "You did?"

"Yeah. They were absolutely thrilled when I told them about you. And, I think it's time—"

"My answer is yes. Yes, absolutely, yes!" The words tumble out like wayward rabbits in a field, and Preston runs a hand through his hair.

"Hah. Okay. Well, they're excited to meet you."

Oh. Calm your nerves, Cherise. "They? As in your parents?" My initial excitement cools, but only by a bit.

"Yeah." A nervous shadow passes over his face. "Um. If that's okay with you? I don't want to assume you're ready to take that step."

"Oh, I'm more than ready." I do an internal face palm. *Nice one, Cherise.*

"Well, that's good to hear." He takes my hand again. "I guess I was worried for no reason."

"I would love to meet your parents. When do you want to do it?"

"Would tomorrow be too soon?"

I nearly choke on my water. "Tomorrow? As in less than six hours from tonight?"

He has enough sense to look sheepish. "They're traveling, and tomorrow is one of the only days we'd all be available."

"What were the other days?"

"The week of Thanksgiving? It felt a little cliché."

"Their earliest availability is in November? Wow, they must travel a lot."

"They retired last year, so that's their plan. Until I make them grandparents."

This time, I do choke on my water. Much to Preston's dismay. I really have the worst timing.

"Eight tapas for the table?" The waiter's is better, it seems.

"You okay, Cherise?"

I wave Preston's outstretched hand away and clear out the liquid threatening to drown me. It'll have to take a number, as the thoughts swirling in my head will surely be the death of me first.

"Sorry, I didn't mean to startle you."

"No! I'm not startled." I protest. "I'm okay. Just had a little water go down the wrong way."

"Okay." Preston laughs, and it lightens the tension. "You ready to pray?"

I nod and bow my head. I'm ready for a lot of things. Most of all, this next step.

32

Going to the Chapel

Saturday afternoon traffic is a nightmare. Preston's folks live in Chapel Hill, a 40-minute slog from my downtown Raleigh apartment when conditions are fair. But it's warming up, the weather is beautiful, and it seems everyone decided today would be a great day for a drive to Jordan Lake. Or the botanical gardens, or wherever else a million cars might travel down West 40 on a Saturday.

Exacerbating the heavy traffic is the fact that I hopped into my car believing I'd planned for every contingency. Preston sprung this meeting on me last minute, but I started prepping as soon as I got home. I picked out the perfect outfit, a modest sun dress with a jean jacket and strappy, white heels. I flat-ironed my hair myself, because I'm not coughing up another $500 for a silk press. I also Googled and rehearsed a dozen topics of discussion deemed appropriate for a first meeting with your fiancé's parents (because I'm ambitious).

What I did not plan for was the less than quarter tank of gas in my car and the horrible traffic. I'm due at the Jones' residence at five, so I've got plenty of time. I blast the AC and my favorite Usher playlist. I skip Confessions Part 2, for reasons that shall remain unspoken.

Twenty minutes and no more than ten miles later, I realize that I'm not going to make it if I don't stop for gas. I signal to get into the right lane, but I'm boxed in by trucks on all sides and nobody's moving. My phone chirps, and I answer it from my dashboard console.

"This is Cherise."

"Hey." Preston sounds apologetic on the phone. "Are you already on your way?"

Uh oh. "Why are you asking?"

"Something came up, and I'm going to be late tonight. But don't worry, everything's fine."

My mind flies in a million directions as I picture what could keep him from coming to dinner at his parents' house. It's Saturday, so it can't be work. "If everything's fine, then why are you gonna be late?" Maybe he's getting cold feet? Or maybe he's meeting up with a side chick? Maybe they've already met, and now he's taking her home, but she lives in Wilmington. Or Greensboro.

"I caught a flat, and it's taking longer than I expected to get it fixed. They're really backed up at the tire place, but said they'd get me in before closing today."

"Oh, okay." I talk myself down. Maybe Usher wasn't the best choice for my playlist. "How late do you think you'll be?"

"They close at five, so maybe an hour late?"

That's a lot of extra time to kill, even for me.

"I would have suggested I pick you up and we go together, but I'm spending the weekend there. I'm really sorry, Cherise. Knowing you, you're probably already halfway there."

"Pfft. No!" *Not yet, anyway.*

He chuckles. "Oh no?"

"I don't know why you'd think that."

"Hmm. Maybe because I know you?"

"What?" I scoff. "You're the punctual one, Mr. Loan Officer."

"I do like to be on time. But you like to have things planned out. I figured you'd leave early, scope out the neighborhood, that sort of thing."

"Dinner is a million hours away. And besides, it's Chapel Hill, not Asheville."

"So, you're *not* on your way?"

I pause. "No-o."

"Sounds like you're in the car, Cherise."

"Well, yeah, I'm in the car. I have things to do. Like, errands."

"Uh huh."

"I've gotta get gas, you know."

"Okay."

"Since someone sprang a last-minute trip on me."

"My mistake. Alright, well, I'll let you get back to it."

"Thank you."

I check the clock as we disconnect. It reads 3:32 p.m., so I've got loads of time before dinner. Traffic clears unexpectedly, but I don't like the gas prices I'm seeing. Maybe I can push it.

My fuel light comes on just as I pass the sign for Chapel Hill. I think I can still make it, but I've got over two hours to kill and zero interest in pushing my car to a station if I don't.

I follow signs for a local place and pull over to a pump. It's a quaint little Family Fare with green pumps and yellow lettering everywhere. I fill up, since the prices are decent, and pretend not to notice the eyes floating my way from the car behind me.

A head pops out of the car's driver-side window. "Hey beautiful."

I turn away, but I make sure I can still see him from the side mirror, just in case.

"Pretty woman like you shouldn't be pumping gas in that dress. You need some help?"

I keep ignoring him, but he doesn't get the memo. I hear a car door open and shut, and a few seconds later, the smell of peanuts and cigarette smoke find their way to me.

"Hey girl, let me help you with that."

I step back when he leans forward. "Nope. I got it, thanks." My eyes dance over to the store, and I catch the eye of the cashier. The stranger beside me finally gets a clue and takes a step back.

"My bad. I didn't mean no harm. You take care of yourself, aight?"

"Mm. Have a nice day."

He returns to his car, but I can feel his eyes lingering on my backside. The pump clicks, and I finish the transaction. The screen flashes "see cashier" when I try to print my receipt. Terrific. I've still got a couple hours to burn before my meetup with Preston, and a bag of salty chips might settle my nerves.

I drive over to a parking spot and head inside, browsing the shelves for salt and vinegar chips. I find them, but then it occurs to me that salt and vinegar chips are not a great choice right before meeting potential in-laws. I opt for a box of Red Hots and head to the counter, but I catch sight of my too-friendly admirer and dip back behind the shelves.

Maybe he followed me inside, or maybe he's just grabbing snacks, too. But I'm not interested in a second encounter, so I slip the Red Hots into my purse and scoot toward the bathroom to wait him out.

After about 15 minutes of handwashing, I pop my head out of the bathroom. No sign of my stalker, so I head to the cashier. "Hey! Can I get the receipt for pump two, please?"

"Someone else is using that pump."

I look out the window. "Right. I got gas a few minutes ago, so could you check from earlier?"

He shrugs. "Does $18.50 sound right?"

Hah, I wish. "No, it was forty something."

He taps on a screen and the receipt prints out. When he hands it to me, his eyes travel from my outstretched fingers to my side. "You gonna pay for the candy, ma'am?"

"The what? Oh!" I fish out the box sticking out of my purse and hand it to him. Heat smacks my cheeks, and a thousand lectures from my mother bounce in my head. "Sorry about that. I forgot they were in there."

"Sure." He doesn't look convinced, which fuels the flames of shame further.

"I was gonna pay for them. But I had to run to the bathroom, and I was in there for, like, 20 minutes, and so you can understand why I'd forget, right?"

He whistles. "Twenty minutes?"

I shake my head. "Not like that. I mean I wasn't actually going to the bathroom for 20 minutes."

"No judgment here, ma'am."

I don't feel like I'm old enough to be called ma'am so many times in a row, but that's a side issue. I need to clear my name. "No, there's no need for that, because I wasn't doing anything in there. It's actually kind of a funny story, if being stalked by weirdos is funny. You see, there was this strange guy who came in here, and he was talking to me at the pump. Do you remember when I made eye contact with you? When I was outside?" He offers a blank stare, so I keep talking. "He was talking to me way too close, and he creeped me out, so I finished pumping, and I came inside, and I grabbed the Red Hots and–"

"That'll be $1.17, ma'am." He hands me back the Red Hots.

"Oh, okay." I hand him my card, and there's an awkward silence as he swipes it in the machine. I should just drop it, but I'm me, so I don't. "He was about six feet tall, red shirt? Light brown skin? Cropped hair? Terrible moustache? He had a couple packs of donuts on the counter, I think?"

"And *he's* the stalker?"

He looks at me with one eyebrow raised, a facial quirk I've come to loathe. I snap my mouth shut, snatch my debit card from his hand, and stalk out the door. Better to cut my losses and save myself from further mortification. I hop in the car, and as soon as I shut the door, all my cleverness comes back. "I'm not a stalker! And I'm only 31! Why does he keep calling me ma'am?" I pull out of the parking spot and to the left toward the road, but slam on the brakes when I hear the screech of a tire. A loud crunch of metal follows.

My heart leaps into my throat as I put the car in park. I didn't feel any impact. I look behind me and my heart drops back down, past my chest and into my stomach. A Ford sedan rests behind me, the front passenger side biting deep into a light pole. A cross hangs from the rearview mirror. *Oh no...*

I've been avoiding him for weeks. This cannot be happening.

Kendi exits the vehicle, slamming the door on his way out. His glare could call down fire from heaven.

33

The Meathead and His Mother

"**I** didn't see you."

"That's what mirrors are for, Cherise. And eyes."

"I said I was sorry, and I'll pay for the repairs. What more do you want me to do?"

Kendi goes quiet as we watch the tow truck driver guide his car slowly up the ramp. The silence is agonizing. I have to fill it.

"You've got pretty good reflexes." He doesn't respond. "I mean, you could have rear-ended me, but you managed to swerve just in time."

"Yep. Right into a pole." He lets out a short laugh, but I can tell there's not a drop of humor in it.

"This isn't all my fault, though."

"Here we go."

"I mean, how fast were you going for that pole to bite into your headlight like that?"

He opens his mouth, then closes it.

"See? Mistakes were made on both sides."

"Don't."

"Both sides have good people."

That gets a chuckle out of him. "Cherise, enough."

But I've found a thread and I'm not letting go. "If we look deep enough, we'll find our common ground. Technically, we both wanted the same thing. To get out of here as fast as possible."

Kendi dips his head. "Alright, you've made your point." He sighs. "Can I trouble you for a ride?"

I check my watch, shamelessly and slowly, before nodding. "Sure. I've got the time. Where to?"

"My mother's house. I was on my way over for the weekend, and there's no way I'm getting my car back today."

I wince. "Yes. Of course. What's the address?"

He texts it to me and I plug it into my phone. As serendipity would have it, it's a five-minute drive from there to the Jones' residence. Kendi finishes up with the tow truck, then slides into the passenger side of my car. His hands carry a wrapped box. "This is for you."

I take the box from him. "What's this for?"

He clears his throat. "It's a bible. I was going to give it to you after the baptism, but..." His unspoken words hang in the air.

Memories of my trauma-inducing baptism rear their ugly heads, and I swallow the lump in my throat. I'm not sure I'm ready to talk about what happened that day. For a little while, I'd forgotten. "Thanks."

Whatever portal to an alternate universe we entered a few minutes ago dissipates, along with the playfulness between us, as I pull out of the gas station. Kendi looms large, his broad shoulders swallowing my mid-sized seats. He doesn't seem to know where to put his hands, and they keep moving in a way that drives me to distraction.

"Focus on the road, please."

I snap my eyes forward and scoff. "I do know how to drive." I can almost hear his eyebrow go up. "How's your mom been doing, by the way?"

"She's doing great. She got the cast off her leg a while ago. Rehab and PT went well, too."

I nod. "That's good to hear."

Kendi clears his throat. "We've missed you at small group. Larry keeps asking after you. You can come back, you know."

I blink away the moisture pooling around my eyes and shrug. "I know."

"We don't have to talk about... that day."

"Thanks."

Kendi clears his throat again. "So, what brings you to Chapel Hill? Work stuff?"

"No. I'm meeting up with Preston's parents for dinner today."

"Really?"

That one word is pregnant with unspoken ones. Disbelief, confusion, surprise, disappointment, ridicule? I mean, I'm only guessing, but Kendi doesn't sound like he's happy for me. "Why did you say, 'really' like that?"

"I'm just surprised. I guess things between you two are serious?"

"Why would that surprise you?"

"For Preston, it doesn't. He's serious about everything."

I wait for Kendi to continue, but he doesn't. He's so infuriating. "Right. Preston is serious about everything. As opposed to me?"

"I didn't mean it like that."

"How did you mean it, then?"

"This is the house, right here."

I pull into the driveway, fuming. The moment I park, Kendi waves and makes his exit. But Kendi knows Preston well, and despite myself, I want to know what he thinks of our relationship. And of me. I get out of the car and follow him.

Kendi puts his hands in his pockets. "You need something, Cherise?"

I need answers. "I need to use the bathroom. If that doesn't put you out, or anything."

"I guess, if you promise not to run me over on the way in. I think I've endured enough damage for today."

"After my side mirror and my fender, I'd say we're even."

"None of those things was my fault!"

"If you hadn't taken my parking space–"

"Again with the parking space?"

"Kendi? What are you doing standing outside, Son?"

We both look up. A beautiful woman with silver hair stands in the doorway, dark hands on her slight hips.

"Hey, Mom." Kendi hops up the porch steps and plants a kiss on her cheek. "Sorry I'm late."

"You didn't say you were bringing over company." The grin on his mother's face is infectious. I smile and extend my hand.

"Hi, I'm Cherise."

Kendi's mother takes my hand with both of hers. "Oh, I am delighted to meet you, Cherise. You can call me Claire. Come inside!"

I hide my snicker as I pass a scowling Kendi and follow his mother through the front door. She must have been baking, because vanilla and coconut coat the air. The house is warm, but not uncomfortably so, with bright, springy hues decorating the corners.

A pot of gold flowers rests in the foyer, and a large abstract painting with purple, black, and white streaks hangs on the living room wall. Wooden frames surround pictures of family, friends, and a smiling, younger version of Kendi.

"The bathroom's that way." Kendi points in a direction, but I ignore him as his mother guides me into the kitchen.

"Now, it's not much, Cherise, but I've got shuku shuku laid out here on the table, and tea's just a kettle of hot water away if you'd like?"

I stare at the small, round confections Claire is offering and grin. "Tea would be lovely, Ms. Claire."

"Ma, she's not staying." Kendi grumbles in the hallway, but it's a small sound.

I grab one from the plate and take a bite. It's crunchy and sweet, with a softer middle, and I know I won't stop at one. "Mmm, these are so good! What did you call them? Shuki?"

"Shuku shuku. They're made with coconut. It's an old family recipe." Miss Claire's grin widens as she pushes the plate closer to me. "I have chamomile, Chai, and English Breakfast."

"Chamomile, please!"

Claire busies herself with my tea, and I help myself to more of the shuku shuku. Kendi pulls up a chair and glares at me. "What are you doing?"

I raise one to his face. "Enjoying some southern hospitality, obviously. You could stand to learn some, you know. Your mom is so nice. I wonder why it didn't rub off on you."

Kendi snatches the coconut ball from my hand. "These are for me."

"Pretty sure this whole plate was offered *to me*."

"No. I asked my mom to make them. For me. Not for you." He slides the plate away from me, but I slide it right back. A brief tugging match ensues, but thankfully, Ms. Claire returns and Kendi lets go.

"Here you are, Cherise. I brought sugar and honey, too."

I take a deep whiff. "Ooh, this smells fantastic. Thank you. For the tea *and* this plate of deliciousness." I bare all my teeth at Kendi, and he scowls.

"Don't you have somewhere to be?"

"Kendi, don't be rude," his mother chastises. "Antagonism is not good for fowls, and it is not good for goats; worse still, it is not good for human beings. Isn't that right, Cherise?"

I nod my head. "Yes ma'am."

Claire nods. "You see? If you watch your pot, your food will not burn. Cherise may be patient, but no one wants a partner with no manners. Keep this up, and she'll cut you loose before Christmas."

"Ma!" Kendi rubs his hand along his neck as I choke on my tea. "We're not like that!"

Ms. Claire makes a face. "Oh?" She looks down at me and up at Kendi. "Well, there's still time." To me, she says, "Cherise, Kendi is like that shuku shuku in your hand. Crusty on the outside, but soft in the middle."

"Mom!"

"Don't let him get away with treating you poorly, though. If he misbehaves, cut him loose. I won't hold it against you. Ashes fly back into the face of him who throws them."

"Please, Mom, just stop."

"Well, if you weren't so bad at this, I wouldn't have to meddle."

I'm not sure how much longer I can hold in my laughter. It feels good seeing Kendi get a taste of his own medicine. He looks like he might pop a blood vessel.

"Cherise and I aren't like that. She's seeing someone else, so stop giving her advice. And stop giving her my shuku shuku!" Kendi snatches the plate and storms out of the kitchen.

I FOLLOW KENDI'S CRUMB trail to the front porch. He's sitting on the porch swing, fiddling with his thumbs. An empty plate rests in front of him on a patio table. So petty.

"Sorry," he says.

I shrug. "It's okay. Ms. Claire's got another batch cooling on a rack. She's gonna pack them for me to go."

"Not about that, exactly. I'm sorry about my behavior today. It was rude."

"Well, I did make you run into a pole. That'd irk me, too."

Kendi shakes his head. "It's not you, it's me."

I sit beside him on the swing. "What do you mean?"

"I don't like having other people in my space."

"I noticed that about you."

"It makes me uncomfortable."

"No surprises there."

"Cherise." He looks up at me with those intense eyes of his, and for a moment, I feel unsettled. I'm not sure what this look means, but I don't like it. "Remember when I told you about why I chose to be celibate?"

I swallow and nod. "Yeah. Um. You said you made a lot of mistakes."

"I did. And the mess I caused was awful. I was selfish, and I hurt a lot of people. People who were close to me. People like Larry, and Maggie. And my mother. So now, I'm very protective of the people I love. I know now that what I do, and who I choose to be with, affects not just me, but them, too.

"You've seen how close our small group is. When one hurts, we all hurt. When one fails, we all feel it. When one has good news, we all celebrate. I love what I have with them, but I haven't forgotten what I put them through."

"What happened, Kendi?" I'm more invested in the answer than I'm willing to admit. While I wait, my own conscience claws at me. But this is different. I love Preston. He and I are meant to be together. And I'm trying to be the good Christian woman he needs, so that's gotta count for something.

Kendi folds his hands together and sighs. "One day I'll tell you about it. Not today, though. Besides, you've got someone waiting on you."

I almost don't catch it, but there's something off in his tone. I check my watch and stand, surprised at how much time has passed. "I do. But if you take your mom's advice, and give it enough time, I'm sure one day you'll have someone waiting on you, too."

Kendi looks at me, and I freeze. There it is again. That look. So deep a girl could drown in it. Is Kendi... falling for me?

That would be extremely inconvenient. Not to mention awkward. I might need to find another small group. Join a different church. Avoid him at work at all costs–

"No thanks."

"Pardon?"

"I'm not interested."

I'm a little lost. "You're not... interested?"

"Nope."

"In what, exactly?"

"Whatever you're suggesting."

"A relationship?" Rude. "Okay, I didn't mean a relationship with *me*, if that's what you're thinking."

Kendi makes a face. "What? No. I meant relationships in general."

I scoff. "Well, that's what I was talking about, too."

He nods slowly. "Okay." An awkward ten-second silence follows. Kendi is the first to break it. "Don't you need to get to the Jones's house?"

"Yep!" I turn on my heels and walk away.

"Cherise. Wait."

Shoot. If he confesses his love minutes before I introduce myself to my future in-laws, I'll punch him in the face. "What, Kendi?" I lace the two words with as much irritation as possible, so he knows I'm not interested.

"Don't forget about the shuku shuku. And come back to small group."

Oh. I nod. "Okay."

"You promise?"

"Yeah."

"Alright. Tell Preston hi for me."

I offer a thumbs up, not trusting myself to open my mouth again. I can't get away fast enough.

34

Me And My Big Mouth

Preston's family home is immaculate. The yard is pristine and neatly trimmed. Black gnomes and fake mushrooms dot the perimeter of the mailbox post. The mailbox itself is a work of art, the metal post curving upward like a vine to the box – which proudly displays the house number and surname Jones in bold, golden letters. The driveway wraps around the yard, with an extension leading to the side of the house. A large, detached garage sits at the back, and I park in front of it, next to Preston's car.

The house looms large and tall; the backyard boasts fruit-bearing trees, a tire swing hanging from the branches of a thick oak tree, and a little woodshop at the back end of the property. No doubt the memories made here are happy and wholesome. My phone vibrates, and for a split second, I consider hopping back into my car and driving away instead of responding to Preston's text. I take a breath, then tap out a reply.

ME: I'm here.

I walk up the back steps on shaky legs, prepared to knock, but Preston swings the door open wide. His smile is even wider as he greets me. "Cherise."

It's going to be okay. I kiss him and he escorts me inside. The back door leads to the kitchen, which is empty except for the simmering pots on the stove and the pan of freshly baked cornbread cooling on the counter. The oven chirps, and I catch sight of a bird roasting inside. It smells like a holiday in here.

I cast a sideways glance at Preston, who's got my hand in his and is tugging me out of the kitchen and into the hallway. "My parents are upstairs, but they'll be down in a bit. Mom told me to keep an eye on the bird, but I think there's time for a quick tour."

I take in the pictures on the wall; a mosaic of family photos. Vacations somewhere tropical, somewhere with snow. A history of firsts. First steps, first bike, first day of school – I count 14 of those, from kindergarten to college. The walls are filled with Preston. Snapshots of his life and accomplishments. Awards and trophies from spelling bees, baseball, tennis, mathletes. His metaphor of him as the sun comes to mind. He wasn't kidding. I bite down on my lip, feeling anxious.

"This is the sitting room here on the left. It's a nice quiet spot when we've got company over. Mom painted the walls a calming blue."

I nod and follow him as he weaves his way through the lower part of the house. There's so much of it, but somehow every space feels full and lived in. It's clean, but there are pens strewn on the table in the dining room, an open laptop and a pair of loafers in the formal living room. A set of keys lay on the table in the hall, right below the row of key hooks hanging from the wall.

"Mom will kill me if I let that chicken burn. Make yourself comfortable here in the family room, and I'll be right back, okay?"

Preston leaves me to myself in the big room with high ceilings and a sectional the size of a small spaceship. I sample its softness, then curl my feet under my thighs and lean back, wondering how many nights Preston spent here with his parents, cuddling on the couch eating popcorn. Or pizza. Would they let him eat on the couch? My mom wouldn't stand for it. No, in Linda Williams' house, couches this nice were for clients. And she kept the walls and shelves clear of what she called "tacky family photos."

"You must be Cherise!" I turn my head and slide my feet to the floor. Preston's mother stands in front of me, gorgeous and smiling, with hands outstretched. I place my hands in hers, and she pulls me into an embrace. "I'm so sorry I wasn't downstairs to greet you. We were scrambling a bit when Preston called to say he'd be late. I ended up putting the bird in later than I'd planned, and then I was a mess and had to get myself ready."

"Oh, it's no problem, Mrs. Jones."

She pulls back and gives me some breathing room. "Oh, call me Thea. Dorothea is too formal, and Mrs. Jones is my mother-in-law. You are gorgeous, Cherise."

"Aw, thank you Thea." Her eyes crinkle at the corners when I use her name. There's a slight sheen to them as she pulls me into another embrace.

"Just one more hug, if you don't mind? I'm so happy Preston met you. He talks about you nonstop whenever we chat on the phone."

I let myself linger in her embrace, and I'm a little sad when she lets me go. "I'm really happy I met Preston, too. You've done an amazing job with him. And this house is beautiful." I gesture toward her mile-high curtains for good measure.

"Well, God is good. I hope you're hungry?"

My stomach growls on cue, and I chuckle. "Maybe just a little?"

"I'd hoped to chat for a bit before dinner, but it's already gotten late, and I don't want to keep you waiting any longer. Preston's dad gets cranky when he hasn't eaten. Like father, like son."

I lift my brows. Preston is rarely cranky, so I'm curious to witness his dad in his hangry state. Thea calls him down as we pass the stairs.

"Jameson, come on down so we can pray and eat!"

"On my way!" A deep voice travels down the stairs, followed by a silver-haired version of Preston. He's a shade lighter, with copper skin and a dusting of freckles across the top of his nose, but the same squared jaw and broad shoulders are present. "There she is!" Preston's dad wraps me in an embrace, and I welcome it wholeheartedly. "Sorry, we're huggers in this family."

"Oh, it's not a problem! My family's the same way." *Why did I say that?*

"Well, I hope you're hungry, because Thea cooked up a storm today."

"Jameson, that's enough." Preston's mom gives him a playful swat.

He chuckles and whispers to me. "She wanted to impress you, so she cooked all her best dishes. You have my thanks." He winks at me and hooks his arm in mine, then in Thea's. There's enough room in the hallway for all three of us to walk to the dining room side by side. As I listen to their playful banter back and forth, a pang of jealousy strikes me right in my gut. My parents can't even stand to be in the same room together.

The feeling continues all throughout dinner as Preston's parents present me with roasted chicken, velvety collard greens, savory black-eyed peas, buttered cornbread, and homestyle mashed potatoes and gravy. A beautiful salad of mixed greens, tomatoes, and avocado slices rests at the center of the table, and Preston's parents take turns offering me second helpings and refilling my cup. They regale me with stories of ski trips and backpacking as a family all over Europe.

Their pride in Preston is clear, their love even clearer. It coats the air with a warmth so thick it smothers all my confidence. Dinner is perfection, but even the slice of decadent chocolate cake Thea places in front of me has trouble finding its way down.

His parents are doting and attentive. Though I know it's mostly for Preston's sake, a part of me wants to believe it's because they already love me. That they see in me a precious daughter, worthy of their attention and overly fussy affection. I want this. All of it. So much that it hurts. I wish my mother kept pictures of me on the wall, that my father held pride for me in his eyes the way Preston's dad does. I can't remember the last time we shared a meal together as a family.

While his parents clear the dinner table, Preston places a warm mug of tea in front of me, stirring in honey to the levels I prefer. "How was everything?"

I look at him, eyes shining. "Everything is perfect."

"It wasn't too much?"

I shake my head. "Not at all. Your parents are really sweet. And my stomach is very happy." I look down at my stomach and give it a pat.

"Everything okay, Cherise?" Preston's mom returns to the table, glancing toward my stomach with a worried expression. "Are you feeling sick?"

I shake my head. "Oh, not at all! I was just telling Preston how delicious everything was."

She waves a hand in dismissal. "Oh, it was nothing."

"It was amazing, Thea. I don't think I've ever had a chocolate cake that good, either."

"Oh, you don't have to say that." She places her hands on her cheeks. "It's nice to hear though."

"Mom, you know we love your cooking." Preston chimes in with a grin.

His dad follows suit, pulling his wife into an intimate embrace. "Yes, Thea. Everything you put on this table was phenomenal." He kisses her deep enough to make Preston and I both look away.

Thea pushes him away with a giggle. "Not in front of the kids, Jameson. Enjoy it while you can, because it'll be back to salad and fish tomorrow."

He makes a face. "Cherise, I wish you could come for a visit every weekend. Though I suppose that would be selfish of us, keeping you from your family. Preston tells us you've got siblings?"

I nod. "Yeah, my older brothers are twins."

Mr. Jones whistles and Thea shakes her head. "I can't imagine how your parents managed it," she says. "One wild boy running around the house is a lot of work, but two?"

"They managed it!" I chirp. "Then they had me a few years later."

"And I'm sure you were a delight!" Thea beams. "I've always wanted a daughter, but it wasn't in God's plan for us."

"Oh, I think it might be in His plans after all." Preston's dad winks at me, and I'm certain he can see the flames in my cheeks.

"Dad." Preston gives him a warning look, and he shrugs.

Thea very expertly pivots. "Cherise, what do your parents do?"

"My mom is in real estate, and my dad is a retired professor."

"Ooh, that's nice. Do your parents travel a lot?" Thea asks.

"Not too much."

"If they need a good travel agent, you tell them to call me. Our agent is phenomenal, and she's always taken good care of us."

"Sure!" My laugh is nervous as I slowly realize that Preston's parents think mine are still together. Probably because that's what I told Preston.

"The way Preston told it, it sounds like your parents are really big on family trips." Preston's dad pulls out a chair for Thea, then slides into the seat beside her.

"Oh?" I swallow, scrambling to remember what exactly I told Preston.

"That's right!" Thea chuckles. "Does your family really spend every Christmas at the Biltmore? I've only been once, and it was gorgeous. I can imagine at Christmas it's even more spectacular."

Right, the Biltmore. I could have said the local Best Western, or the mountains, or any number of vague things. But no. I chose a very popular, very expensive historical site that's essentially a castle from yesteryears. "Yeah, it's kind of a tradition for us."

"It's one of the things that I found really unique about her." Preston kisses my hand and laughs. "It's not just Christmas. What was it you said to me? I thought it was so interesting, I couldn't get it out of my head. Fourth of July at home. Juneteenth at Big Mama's. Thanksgiving at your maternal grandparents, and Christmas at the Biltmore. Did I get it right?"

Oh. My. God. I nod, very weakly. "Yup, that's right."

"That's so wonderful!" Thea grins. "Tradition is very important in a family. Every winter we'd take Preston skiing. Have you ever been skiing, Cherise?"

"No ma'am, I haven't."

"We'd love for you to join us if your schedule allows it. We usually go in January."

"Oh, but February might be better at the summit. Especially for someone who's never been on the snow."

"I don't know. I think earlier in the snow season would be better than later."

As Preston's parents go back and forth about the best time to take an inexperienced skier to the summit, my mind begins to swim. I can't believe Preston remembered what I told him. *I* couldn't even remember what I told him.

The anxiety I felt earlier in the evening returns with a vengeance. I'm going to ruin this. Preston's perfect, and so is his family. They're perfect and wonderful and so well put together and what am I? I'm a mess. My family's a train wreck. My parents barely acknowledge my existence.

I gulp down my tea, hoping the chamomile will soothe my growing panic the way it soothes my throat.

Preston glances my way and leans in toward my ear. "You okay?"

I nod. "Of course."

He stares at me for several seconds, his keen eyes practically dissecting my soul, then leans back into his chair. "Mom, Dad? Thank you so much for dinner. I think Cherise is a little tired, and she's got a long drive back."

"Oh, look at us, gabbing on and on." Thea is apologetic. "It's been a pleasure, Cherise."

Preston's dad nods. "We've really enjoyed having you over. We should get together again real soon. We'd love to meet your parents, too."

"Jameson, don't pressure the girl." Thea scolds him.

"Oh, definitely!" I nod my head. "My folks would love that."

"You think so?" Thea looks so hopeful, I want to squeal with happiness. His parents really do like me.

"Sure! Next time we can get together with my folks and have a big dinner." *Stop talking Cherise.* "My mom loves hosting and baking and all that stuff."

"You don't say?" Thea leans in. "What's her specialty?"

Shut up. Shut up. Shut up! "Um. Well, she makes a lot of baked goods. But if I had to pick just one, it would definitely be her chocolate chip cookies."

"Are they really good?"

The last time I spotted Linda Williams near a stove was the day of my eighth-grade bake sale. The prepackaged cookies didn't even need to be baked, but she placed them in the oven to 'warm them up.' She still managed to burn them, and ended up just making a financial donation.

Prior memories tell a similar story. Burnt casseroles, crunchy eggs, a custard pie that somehow exploded in the oven. I should shut my mouth, but instead, I look Thea dead in her face and tell her, "My mom's cooking skills are unbelievable. Everything she makes leaves me speechless."

"Oh, then we've got to swap recipes! When do you think would be a good day for dinner?"

I tilt my head. "Pardon?"

"We've got a flight to Venice scheduled for next Monday, but if we move some things around, we could try for the weekend." Thea's practically jumping with excitement.

"Okay, yeah. Sure."

"How's next Sunday sound?"

Preston's dad rubs his chin. "I've got golf that afternoon, but I can cancel."

"And I can always skip the aerobics class at the Y. So how about it, Cherise?"

"Next Sunday?"

"Do you think it's too soon?"

For me to convince my mom *and* my dad to not only be in the same space, but to pretend to be a happily married couple for the sake of their daughter's happiness? No, seven days is not enough time. Seven lifetimes wouldn't be enough time. But Thea looks so earnest, and I just can't say no to her. "I'm sure my parents would be delighted."

"Great! Just be sure to confirm with them first, then get back to us, okay?"

CHERISE AT THE ALTAR

I feel lightheaded as I nod my agreement. What have I gotten myself into?

35

Dare I Even Ask?

T here's no way I can ask my mom to help me over the phone. The fact that she barely answers my calls aside, it would be too easy for her to hang up mid-explanation, or feign a bad connection. No, I need to do my groveling in person. And in public so she won't cuss me out.

I clear my morning on Monday and head straight to the office of Linda Williams Realty, Ms. Linda Williams presiding. Mom's with a client, so when she spots me outside her office, she sends a clear message with her eyes while maintaining the smile on her face.

I know the look. It's a dismissive shift from left to right. I call it the I-don't-have-time-for-you eye roll, and it still stings the same way it did when I was a kid. Mom stands, shakes her client's hand, and escorts her to the door. I step aside, waiting patiently for them to wrap things up. She waits until her client is several steps away before whispering to me.

"Cherise, now's not a good time."

"Busy morning?"

"I've got another client coming in soon. Do we have an appointment I'm not aware of?"

Ouch. "Um, no. I actually just need to ask you for a favor."

Mom almost rolls her eyes but catches herself as her client waves one last time before leaving the building.

"Thank you, Linda!"

"Oh, it's my pleasure! See you at the showing tomorrow." The way mom switches on and off is scary. Her smiling face morphs the moment her eyes land on me. "Cherise, you should have called."

"You don't answer when I call."

Mom huffs. "This again? Honestly, it's a good thing you're not the marrying type. You're entirely too needy."

I ignore the dig and plow forward. "That's actually why I'm here. I've met someone, and–"

Mom snorts. A sound I was not expecting. "You're serious?"

"Um, yeah. His name is Preston and things are getting pretty serious between us."

"Oh honey." Mom walks back into her office, shaking her head. "How many times have I told you not to attach yourself to any man? You're much better off on your own."

"Mom, would you just let me finish?" I follow her inside and close the door. "Preston took me to meet his parents this weekend."

"How charming." I give Mom a look and she throws up her hands. "Fine. Sorry. Go ahead, Cherise. I won't interrupt again."

"Thank you." Despite my mom's expertise at speaking through facial expressions and body language, I continue. "Preston's parents are great, and they want to meet you and dad this weekend for dinner. On Sunday."

Mom drums her fingers on the table. "Is that all?"

Now for the hard part. "There's more. I kind of told Preston, and by extension his parents, that you and Dad are still together."

Mom lets out an expletive. "You can't be serious."

"I know how this sounds. But Mom, I really like Preston, and I'm asking you to help me out."

"Absolutely not."

"Mom, it's just one dinner."

"This is gonna blow up in your face, Cherise. Your father and I can't stand each other, and there's no way he'd even think to agree to this."

"Dad's already on board."

That gets her attention. "Your father said he's okay with this?"

"Yes!"

Mom's eyes narrow. "Assuming your father *actually* shows, where are we meeting? You know your dad is picky, and I can't waste a whole Sunday driving up to Wilmington because he wants to eat at his favorite crab spot."

I let out a short laugh, despite knowing this next part will be a hard sell. "You won't even have to leave home, because I told them you'd cook for us."

That earns me a second expletive, followed by my full government name. "Cherise Michelle Williams, have you lost your mind?"

"I know this is short notice, but–"

"Short notice? That's the least of my concerns. You're *lying* about us, and on top of that you expect me to cook like some matriarch of the 1950s? Have I taught you absolutely nothing? Because this defies logic and sense. Just tell them the truth and be done with it."

"I know this sounds messed up, but Mom, I really like Preston. His parents are amazing, and when they asked to come over, I panicked, okay? I will tell them the truth, but for now can you just please, please, please say yes?" Mom's eyes narrow even further, and I shrink. *Time to grovel.* "Please, Mom? Just this once can you not be Linda Williams, proud, independent black woman and just be my mom? Please?"

I think I've struck a nerve, and hope bubbles up inside me. It lasts for about three seconds. As Mom's eyes narrow into slits, the hope inside of me dies.

I STARE AT THE NUMBER on my screen as I sit in my car, nursing my wounds. I haven't called my brother in ages, but Jeremy is my best chance at getting Dad to come to dinner. Mom rarely picks up when I call, but Dad picks up even less. Not that I call him much. There's the obligatory Father's Day call, and I check in during the holidays, but our conversations tend to languish after a few minutes of small talk.

Not that my talks with Jeremy and Jason have fared any better. Jason only calls for favors, and Jeremy calls to gripe about Mom when she gets too nosey. I don't know how three siblings with the same mother can have such different relationships with our parents, but that's where we are. I shove down my growing apprehension and dial Jeremy's number.

After three rings, the line clicks and I hear an abrupt "What?" on the other end.

"Hey Bro." I have to force myself to sound upbeat. "How's it going?"

"Something wrong?"

I scoff. "No, why would anything be wrong?"

Jeremy starts talking to someone else in the room, and for a few minutes, there's just static and random shuffling.

"Hello? Jeremy? You still there?" I tap my fingers on the steering wheel and wait another minute. "Hello?"

"Yeah, sorry. My roommate keeps borrowing my charger, and now I can't find it. My phone's on five percent, so you've got five, ten minutes tops. Spill it."

I clear my throat. "Yeah, okay. So um, I need you to do me a favor and ask Dad to come to dinner at Mom's house."

Silence answers me.

"Jeremy, did you hear me? Hello?"

Jeremy mutters something to his roommate before returning to the phone. "Uh, Cherise, have you met our parents? They'll kill each other."

"Jeremy, please just ask him. Mom said she'd do it, but only if Dad agrees."

"Wait. *Our* mother, the woman who gave birth to us, told you she'd have dinner with *our* dad?"

I swallow and nod, though he can't see me. "Yeah. It wasn't easy getting her to agree, but she said if Dad's willing to suffer through a meal, then she'll do it, too."

"I don't believe it."

Probably because I made it up. "Please, Jeremy, just call Dad and ask him, okay?"

"Why do you want them to have dinner so badly?"

Jeremy's tone is patronizing. And herein lies the problem with my brothers. They are incapable of taking me seriously. Ever. And they know where all my buttons are, because they've pushed every one of them. Multiple times. I know the second I tell my brother why I want our parents at dinner, he'll have something snarky to say about it. But with less than a week to make this dinner happen, I need him. "I met someone."

There's a brief pause, followed by a snigger. "Okay, you got me. What's the real reason?"

I bite down on my lip. "That's the reason. My boyfriend and I have been dating for a while." More snickers. "And this weekend I got to meet his parents. Now they want to meet mine."

At this, Jeremy all out howls. "Are you kidding me?"

"Jeremy, it isn't funny."

"First of all, I've seen some of the guys you've dated, so I'm a little worried. Either he's crazy or he's slumming it."

"Preston isn't slumming it. And he's of sound mind and body."

"Whatever. If he's decent and he's not crazy, he's not gonna last a night with our parents. You remember your graduation party, Cherise?"

I do remember my high school graduation, and the humiliating shouting match that occurred between my parents in front of all my peers. I also remember Linda and Gregory Williams being the picture of decorum for Jeremy and Jason's joint celebration.

"You sure about this?"

"Yes. So please pass along the message. Mom's house. This Sunday at seven."

"Dinner will be a wrap by eight. Seven thirty if Dad brings up his golf clubs. He's still pissed Mom managed to swipe them in the split."

"That's another thing. They need to pretend they're still together." Before Jeremy can get a word in, I add, "It's just for one dinner. And Mom swore to be civil."

"Dad's never gonna go for that."

He's not wrong. But I have a plan. Once Dad makes a decision, he tends to stick with it. If I can get him to agree to dinner with Mom, I can fill him in later on the details. "Just ask him about dinner. Leave out the last part. I'll talk to him myself about that."

"Alright. One last question before my phone dies. What's in it for me?"

I blow out an exasperated breath. Brothers. "What do you want?"

Jeremy hums a full minute. "I'll let you know."

"Jeremy, just tell me what you want." As I say the last word, the line goes dead in my ear. I catch the time on my screen and wring my hair in frustration. I've got to head to the clinic. Mom's resounding 'no' is still ringing in my ears, but I'm playing the long game.

I tap out a text.

ME: Just got off the phone with Dad. He wants to know what dish he should bring.

Mom doesn't reply, but I can see that she's read the text. I know how dangerous it is to get caught in between my parents, but Dad's the only person I know who can get a reaction out of her. My happiness isn't enough to motivate her to cooperate, but being showed up by my dad - or, heaven forbid, seen as less accommodating - would slowly eat away at her. At least, that's what I'm banking on.

My phone buzzes, and I stare at the screen. I blink once, twice, a third time as I reread the text.

MOM: Just one dinner.

36

D is For Disaster

I walk up the steps to Mom's condo and take a deep breath before pressing the call button. Mom's voice floats out on the intercom. "You're late."

"Sorry," I mumble, hardly waiting for the buzz of the lobby door before yanking it open. My backpack gets caught as it slams behind me, and it takes a little finagling to wiggle it free. I'm a bundle of nerves as I take the steps, two at a time, to Mom's unit.

She flings open the door, hair wisped around her temples, a frenzied look on her face. "You said you'd be here at noon. It's almost three." She pulls me by the arm into the house, and I let her, feeling a little giddy to have Linda Williams actually need me.

The moment dims in the light of the kitchen, where a mess of overflowing pots and pans litter the stove and something sticky drips from the counter. Mom pushes me toward the kitchen. "This is a disaster."

I shake my head. "No, we can fix this." I sift through the pots, careful not to slip on the melted chocolate dotting the floor. There's nothing salvageable in the pot of burnt, undercooked black-eyed peas, the blackened cornbread, or the pot of mush I can only guess was meant to be some kind of soup.

Mom throws up her hands. "I can't serve any of this. I called you a dozen times, and you didn't pick up! Didn't you check your messages?"

I slip my phone out of my backpack and check it. It's on silent mode, but the notification bar flashes with missed messages. Two of them from Preston, one from Kendi, and the rest from Mom. "I'm sorry. I got caught up working on something."

"This is *your* dinner! What were you doing that was so important?"

I unzip my backpack and pull out several framed photos. "I was doing this." I head to the living room with the photos and begin replacing Mom's nondescript artistic frames with my photoshopped memories. Past my eighth birthday, I have no pictures of all five of us together, so piecing everything together took the better part of two days.

"What are you doing?" Mom clucks as she stares at the photos. "This is ridiculous, Cherise. Dinner is ruined, anyway, so why don't you just call the whole thing off?"

I lower the picture in my hand and sigh. "I can't just cancel, Mom. Preston and his parents will both be here in a few hours. We can salvage dinner. I'm sorry I was late, but I'm here now."

"I have been slaving away in that kitchen all afternoon like some tottering housewife, and I'm not spending another minute in there."

"Mom—"

"No, I won't do it. As a feminist, the idea is offensive, and as your mother—"

I scoff. "As my mother? Really? Now you want to be my mother?"

"I have always been your mother, and you and I both know how stupid this is. You're going through all of this trouble over a man you don't even need."

I toss the photo on the couch and glare at her. "But I do need him."

"No woman needs a man, Cherise. Not really. And especially not you. That's not how I raised you."

I know being a single mother isn't easy. But years of emotional anemia have done a number on my heart, and I'm tapped out. "Maybe if you took even a second of your day to think about me, I'd believe that. But I've never been a priority to you. I've always been an afterthought or worse, a burden."

Mom scoffs. "Honestly, Cherise. It's really hard to talk to you when you get like this. You throw these little pity parties and tantrums, expecting the world to revolve around you. Well, it doesn't. The sooner you realize that, the better off you'll be."

"I've always known I'm not the center of the universe, Mom. I know I'm not the sun. I'm not even a planet in your solar system. You've made that abundantly clear."

Mom unties the apron from her waist and neck and tosses it to the floor. "You've got some nerve. I'm doing this, all of this, for you." Mom gestures toward the kitchen, then glares at me. "You asked me to prepare this farce of a dinner, and I agreed to it, but that doesn't mean everything's going to go your way. If you want dinner so badly, we can order out. I don't know why I even bothered."

Mom walks away in a huff toward the kitchen, and I follow her. "I don't know, either. But for the 30 seconds you actually cared, it felt nice."

Mom rolls her eyes. "Oh, here we go."

"It feels good to have someone sacrifice for you, to go out of their way for you, to actually want to be around you. And that's what I have with Preston. He cares about me and does things for me that no one ever has. Not you, not Dad, not anybody.

"His family is so beautiful and so warm, Mom. They take vacations together and eat meals on Sunday, and I want to be a part of that. And if pretending for a few hours that your daughter exists is too much for you, then fine." I walk back to the living room, eyes brimming with unshed tears, and pull a picture from the wall. I plop it onto the sofa, swipe at my face, then grab another. It's a picture of my first - and last - high school chorus performance. Mom and Dad are in the background, thanks to the power of cut and paste, but it's a farce. They were never there, and I took a bus home alone that night.

Pain squeezes my chest and I tug the frame off the wall. I remove another, and another, and when I get to the last one, Mom places her hand on mine.

"Cherise, just hold on." I lower my hand. Mom sighs and scratches her head. "If it means that much to you, I'll..." She hesitates and stares at the kitchen. "I'm just not good at this."

I catch a flash of something in Mom's eyes. Worry? "You're not good at what?" I ask.

"Cooking, for starters." She shrugs and smooths the hair on her head. "I'm not comfortable doing things I'm not good at. I tried to be a good housewife once, and the kind of mother mine was when I was growing up. But it's just not in me."

"I've seen you with Jeremy and Jason, Mom. You don't treat them the same way you treat me."

She shrugs. "It's different with the boys."

"Sorry I was born a girl."

Mom lets out a long sigh. "Cherise, I'm trying here. Can't you meet me halfway?"

I stuff my feelings down and nod. "Fine. I'll start working on the chicken. Is it in the fridge?"

Her eyes go wide before she rests her palms on her face. "I knew I forgot something."

I groan, then let out a slow breath. Mom looks like she's ready to bolt. If I want this dinner to be a success, I need to keep my cool. "That's okay. We can just buy one from the store, right? I'll head out and grab a few things."

"I'll grab them." Mom clenches my arm. "There's a bunch of stuff that still needs to be cooked, and we both know what will happen if I try to cook it."

She's got a point. "Okay. You go to the store, and I'll start on..." I stare at the kitchen. There's not a clean surface in sight. "The dishes, I guess." Mom's already out the door before I can ask her where she keeps her cleaning gloves.

"I THINK THIS IS GONNA work." I stare at the giant bird resting on the counter and cover it with foil. The meal will be a bit leaner than I'd hoped, but there's a fresh batch of golden cornbread ready to serve, a pot of creamed corn, and cookies in the oven, courtesy of Pillsbury. Mom's working on a green salad, and Dad should be arriving any minute with macaroni and cheese.

I remove my apron and head to Mom's bathroom to freshen up. I apply a layer of gloss and some sheen to my curls, then spritz with a bit of body mist. "You've got this, Cherise," I say to myself in the mirror. My phone buzzes in the pocket of my dress (yes, it has pockets!) and I read, then reread the text from Preston.

I rush out of the bathroom and into the dining room. "Mom, how much time before you're done with that salad?"

"Why?"

"Preston's on his way, and we haven't even started setting the table yet!"

Mom looks at her watch. "But dinner's at seven."

"Ugh, I should have known he'd come early."

"Well, that's not my fault!"

"Mom, we need to set the table! Where are the good plates?"

"They're above the cabinets."

I stare at the box of China sitting on top of the cabinets. "You didn't take them out yet?"

"Cherise." Mom glares at me. "I'm trying my best here, but if you raise your voice to me one more time, I'm done."

I lower my head. "I'm sorry. I'm just freaking out a little."

"Freak out as you bring down the China. It's more productive that way."

I mutter, under my breath, and grab a stepping stool. "You know I can't reach all the way up here." I heft the box out of its spot, displacing a few dust bunnies on the way down. "Ugh, dust, too?" I glance at Mom, who's unfolding a tablecloth to put on the dining table, then turn back to the box. It hasn't even been opened. "Guess I gotta find scissors, too. And where is Dad?"

I got a confirmation from Jeremy that he'd be here, but I'd waited until this morning to call him and tell him the details – making sure it was early enough for his Do Not Disturb mode to still be active and the phone to go straight to voicemail. Because, spoiler alert, I'm a coward.

My phone buzzes again, and I put it on the counter and hit the speaker button so I can keep looking for the scissors.

"Cherise, what on earth is this message you left on my phone? I'm supposed to do WHAT with your mother? Dinner is one thing, and you're really pushing it with dinner, but what? Pretend that I'm still shackled to that old harpie–"

I try to take the phone off speaker, but Mom swipes the phone before I can get to it.

"That's pretty rich coming from you, Gregory. And why aren't you here yet? Dinner starts at seven and we're waiting on you."

"You can keep waiting, Belinda the Witch, because I'm not choking down a dry casserole and pretending I like it. I don't have to anymore, and I've got a paper framed on my wall to prove it."

"Guys, don't." I try to mediate, but Mom's already riled up.

"And I've got a paper that says I don't have to listen to your drivel all night long and pretend to like it, either. Speaking of things I don't have to pretend to like all night long–"

"Okay, Mom!" I snatch the phone from her and speak quickly into the phone. "Dad, this is really important to me, and you promised to come to dinner. I need you here."

"Jeremy said dinner would be at your mother's house, but that she wouldn't be there for more than a half hour because she had a showing."

I rub my temples. "He said *what*?"

"I was told I'd only have to put up with her for a half hour, not for the whole night, and certainly not while pretending to be a happy couple."

"You're so good at pretending, though." Mom's words are laced with venom. "You did it for most of our marriage, what's a couple more hours?"

"Mom..."

"I wouldn't have had to pretend if you'd been a better wife."

"I did the best I could. And considering I was competing with a skinny office aid half *both* our ages, I think I did pretty well."

The phone goes silent for a moment, and I stare at it, reeling. "Dad, you cheated on Mom?"

Dad clears his throat. "Linda, I told you that was just one time."

Mom scoffs. "Why would I believe that? Why would I believe a single word that ever comes out of your mouth? I gave up *everything* for you, and you–" Mom shakes her head. "I can't do this." She starts walking out of the kitchen, and I stare after her, numb.

"Mom, wait. Preston's gonna be here any minute."

"Have dinner without me. I can't be in the same room with that man."

"You won't have to." Dad's voice is brusque. "I'm not coming."

"Good!" Mom shouts from the hallway.

The line goes dead. Mom must have taken half the air out of the room with her, because I find it hard to breathe. I'd known Mom and Dad didn't get along, but in the way that every kid knows when there's tension between their parents. In the silence at meal time and the clipped tones of conversations. I always thought they were just too different, or too much alike. Mom too independent. Dad too ambitious.

I always assumed they'd grown apart. I never considered the possibility that Dad betrayed her trust. My mom is the strongest person I know. I've seen her yell and hold her own, but I've never seen her cry. Never seen her broken pieces. It should bring me a little comfort to discover my mom is human after all, but it doesn't. It scares me. I thought I had Linda Williams figured out. Turns out I don't know her at all.

I walk down the hall and knock on her door. "Mom? Can I come in?"

"I have a headache, Cherise."

"I'll bring you some medicine." I find some ibuprofen in the bathroom and bring it to the door with a glass of water. "Mom?" I open the door, and she's at her desk, perusing through a sea of MLS numbers. "Mom, what are you doing?"

She shrugs. "There are some new houses on the market. I need to jump on the properties early."

"I brought you some medicine."

"Just set it over there on the dresser."

I do, and I fill the silence that follows with my growing panic. "Preston will be here any minute."

"I'm not doing it."

"But we worked so hard on everything, and Dad says he's not coming, so—"

"It doesn't matter. I never should have agreed to it."

"But Mom."

"Cherise, why do you want this so bad?" Mom turns around and stares at me, and for a moment, I see it. The pain in her eyes, the unshed tears. "Why even bother? I spent years with your father, striving to be everything he wanted me to be. And where did it get me?" She swipes at her face, then smooths her hair. "Just focus on yourself. On accomplishing your own goals. Don't worry about changing yourself for someone who's just going to hurt you in the end." Her voice cracks at the last part, but then the mask returns. "Thanks for the medicine. I'm sorry about dinner, but I'm not doing it."

"Mom, you promised." The smoke alarm interrupts our conversation. The smell of burning sugar hits my nose the same time Mom's eyes go wide. "The cookies!" I rush to the kitchen and turn off the oven while Mom begins fanning at the smoke alarm.

"Open the window!"

I lift the single, small window over the kitchen sink. I carefully open the oven, covering my nose as another plume of smoke wafts up. Black disks wink up at me, and I frown. Mom pulls them out and dumps the pan in the sink. "This was a bad idea from the start." She shakes her head. "Don't worry about the mess. I'll clean up later." Mom returns to her room without so much as a second glance, and I stare at the pan simmering in the sink. The doorbell rings, and I let out an expletive.

This is an absolute disaster. And now Preston's parents are going to find out just how dysfunctional, and baking-averse, my family is. A second ring echoes through the living room, and I make my way slowly to the front door. I swallow the lump in my throat, put my hand on the knob, and twist it.

Preston greets me with a smile. "Hey, Cherise."

"Hey." I'm sure he can hear the strain in my voice, because his eyebrows dive down the bridge of his nose.

"Everything okay?"

I shake my head, then look behind him, searching for Mr. and Mrs. Jones. "Where are your parents?"

"Oh, didn't you get my messages? There was a mix-up with their flight, and they had to hop on a plane this morning. It's just me."

I swallow, not sure what else to say just yet. All this stress, and his parents weren't even coming?

He takes a step closer to me. "Cherise? What's wrong?"

I clear my throat. "It's fine. I was actually gonna call you. My mom's not feeling great."

"Oh. I hope it's nothing too serious?"

I shake my head. "I don't think so, but I don't think we'll be having dinner anytime soon."

Preston wraps me in an embrace, and the tears I've been holding at bay break loose. "Hey, it's okay." He kisses the top of my head and squeezes tighter. "I know how important this dinner was for us, but these things happen. Don't stress over it, okay? We can have dinner, just the two of us." He tilts my head up, and I revel in the kiss that follows. I don't deserve him. I don't deserve this. And for the hundredth time, I realize that sooner or later, I'm going to have to tell him the truth. My parents aren't going to magically start getting along, and this evening proves it. I need to fess up. And not just about my parents.

"Dinner sounds great." I sniff, and swipe at the tears on my face. "Sorry. I'm just a little worried."

Preston nods. "About your mom? Think we should bring her some soup or something? Or, if you'd rather stay here?" Preston puts on a brave face, but he doesn't let go.

I don't want to stay here and pretend to take care of my not-sick mother, so I shake my head. "I'll bring her something later. She's resting right now."

"Okay." He kisses me again, and I follow him to his car.

After dinner. Just one more dinner, and I'll tell him. More tears fall, but I let them. I think I can let myself off the hook, just this once.

"Cherise?" Preston turns and looks at me, his eyes searching my face. For what, I don't know, but I drop my chin, feeling exposed. He bends down, leaning closer until our noses touch. "Cherise?" His voice goes soft, and my breath hitches. I let my eyes wander back to his, and he smiles. "I love you."

Warmth fills me from the tips of my toes to the crown of my head and back. I still can't breathe, though.

He kisses my cheek and says it again. "I love you, Cherise." The words echo in my ear as he repeats them over and over, showering my face with kisses.

He's never said the words before. I stand there, dumbstruck and oxygen deprived, as he confesses his love to me. I'm elated, and at the same time, terrified. Because I know how selfish I am. I spent the whole evening thinking of myself, and I can already feel the resolve I had a minute ago slipping away into the night air. If I were brave, I would be honest and hope that Preston's love for me is stronger than the lies I've told.

But I'm not.

37

Doubling Down

If someone told me a year ago that I'd be spending my summer attending church and small group meetings, I would have laughed them out of the Triangle. But for the last two months, that's exactly what I've been doing. I may be a chicken, but I am not ungrateful. And I'm more determined than ever to become the woman Preston deserves. If that means copying down every word that comes out of Kendi's mouth at small group and filling every journal I own with scriptures - and notes, and Christian artists, and musicians, and podcasts - then I'll do it.

I've signed up to volunteer for the fall festival in a couple of months, as well as the women's conference happening the following spring. I asked Kendi for a membership application for the church, and he'll get that to me tonight. Things are progressing well, despite the secrets piling up.

"Does anyone have anything to add before we wrap up our study of Luke?" Kendi scans the group, and his eyes land on me. I resist the urge to slump in my seat, but I don't volunteer, either. The book of Luke is full of stories that mostly confuse me. I enjoy listening to the group discussions, and I hope some of it is rubbing off on me, but I've found I have better success in conversations when I stick to mimicking the verses and thoughts of other people. Larry being the exception, of course.

"I really love the story of the tax collector," Asia chimes in. "It reminds me of how much God cares about us, to the point where he's willing to overlook our faults when we come to him with a sincere heart. Imagine if we had to get ourselves right before coming to God. No one could ever manage it."

"I grew up in a church where you couldn't even be baptized without proving your Christianity first." Zev's voice is soft as he speaks. When I first started coming, he was always quiet. But in the months since, he's become more vocal.

"What do you mean, 'prove your Christianity'?" I ask. I wonder if that's something Kendi's left out, or if I've missed something. Is there a test I'm going to have to take?

Zev shrugs. "If you had a tattoo, you had to get rid of it. You had to quit smoking and drinking, and you couldn't wear shorts or flip flops to service. Things like that. And if anyone in the church spoke against you being baptized, they wouldn't let you do it."

"Oh." Well those sound easy enough to navigate, and I've already been baptized. Sort of. If there are any tests like that, I should be able to skate by.

"But none of those things really proves your Christianity, and that's not what baptism is about anyway." Zev shakes his head. "I've really enjoyed this study of Luke and being in this small group, because it's helped me to better understand my faith. It's not about what you do. Living a certain way isn't how we are saved, and it doesn't justify us for baptism. Accepting Jesus and what he did for us on the cross is what saves us. Baptism is a celebration of what's already been done by Him, not what's been done by us. And living right is a result of our salvation, not a prerequisite for it."

I nod along with everyone else, pretending the queasy feeling in my stomach isn't there. Kendi leads the group in prayer, and we dismiss for the evening. I hang back as everyone shuffles out, but when Kendi looks up at me, I feel like running.

"Hey, Cherise. I have the membership application in my office. Give me a few minutes to clean up, and I'll get it to you, okay?"

"Okay." I nod and watch him take the additional folding chairs out of his living room and place them in a side closet. I'd help, but I just got a new gel set and I'm not taking any chances.

"You okay, Cherise?" Kendi pauses and waits for my response.

I nod again, but the pit of my stomach twists tighter than the Bantu knots on the top of my head.

"You seem a little off tonight." Kendi returns to the living room and slides into a lounge chair. "Wanna talk about it?"

"Oh, I'm fine." I flash a bright smile, but it slips as soon as I make eye contact with him. I avert my gaze, searching for something to do. There are still cups on the table, so I start there. "I'll just take these to the sink."

"Sure." Kendi stays in the chair a minute longer, watching me gather the cups. "If you're nervous about becoming a member, I want you to know you've got nothing to worry about."

"Pfft." I scoff. "Why would I be nervous?"

He shrugs. "I dunno. Sometimes big decisions, like getting baptized or joining the church, can feel really scary."

My mouth goes dry, and I swallow. "Uh, yeah. Okay."

"What's got you worried, Cherise?"

I guess he's not gonna let this go. But I'm not really sure what's got me so pent up tonight. Things are going well with Preston, and I'm starting to not hate being around Kendi, too. I'm still a little lost in bible study, but I'm managing okay.

Maybe that's it. Maybe I'm waiting for things to fall apart. For that proverbial shoe to drop. Every time I find a sliver of happiness, something happens to stomp it out of existence.

"Cherise?"

I clear my throat and sigh. "I'm okay, Kendi. Really."

He stands, and though I refuse to make eye contact, I know he's looking at me. Waiting for me to fess up. But Kendi has a way of drawing things out of people, and once I start talking, I'm afraid I won't stop. The last thing I need is to slip up and say the wrong thing. I'm no stranger to self-sabotage, and I know when to keep my mouth shut. Most of the time.

Eventually, Kendi heads to his office and brings me the membership application. He hands it to me with a look, and I accept it with a dip of my head. "Thanks."

"When you're finished filling everything out just get it back to me, and I'll take it to the church secretary for processing. Any questions, I'm just a call or text away, okay?"

"I got it." I inch my way to the door, apprehensive once I realize that Kendi is right behind me. I turn toward him and raise the application packet. "Thanks again for this."

"I'll walk you to your car."

"Oh, no need."

"I want to talk to you about something."

Another knot forms in my gut. What could he possibly want to talk to me about? "Okay," is all I manage to squeak out. He follows me through the hall and out of the apartment complex. We're halfway to the parking lot before I realize he hasn't said a word.

When we reach my car, he clears his throat. "Can I ask you something, Cherise?"

"Sure," I mumble as I rifle through my purse in search of my keys.

"Why was Preston the only person at your baptism?"

My hands start to shake. Which makes finding my keys a hard task, but I concentrate on the dark recesses of my bag and try to conjure up an acceptable answer to Kendi's question. What's his game? What should I say? I need time to think. "Preston wasn't the only one there. There were a lot of other people there."

"That's not what I mean. Preston was the only one there for you."

I know what he meant, but I'm still at a loss. Luckily Kendi's willing to fill in the gap.

"I've noticed that you always come to church alone or with Preston. And you never mention any friends or family when we have discussions. So, I've been thinking about why."

I'm caught. He's figured it out and now I'm going to have to—

"Cherise, breathe." Kendi's hand on my shoulder pulls me out of my head for a moment. "This isn't an interrogation. I just want to check in with you."

I nod. "Okay. But I told you I'm fine."

"Your face says otherwise. And normally, I wouldn't pry, but you've got me a little worried. There's usually one of two scenarios in cases like yours."

"What do you mean 'cases like mine'?"

"Cases where you either deflect or share something vague about your family and friends during discussions. I've been leading groups a long time, and I could be reading it wrong, but I'm worried that you're not sharing that part of yourself because you're ashamed of them. Or maybe, because they're ashamed of you."

I blink. "What?"

"Cherise, your faith is nothing to be ashamed of. If you're afraid to tell your family and friends about it, I want you to know that you've made the best decision you'll ever make. You belong to God's family now. And being in the family of God is worth more than the approval of anyone else in our lives.

"I also want you to know that sharing your faith with others is a necessary part of our spiritual growth. None of us has a perfect life. Families are messy. Friendships are complicated. People are lost. But they're all welcome in God's house, baggage and all. So don't be ashamed of them, and don't be ashamed of you. We're here to bear one another's burdens. Even if those burdens are the people closest to us. You can talk to us about them, and invite them to join us, too."

I can't imagine inviting anyone I know to church. Especially not my family. No, it's best to keep them tucked away and hidden. But I nod at Kendi anyway. "Thanks. I really appreciate that."

"If you ever want to talk, I'm here. I hope you know that?"

"Yep. Well, I better get going, before it gets too late." I finally locate my keys and retreat to the safety of my vehicle. Though he's way off base, Kendi's heart is in the right place. Knowing that makes my already pretzeled gut knot up even further. This guilt is going to give me ulcers.

But I made a promise to Preston, and to myself, that I'd become the Christian woman that he needs. If I'm going to do this, I have to do it right. I'm not bringing Shantell to small group, but I could bring her up in a discussion or two. Ask for prayer for Adrian, whose biopsy has been rescheduled twice already. I might not be a perfect Christian, but I can swing being a passable one. Probably.

Maybe?

38

Happy Birthday To Me?

I'm so grateful for my brown skin. The number of times heat has passed through my cheeks since dating Preston is as high as the annual hot air balloon festival. Tonight is no exception.

Last year's birthday was a complete bust, but this year I have Preston Karrington Jones at my side, and he's pulling out all the stops. He sent flowers to the clinic, took me out for lunch, and is currently crooning in octaves I didn't know existed from the stage of my favorite restaurant. They typically host a live band, but Preston called in a few favors so he could serenade his sweetheart on her birthday. His words.

He's looking right at me as he sings the lyrics to his favorite song, Everything I Do by Bryan Adams. I've got to admit, though it's not my typical flavor, the song is growing on me. This night, this feeling, is everything. Preston loves me. Really, really loves me. Our relationship is proof that a happily ever after is possible for me. That Garrett wasn't my last chance and Calvin wasn't the next best thing. Preston's love is a gift. One I won't take for granted. I'm holding on with both hands and never letting go.

The dining room applauds as Preston wraps up the song. A few feminine eyes follow him to our table, but his eyes are only on me. He kisses me, long and deep, and I swoon a little.

"I love you," he whispers in my ear before sliding next to me. I smile as the waitress appears.

"What can I get you to drink tonight?" she asks. "We've got a tipsy pumpkin special for the season, made with pumpkin syrup, bourbon, bitters and a dash of spice. Or if you're not a fan of pumpkin, the spooky mimosa is a crowd favorite. It's served with absinthe mist."

"Ooh," I squeal. I've been wanting to try one of their seasonal drinks. I wonder if Preston will mind if I order both? I open my mouth to answer, then shut it, remembering who I'm with. Preston doesn't drink, and as far as he knows, neither do I.

"Lemonade for me," Preston says. "And for the birthday girl, whatever she'd like." He winks at me and I die a little inside. I really want that tipsy pumpkin, but I don't want him to think less of me.

"Those specials sound lovely, but I'm going to go with a lemonade, too," I say.

"You sure?" Preston pushes the menu toward me. "It's your birthday, Cherise."

"I like lemonade," I say. "It's fine."

"Yeah, but your eyes lit up when she was talking about that pumpkin drink, and I'm sure they can make it virgin, right?" Preston looks at the waitress for confirmation, but she shakes her head.

"Actually they can't. Sorry." She holds up her hands.

"Wow, really?" Preston frowns.

"It's served in an actual pumpkin, and I don't know the alchemy, but the alcohol is what makes the drink work."

"Oh, it's alchemy." Preston nods. "And the spooky mimosa? You can't make that virgin either?"

"It's basically orange juice without the alcohol." She shrugs. "You want orange juice, birthday girl?"

"Lemonade it is!" I try to let out a good-natured chuckle, but I'm not sure I pull it off.

"Cherise, you don't have to drink lemonade on your birthday. I'm sure they've got other drinks on the menu."

As a frequent patron of this establishment, I've tried pretty much everything they have. And anything without alcohol is essentially trash. I don't have the heart to tell Preston that, though, so I let him scan the drink menu and pester the waitress for a few more minutes.

"You guys don't have any milkshakes or anything?" he asks.

"Milk based drinks are seasonal, so what you see on the menu is what we've got."

Preston looks at me and I force a smile. "Preston, it's really okay. Lemonade is fine."

He sighs. "Alright. Then lemonade for both of us."

Our drinks arrive, followed by some of the best wings in Raleigh, but I have to force all my smiles. I told Preston the lemonade was fine, but I don't know. I guess a part of me wanted him to secretly order a tipsy pumpkin for me, anyway.

But why would he? The Cherise he knows doesn't drink. Maybe if I ordered it, he wouldn't mind. But I've worked so hard to stay in sync with him, and I don't want to screw things up. Not now. Denying this small piece of myself shouldn't be so hard. Preston shows up for me in the ways that really matter. I can give up this one thing for him. It may be my birthday, but really, it's just one night.

39

Broken Bits

I'll turn in my membership application as soon as Kendi wraps up bible study tonight. It's been sitting in my purse for months, and I don't know why I've been dragging my feet on it. Kendi's reminded me multiple times. Maybe it's guilt. Maybe it's fear. Maybe it's a little bit of both?

I wait until everyone's trickled out before approaching him.

"Everything okay, Cherise?" He frowns at me, and I fiddle around in my purse.

"Everything's great. I just need to give you this." I hand him the membership packet. "Sorry it took so long to get it back to you."

"No problem." He sets it down on his coffee table, then looks back at me. "So, everything's good?"

I nod. "Yeah, everything's fine."

"And you and Preston? Everything's going good there, too?"

Don't panic, Cherise. "Why?" I ask the question in what I hope is a normal pitch. Kendi never asks about me and Preston. "Did he say something?"

Kendi hesitates a hair too long before saying, "No. Uh, no. Everything's fine." It isn't like Kendi to lie, but his body language is too fidgety to miss. Whether he's lying to spare my feelings or to keep Preston's confidence is anyone's guess. But he's definitely hiding something.

"What is it?"

Kendi opens his mouth, then closes it.

A cold sweat breaks out on my palms. Kendi knows something I don't about Preston and me. But what could it be? I've been so careful the last few months. I've cut down on squad time to focus on our relationship. I've been doing extra bible study, and I've even started working on a plan to tell Preston the truth about my divorced parents. That lie's been allowed to run wild too long already, and it's not the kind of secret I can keep. My parents are outside the limits of my control.

In the meantime, I'm doing everything I can to change myself and be the woman Preston deserves. But none of that matters if he's having doubts about us.

"Come on, Kendi." I try to keep the tremor out of my voice. "If something's wrong, you could at least give me a heads up."

Kendi's eyes go wide. "No, it's nothing like that. Sorry. It's nothing, really. Nothing for you to worry about, anyway."

"Oh."

"I'll make sure I get this application to the church office and get the process started, okay?"

I exhale and shrug. "Sure. Yeah. Great."

"Okay, great."

"And you're sure Preston didn't say anything about us?"

Kendi shakes his head. "I'm sorry I said anything. I didn't mean to make you worry. I was just checking in."

"Okay." I say the word slowly, waiting to see if Kendi will expound further. He doesn't. "Well, I'm off, then."

"Good night, Cherise."

I leave Kendi's apartment feeling more anxious than ever. Preston definitely said something to Kendi about me. But Kendi wouldn't tell me not to worry if it were something I should worry about, right?

He's not the meathead I originally thought he was, but he's not exactly the greatest communicator, either. Unless it's related to the Holy Trinity, that is.

I get a text from Shantell with wine emojis, but I send her a text back with a frownie face. I've got to memorize the notes from this evening's study, then jump on a video call with Preston. He's been out of town at a conference all week, and I don't want to miss his call.

Shantell sends me a crying emoji, followed by a string of inappropriate emojis rounded out with a middle finger. I roll my eyes and don't bother to respond. Seconds later, Shantell's face pops up on my phone screen. She calls again when I don't pick up, and three more times by the time I get home.

Just as I'm about to set up my laptop to call Preston, she calls again.

"Yes?" I answer after the fourth ring.

"What up, Tellie Tubbie?"

Of all the nicknames I've been given over the years, I hate this one the most. And Shantell never uses it unless she's pissed off. "Why are you blowing up my phone, Shantell?"

"Haven't you been getting Adrian's messages?"

I scroll through my phone, searching for the missed messages. "I don't see anything from Adrian."

"Well, maybe she would have messaged you if you actually answered your phone these days."

I sigh. "You know I've been busy, Shantell."

"Too busy to care if your friend has cancer? She got the results back today."

It seems no matter what I do, my stomach is determined to be unsettled. Shantell's words finally click, and I feel two inches tall. "Adrian's test results. For the biopsy?"

"Yeah. Her results are in the app, but she was too scared to look, and she missed the doctor's call. She wants us to look together. Tonight."

My laptop begins to chime, and Preston's avatar pops up. "Shantell, I can't tonight. Preston is calling, and–"

"You can call him back tomorrow."

"I haven't talked to him all week, and his schedule's been really tight. Tonight's our anniversary, and–"

"Cherise, are you kidding me right now?"

"Tell Adrian I'm sorry, okay?"

Shantell begins to say something, but it's cut off by Adrian's voice."

"You know what, Cherise? If I have to explain to you why bringing your sorry butt over here is more important than chatting with your boyfriend, then frankly, you can stay right there."

"Adrian?"

"I thought we were friends. Guess I was wrong."

"Adrian, I'm really sor–" The line disconnects, and I stare at the phone. This is really bad. I didn't even know Adrian was capable of raising her voice.

My computer chimes again, and I answer Preston's call. "Hey, Cherise." The way his face lights up when he sees me fills me with warmth.

"Hey, Preston."

"It's so good to see your face. I've missed you."

I nod. "Yeah, me too."

Preston tilts his head to one side. "Everything okay? I'm sorry I've been so busy the last few days. I left the evening session early to try and catch you today. The time difference over here on the west coast makes it a little tricky."

"Yeah. Um, Preston? I actually have to go."

His face clouds, and it makes my heart break. "Oh. I'm sorry. Did I get the time wrong? I thought we were scheduled for right after small group."

"We were, but something came up, and I have to go."

"Oh. Okay." He clears his throat. "I'm sorry to be out of town on our anniversary. Do you have to leave right away?"

I close my eyes, as if that will minimize the hurt in his voice. "Yeah."

"Alright. Well, I'll see you when I get back."

His statement sounds more like a question. I want to reassure him, but I don't know how to explain it. I don't talk to Preston about Shantell and Adrian. A few breadcrumbs in small group is one thing, but if I share my friends with Preston, he'll ask questions. Then, he'll want to meet them, and then Shantell will say something out of pocket. It's better to keep these parts of my life separate.

"Cherise?"

I nod my head and smile. "Of course. I'll see you when you get back."

"Okay. I love you."

"I love you, too."

I end the call and grab my keys. Shantell's place is a 20-minute drive from my house, and Adrian's is 15 in the opposite direction. I don't know where the two of them are, so I try Adrian's place first. I get no answer when I ring the doorbell, so I call Adrian's phone. No answer there, either. When I call Shantell, it's the same. I ring Adrian's bell again. Still no answer. I hop back into my car and head to Shantell's.

By the time I'm at her front steps, an hour has passed, and I still can't get either of them on the phone. I curse Raleigh's Friday night traffic and press Shantell's doorbell. Since she's my cousin, and I know it will drive her nuts, I ring it a million times in a row.

My strategy works, because I hear her stomp toward the door. She swings it open and scowls at me. "You've got a lot of nerve, little girl."

I take a step back as Shantell approaches, hands on her hips and fire in her eyes. She's not the type to swing on me, but I'm not the type to take chances, either.

"What's wrong? Did Preston not answer your call?"

"He called me, but–"

"But what?"

"I told him I'd see him tomorrow. Look, I'm sorry."

"Yeah, what else is new?"

I wait a beat. "How's Adrian?"

"How do you think, Cherise?"

"Shantell, I know I messed up."

"That's not the problem. Everybody messes up. You made a choice. And that choice was Preston. You chose him over your best friend. Which is already sad enough, but the fact that you put him over everybody, including yourself, is just pathetic."

I let out a laugh, but her words strike a nerve. And I guess there's some truth to the old adage about hurting people. "That's rich, coming from you. The person who literally launches herself at every man that breathes, because she's got daddy issues."

Shantell points her finger at me. "You can go to hell." She turns around and walks back inside, slamming the door shut behind her.

I stare at the closed door a long time before I finally go back to my car. We've had fights before, but Shantell and I have always had a quiet agreement between us. Our broken pieces aren't weapons we use to wound each other. Shantell's relationship with her dad is one of those broken pieces, and those words never should have left my mouth. But they're out now.

And I'm not sure how to take them back.

40

Big Mama's House

I haven't stepped foot in Big Mama's house since I was a kid. I'm not sure what occasion led me to darken the 'Blessed' welcome mat at her front door last, but I do remember holding a casserole in my hands. I held on tight, a towel pressed between my fingers and the warm dish. Mom and Dad stood right behind me.

On the surface, the casserole looked edible. A beautiful, hand painted porcelain dish on the outside, covered by a glass top with large, curving leaves carved into it. A golden, cheesy crust gleamed proudly just under the lid. But the casserole came from my mother's kitchen, and the moment Big Mama laid her eyes on Mom's humble offering, her nose tilted into the air.

"Set it over there, Cherise."

Over There is Big Mama code for out of the way. A large, sturdy table sat in the middle of Big Mama's dining room, and the smells coming from the covered dishes made my mouth water. Brunswick stew, potato soup, fried chicken, homemade cornbread, creamy mac and cheese, greens I knew would send me straight to heaven. The table practically groaned with the weight.

But the steady oak held fast and, with a little shuffling, I could have squeezed Mom's dish in. But Big Mama had banished it to Over There. To a deserted, uncovered table with paper products, empty pots, a stack of aluminum pans and a goopy, gray pot of something I couldn't identify.

The tension at my back as Mom watched me set her dish Over There could have suffocated the whole room. No argument followed, just a succession of sniffs and sighs. I joined the sea of people flowing in and out of Big Mama's backyard and pretended to enjoy myself. Pretended that the argument I heard that morning had just been Mom and Dad letting off steam. Divorce came up every once in a while, in the heat of an argument or two, but things always calmed down eventually.

The one silver lining I could always rely on at Big Mama's house was Shantell. She'd corner me and force me to listen to her gossip about all of our cousins. Sometimes we were bold and would sneak into the kitchen to get first dibs on Big Mama's signature dessert – her banana pudding.

If I'd known it would be my last taste, I would have sprung for more than a spoonful that day. Mom and Dad had a big fight in the yard, in front of Big Mama. Things got so heated that Big Mama told my mother not to set foot in her house again. Mom never did. Which, by default, meant neither did I.

I wasn't unwelcome, per se. But my absence seemed to make little difference to Dad's side of the family.

Now, I'm standing on top of Big Mama's welcome mat. It's worn with age, but I can still make out all the letters in 'Blessed' if I squint. I carry no dish in my hand, I know better than to try. Big Mama has a way of speaking without words that leaves you thoroughly spoken to. I don't come empty handed, though. I've got two bottles of sparkling grape juice, one white, one red. It's the only kind of vine Big Mama accepts in her house, and I need to win her over if I'm going to convince my cousin to start talking to me again.

I ring the bell, not an easy feat with bottles in my small hands, and Big Mama opens the door with a wide grin.

"Cherise?" The smile dips a little as she looks past me.

"It's just me, Big Mama. Mom's not coming."

"Hmph. As if she'd ever darken my door again. Miss Linda Williams is too good for this family." Big Mama huffs, and then her eyes find mine again. "It's good to see you, Baby Girl. Come on inside out of the cold."

I follow her through the foyer and into the dining room. Big Mama's tables are always bountiful, but Thanksgiving is on another level. She takes her matriarchal role very seriously, and there's not a cousin within a hundred-mile radius that isn't welcome. It seems all of them are present. Her backyard, the living room, the family room, and the basement below us rumble with the sounds of laughter and conversation.

Big Mama scrutinizes my offering and chuckles. "So sweet of you to bring something, Cherise. I like the red better than the white, but at least it's consumable. You've got more sense than your mama, I see."

I ignore the dig at Mom. "Is Shantell here?"

"Mhm. She's down in the basement cackling."

I make my way downstairs, searching for the blue of Shantell's new extensions. She and Adrian still aren't talking to me, and I'm not sure how much more I can take.

We spot each other at the same time, and for a few seconds, she looks happy to see me. The look is quickly replaced by a scowl and she turns away, looking far more interested in Great Uncle Jerry's birdwatching story than any normal person should.

"So, you see, the cardinal is the state bird for North Carolina, but the real beauty of the state is the goldfinch."

I clear my throat. "Shantell."

She ignores me and leans closer to Uncle Jerry. "That's really interesting. Uncle Jerry, how many did you spot last Sunday?"

Uncle Jerry squints in concentration. "Well, now, it's gotten colder, so you don't see too many goldfinches around. But I did spy one way up high in a tree at Umstead. Almost missed it. There were a few chickadees, and I thought I spotted an indigo bunting, but it turned out to just be a blue jay. I must be getting old. No proper birdwatcher would ever confuse the two, and I'm embarrassed to say I did."

I clear my throat again. "Shantell."

"What about ducks? How many kinds of ducks are there in North Carolina?"

Uncle Jerry lights up at this. "Oh, well now, let me see. You've got the wood duck, which has copper feathers with a white border, and–"

"Uncle Jerry, I'm so sorry to interrupt." I step between the two. "But I've got to borrow Shantell for a bit."

I snatch her by the wrist and pull her away from Uncle Jerry. Shantell scowls at me, pulling back, but I keep tugging until we're in the privacy of one of the basement rooms. "Can we talk now?"

Shantell crosses her arms. "Excuse you, but I was already having a conversation."

"You do not want to spend your whole Thanksgiving talking about birds, Shantell."

"Well, I don't want to talk to *you* about anything."

"You're a liar. You're over a foot taller than me and twice as strong. If you really didn't want to talk, I wouldn't have been able to get you in here."

Shantell sniffs, but she uncrosses her arms.

"Shanty, I'm sorry." I step closer to her. "I realized I was being ridiculous as soon as Adrian hung up on me, and I came over right away."

Shantell frowns. "You took over an hour to get to my house."

"Only because I went to Adrian's house first. And then I got stuck in concert traffic, and the downtown traffic on Fridays is a nightmare."

Shantell shakes her head. "Whatever. You should have taken the highway instead."

"I know, but the left turn is blocked by that big tree near Adrian's house, and you know I'm not an aggressive driver."

Shantell sighs. "I keep telling you to nose your car out when you're on that street. It's the only way people will let you in. So long as they're more than 20 feet away, they'll slow down."

"But I can't see that far down because of the tree."

Shantell clucks at me. "My poor, short cousin."

I rub my shoulders. It's a lot colder in the basement than it is upstairs.

"My poor, short, anemic, stupid cousin." Shantell sighs. "Where's your jacket?"

"Upstairs."

"You know the heat doesn't work well down here. You should have just kept it on."

"I forgot. And it's hot upstairs." I wait a beat, fearful to ask the next question, but aching to know the answer. "About Adrian? Her test results? Did you look at them?"

"Pfft. Wouldn't you like to know."

"I do." I hiccup, and take a step forward. "I really want to know. I want to be there for her. Especially if... if..."

Shantell's face softens and she sits on the bed, patting the space beside her. I sit next to her and wipe my eyes with my fingertips. "Oh, goodness, girl." Shantell grabs a box of tissue from somewhere and hands me a few sheets. "Honestly, you don't deserve to know."

"I know," I cry.

Shantell seems satisfied with this reply. "Since you're begging, I guess I can tell you that Adrian's results were inconclusive."

"Inconclusive?" I blow my nose. "What does that mean?"

"It means they have to do another biopsy."

"Oh. Poor Adrian! Is she okay?"

"No. She's a mess, which is saying a lot for Adrian. She's the least messy between us. But she's scared." Shantell sighs. "And she misses her best friend."

I perk up at that. "Really?"

She nods her head. "Yeah. She wanted to call you the next day, but I talked her out of it."

"What? Why?"

"Because you deserved to get iced out, Cherise. Look, I love you. I really do. But you can't treat the people you love like they're expendable."

"I know. I'm sorry."

"Good. You should be."

"Truce?"

Shantell taps her chin with her finger. "Maybe. But it'll cost you more than a little groveling to get back into our good graces."

"I've got boxed wine in my trunk."

"God bless you. I'll text Adrian now."

41

Kind of A Big Deal

I love December. I mean, it's cold and it's gray and sometimes, especially in the south, the weather is completely nuts. But between the Christmas lights and the cinnamon smells and the tiny towns and store displays, I can't help but feel lighter. I've got some vacation time coming up at the end of the month, Adrian and Shantell are finally speaking to me again, and I'm looking forward to planning something special with Preston. I'm not sure what his traditions are, but I'd like us to at least exchange a gift and have a nice dinner. Dancing would be fun, too.

Friday night, I skip small group to cook for him. He rings my bell and the first thing I see when I open the door is a basket of red roses.

"These are gorgeous!" I gush as I take the basket, which is heavier than I calculated. Preston has to take them from me and carry them to my living room.

"They've got nothing on you." Preston brushes his lips against my cheek as he sets down the basket. As soon as his hands are free, he wraps them around my waist and pulls me close. "I've missed you, you know."

"Yeah?"

He moves in for another kiss, this one long and lingering, and I wrap my arms around his neck. We come up for air eventually, thanks to the oven timer, and he plants a final kiss on my nose. "What's for dinner tonight?"

"It's a surprise."

"Yeah? That's funny. I have a surprise for you, too."

I smile on my way to the kitchen. "Ooh. What kind of surprise?"

"I'll tell you after dinner."

I open the oven door and pull out the baking dish. A loud hiss of steam whines from the bird when I slide a knife into it. I don't think it's supposed to make that sound.

I wrap the top of the chicken in foil to rest and check on the wild rice and mushrooms simmering on the stove. A plume of dark smoke starts me gagging, and I quickly replace the lid and turn off the eye as Preston saunters into the kitchen.

"Everything okay?"

I smile and nod. "Uh huh. Everything's great!"

He hesitates a moment, then nods. "Okay."

Forty minutes later, I pay the pizza guy, tipping him extra for the fast delivery. It isn't what I wanted, but I'd rather serve him edible food than force him to choke down dry chicken and burnt rice.

Preston says grace, and we eat greasy pizza on fancy plates, because I still have high aspirations for the evening. "Sorry about dinner, Preston."

He chuckles. "No worries, Cherise. Everyone has off days."

I bet his mother's never had an off day in her life. But I keep that thought to myself. "I actually wanted to talk to you about something. Christmas is coming up, and I wanted to see if you had any plans for the holiday?"

Preston freezes mid-bite. "Um, actually." He sets down his pizza. "I was going to talk to you about that tonight." He smiles, but in a nervous way. Like he's not sure how I'll react.

"What is it?"

He clears his throat. Takes my hand. Rubs it in slow, distracting circles. "Cherise, you and I have been through a lot together. And I think we've grown a lot as a couple. So, I thought, maybe, this Christmas we could go on a trip together."

"A trip?"

He nods. "I know you usually spend Christmas at the Biltmore with your family."

I nearly choke on my soda. "Um, yeah."

"So, I booked us a room there the weekend of Christmas."

My world starts spinning. "This is your surprise?"

He looks stricken. "You think it's a terrible idea."

I shake my head. "No! I love your surprise. I actually wanted to talk to you about spending Christmas together, so this is perfect."

Preston's grin nearly splits his face, and he leans forward and kisses me. "I love you, Cherise Michelle Williams." He whispers this in my ear before moving back to his seat.

The words send a shiver up my spine and down again. Preston wants to spend a weekend with me. This is good news.

I can't wait to tell my squad.

SHANTELL POPS OPEN another bottle of champagne as we celebrate Adrian's test results. I lift my glass to partake in the libations. Adrian does the same, and as soon as Shantell refills her glass, we clink them all together.

"How's it feel to be cancer-free?" Shantell does a little dance and Adrian giggles.

"Fantastic." Adrian sips from her glass slowly. "I'm so happy I could burst." And she does. Shantell and I coo at her as she drowns our shirts in a puddle of tears. It feels good to have both women at my side. And I'm beyond grateful for Adrian's good news.

"I don't know what I'd do without you both." Adrian sniffs and shoos us away while she blows her nose. "But enough about me. What's going on with you two?"

"Well, we're finally breaking ground on a new daycare." Adrian and I cheer at Shantell's news. "It's been a long time coming, but it's gonna be a lot of work on the front end. You may not see me as much come January."

Adrian laughs. "Cherise and I won't let you drown yourself in work. We'll kidnap you if we have to."

"That's right!" I chime in.

Shantell gives me a pointed look and smirks. "Fair enough. And if you flake on us again, Adrian and I are pulling up on you, you got that? Don't forget, she's got bricks in her trunk."

I nod. "Yes, and one day we're gonna unpack that. But I promise I'll never flake on you ladies again. I love you."

"Aw, we love you too." Shantell and Adrian come in for a hug, and we awkwardly try to balance our drinks in the process. "So, Cherise, spill it."

Adrian grins at me. "Yup. It's plain as the nose on your face. You've got something to tell us."

I nod, unable to hold back any longer. "Preston wants to spend Christmas together. At the Biltmore. For a weekend!" I press my knuckles against my face and squeal.

Shantell's lips draw into an O, and she and Adrian exchange a glance.

"What? What's that look for?"

"Preston's finally making his move." Shantell gives an approving nod. "Took him long enough."

"What are you..." My face goes hot at the lascivious look on Shantell's face. "Oh. You think?"

Both Adrian and Shantell nod.

Adrian snorts. "I guess the celibacy's over."

It's strange that this didn't occur to me sooner. I shake my head. "No, I don't think so. I mean, he and I haven't discussed that subject in a long time."

Shantell taps her chin. "Okay. I need details. How many rooms did he book?"

"Just the one as far as I know."

"And how many beds in that one room?"

"That doesn't mean—"

"And how many nights are we talking?"

"Friday to Sunday, so two nights."

"Two nights, plus one room, divided by one bed. Adrian, what does that add up to?"

"That adds up to mischief, Shantell."

"Yes, ma'am. The sinful kind." Shantell giggles.

I press my fingers to my temples. "Oh. I need to prepare, don't I?"

"Don't worry, Cuz. I know it's been a minute, but I've got you."

Shantell runs down a list of necessities for me to pack, then agrees to text me the list so I don't forget anything. I'm not totally convinced that this weekend will be anything but chaste, but I can do my own math. And if my calculations are correct, something's bound to happen. Something big.

42

Incomplete

Kendi's apartment is warm, a fact I am grateful for. It's a stark contrast to the frigid cold front stirring up outside. It's not uncommon for Raleigh to be cold mid-December, but the biting, icy shockwaves of winter don't usually hit until late January. Larry and Pam are absent this evening. A few others didn't make it out tonight, either, leaving a smaller, more intimate group. Kendi, Asia, Zev, and me.

"This will be the last meeting until after the holidays," Kendi announces. "I'll be spending Christmas with my mom, but if any of you needs me, I'm just a text away." He opens his bible and smiles. "Since it's a really small group tonight, I thought we'd go around the room and read our favorite verse or passage of scripture and talk about it a little. I'll go first. My favorite passage of scripture comes from Psalm 139. I'll just read a few verses from the NIV.

'You have searched me, Lord, and you know me. You know when I sit and when I rise; you perceive my thoughts from afar. You discern my going out and my lying down; you are familiar with all my ways. Before a word is on my tongue you, Lord, know it completely. You hem me in behind and before, and you lay your hand upon me. Such knowledge is too wonderful for me, too lofty for me to attain.'

Kendi closes his bible and looks up at us. "What I love most about this passage is how it reminds me that God knows me best. Better than any other person ever will. Better than I even know myself. He knows the secrets I carry, and the failures weighing me down, and he chooses to love me anyway. So when I mess up, or when I'm struggling with something, I read this verse and remember that I am thoroughly known and genuinely loved by the God of the universe."

I blink, surprised by the tears welling in my eyes. It's a beautiful passage. And how many times have I wanted the same thing? For someone to know me and love me? Really love me? I have that with Preston.

Except it's a lie.

I swipe at my eyes and listen as Asia shares her verse. "My favorite comes from 2 Corinthians 5:17. It says *'Therefore, if anyone is in Christ, he is a new creation; old things have passed away; behold, all things have become new.'* What I love about this verse is the promise. That we're not stuck with our old, selfish, sinful selves. God promises to make us new. It's something I've really struggled with over the years. Falling back into old habits, wondering if I'm really saved, or if maybe it didn't take the first time around. I understand now that it's a process, but I look forward to what Jesus is going to do in me, to change me from the inside out."

Zev nods and glances my way. "Hey, Cherise, you mind if I go next?"

"No, not at all." I have no idea what verse to pick. I've memorized a lot of them, but I couldn't say that any one of them is my favorite.

"My verse is from Romans 5:8, which says *'But God demonstrates His own love toward us, in that while we were still sinners, Christ died for us.'* Growing up the way I did, I always had it backwards. I thought I had to work to be worthy. But God loved us before we were worthy, and that's freed me in so many ways. It's changed my whole perspective of faith and helped me to be more gracious toward others."

I nod my head, still scrambling for a verse. I want to impress the group, show them I'm one of them, but I'm drawing a blank. A silence settles over us as they patiently wait. But I'm at a loss.

Finally, Kendi clears his throat. "Cherise, do you want to share a verse?"

I laugh. "Um, I'm having trouble picking. There's so many great ones, you know?"

He nods. "What about from some of our recent studies? Anything in particular that stuck out for you? A story, a verse? It can be anything at all." Kendi stares at me as if he's searching for something.

"Um, I liked all the stories, really. It's hard to pick just one." I plaster on a smile to mask my slowly rising terror. I'm afraid to open my mouth again. I know something stupid will come out if I do. Kendi keeps staring at me, waiting. My eyes shift to Asia and Zev, hoping they'll throw me a lifeline, or a hint. *Something.* But they seem oblivious to the silent war playing out in front of them. Asia gives me an encouraging smile. Zev leans in, patiently waiting for my response.

I glance over at Kendi again. His gaze narrows, and then he straightens. "It's okay, Cherise. You don't have to share if you don't want to."

"Oh, it's not that. I'm just having a hard time picking."

Kendi nods, and his expression returns to something closer to friendly. But there's a tightness to his features that makes me feel as if I've disappointed him, somehow. Was this some kind of test? If so, I'm pretty sure I failed it.

"I've got presents for everyone." Kendi's voice is cheery and upbeat as he passes around small boxes. He hands me mine last, but as he says "Merry Christmas," our eyes catch. And there's that look again. This is going to drive me nuts.

Music and games follow, and since it's just the four of us, we end the night with a round of cards. Uno, to be precise.

"House rules?" Asia asks as she shuffles the gargantuan deck.

Kendi nods. "Two card penalty, stacking is legit, skips are personal. Any questions?" I have some, but I don't want to draw Kendi's attention to me any more than I need to.

TURNS OUT A FRIENDLY game of Uno with a Christian small group is cutthroat. I've only ever played Uno using the official rules, so Kendi's house rules trip me up. Between the draw two stacks, the draw four stacks, and the unrelenting skips I endure from both Kendi and Zev, I end up with 20 cards in my hand by the time Kendi drops his last one. I fare a little better in the second round, with only 19 cards in hand. I almost win the third round, but Asia calls Uno before I do, Zev skips me, then another round of merciless stacking puts my numbers back up to the double digits.

As I nurse a silent grudge against the boys for ganging up on me, Zev and Asia say their goodbyes by the door. I tuck my gift from Kendi into my pocket book and wait for a hole to open up so I can squeeze through it. Preferably without any more contact with Kendi for the rest of the year.

Asia dips out first, and I see my opening. But before I can slip out, Kendi taps my shoulder. "Cherise, you got a minute?"

Suspended in place, I consider pretending I didn't hear him and running out the door.

"Goodnight Cherise!" Zev waves at me. "Merry Christmas!"

"Merry Christmas, Zev!" I return an awkward wave of my own, mortified as he closes the door behind him. So much for running away.

"This will only take a minute."

I spin around on my heels, watching as Kendi pulls a stack of papers from the coffee table drawer. "Yeah? What's up?" I inch closer to the couch, but I keep standing. Easier to flee if I'm standing.

"I got a call from the church office this afternoon about your membership application. Looks like you left off some information."

"Oh." That's all? "What, did I forget my birthdate or something?"

"Uh, no." Kendi sits in his chair and points to the couch. "You can sit."

I lower myself onto the soft cushion. "I thought you said this wouldn't take long."

"It shouldn't be more than a minute or two." He shuffles through the pages. "So, the church secretary made a few notes. You left off the date of your conversion, and your testimony of faith is missing."

"Oh." I guess those parts weren't optional. "Well, I'm not exactly sure what they meant by that."

Kendi's not buying it, though. "I know sharing something so personal might be intimidating, Cherise, but you don't have anything to prove here. You don't have to give every detail, and you don't have to have some big, elaborate conversion story. Just whatever's most important about the day you gave your life to Christ."

"The actual date?" I bite my lip. "I don't remember the exact day."

He shrugs. "That's okay. Do you remember the month?" I don't answer right away, and Kendi scratches his head. "The year?"

"Last year." I blurt the words out before the line in the center of Kendi's forehead gets any deeper. "It was last year in the spring."

He scribbles something down on my application, I'm guessing the approximate date, then looks back at me. "Okay. Tell me about what happened?"

I squeeze the leather straps of my bag. "That day? Okay. Well, um. I was not doing great, obviously. I was lost, but then God found me. And so I became a Christian."

Kendi waits a beat, then rubs his chin. "Can you be any more specific than that? I mean, what happened? Who told you about Jesus? Were you alone? Was someone else involved? What was going on in your life at the time? What does your salvation mean to you?"

"You want the whole story, then?" He nods. I swallow. "Okay. Yeah. The whole story. Well, I was in a dark place. Um, a bar, actually."

"Okay." He begins writing.

"And I was singing that day, in the bar. My boyfriend and I had a fight backstage, and before I knew it, I was running away. I was scared, you know? I didn't know what to do. And so I hid in this church, and the women there kept me safe and told me about God. I sang with them, and I helped them to sing, and–"

"Cherise, hang on." I look up. Kendi has stopped writing. He's actually glaring at me now.

"What?"

"You're not taking this seriously."

"Of course I am. Why wouldn't I be?"

Kendi works the muscles in his jaw. "You're giving me the plot from Sister Act, for starters."

Crap. "No, I'm not." Kendi glares at me until I cave. "Okay, maybe there are a few parallels. But what difference does it make what I put on the application, anyway? I thought this was a formality."

"Cherise, if you're embarrassed about your story, don't be. I told you, it doesn't have to be perfect. It just needs to be yours. And I never try to push people to share their private thoughts before they're ready, but this is important. For the church process, and for you, too."

I fold my arms across my chest and sigh. "I don't know what to say."

"Is it because you're ashamed?"

I close my eyes and sigh in frustration. "Why do I have to have a conversion story, anyway? Isn't all of this a process? Why do I need to have a day that I made a decision? What if I just eased into salvation, instead?" I look up at Kendi, then immediately look away. I should have run when I had the chance.

Kendi's voice goes soft. "You don't know what to say, because you've never made a decision." It isn't a question. It's a statement. One I have no argument against. But that doesn't stop me from trying.

"I'm doing the work, Kendi. I'm coming to small group. I'm going to church. I'm reading the bible and trying my best to be a good person."

He stands and walks over to me. "Cherise, none of that matters if you've never made a decision to follow Christ. This isn't a system you can game, or a loyalty program where you can earn points for doing all the right things. It's about acknowledging your sins and coming to the realization that you need a savior. That you need Jesus. How is it you've been coming here for months and still missed this?" Kendi's fingers run through his hair, a clear sign of his frustration.

I stand on shaky legs so he won't tower over me quite so... toweringly. "I'm here, Kendi. I keep coming back because I choose to be here. Maybe I don't have the same faith you guys have, but I have just as much right to be here as everyone else."

"Sure, Cherise. You can come to the meetings, you can join in on the discussions, but until you actually give your life to Christ, you're not a Christian." Kendi freezes, then steps closer to me, an accusing look on his face. "Does Preston know about this?"

No, please don't connect those dots. "What difference does it make?" I stammer and stumble a bit on my words. "I'm doing all the things."

"Cherise, you've got to tell him."

I shrug. "As far as I'm concerned, there's nothing to tell."

Kendi's expression goes dark. "Is that why you've been coming here? To trick Preston into thinking you're something you're not?"

I shake my head. "No, of course not."

"Then why? Why did you come to me that day asking to join my small group?"

I cannot tell Kendi that what he thinks of me is true. Because the second I do, he'll tell Preston, and that will be the end of everything. I can't let that happen. "Because Preston had such good things to say about you. And I was curious. I wanted to know why he was so devoted to his faith." I keep talking, desperate to plead my case. "And now I know. I've listened to you and the others talk about your faith for months, and I want what all of you have. I'm trying my best, here."

Kendi studies me a moment, and then his face softens. "Preston thinks you're a believer, Cherise. He thinks the world of you, and you've been lying to him." Kendi takes my hands in his. "I know you're scared, but you have to tell him the truth."

I lower my head, and the tightness in my chest eases a bit. He isn't throwing me out, at least. "I know. And I will tell him. I promise."

"Don't wait, Cherise. Talk to him. Tonight."

I pull my hands away. "Tonight? Why tonight?"

"The sooner you do it, the better."

"But–"

"Cherise, I get why you didn't tell him. But Preston's my friend. My brother in Christ. I don't want to get involved, but if I have to–"

"If you don't want to get involved, then don't get involved." The ice in my voice surprises even me.

"Cherise."

"Where do you get off?" I match his glare with one of my own. "Just because you've decided to be miserable and alone doesn't mean you have the right to ruin everyone else's happiness."

"You *can't* keep lying to him."

"And I told you I won't! But Preston and I are happy, Kendi. We're really happy, and if you tell him, you'll ruin that. Not just for me, but for him."

"Your happiness isn't real if it's based on a lie, Cherise. This isn't about me. It's about you doing the right thing before he makes an even bigger mistake." Kendi pauses then, and shakes his head. "I can't just do nothing."

"You're not doing nothing!" I tug at my hair. "You're just giving me a little time."

"You've been dating for months, Cherise. You've had plenty of time already. If you were going to tell him, you would have done it by now."

"I will. I swear, Kendi. I love Preston, and I would never do anything to hurt him."

"If you wait any longer, that's exactly what you're gonna do."

I can't let him ruin this for me. If Kendi wants to fight me on this, well, I'm not above playing dirty. "Is this really about Preston? Because from where I'm standing, what happens between us has nothing to do with you."

"He's my friend."

"Larry and Pam are your friends, too. Do you butt into their relationship? Do you butt into anybody else's private business, Kendi? If I didn't know better, I'd think you were jealous."

Kendi scowls. "I'm not jealous."

"You've never liked us together. I think you *hate* the idea of us together."

He rubs his temples. "That's not true. I've always had my doubts, but that's not the same thing."

"Then prove it. Preston means the world to me, and I promise to do the right thing. But if you take that chance away from me, it's as good as saying you hate me."

Kendi stares at me a long time, then steps back. He grabs my membership application and hands it to me. "You should hold onto this. There's no point turning it in."

"Kendi."

"It's getting late. You should go."

"Please don't tell him."

Kendi stares at his feet, then rubs his jaw. "Preston loves you, Cherise. If you care about him like you say you do, you need to tell him."

"I swear it. I'll tell him."

"Don't wait until your trip. Tell him before you go. I won't lie for you, but I can give you until then."

I nod. "Thanks."

I walk myself out, but it isn't until I reach my car that I begin to wonder. How does Kendi know about our trip?

43

Just the Two of Us

I can't keep this up. Every day I wake up in a cold sweat, wondering if Kendi will break his promise and out me to Preston. Every time I get a text from Preston, a cold terror grips me by the throat. The relief I feel when I see it's just confirmation of a last-minute trip detail is eclipsed by the panic that follows.

Sooner or later, he's going to find out the truth. Kendi said he'd give me time, but he also said he wouldn't lie for me. My plan to become the woman Preston needs is still in effect, but unless I figure out a way to make Kendi think I've confessed without actually confessing, I'm screwed.

Tuesday, I see my last patient for the year. Natalie is as cheery as ever, the weakness in her ankle all but gone as she tumbles around on all my equipment. She won't need to come back after today. Strictly speaking, her mother could have ended her therapy months ago, but Natalie enjoys her sessions, and their insurance covers them, so her mother insisted they keep coming until the end of the year.

"Show me another of those famous tumbles!" I cheer Natalie on as she tucks her head to her chin and does a somersault on a blue mat. I clap and give her a high five when she stands, and she wiggles her ankle at me.

"See how strong it is?"

I nod. "Yup, super strong! You've been doing a great job with your stretches and exercises."

"Yup!"

"Well, I think all that hard work deserves a reward, don't you?"

She nods her head. "Yup!"

I tap my finger against my lips. "Well, why don't you take a peek underneath that cot over there by the wall?"

Natalie's face lights up, and she rushes over, dipping her head under the cot. "There's something under there! It's a present!" She looks back at me. "Can I get it?"

I nod, and she pulls out a box wrapped in red paper and a yellow bow. Her mouth stretches into a wide grin. "This is for me?"

"Yes, it is!"

She looks to her mother. "Can I open it now?" Her mom gives her a thumbs up, and Natalie tears open the paper, cooing with girlish shrieks as she sees the ballerina on the box.

"This is a music box, Natalie. And the ballerina on top is Misty Copeland. She worked really hard to become a ballerina, just like you worked hard to make that ankle strong. I want you to remember to always work hard for what you want and do your best, okay?"

"I will." Natalie squeals and hugs the box to her chest. "I love her!"

I smile as I walk Natalie and her mother out for the last time. Something in me aches at the sight of them hand in hand. How long before I have my own daughter?

"I'm going to miss that little girl." Tammie chuckles and stands to stretch. "Got any big plans for the holidays, Dr. Williams?"

I nod. "You could say that."

"Well, I hope they're filled with plenty of good things. I'll see you in the new year."

I finish out some paperwork in the office, then head over to Shantell's house for a pep talk. She swings open her door with flair when I ring the bell. "Cherise, darling. Welcome."

"Hey Shanty."

"Ooh, by the time I'm done with you, Preston won't know what hit him."

I don't mention my conversation with Kendi. Instead, I pretend all is well and let her talk me into lingerie and see-through slips and lipstick shades that are far too flashy for me. We giggle and sip wine, and at some point I snuggle against her on the couch with a blanket and a haunting suspicion that none of this is going to matter in a few days.

I PLAN TO TELL PRESTON on Wednesday. Then again on Thursday. By the time we meet up Friday morning, I've lost my nerve. Again. I feel the weight of time as it pushes against me. I know I need to tell him. I don't have a choice. But Preston has been so good to me this week, so unbelievably tender and sweet. Each kiss feels like a promise, every caress a profession of love, every word a poem written to encourage me.

He takes my hand in his as we stand next to his car. It's packed full with one of his suitcases and three of mine. "You ready?" He kisses each knuckle softly, then plants a kiss on my cheek.

I respond with a giddy nod. "As ready as I'm gonna be."

"Oh, do you mind if we make a quick stop on the way?"

"Sure. Where are we stopping?"

"I was gonna stop by Kendi's place real quick. I wanted to borrow something from him, but I haven't been able to get a hold of him. I figured I'd stop by and see if he's home."

All the expletives I know crowd at my throat, and, with some effort, I shove them down. "Kendi's at his mother's house, actually."

"Oh, really?"

I nod. "Yup. So, no need to stop there." I'm not sure when Kendi planned to go to his mom's house, but I don't want to take any chances.

"Okay. Never mind, then."

Bullet dodged, I slide into the passenger seat and let out a slow breath. It sounds like Kendi's dodging Preston's calls to give me time to come clean. Which is good news. But how much longer will he wait?

I have to tell him. "Preston?"

He turns toward me from his spot on the driver's side. "Yeah?"

"I need to tell you something."

His phone buzzes. "Oh, that's Kendi calling me back. Hang on a sec." He slides his finger across the phone icon to take the call. "Hey Kendi! You're a hard man to get a hold of these days. Listen, are you home? I was wondering if I could borrow your–"

I slap the phone out of his hand, and it tumbles in between the door and the seat. Preston and I both stare at the offending hand, mouths equally wide with disbelief. I blink and give my head a shake. "Sorry. That was really weird, wasn't it?"

"A little." Preston speaks the words slowly, then puts his hand on my temple. "You feeling okay?"

"A little anxious, maybe." I stare at the space where his phone is stuck. "This weekend is a really big step for us."

Preston fishes his phone out, then stares at the cracked screen. "Looks like I won't be using this anytime soon."

"I'm sorry. I'll pay for it."

"Nah, it's time for a new one, anyway." He chuckles. "Though, if you didn't want me on the phone, you could have just said so."

"I'm sorry."

"I'm sorry, too. I cut you off when you were trying to tell me something." He shifts, giving me his full attention as he takes my hands in his. "What is it?"

Now's my chance to come clean. And a few minutes ago, I would have. But now Preston's phone is broken. Which means Kendi won't be able to get a hold of him until after this weekend is over. This trip really is a big step for us. And without Kendi's threat looming over me, I might actually be able to enjoy it.

Preston's worked so hard to make this weekend special for us, even curating a playlist for the way there and the way back. There's not a single Usher song on it, but it's the thought that counts.

"Cherise?"

I kiss him, trying my hardest to convey all my feelings as I do. He smiles as I move back, then pulls me forward to return the favor. We stay like that for a while, kissing and holding each other, until my phone buzzes. Preston pulls back, and I pull it out of my purse. A quick glance tells me I've got a message from Kendi, and I immediately switch off the power. "I don't want us on our phones this weekend."

Preston chuckles. "That won't be a problem for me."

"That's what I wanted to say to you before. No phones." It's a weak lie, but Preston nods before kissing me one more time.

"We've got a tour scheduled for right after we arrive, so we'd better get going." Preston starts the car and pulls away, his right hand enveloping mine as we head out into the morning traffic.

44

The Biltmore

There are some things you just know. No one has to tell you. It's as sure as the humidity on a summer day in the south. A feeling in your gut. A tingle in your fingers. A premonition of some unspoken secret.

The Biltmore is beautiful. Steal-your-breath-away-and-hide-it-in-a-sea-shell-level magical. I've never had an affinity for castles, but standing on the grounds looking up at the peaks of each little tower makes me want to live in one. The inside is decadent. Rich hues, arched ceilings, dizzying staircases. Add to that the sparkling joy of Christmas lights and holiday festivity and, well, the Biltmore immediately becomes my favorite place. Something big is going to happen here. I know it.

The longer I walk with Preston through the grand halls, touring the grounds, the more stupid I feel. Every Christmas at the Biltmore? On a college professor's salary?

"This place is amazing, Cherise." Preston leans toward my ear so only I can hear. "I'd better up my game."

"You don't have to do anything else," I say. "This is perfect."

"Yeah?"

"I'm here with you. I don't think it can get any better than this."

Preston chuckles and tilts his head. "I might surprise you."

The tour lasts over an hour, and after our long drive, the call of nature bears down on me like an ankle weight on an ant's back. I excuse myself to the lady's room and hope to heaven I don't shame the family name before I reach the toilet.

On my way out, I catch the back end of a person's profile. One I've known all my life and would never expect to see here. Not in a million years. *What is Dad doing here?*

As I step further into the lobby to follow him, Preston clutches my hand.

"Hey. You ready to do some more exploring? I know this is all probably old hat for you, but I figured you wouldn't mind indulging me?"

I nod, and the excitement growing in my belly spreads up my neck and into my cheeks. If Dad's here, that means something really big *is* happening. Preston tugs me out of the building and back onto the grounds, where we explore the gardens and enjoy the twinkling lights. I've never needed to use the word sprawling to describe anything, but that's what the Biltmore is. A massive, abundant, unending sea of rolling hills and grand structures.

"We're staying at the Village Inn tonight," Preston says. "But we'll have dinner at 6 in the dining hall. We have plenty of time between now and then, and we've got all weekend to enjoy the spaces." We walk in a comfortable silence, taking in the grounds at a slow, even pace. I could stay like this with Preston forever. My stomach has other ideas. This time it wants to be fed. Preston obliges it, and me, with a meal at one of the estate's seven restaurants.

"We'll need to dress up for dinner." Preston swipes one of the cherry tomatoes from my salad. "But I guess you already know that."

I hadn't known that, but since I've allegedly spent every Santa day here, it stands to reason I should. Thank God Shantell convinced me to pack some formal wear.

The rest of the afternoon is a blur as we check into our room and get ready for the evening. Preston comes in and out, claiming an interest in the history of the estate. I know he's up to something, though. I take my time getting ready, wanting everything to be perfect.

By the time dinner rolls around, I think I'm pretty close to it. From the updo crowning my head, and the swishy chiffon hugging my curves, to the silver heels molding my feet, I'd say I've outdone myself.

Judging by his reaction when he walks back into the room, Preston agrees. He stares at me a full minute before speaking. "Oh babe, you look..." His eyes float over my dress, and I can tell he's at a loss for words.

I decide to help him out. "Perfect?"

He nods. Then clears his throat. "I need to get ready." He grabs the suit laid out on the bed, stopping to kiss my neck on his way to the bathroom. "Don't want to mess up your lipstick." He smiles softly, then pulls away and into the bathroom. I decide to wait outside the room, finding the sounds of the shower and the imaginings that follow too distracting.

I head downstairs to wait for him in the lobby. To my surprise, Linda Williams of Linda Williams Realty is also waiting in the lobby.

"Mom?"

"Cherise!" I find myself enveloped in a hug. Not an unpleasant feeling, but certainly unexpected. "Sweetheart, you look gorgeous!"

"What are you doing here?"

"What do you think?" She winks at me. "Your father and I spend every Christmas at the Biltmore, honey."

Oh, no. "Preston called you?"

"He apologized for interrupting our tradition, but promised to take good care of you this weekend and invited us to join you for dinner this evening." Mom's eyes sparkle with excitement. "I have to say, I was skeptical at first, Cherise, but Preston leaves a good impression." She looks around the lobby and grins. "And this place is amazing. I always thought it was just a tourist trap, but it's really remarkable."

"What did you say to him? And is Dad really here with you?" I need to be prepared for whatever happens tonight.

"God, no. Your father came on his own. Your brothers are on their way, and we'll divide ourselves between the two rooms Preston booked for us."

My stomach drops to my ankles at this news. "My brothers are coming? Here?" This is going to be a disaster.

"I think it's sweet, Cherise." Mom's voice dips down to a whisper and she steps closer. "And I've been meaning to talk to you. About what happened that day with dinner. I've been giving it a lot of thought."

"Now's not a good time, Mom." I shake my head and search the lobby, anxious I'll spy another member of the Williams family popping out of the topiaries. "I need to think a minute."

"Did Preston not tell you we'd be coming?" Mom's brows dip with worry, then lift in apparent delight. "Ah."

"What do you mean, ah?" I force my hands to my sides to keep them out of my hair. It took over an hour to get this style just right, and a series of frustrated tugs will undo all my hard work.

"Nothing." Mom grins, but doesn't enlighten me. My fingers begin to creep up the back of my neck, but Mom grabs them and cups them in her hand. "Don't worry, Cherise. Your Dad and I have called a cease-fire, and your brothers promised to behave."

"They don't know how to behave," I mutter.

Mom gives me a pitying look. "We'll play along for the evening, but you know you've got to tell him the truth sooner or later."

Right. "I know. I'm going to tell him."

Mom gives my hand another squeeze. "I'm happy for you, Cherise. I really mean that."

I sniff and fan my face, not wanting the sudden wave of emotion to overtake me. Mom's never been this sentimental before. Maybe seeing how much Preston loves me, and how far he's willing to go to make me happy, will make my own family realize that I am, in fact, a worthwhile person. That I am enough.

PRESTON WALKS BESIDE me into the dining hall, our hands intertwined. Mom and Dad will be along later with my brothers, but for now we're the only two people in the room. I stare at the table, mouth slightly agape, as trays of decadent hors d'oeuvres stretch out in front of us.

Preston kisses my hand and escorts me to my chair, pulling it out for me to sit. This feels like a fairy tale. Dozens of roses decorate the centerpiece, surrounded by shining flatware and hand-painted plates. The tableware looks like it may actually begin singing and dancing. "I made a few special requests for tonight." Preston smiles and kisses my cheek. "I hope you like them."

"I'm sure I'll love them." I touch my cheek and grin. "I can't believe how amazing this place looks."

"Is this your first time in the dining hall?" Preston waits for an answer, and I tilt my head to the side. Then I remember. Oh.

"Oh, no! But they do things a little differently every year, and this time they've really outdone themselves. There must be twice as many lights now. Hah." I take a sip of water from a glass. *Nice one, Cherise.* I'd better be on guard the rest of the night, or I'm going to embarrass myself.

"Hey Sis!" My brother Jeremy's voice is syrup as he plants a kiss on my cheek and plops into the seat beside me. He looks halfway decent in a suit, but the smirk on his face ruins the whole look for me.

For Preston's sake, I greet Jeremy with a warm smile and a hug. "Jeremy! What are you doing here?"

"Didn't he tell you we'd be here?" Jeremy winks at Preston.

"Sorry, Cherise." Preston squeezes my hand. "I wanted it to be a surprise."

Jason slides into the chair beside Jeremy and waves. "Hey Sis. Mom and Dad are on their way. He needed help with his tie or something."

More likely, they needed to get their stories straight. "Preston, I can't believe you invited my family to dinner."

"Cherise!"

Preston's smile is sheepish as the voice of his mother chirps behind me. "Not just your parents. Mine, too."

I turn around in my seat. "Mrs. Jones! I mean, Thea. Hi."

"Cherise, you look gorgeous. Don't stand up, I'll come to you." She reaches down to hug me, then follows her husband to the opposite end of the table.

My insides are on fire. My family is here. His family is here. This can only mean one thing. *It's finally happening.* Mom and Dad show up a few minutes later, their eyes and mouths strained enough for me to know that they've been arguing. But if Mom's word can be trusted, they'll be civil tonight. At least in front of the Jones family.

As soon as Mom and Dad take their seats, Preston stands up. "Thank you all for making it out tonight. To the Williams family, thank you so much for allowing me to interrupt your tradition and bring my parents to celebrate together. I'm sorry we couldn't share a meal sooner, but I'm glad everyone's here to share in what I hope will become our special day."

Preston looks at me, and my heart turns to jelly.

"Cherise, we've had our ups and downs this past year. But as I've gotten to know you better, I've learned that you are more than just a beautiful, intelligent woman. You're resilient and you're kind. You're funny, and you genuinely care about others. You've got a sweet, Christlike spirit, and it would be my honor if you would allow me to share more days like this with you. I love you. And, if you'll have me..." Preston pulls a box from the roses on the table and kneels in front of me. He opens the box, and a dazzling ring winks up at me. "Cherise Michele Williams, will you marry me?"

I've wanted this for a long time. Ever since that day I watched Garrett and Brianna tie the knot, I've longed for this moment. The moment when someone who cares for me, truly and deeply, professes his love in front of God and everybody, sweeps me off my feet, and whisks me off into my happily ever after.

Preston is on his knees, waiting for my answer. Everything I want, everything I've worked for, is right in front of me. My breath hitches in my throat. There's so much I need to tell him. So much he deserves to know. Kendi's words echo in my brain.

He thinks the world of you, and you've been lying to him.

The seconds tick by. Preston blinks, a worried look shadowing his face. Seeing it snaps me out of my trance and I move toward him.

"Yes."

His mouth twitches up. "Yes?"

I nod. "Yes, I'll marry you. Of course I'll marry you."

He kisses my hand, then slides the ring onto my finger. Relief floods my insides as we embrace. It's going to be okay. I'll figure out a way to tell him the truth. But not tonight. Tonight, I just want to enjoy this time together. Him and me. Happy.

45

Jonah and the Big, Fat Lie

Dinner is a blur of sounds and smells. Mom is charming. Dad is pleasant. My brothers are funny without crossing lines. It's as if they've all been cast under a spell. Or maybe Preston just has a way of making people want to be better. I don't know. But the ache in my belly gives way to joy as the evening progresses and my family acts, well, normal.

Dad does an amazing job avoiding any specifics about past visits to the Biltmore, I'm guessing thanks to Mom's coaching. Jeremy and Jason stick to sports and the weather, and, to my relief, don't say a word about any of the embarrassing events of my childhood.

Preston's family is all charm and grace, and they weave in and out of topics like professionals, sharing stories about their travels and only asking safe questions. Maybe Preston has coached them, too.

Our parents will leave in the morning, and the question of whether or not we'll have breakfast with them is left open-ended.

"We'll be heading out around nine," Thea shares. "We'd love to join you and Gregory, Linda, if you're available."

Dad shrugs his shoulders, and Mom offers a placating smile. "Gregory sleeps in most mornings, but if he's up, then we'll give it a try."

The parents disperse to their quarters, and Preston and I take the scenic route back to the parking lot. The evening lights are even more beautiful against the sky's inky backdrop. Preston squeezes my hand, and we stop walking. He wraps his arms around my waist and rests his chin on my neck. "Thank you for saying yes."

I laugh. "What else would I say?"

"For a moment, I was worried you'd say no. I'm not sure what I would have done if you did."

"Well, now I guess you'll never know."

Preston rubs my shoulders, and I shiver. It's cold. Too cold to be walking around with no jacket on. As if he can read my thoughts, he wraps his suit jacket around me, and we walk the rest of the way to his car. He's quiet on the drive back to the Village Inn, and I begin thinking about our sleeping arrangements. There's only one bed in the room.

When we arrive, Preston helps me out of his jacket and puts away my shoes and bag. The air between us feels heavy and charged as we move slowly around the room. Our shoulders touch as he brushes past me and toward the air conditioning unit.

"Sorry," he says.

"Oh, it's fine." I fiddle with the pendant on my necklace and make my way to the dresser. I pull open the drawer with my night clothes and stare at each skimpy garment. It seemed like a good idea while Shantell and I were packing for the weekend, but now I'm not sure. I look up at him, examining his back as he punches a few buttons on the unit.

"I tend to get hot at night, so I can sleep on the sofa over here by the AC."

"Oh, okay." My smile lacks enthusiasm, and my shoulders deflate. I shut the dresser drawer and sigh.

"Or." Preston turns and looks at me. His eyes find mine, and he closes the distance between us – one slow, tentative step at a time.

My whole body tingles as he inches closer. He leans over me, pressing his forehead against mine. I echo his word in a whisper. "Or?"

"If you wanted, you and I could be together, tonight."

I look up at him. "Are you sure?"

He nods. "I love you, Cherise. And now that we're engaged, I've made you a promise. You can trust me, and I can trust you."

Preston thinks the world of you, and you've been lying to him.

I shake my head against the invasive thoughts, but Preston misunderstands my movement and takes a step back. "We don't have to do anything. Things can stay the way they've been, and that's fine with me. I thought, maybe just for tonight, if you wanted to?"

"I do." I step into his space and kiss him, pressing my body against his. His eyes widen, and he smiles against my lips. His hands find the small of my back, and he pulls me even closer. Our movements grow more urgent as we move toward the bed.

Preston's kisses are tender as he guides me to the pillow. His touches are gentle, but that doesn't stop them from sending fire through my skin. The pins in my hair are uncomfortable, but I don't want to give him a reason to stop. He's made me a promise, and he's mine now. I don't want to give him up, not even a little. Tonight, I'm the one who matters most. He loves me, and he wants to make me happy.

Your happiness isn't real if it's based on a lie.

His lips brush against the bare skin of my neck, his nose grazing my ear as he kisses a fiery trail to my shoulders.

You can't keep lying to him.

He finds my mouth again, but Kendi's voice keeps rattling around in my brain. *You have to tell him the truth.*

Ugh, stupid Kendi!

Preston freezes. "What?"

Please don't tell me I said that out loud. "What? What is it?"

Preston's eyes meet mine, searching. "You said Kendi."

I shake my head. "No, I didn't." Preston sits up, and all the places where our bodies touched begin to cool. I sit up, too, as a growing panic spreads into my lungs.

"Cherise. You said Kendi's name. I know what I heard."

"No, I–"

"Is there something you need to tell me?" The change in his voice is chilling.

"No. Preston, you've got nothing to worry about."

He nods. "I might believe that if another man's name didn't just come out of your mouth. If something's happened between you two–"

"No. Never. Not in a million years."

"You two have spent a lot of time together the last few months." Preston's voice drops to just above a whisper. "I'm not saying it did, but if something happened, even on accident, you can tell me."

He's trying to be brave, but I can see the hurt in his face. And I can't let him think the worst of me. "Preston, I would never do that to you. I swear, it's nothing like that."

"Then what is it?"

I lick my lips, then press my fingertips together. "I did say Kendi's name, but it's really not what you think. Something he said keeps bugging me, that's all."

"What did he say to you?" I can tell by the way Preston's looking at me that he isn't buying it.

This isn't the way I wanted tonight to go. But I know the ache that comes with betrayal, and I can't do that to him. I won't. My hands shake with pure terror, but I force my words out with a laugh. "It's kind of a funny story, actually. Kendi and I had an argument over my membership application for the church."

"Why would you argue about that?"

I smooth out the bedsheets beside my leg. "Well, Kendi said I needed to fill out the section for my testimony of faith. But I left it blank, because I don't have one."

Preston blinks. "What do you mean, you don't have one?"

I stare at a spot on the rug. "I don't have one, because I haven't really made a decision yet."

"You... what?"

"I've been trying, Preston. Really trying." I place my hand on his shoulder. "And I'll keep trying. I promise."

He stands up, putting even more distance between us. "I'm a little confused. Cherise, what are you saying? Are you not a Christian?"

"Preston, I know this is really important to you, and I'm sorry I lied, but–"

"So, you've been pretending this whole time?"

I join him on the rug. "I know how it sounds, but honestly I did this for you. For us."

"Cherise, my faith isn't something I take lightly. I told you that from the beginning. How could you lie about something like this? Do your parents know? Have you been lying to them, too?"

Right. My parents. I struggle to work out the words as Preston stares, waiting for an explanation. "Actually, there's something else I've been meaning to tell you." I lower my head. "About my parents? They're not Christians, either. They're not even together. They've been divorced for years."

Preston runs a hand over his mouth. "I see. So all the family trips you talked about?"

"They never happened."

"And Christmas at the Biltmore?" I shake my head, and Preston lets out a dry laugh. "So, you really lied about everything?"

"Not everything." I reach for his hand, desperate for the warmth of his fingers. "Not about us. Not about how I feel about you. Preston, I love you." He scoffs, but I take a step closer to him. "That's why I'm doing everything I can think of to make you happy. I got baptized, I go to church, I go to small group. I barely hang out with my friends. I always make sure we do what you want to do, listen to the music you like, go to the places you want to go, eat the things that you want to eat. Lots of people take interest in their partner's hobbies. That's what any good girlfriend would do."

"My faith isn't a hobby. It's the core of who I am. I need to be with someone who shares the same faith. Someone who puts God first and will encourage me to do the same."

"And I can be that someone, Preston. Just give me a chance. I'll be a good wife. I'll do whatever it takes to be the woman you need, I promise. Nothing has to change. We can still be together."

"You can't be a Christian without Christ, Cherise. It doesn't work like that. It isn't something you do for me. Your relationship with God is personal. It's something that happens in your heart, not a list of things that you do. You not understanding that very basic thing is proof that we can't be together."

It dawns on me that Preston is breaking up with me. We've been engaged less than a day, and he's already ready to throw me away? "No, Preston, you don't understand. I love you. I really do. I'm sorry I lied, but I was scared, okay? I thought if I told you, then you wouldn't want to be with me. And besides, you were the one that assumed I was a Christian and asked me out first. I was falling for you so fast, and then you told me I had to be a Christian and I panicked."

"I told you why my faith is important, Cherise. And I admit I made an assumption in the beginning, but you've had plenty of opportunities since then to come clean."

"I know, and I'm sorry. But I tried. I really tried to tell you."

He glares at me, and I shrink back. "When? When did you try to tell me, Cherise? When I told you about Kendi's small group, you could have fessed up then. Or how about when I asked you if you were a new believer? Or one of the countless times we were alone together? For you to go this far..." Preston looks up at the ceiling. "You got baptized with no real conviction. You're a fraud, and you've made a mockery of my faith and of me. Do you really think that's what I wanted? For you to pretend? For you to manipulate me to get what you want?"

"You gave me no choice. If I didn't lie, I would have lost you. And you're the best thing that's ever happened to me. I've never been with anyone who makes me feel the way you do. I love you, and I know you love me, too."

Preston shakes his head. "It isn't real."

That stings. "Yes, it is."

"No, it's not! I don't know you, Cherise. How can I love you when I don't know who you really are?"

"You do know me, Preston."

"What's your favorite song?"

"What?"

"Your favorite song? I'm guessing it's not *Joyful, Joyful*, right?"

"Well–"

"And when I told you about my parents, you said you knew exactly how I felt. What did you mean by that?"

I have no answer for him.

"Everything I know about you is a lie. Everything I love about you is tainted with the knowledge that you lied, not just about the most important parts of you, but the little things, too."

"What was I supposed to do?" I shout the words, feeling desperate, needing to be heard. "You have no idea what it's like to be me. To have parents who barely acknowledge your existence, and men who only see you as an easy score, and boyfriends who tell you you're too much because you want to wear matching shirts. I love drinking wine and snuggling on the couch, and having sex, and listening to the nastiest songs Usher has to offer. I cuss, and I wear sleeveless dresses, and before I met you, I could count on one hand the number of times I'd been to church. I'd never read the bible, or even heard of Joshua and the whale."

"It's Jonah, Cherise."

"Okay, Jonah. I admit, I don't know a lot about church or God, and I know it was wrong to hide these things from you. But everyone who's supposed to love me always says the same thing. That I'm too much or not enough. So yes, I lied. I hid the parts of myself that I thought you wouldn't like, because I want this to work. I want you, Preston. I want to marry you, and have a family with you."

His eyes soften as he watches me cry. I swipe at the tears running down my face, and for a moment, he looks like he might reach out to me. His hand moves up, then falls back to his side. I know it's flimsy, but if there's even a sliver of a chance, I've got to try.

"Preston? I'd like to use my wish now."

"What?"

"You owe me a wish. From when we first started dating, remember? I'd like to use it now. Just give us a chance. Please? I know I messed up, but my heart was in the right place."

He scoffs and shakes his head. "Your heart was in the right place? Cherise, when exactly were you going to tell me the truth? When we got married? During our honeymoon? After our first kid? Never?"

The truth lodges in my throat. I keep it there until it dies. I *can't* lose him. "Preston, I'm sorry."

"I don't understand this, Cherise. I could never be happy with someone I couldn't be myself with. Is that what you really wanted? A life where you'd always have to pretend? Where you could never let your guard down? Never be yourself? I trusted you. I was vulnerable with you. I wanted to share my life with you. And I thought you felt the same way about me, but I was wrong."

"I want all those things, too."

"No, you don't. If you did, you would have been honest with me. Your heart wasn't in the right place, and you didn't do this for us. You did this for you."

"I told you I was scared."

"You're not the only one who's scared, Cherise. Don't you think I'm scared, too? Being in a relationship is scary. Being vulnerable with someone is scary. Risking having your heart broken is scary. But I'm not willing to spend the rest of my life with someone I have to hide from. And I don't understand why you would."

He's not wrong. I have been hiding myself from him. But now that everything's out in the open, maybe we can start fresh. "I'm sorry, Preston. I promise to do better from now on. No more hiding, okay? I won't lie to you again. I swear."

His eyes go wide. "No, Cherise. I can't be with you."

"I know you're mad, but we can work this out."

He shakes his head again. "I don't know you. And if you think I can be with you now, after lying to me about your faith and everything else, then you don't know me either."

"You know the truth now. And I can work on my faith. I can–"

"Just stop!" Preston rubs his face. "It's over."

No. It can't be over. Not after everything we've been through. Not after everything I sacrificed to get to this point. "Please don't do this. Don't throw me away. What about forgiveness? Isn't that part of being a Christian, too? I made a mistake, and I'm asking you to forgive me. Maybe I'm a bad Christian, but that doesn't mean we can't make this work."

Preston frowns at me. "So you want me to remember the parts of my faith that suit you and ignore the parts that don't? Never mind what I need, so long as you get what you want, is that right?"

I shake my head. "That's not what I meant."

"Marriage is about being a partner to your spouse. Being a friend. Being someone they can share their whole self with." Preston's eyes harden. "Keeping yourself from me, lying to me, tricking me so you can get what you want, none of that is love. It's selfish, and it's the worst kind of manipulation."

I can't bear to look at his face, so I turn away, placing a tentative hand on his arm. Speaking is hard. All I can manage is a broken whisper. "Preston?"

His fingers touch my skin, briefly, as he removes my hand from his arm. "You're not a bad Christian, Cherise. You're a shitty human being."

All the air leaves my lungs. A moment later, Preston leaves, too. I slink down to the floor, shaking, as I wait for my brain to remind my body how to breathe.

46

Too Much To Unpack

When I open my eyes, it's dark. I'm curled up on the floor next to the bed, throat dry, eyes itchy, arms and legs freezing. I stand up and switch on the light, but it's obvious I'm alone in the room. I head to the bathroom, noticing the absence of Preston's shoes. Not just the ones he walked out in, but his slippers, too. I check the closet by the door, then check the drawers. His clothes are gone. He must have slipped back in at some point and packed his things.

I check my phone for messages, but there aren't any. Then I remember his phone is broken, so there wouldn't be any messages from him, anyway. It's early morning, just a few minutes shy of five o'clock, but I can't bear to stay here. Either Preston left, or he's in a different room. Either way, the message is the same. He's done with me.

I let out a whimper as I pack my belongings into my suitcase. As long as we've been dating, I've never heard Preston utter a harsh word. Not to me, not to a stranger, not to anyone. A fact that makes what he said to me last night even harder to bear.

But is he wrong? I did lie to him. Repeatedly. And despite what I told Kendi, and my mom, and anyone else who suggested I tell Preston the truth, deep down I know I never would have. Because deep down, I've always known that who I am has never been good enough. Will never be good enough.

I need to go home.

Once I'm finished packing, I hightail it out of the room and toward my mom's suite. I don't know what I'll say to her, but maybe if she sees I'm in distress, she won't ask too many questions.

The door opens just as I get ready to knock, but to my surprise, Dad stands in front of me.

"Oh. Cherise. What are you doing here?"

I stare at him a beat. Note the empty ice bucket in his hand. "Sorry. I thought this was Mom's room. I'll go check the other one."

He looks away, clears his throat. "This is the right room. I just needed to ask her something."

At five in the morning? "Oh. Okay."

"Gregory, why are you standing at the door?" I spy Mom behind him, dressed in a robe. She freezes when she sees me. "Cherise?"

I turn around and head toward the other room. Whatever's going on between my parents, I can't deal with it right now. I'll have to get one of the twins to take me home.

The room is at the opposite end of the hall. I bang on the door and wait for one of them to let me in. "Jeremy? Jason? Wake up!" I keep banging on the door until I hear shuffling feet.

The door swings open and Jeremy scowls at me. "What is it, Shell Breath?"

"I need you to drive me home."

Jeremy raises an eyebrow, then looks down at his watch. "Maybe in a couple of hours."

"No. Now."

Jeremy begins to protest, but hesitates when he gets a good look at me. His eyes drop to my suitcase, then circle back to my face. "Give me ten minutes." He opens the door wider and lets me inside. "Just gotta pack and pee, alright?"

I nod, not trusting my voice. Jason is passed out on one of the two beds, but Jeremy smacks him on the back of the head on the way to the nightstand. "Yo, Jase. Ride back with Dad or Mom. I'm heading out early."

Jason mumbles something incoherent and lifts up his thumb. Ten minutes later, I'm following Jeremy to his car. He loads up all of my suitcases into his trunk, followed by his duffel bag, then opens up the rear passenger door for me. I slide inside, staring out the window as he starts the car.

"You owe me."

"K."

"That's two now, including asking Dad to that dinner. I know he never showed, but that's not my fault. I held up my end, so it's still a favor."

"K."

"Speaking of Dad." Jeremy wiggles his eyebrows at me through the rearview mirror. "Did you know him and Mom hooked up last night? They kicked Jason out and everything."

"Could we please not talk, Jeremy?" As soon as the words leave my mouth, the floodgates open up, and the tears I've held at bay rush out in heaving sobs. Jeremy obliges and doesn't talk to me anymore, just sends furtive glances my way from time to time. As we wind through the curvy roads of the Biltmore Estate, I catch a final glimpse of the big house and its enchanting towers. But whatever spell was cast last night has broken, along with all my dreams of happily ever after. There's no princess at the end of this story, just the shattered bits of a smashed pumpkin.

47

Unblocked

"You know what you need to do, right?"

Shantell sips her boba tea and smiles at me. With the new year days away and absolutely zero plans in place, I've run out of ways to fill my vacation. Adrian has plans to visit her parents and will fly out tomorrow. Shantell has been busy with her daycare and will also be going out of town for some much-needed leisure.

"I don't know what to do, that's why I'm asking you two." I sink my head into my hands. It's been four days since I last spoke to Preston, and I'm not sure what to do with myself. He isn't taking my calls. I keep hoping it's because his phone is still broken.

Shantell's smile broadens. "You need to have revenge sex."

"What?"

Shantell nods. "You know what that is, right? I mean, I know it's been a while, but you haven't forgotten?"

"Yes, I know what it is."

"K, just checking. Adrian, what do you think?"

"Agreed." Adrian stirs her iced tea and sighs. "Preston did a number on you, and I think you need a hard reset."

Shantell mimics Adrian's words, emphasizing the last two. "Yes, ma'am. A hard reset."

"But I don't want a reset. I want Preston back." I sniff and rub my face with my fingertips. "What am I supposed to do without him?"

"Girl, move on." Shantell rubs my back. "He wasn't for you."

"*Nobody's* for me."

"That's not true," Adrian says. "You're amazing, Cherise."

I wish I could believe them. But honestly, I don't feel amazing. What I did to Preston was wrong. And looking back, he was right about me. I tried to manipulate him into thinking I was something I wasn't, and it backfired.

I look up at Shantell and Adrian. They're both showering me with compliments I don't deserve, telling me things about myself that just aren't true. I don't deserve them, either. Especially after the way I treated them. I put my relationship with Preston above our friendship, but they're still here. It makes my heart hurt to think of it. I let Adrian down when she needed me most. I hurt my best cousin when she didn't deserve it.

Preston's words hurt, but he was right. I'm a terrible person.

I STARE AT MY PHONE, and a small voice in the back of my brain reminds me that this is a bad idea. But I'm already in the gutter, and it's lonely at the bottom. I unblock the number and dial it, silently hoping no one picks up on the other end.

The line clicks on. "Hello? Cherise?"

"Hey, uh, Brunswick. How are things?"

"Oh wow. I wasn't expecting your call. What's it been, like, a year now?"

"Yep. About that long. So, what's new?"

"Well, I've managed to whittle it down to just Loki once a month."

"Wow." Even Brunswick is growing as a person. "That's, um, incredible."

"Yeah. I've been working really hard on that. Cherise, I'm really glad you called."

"Yeah." I say the word slowly. *Just spit it out, Cherise.* "Brunswick, I was wondering if you'd like to get together?"

"Yeah! When? Where?"

"How about your place?"

Brunswick hesitates. "My place?"

"We don't have to."

"No, that's okay. Sometimes Jimmy doesn't like extra people in his space, but if it's you, I'm sure it will be fine."

"Jimmy?"

"I introduced him to you on our date, remember?"

Right. His other little action figure. I'd almost forgotten. The voice in my head screams at me, but I ask Brunswick for his address, anyway. I blew it with Garrett, I couldn't get Calvin to stay, and my relationship with Preston imploded. Maybe Brunswick is the best I can hope for.

48

New Year, Same Old Me

The new year promises new beginnings and a fresh start for many. But for me, it feels more like a ticking clock. Another year gone without much to show for it. I'll be 33 when my birthday comes in October. I'd hoped to start a family by now, but I've all but given up on that.

Getting through the day is all I can manage.

Tammie smiles at me as I walk into the clinic, and I try my best to put on a brave face. If it's strained, I can't help it. It's the best I can do.

"Happy New Year, Dr. Williams!" she chirps.

"Same to you, Tammie. Can you do me a favor and thin out my appointments this week?"

"Sure! Everything okay?"

Not at all. I'm slowly spiraling into a void, and being here at work feels overwhelming. Thankfully, I've got a light day today. One client in the morning, one in the afternoon. But I need to answer Tammie. "Everything's fine. I've just got some personal things to deal with this week."

"Alright, I'll make some calls and shuffle things around."

"Thanks, Tammie." As soon as I reach my office, I cup my face in my hands. "Get it together, Cherise. You just need to get through today. Just one day, and then you can go home." Maybe not the best thing to tell myself, considering how empty my apartment is.

Preston hasn't reached out, not even once. And he's never left anything of his in my apartment, so there's no lingering trace of our relationship for me to hold on to. Just sterile, empty spaces and blank walls. A carbon copy of my mother's apartment. It's a sobering thought.

I send out a text to Brunswick to see if he's free this evening. Wading through action figures and Marvel-centric conversation beats eating dinner alone.

He texts me back right away, and the message is followed by a picture of him and Jimmy. I cringe when I read the next line of text. "We can't wait to see you!"

Brunswick's obsession is concerning, but at least he's seeing a therapist. And there are worse things. *Worse people, too.*

My eyes and nose start to burn, and my throat feels thick. I swallow, but it doesn't help. A wayward sob escapes, and my resolve breaks. I shouldn't have come in today. I should have cancelled all my appointments and stayed home. Away from the sunshine and fresh starts and hopeful faces. I can't smile for my patients and encourage them to heal when everything in me wants to shrivel up and disappear.

I send a message to the other PT to see if she can cover my patients for today. It's short notice, but she messages me back a thumbs up. I send a message to Tammie, knowing I won't manage a complete sentence on the intercom in my current state, then gather my things and slip out the back way.

As soon as the wintry air hits my face, I crumble to the ground, placing my fist in my mouth to muffle my whimpers. I can hardly breathe, my heart hurts so much. I thought if I came to work and got back into a rhythm, that it would help. That I'd feel more normal.

But I was wrong. I'm all wrong, and I don't know how to fix it. Things got so twisted between Preston and me. I'm sure he hates me, and now I think I hate me, too.

But I can't just walk out of my skin and be someone else. On the inside, I'll always be me. Inadequate, insufficient, me.

My whimpers give way to sobs, and I know I should leave, but I can't get my legs to work. So, I sit on the back step of the clinic and cry until my eyes are dry and my sleeve is soaked and the snot dripping from my nose crusts over. I guess there's one silver lining to being alone. No one's here to see me like this.

"Cherise?"

Oh God, please no. I hide my head in my arms and pretend I can't hear Kendi's voice.

"Cherise, are you okay?"

Obviously not, Meathead. "Just go away."

Kendi sighs, then, to my absolute horror, sits next to me on the cement stoop. I shift away from him, scooting as far as the space allows without falling. He doesn't say anything. We sit there in silence for a long time, so long that I wonder if maybe he's left and I didn't hear it. I peek out over my arms. He's looking out at the parking lot, his face pensive, his hands folded in front of him.

"Why are you still here?" I ask. Because I'm genuinely curious. Kendi has just as much right to be upset with me as anyone. But he doesn't look upset. He looks worried.

He turns toward me, and I hide my face again. "I wasn't sure if I should call you. I'm sorry I didn't."

Not what I expected to hear. "Why would you call me?"

"To make sure you were okay." Kendi goes quiet again, then says, "Preston told me about what happened."

My crying begins afresh at this news. Of course he told Kendi. I can only hope he left out the more vulnerable parts of our exchange.

"What you did was wrong, Cherise. Really wrong. And you hurt a lot of people. Preston, his parents. Me."

"Thanks for the pep talk." My sarcasm is unwarranted, but what can I say? Kendi brings out the best in me.

He sighs. "I was wrong, too. I had my suspicions about you, but I figured you were seeking, so what would it hurt? I should have told Preston the moment I learned the truth. But I didn't, and I ended up hurting him, too."

I look up at him, despite the state of my face. "What do you mean? You didn't do anything wrong."

"Preston and I are friends, Cherise. More than that, we're brothers in Christ. I should have told him the truth."

"Why didn't you?"

"I'm not sure yet. Maybe I wanted to give you a chance to come clean. Or maybe I was being a coward. I knew it would hurt him, and I didn't want to be the one to do it." Kendi lets out a sigh, then looks at me. "The point I'm trying to make here is this: I understand how you feel. And I want you to know that as wrong as everything is right now, there's still hope."

"There's no way Preston will ever forgive me."

"I'm not really talking about Preston. I'm talking about faith."

I sniff. "In case you've forgotten, I don't have any."

He nods. "I know, Cherise. But that can change at any moment. God draws us in with loving kindness, and a life in Christ is one of grace and forgiveness. I know you started coming to small group for the wrong reasons, but you're always welcome to come back for the right ones."

I shake my head. "I can't go back there. I can't face everyone now, after everything."

"What happened between you and Preston can stay between us. I won't share anything you don't want me to. So far, all they know is that you're dealing with something personal."

Kendi didn't rat me out to the group? I'm not sure why it matters to me so much, none of it was real. But it's a relief nonetheless.

"Whenever you're ready, we'd love to have you back. And if you ever want to talk, I'm here."

"Preston hates me."

Kendi's silence is damning.

I don't know what I expected him to say, so I just keep talking. "I really messed up. And I know I deserved it, but I can't get Preston's words out of my head. He called me a–" I can't say the words out loud. Hearing them in my head is enough.

"I know what he said." Kendi's voice is soft. "Cherise, I won't make excuses for what either of you said and did that night. And I don't know what the future holds for the two of you. What I do know is that you have an opportunity here to acknowledge that you were wrong. That you went down the wrong path. But there's another path available to you, if you're willing to accept the help."

"Why are you even talking to me?" I scowl at him. "I lied to you. I lied to everyone. I told you I was curious about Preston's faith, but that was a lie, too. I never cared about any of it. All I cared about was tricking him into loving me so I wouldn't be alone."

"Cherise."

"Don't you get it? I'm not interested in any of this God stuff, so just leave me alone." I finally find my legs again and launch myself off the stoop. It's a wobbly move, and Kendi grabs me before I face-plant into the gravel. Salt in the wound.

I tug my arm out of his grip and stomp away, toward the front parking lot. I feel his eyes on me as I round the corner, but he doesn't follow. At first, I feel good about walking away. It's not often I'm the one to do it. But Kendi is the only real connection with Preston that I have left. Cutting ties with him feels like the last nail in the coffin.

I walk to my car, feeling hollow – as if something's scraped away my insides and left just the husk.

49

A Remarkable Descent

Being empty is worlds apart from being heartbroken. After my breakup with Calvin, I was devastated. Like a pincushion in a world full of needles, I felt *everything*. Songs, fruits, random smells, words or phrases were all painful reminders of what I'd lost. The slightest thing could set me off and turn me into a pile of mush. For a long time, I couldn't even hear his name without breaking down.

The world is much easier to manage with a hollowed-out heart. Work is bearable, for the most part, and my life eventually returns to the ebb and flow of pre-Preston times. I join my friends for drinks at the club. Sometimes I have to force my laughter, prop a smile on my face so they won't pry. I haven't told them about Brunswick. I'm sure they won't approve, and besides, I don't want to risk my newfound emptiness.

I don't want to fight anymore. I don't want to think about whether or not Brunswick measures up to Garrett, or Preston, or anybody, because any time I think about measurements and weights, I remember how poorly I've measured up. That makes me feel sad. And I'm tired of feeling sad.

Shantell invited me out tonight, but we're not meeting at a bar. We're meeting at a café. A quiet one. The kind where people talk and hold interventions instead of dancing themselves into oblivion under the pulsing beats of a speaker.

I show up to the café, anyway, with a big smile and a chirpy tune. "Hey girl besties!"

Adrian and Shantell offer muted smiles in return. This is definitely giving intervention vibes.

Adrian is the first to speak. "Hey Cherise. How are you doing, honey?"

I shrug. "I'm doing great. I've got two new clients at work, and I'm pretty sure I can get a referral out of one of them for a third."

"That's cool." Shantell drums her fingers on the table. The waiter comes over and takes our orders. He's pretty cute, but Shantell doesn't even try to flirt with him. Not a good sign.

"So, what's up?" I try to sound nonchalant as I look from one woman to the other.

"Cherise, you know we love you," Shantell says.

My stomach curls. Nope, not good.

"And after what happened with Preston–" Adrian stops midsentence, as if waiting for my permission to continue.

"Girl, it's fine," I say. "You can say his name. It's not like it was with Calvin. I'm fine."

"Yeah, about that." Shantell sighs. "I'm gonna be honest with you, Cherise. We're worried."

I laugh. "Why? I told you, I'm completely fine."

"Yeah, and on the outside you *seem* fine," Shantell says.

"But something's off." Adrian adds. "You've been really peppy lately."

"You go out with us every time we want to go to the club, which isn't like you."

"And you've been dodging our questions about whether or not you're seeing someone new."

I'm starting to feel cornered. Which means I'm starting to feel. Which is the last thing I want. "I need you ladies to back off, okay? I told you I'm fine."

Adrian frowns. "Cherise, you're not fine. You've been drinking a lot lately."

"So what? Shantell drinks way more than me."

"But that's normal for me," Shantell says. "You don't get down like that."

"You also don't go home with strangers," Adrian adds. "But the other night you didn't leave with us."

"I'm sorry, aren't you the ones who told me I needed revenge sex?"

"Revenge sex, not scary get-yourself-killed sex." Shantell shakes her head. "This isn't like you. You weren't like this before."

"Well maybe I don't like who I was before. Maybe I want to be someone different."

"Cherise, don't be mad." Adrian's tone is so patronizing, I can't stand it.

So, I stand up. "I've gotta go."

"Cherise, don't leave," Shantell stands up, too. "Look, we just don't want to see you get hurt."

"I can take care of myself, thanks." I run out of the café before they can see my tears. Before the feelings get too strong. Why can't they just let things be? I dial Brunswick once I'm in my car and let him know I'm coming over. At least he understands the need to pretend.

I CAN HEAR MY PHONE buzzing, but I can't see it. I try to lean to my side, but the hand resting across my chest has me locked in. The buzzing stops, and I rub at my eyes. A zombie poster plastered to the slanted ceiling greets me, catching me off guard though I've seen it at least a dozen times. Brunswick's apartment is really just the finished attic of his grandparents' home. Inflation being the way it is, I can't say I blame him for this one. But the poster is unnerving.

As are the sea of toys dotting his floor in what Brunswick describes as strategically placed sight lines. In case of an attack. From what, is anybody's guess.

I peel away Brunswick's sweaty arm and search the room for my belongings. Not an easy task in the semi-darkness. I step on something sharp, but stop just shy of shouting an expletive. Stupid toys.

My phone lights up again, and I grab it on my way out. I've got a voicemail. The house is quiet, save for the creak of my feet as I descend the stairway. Which makes Mom's confident voice ring all the louder as I listen to her message.

"Hey honey, it's Mom. Listen, I was wondering if you have time for lunch this week? Give me a call back."

Odd. She rarely calls, and when she does, she's never trying to make plans to get together. Only trying to get out of them. I stare at my phone a moment, wondering if maybe Mom's having a midlife crisis. Or maybe she dialed the wrong kid?

"Cherise."

I drop my phone and turn around, heart pounding, fists raised. Brunswick stands on the last step with a scowl on his face and a couple of toys in his hand. "Brunswick, you scared the bejesus out of me."

"What have you done, Cherise?"

I shake my head. "What?"

He holds up the objects in his hands, and I note that they are not toys, plural, but the broken pieces of a single toy. One I've grown embarrassingly familiar with, because it's his favorite.

"Oh. What happened?"

"You tell me." Brunswick's face is a storm. "Last night, Jimmy was perfectly fine. I put him on his spot on the dresser, same as always, but this morning I turn over to get a sip of water, you're gone, and he's... he's..."

"Brunswick, I don't know what to tell you."

"You could tell me you're sorry, for starters."

"Sorry for what?"

"For breaking Jimmy!"

Is that what I stepped on? "I didn't break your toy, Brunswick. And even if I did, you've got a hundred toys all over your floor. Would it kill you to clean up a little?"

"Not a toy. I've told you a million times he's a collector's item."

"He's a toy."

"He's my friend! And you ruined him."

The look of betrayal on Brunswick's face cuts me deeper than I expect. "Hey, listen, Brunswick."

"I don't think this is gonna work."

"Wait, what?"

"Jimmy said you were jealous, but I didn't listen. And now this happened, and I don't think I can forgive you. So please leave."

My jaw drops open. "You're asking me to leave?"

Brunswick lowers his head. "Yeah."

I pick up my phone and slink out the door under Jimmy's watchful eyes. This is a new low, even for me.

50

Never Enough

E ventually my phone stops ringing. I guess if you ignore people's calls long enough, they take the hint and leave you to wallow in your sorrows in peace. One month bleeds into two, and now I'm not sure if I'm ignoring Adrian and Shantell because I'm angry or embarrassed. Maybe both? Angry because they tried to handle me. Embarrassed because they were right to try.

Not that it stops me. Raleigh night life has plenty to offer, and it's getting harder to stave off the pain. Monday morning I'm functional. I help all my clients with the professionalism I've fine-tuned over the years, smiling, nodding, and reassuring at all the right moments.

Monday night, I'm knocking back margaritas and sweating in a dark box as I dance with strangers. The music makes the windows vibrate, but I'm grateful for anything that can drown out my not-so-quiet thoughts. Including the short, oak-skinned brother with a patchy goatee giving me sideways glances on the dance floor. He moves in closer, and I let him dance with me. He's got an inch on me, maybe two, and his hands graze places no gentleman would dare. But he's here in front of me, and that's all I can ask for.

At this point, my Five G standards feel pretentious. I'm not a prize worthy of anyone's efforts. Not Garret's, not Calvin's, and certainly not Preston's. I was rejected by Brunswick, of all people! If I can't get a delusional man-child to hold on to me, I'm hopeless.

Brunswick called exactly one time, and that was only to accuse me of stealing one of his limited-edition Marvel action figures. I denied it, vehemently, then called him a lot of ugly things and hung up the phone. Afterwards I had a big laugh, an even bigger cry, then threw the stupid Spiderman in the trash.

Did I swipe it from the hallway shelf out of spite as he kicked me out? Yes. Did it make me feel better? For about five minutes, yes. And then, not so much. Stealing toys is a weird flex, and I can't even brag about the larceny since he called me on it the same day. I guess I couldn't get one past Jimmy, after all. I still see that creepy toy in my nightmares.

"My name's Philip." The guy I'm dancing with shouts into my ear, and I wince. He smells like a smoker. That's going to be unpleasant when I kiss him later.

"I'm Cherise!" I inch closer to him while we dance, sending him all the signals that I do not want to go home alone tonight. He seems to pick up on them, but then, someone grabs him by the shoulder and whirls him around.

An angry woman several inches taller than both of us glares at me while she speaks to him. "I thought you were hanging with the *boys*, tonight. This isn't the bowling alley, Philip."

"Babe, how did you..." Philip casts a glance my way, then hangs his head and follows the girl out. She spares me another lethal look as she tugs him away.

That could have been worse. Judging by the size of her foot, she could have stomped me into the ground if she had a mind to. Not wanting to press my luck, I call it a night and slink out of the club.

THE HOLLOW SPACES IN my chest are fickle. Some days, they fill up with irrational rage. The kind that can spill over unexpectedly as a harsh word to a client, or a rant against the old lady at the grocery store who touches every fruit before picking the one she wants.

Other days, those spaces are as hollow and vacant as the parking lot at the old K-Mart on Blue Ridge. On those days, if you listen close enough, you can hear the wind whistle through my threadbare soul.

But this constant bouncing between two extremes has left me feeling unstable.

Preston still hasn't called. I've left messages. Dozens of voicemails. Physical traces of my desperation in the form of texts and long emails that would make every feminist cringe.

I don't understand how someone can love you so deeply and fully, and then just... not. No phone call. No hesitation. He's completely shut me out. And I guess that's what hurts the most.

I thought if I loved him enough, letting me go would be hard. So hard that he'd bend the rules for me and cling to me the way I clung to him.

But he didn't. And with one slammed door, he erased an entire year of my life like it was nothing. I put everything I had into our flimsy, fragile love, but I've got nothing to show for it. And I've got nothing left in me.

It's Sunday.

My head hurts, and though the bottle next to my bed has a lot to do with it, the crying doesn't help. A lurch in my stomach sends me running to the bathroom with little regard for the contents of my nightstand. I almost don't make it in time, but thankfully the toilet lid is already up, saving me a few precious seconds before I empty out my insides.

I'd hoped settling in with my favorite vintage and a box of pizza would help me sleep. But unless you call polishing off an entire Sicilian pie solo an accomplishment (yay me), my efforts were in vain. And, like all my life choices, I'm really regretting it now.

Another crying fit follows, and it's just a matter of time before my head splits open. There's ibuprofen inside my nightstand. Definitely not a good idea on an empty stomach. An even worse idea after a night of drinking. But the pulsing throb in my cranium trumps everything, including the D in my DPT.

I crawl toward my nightstand on all fours, too dizzy to stand. I stink, my room's a wreck, and the clutter from the top of my nightstand is staring at me from the floor.

Normally the space beside my bed is clean and clutter-free, but over the last few weeks, it's become the graveyard for all the things I no longer want to deal with. Piles of mail, an anniversary card from Preston that I pulled out to burn but couldn't, the bible Kendi gifted me after my phony baptism, my car keys.

Ugh, my car. It'd take a forklift to remove all the fast-food wrappers currently piled on the floor. Everything's gotten away from me.

I look at the card from Preston, letting my fingers glide over the large, embossed lettering on the front that says "Happy Anniversary." I open it, because I love torturing myself.

To Cherise. Getting to know you over the last year has brought me immeasurable joy. I look forward to discovering more in the years to come.

Love, Preston

I whimper as I read the note again. We spent a whole year together, but he never really got to know me. Not the real me. And honestly, after a year of pretending, I'm not sure who the real me is.

If I don't know who I am, how can anyone else truly know me? Or even love me? No matter how much I wanted my happily ever after with Preston, I know now that I was lying to myself.

I rip the card in half and tilt my head back, resting the base of my neck against the mattress. My head is throbbing, but my heart feels even worse. Real or not, losing Preston hurts. And I don't know where to go from here.

I whisper a plea into the air. Silence answers me.

After a few more minutes, I decide I've reached my pain threshold and return to my search for ibuprofen. I find the bottle in my nightstand drawer, but my shaky hands struggle to hold it. I drop it square in the middle of my bible, which is resting conspicuously on the top of a pile of junk on the floor. I reach for the bottle, but one of the verses in red catches my eye.

God, have mercy on me, a sinner.

I pause. Something in me, something desperate, holds on to those words and refuses to let go. I scan the passage, reading it where the red letters begin:

"Two men went up to the temple to pray, one a Pharisee and the other a tax collector. The Pharisee stood by himself and prayed: 'God, I thank you that I am not like other people – robbers, evildoers, adulterers – or even like this tax collector. I fast twice a week and give a tenth of all I get.'

"But the tax collector stood at a distance. He would not even look up to heaven, but beat his breast and said, 'God, have mercy on me, a sinner.' "I tell you that this man, rather than the other, went home justified before God. For all those who exalt themselves will be humbled, and those who humble themselves will be exalted."

I remember taking notes on this story one night during small group. It hadn't made much of an impression then, but reading it now, I feel something akin to hope. Maybe it's the familiarity of the story, or maybe I'm just really struggling. But I've messed up pretty bad, and I'm willing to try anything at this point. Maybe I should go to a temple and try to pray.

I don't think they'll kick me out of church. I look like the food that gets stuck in the garbage disposal, but that's okay, right? I still rinse my face and tie up my hair, just in case. RCF is the only church I know, so that's where I decide to go.

I hop into my car before I can change my mind. I'm not sure what I'm expecting. I know I've screwed up, but I'm tired of feeling this way, and I don't know where else to turn. Kendi said I was always welcome. I hope he meant it.

51

At the Altar

I get to service late. The pastor is wrapping up his message as I find a seat in the back of the sanctuary.

"As we close this morning," the pastor says, "I'd like to extend an invitation to everyone here. Maybe you came here because you're in a desperate situation, like the tax collector in our story today."

My breath catches. That's got to be a coincidence, right?

"Maybe you see yourself as the tax collector. You realize that you're a sinner, in need of salvation and grace. In need of mercy from God. Maybe that was your prayer this morning. For God to help you, to rescue you from your sin. From yourself."

I look up at the pastor.

"If this is you, now is your chance to come to the altar. Come talk to your Creator, the one who knows you inside and out. The one who never leaves us or forsakes us. The one who loves us fully and completely."

I lick my dry lips and stare at the altar. Can I do it? That's why I'm here, right? But my feet don't seem to agree. Someone else in the congregation stands and walks to the altar. A couple more people go. I watch them, feeling a tug to join them, but I stay in my seat.

CHERISE AT THE ALTAR

I came here hoping to feel better, but as I watch people walk down to the altar, I realize that's not really what I want. I'm tired of chasing a feeling, of pretending, of chasing after ideas and hoping they'll make people stay. I lied to myself before, and look where it got me? I don't want to lie to myself anymore.

I want something real. And I'm not sure if this is.

The pastor prays a prayer and the service ends. People shuffle out of their seats and leave the sanctuary, but I stay. I watch a few smaller groups linger in conversation, quietly waiting. I'm not sure what I'm waiting for, but I stay. Eventually everyone leaves, and the only sound in the sanctuary is the hum of the fans and the buzz of the lights hanging overhead.

I stare again at the altar, wondering. "God," I whisper. "I want to believe there's someone who can love me unconditionally, but I'm just not sure. If you're real, if any of this is real, please show me." I sniff and wipe my face. "I'm sorry if that sounds arrogant. I just, I need to know that it's not a waste. I spent the last year wasting my time on a lie. And I know my life isn't worth much, and I'm not very special, but Kendi says you love me. If that's true, then I have to think you'd want me to really believe in you, not just pretend or hope you're real, but really know. So, if you could help me out?"

The lights above my head go out. I turn, and the lights to my left and right go out as well. The stage lights go off next, and soon the only light left is the one illuminating the altar. I wait for it to go out, too, but it doesn't. It stays. The lights outside the sanctuary go out, but the altar continues to glow in the soft light.

I wait another minute, expecting the light to turn off at any moment. But it doesn't. Everywhere else is dark, and the longer I stare at that one illuminated spot, the more it seems it's meant for me.

Go.

I'm not sure if the thought is in my head or not, but I stand to my feet and hedge into the aisle. I swallow the lump in my throat and keep my eyes on the altar as I step forward. One step after another. The closer I get, the shakier my legs become.

When I reach the altar, I kneel. As I do, a weight bears down on me. Like a boulder at my back, it squeezes the air from my lungs. I feel the heaviness of all I that I am, and all that I am not, and it hurts.

I'm selfish. I'm a liar. I'm not good enough. I'll *never* be good enough. I'm a pretender, a fraud, and a fake. I don't deserve something real.

But I'm here. And as much as I know what I'm not, I also know that I need to be here. I need to be forgiven. To have someone see me, through and through, and still choose me. And that need keeps me at the altar despite the pain in my chest.

I know I don't deserve it, but like the tax collector in the story, I ask anyway. I open my mouth and, not knowing what else to say, I recite the scripture. "God, have mercy on me, a sinner."

I cry, and I cry, and I cry. Right there on the altar, confessing everything I've done wrong, every hurt I've felt. Every lie, every half-truth. Every heartbreak and frustration. It's a garbled mess, but I can only hope that God is listening, and that He speaks the language of the brokenhearted.

I stay there, pleading and crying, until I run out of tears.

52

This Little Light of Mine

A hand grabs my shoulder in the dark. I jerk forward and bright light floods my face.

"Oh, I'm sorry." A short woman moves the flashlight away from my face and retracts her gloved hand. "Miss, are you okay? Did you get stuck in here?"

I look around, disoriented. I'm still in the sanctuary and it's dark, except for the flashlight. I stand and smooth out the flat side of my hair. My throat is sore and my eyes itch, but I feel lighter. The weight on my shoulders is gone.

"I must have fallen asleep."

"Yes, you were snoring. I came to clean the classrooms, but I heard something from here. You shouldn't be here, you know. The church was locked up hours ago."

The woman clucks and begins texting someone on her phone. "They're supposed to check for stragglers before they leave." The rest is in Spanish, and I don't catch it. Another woman comes through the sanctuary doors and shouts to her. She replies, and the woman flips a switch, turning on the stage lights.

I squint at the lights, then turn back to the woman. "I'm sorry. There was still a light on when I was here, so I didn't know everyone had left."

"Which light? All the lights were off when I came."

I point to the light above the altar. "This one."

She squints at me. "The stage lights?"

"No, just this one."

She looks at the stage, then looks at me. "There's no 'this one' light. Only the stage lights."

I shake my head. "I'm sure the stage lights were off. Just the light above the altar was on."

She shakes her head and says another phrase in Spanish. "Listen, there's only four lights. Three for the sanctuary, one for the stage. Watch." She shouts to the other woman again, and the woman flips three switches, illuminating the sanctuary one section at a time. She then flips a fourth switch, and it turns off the stage lights. The light above the altar goes off with them.

"They aren't separate," I say.

She smiles and gives me a thumbs up. "Now you see. Come on, let's get you out of here."

I look back at the altar, and warmth floods my insides. The lights aren't separate. Which means...

"Come now, Miss. Do you want me to call someone for you?"

I shake my head as she guides me out of the sanctuary. I can't believe God answered my prayer. I start to laugh, startling the woman walking beside me.

"Are you alright?" she asks.

I nod my head. "I'm better than alright. I'm... happy." And it's true. Because I've just discovered something amazing.

53

This Is My Story

It's dark outside. Even so, I worry that I won't catch Kendi before he goes into work this morning. I'm guessing he'll be in by five, but I really don't know. I stay in my car to keep warm, my eyes scanning the entrance of the parking lot for Kendi's beat up Ford.

I'm nervous, I'll admit. And after the way I spoke to him, I wouldn't blame him if he told me to find another small group. But I'm banking on Kendi practicing the forgiveness he preaches. He's proven pretty reliable so far.

Light floods the parking lot and I pull out of my space, following the maroon car around back. I park beside him and step out.

Kendi gets out of his car with a look of surprise. "Cherise? What are you doing here this early?"

"I wanted to talk to you."

He stares at me a moment, his eyes searching mine. "Okay. You wanna take a walk?"

Not really. It's still freezing, despite it being March. But I guess I hesitate long enough for Kendi to figure it out.

"Never mind. Come on inside. I've got a few minutes, and we can talk in the break room."

I follow him into the fitness center and to the employee section. There are only two other employees inside, one of them on his way out, and they greet each other with some kind of Meathead Code I can't cipher.

Kendi pours himself a cup of hot water. Nothing else in it. No coffee, no tea. Just hot water. "Can I get you anything to drink?"

"No. It's a little too early for anything. And I wanted to tell you something."

He gestures to a pair of chairs at a table, and we both sit. "What's on your mind, Cherise?"

I want to blurt out all the good parts right away, but I know I need to start with an apology. So, I tamp down on my excitement and work on the hard parts first. "Kendi, I was wrong. I never should have done any of the things I did to you, and to Preston, and I'm sorry. I'm also sorry about all the awful things I said to you. Even when you were trying to comfort me, I was rude, and mean, and I am really, really sorry."

"Okay." He hands me a tissue, because of course I'm in tears now.

"I know you probably hate me now, but please don't. I really don't want you to hate me."

"It's alright, Cherise. I'm not upset about any of that. I mean, I was frustrated, sure, but nothing that would make me hate you."

"That's good to know. Because I went to the altar on Sunday, and I told God everything. I asked him to show me He's real and he did. And I asked him to forgive me, and I really think He has. And I really could use your help with figuring out where to go from here."

A slow grin breaks out on Kendi's face. "Cherise, are you serious?"

I nod, smiling despite the tears running down my face. "Yeah. And I know it's shameless, but I was kind of hoping that offer to come back to the small group still stands?"

"Of course! Cherise, this is fantastic. I'm happy for you." He waits a beat, then cocks his head to one side. "Do you mind telling me about what happened? I mean, what led you to that decision?"

"Everything, really. I got to this place where I knew I was all wrong, but I didn't know how to fix it. I hurt so many people, and I felt so lost. I went to the church feeling sorry for myself. But something changed while I was there."

Kendi nods but doesn't interrupt.

I laugh, thinking about the irony of my situation. "It's funny, you know. I had this idea in my head about my happily ever after. I thought I'd be happy if I just found the right person. And in some ways, that was true, I guess. Just not in the way I thought. I had all this weight on me from all the things I'd done wrong, and all the ways I felt unlovable, and God took all of that. I went to the altar, but there weren't any church bells or flower arches. Just God.

"And when I got up from the altar, I felt so loved. Really and truly loved. I don't deserve any of it, and I know I haven't earned it, but I just feel so grateful, Kendi. And I want to show God how grateful I am, but I'm not really sure how." I accept another tissue and blow my nose. "I know I messed up, but I really need your help. Do you think you can give me another chance?"

"Cherise, nothing would give me greater joy than to help you in your walk with God. And I'm sure everyone in small group will feel the same way. You're not alone. You're a part of God's family now."

I nod. "Thanks, Kendi."

"Anything you need, we'll help you, okay?"

"Okay."

"And I'm only a few steps away, though you've come over enough times to know that."

I laugh. "Yeah. Sorry about that."

"Don't be. Even though your motives weren't the best, I'm glad you saw me as someone you could come to for advice."

"Kendi, you lead the small group studies and half the activities at the church. You're kind of a big deal."

He chuckles. "Things weren't always like this for me. I've been where you are, and that was after I'd already given my life to Christ. I messed up a lot, and I'm still working my way through that. So, I want you to know, you can always come to me. Doesn't matter how bad it is."

"Okay, I'll keep that in mind."

Kendi looks at his watch. "I'd better clock in. Come to small group this Friday, okay?"

I nod my head. "I'll be there."

I wouldn't miss it.

54

The Second Time Around

Friday's study leaves me in tears. I'll admit, I'm a bit of a crybaby, but also, these are happy tears. Larry and Pam recount the disastrous events of their twice-delayed-honeymoon-slash-anniversary-trip – missing luggage, freak hurricane, sharing a hotel room with a pair of strangers due to a double-booking – but their account leaves us all laughing. They both seem happy, despite their misfortune. And though I still feel the sting of my own failed relationship with Preston, it doesn't keep me from sharing in their happiness.

I'm glad to be back. Zev and Asia were the first to greet me this evening, and they showered me with love by way of hugs and hundreds of questions. I answered some, but promised to share with the whole group at the end of bible study.

Tonight's study is in Romans, which is fitting. I listen to the scriptures being read, and I am again filled with gratitude. To be loved by God, forgiven, and in this room, with this group of people who have opened up their hearts and homes to me.

Kendi reads Romans 5:8 to us. *"But God demonstrates His own love toward us, in that while we were still sinners, Christ died for us."*

I've heard the scripture before, but this time the words really matter to me.

Kendi says a prayer to end the meeting, then invites me forward. "Hey guys, Cherise wanted to talk to everyone before we leave tonight. Cherise?"

I look at all the faces in the room and will myself not to cry. At least, not until I've gotten all the words out. "Hey everyone. Thank you so much for all your prayers and encouraging words. It means so much to me that you all think about me even when I'm not here."

"Of course! We love you, Cherise." Asia blows me a kiss, and I lose a bit of resolve.

So much for not crying. "I have something to confess. You guys are all so amazing, but I've been lying to everyone." I pause to compose myself. They won't understand a word of it if I blubber through it.

"I started coming to this small group, because I liked a guy who was Christian. And I thought if I pretended to be a Christian, too, then that would keep us together. But after meeting you guys, I realized there was so much more to it. And I knew I was wrong to keep lying to everyone, but I did it anyway, because I thought maybe I could just imitate what you guys do and that would be enough. But of course, it all blew up in my face.

"Now I know God is real, and this is real, and I want to be a part of it. For real. I'm sorry I lied to everyone, and I hope you can forgive me. Um, that's basically it."

"Oh, Cherise." Asia is the first to stand and pull me into a hug. "I forgive you, and I love you." Zev, Pam, and a few others follow suit, and before long I'm surrounded by a sea of arms, echoing the same sentiment. That I'm loved. That I'm forgiven. That I'm welcome.

Mascara was a poor choice.

CHERISE AT THE ALTAR

THE WATER IS AS COLD as I remember it, but this time I'm prepared. My curls are tucked securely in a bun, my face is free of make-up, and my heart is in the right place. I look to Kendi, who's standing waist deep in the water with an unreadable expression on his face. Then I look out.

Zev, Asia, Pam, Larry, and a few other members of our small group are here, each of them offering an encouraging smile or wave of their hands. I'm glad none of them got to witness the last baptism. And not just because it was one of the most embarrassing moments of my life. I didn't understand what baptism meant, and I had no business being there in the first place. Now I know why I'm here.

I walk slowly until I'm standing right in front of Kendi. He looks at me with a solemn expression on his face. "Cherise, have you accepted Jesus Christ as your Lord and Savior?"

He furrows his brow, waiting for my response. I nod my head. "Yes."

He smiles, then places his hand on my back. "You ready?"

I cover my nose with my hands and nod.

"Then Cherise, I baptize you in the name of the Father, the Son, and The Holy Spirit." Kendi winks at me, and I fall into the water.

I SIT ALONE AT A TABLE, waiting for my iced tea to arrive. I keep staring out the window, then staring at my watch. I asked them to come at noon. It's 12:05 p.m. I worry they won't come. But part of starting fresh is making amends. And I have a lot of ground to cover.

The bell over the door chimes, and I smile. Shantell and Adrian arrive together, both donning fashionable sunglasses that I know came from the dollar store. Shantell is wearing a faux fur coat. Adrian is wearing gloves and carrying her fanciest purse. They're going to put on a show. It's a very good sign.

Shantell does a runway pose when she stops by my table, then looks up into the air, sighs loudly, and slips off her sunglasses. Adrian stops beside her with a bored look on her face. She keeps her glasses on.

"Adrian, please inform the peasant below me that I tire of her."

Adrian lets out a sigh. "I would, except I am also tired of her."

"How unfortunate. I guess we'll just talk to each other then."

"Sounds like a plan."

I interject. "Hey girl besties."

Shantell tilts her head to one side. "Adrian, did you hear something?"

Adrian shakes her head. "Not a word. You know I'm hard of hearing."

"Sounded like a little rat squeaking. One that's incredibly annoying and probably really short in stature."

"Hey!" I scowl.

"Well, if it was a rat," Adrian huffs. "I definitely don't want to be here. Rats and restaurants are a bad combination."

"Yes, they are," Shantell agrees. "I mean, if someone wanted to *grovel* and beg forgiveness, they should at least pick a decent establishment to do it in."

"One that serves fancy options like crème brûlée and lamb shank, not sandwiches and iced tea."

Shantell shrugs. "Well, the boba tea is pretty nice."

Adrian giggles. "And I do enjoy the panini breads. So fresh!"

Shantell sighs. "Well, I suppose we could lower our standards a bit, provided adequate refreshments are offered."

Both women wait. I chuckle and throw up my hands. "Lunch is on me."

Shantell slides off her coat and slides into a chair. "That settles it, then. Where's that cute waiter at?"

Adrian sits down as well and grabs the menu. "Hm, I think I'll have a sandwich, but I also want soup and the special."

"We should probably get some wings, too."

"Oh, of course!"

The waiter comes over, and I listen gratefully as both ladies rack up a sizeable lunch bill. My eyes well up with tears as Adrian takes off her gloves. "Thanks for coming, ladies." The words come out choked, and Adrian breaks character and coos at me.

"Oh, Cherise," she says, grabbing my hand.

Shantell slaps her hand, and Adrian releases mine. "Nuh uh, Adrian, we talked about this. Ahem." Shantell turns toward me. "Don't you have something to say to us, Little Miss I Don't Answer The Phone?"

"I'm sorry. I'm really, really sorry. Everything got really messed up with Preston, and I was spiraling, and I'm sorry I cut you ladies out. Really and truly."

Adrian tries to put on a stern face, but I can tell it's hard. Shantell has a scowl on hers, but it's soft at the edges. "Well, you should be sorry. Do you have any idea how much money I've had to spend on meals lately?"

"I'm sorry. And I am happy to cover lunch today and any day we're together."

"Well," Shantell throws the word out as a final chastisement, then thanks the waiter for bringing out her boba tea.

"There's something else I want to tell you ladies." This part I'm a little nervous about. "I spent a lot of time feeling sorry for myself and feeling lost and upset about everything that happened with Preston. But I went to church, and I prayed and asked God to help me and forgive me. And he did. So I gave my life to God and I'm a Christian now. No more pretending."

Shantell nods as she sips her tea. "Okay."

Adrian's lip draws into a thin line. "Okay."

"Okay." The words left unsaid are there, hanging in the air like overripe fruit on a hot summer day. But they'll have to wait. For now, it's enough to share a meal with my two favorite people. "Do either of you ladies have any big news?" I ask.

Shantell raises her hand. "I do! Guess who was nominated for a small business award?" She points at herself and Adrian and I clap.

"Congratulations!" I say. "When do you find out if you win?"

"This summer. If I win, the daycare will get ten grand in grant funding, plus be featured in the SBA magazine."

"That is fantastic news!" Adrian clears her throat. "I also have some news."

The serious look on Adrian's face gives me pause. "What is it?"

"Remember that Jonas Brothers concert you all took me to for my birthday last year?" Adrian clears her throat and pulls out a cd from her purse. "Well, I stood in line for hours after the event to get my album signed, but they turned everybody away at the last minute."

"I remember the texts about that," I say, not sure where this is headed.

"Well, I sent a very strongly worded letter to management about the whole thing, and after months of nothing, I finally got a response." She holds up the album, which has a scribbled autograph across the front. "They apologized and sent me a complimentary special edition, plus VIP passes for the next concert!" Adrian squeals. It's a strange sound, because Adrian never squeals, and Shantell and I are left speechless.

"So, your news is a copy of the Jonas Brothers' last album signed by the Jonas Brothers?" Shantell quirks her eyebrow up.

"Not all of them signed it. Just Joe. I would have preferred Nick, but other than that, it's perfect!"

"Well, I'm happy for you, Adrian," I chuckle. "And how many VIP passes did they give you?"

"Just two." Adrian frowns. "But I don't want that to come between us."

"Oh, it won't," Shantell shakes her head. "I know you'd prefer to take me, but I couldn't possibly deny Cherise the opportunity to grow in her knowledge of the Jonas Brothers."

"Oh, Shantell, I know what a big fan you are of cute brothers." I wink. "Please don't worry about me. You deserve this opportunity way more than I do."

Adrian interjects. "Did I mention there's an all-you-can-eat buffet backstage?"

Shantell blinks. "On second thought, you're right, Cherise. I do deserve this opportunity more than you."

I shake my head. "Actually, I think you were right, Shantell. I don't know nearly enough about the Jonas Brothers, so it's probably better if I go."

Our food arrives as Shantell and I take turns vying for Adrian's extra pass, and we call a truce to eat. I don't know how the dynamics of our trio will change in the months ahead. All I know for sure is that I love these two women, and I won't let another man come between us again. Not even Nick Jonas.

Epilogue

I haven't had the greatest luck with men. And I am obnoxiously good at screwing up. But there's one thing I am eternally grateful for, and that is God's timing.

Preston called me this morning and asked to meet. It's been six months since our breakup, and I've had a lot of time to reflect, and to grow. That said, I'm more than a little nervous as I walk into the same Starbucks we met in when he returned my jacket over a year ago. Somehow, it feels longer.

I spot him near the window, and our eyes meet. He gestures toward the seat beside him, and I walk forward. He looks good. A part of me resents that, but I can honestly say it's really small.

"Hey, Cherise."

Okay, so Preston's voice still has an effect on me. It's smooth as churned butter, and since I'm being honest, I do swoon a little. "Hey."

"Thanks for agreeing to meet with me. Can I get you something to drink?"

I shake my head. "No, I'm not staying long."

"Okay. How are you?"

I'm not sure where to start. Is he asking because he genuinely wants to know, or is he just being polite? I suppose, either way, the answer is the same. "I'm good. Really good, Preston."

He nods, and I wonder if that's relief in his eyes. "Good, good." He rubs the back of his head slowly. "I guess you're wondering why I called you?"

"Yeah. You never replied to any of my messages."

"I know. I needed time."

I lower my head. "I get it."

"I'm sorry, Cherise."

That sends my head snapping back up. "You're sorry?"

"For what I said to you. That was wrong. I was angry, but that's no excuse. I never should have said what I said to you, and I'm sorry."

I didn't know what to expect coming here. An apology wasn't even on the list. "I lied to you for over a year, Preston. You don't owe me an apology."

"Yes, I do." His eyes are intense, and for a moment, I wonder if maybe he's spent the last few months in as much agony as me. "And not just about what I said, though Kendi ripped me a new one about that. I wasn't ready to hear it, but he was right about a lot of things. I was moving too fast. I ignored all the signs that right now feel glaringly obvious and charged ahead anyway. Because I wanted you. I really wanted to be with you, Cherise. I wanted things to work between us. And I let that desire cloud my judgment. But that's not on you. That's on me."

There's a lot to unpack in what Preston's just said, including Kendi's involvement, but I don't want to rehash the past. His apology, whether I deserve it or not, comes as a relief. "I really am sorry for what I did to you, Preston. I shouldn't have tried to trick you. But everything's changed because I met you. I've got this new life in Christ, with people who love me and encourage me, and part of that is thanks to you. I didn't start on this path for the right reasons, but if I'd never met you, I don't know that I would have ever come to this decision on my own. So, thank you for that. And please forgive me for the pain I've caused you."

"I do, Cherise. Can you forgive me?"

I nod. "Of course."

He smiles softly. "So, no more pretending? You've really made a decision to follow Him?"

"I have. And I'm not sure what's next, but that's okay. I don't have to worry about being too much or not enough. I don't have to pretend to understand when I don't, or force myself to fit into a box. I can just be myself with God. And that makes me happy."

"That's good. I'm glad to hear it." Preston looks like he wants to say something else, but he hesitates.

I stand up, not wanting to linger. "Thank you for this, Preston. I really appreciate you talking to me."

He looks down at the table and nods. "Same here. I wish you all the best, Cherise." He stands and extends his hand. "Take care."

I shake his hand, then leave. If Preston had called a couple months ago, I might have begged him to take me back. But now, it's the least of my concerns. I don't know if we'll cross paths again, and I'm okay with that. I'm grateful for what I have, and I'm curious to see where this new life in Christ takes me.